CRESTING THE SUN

A Sci-Fi / Fantasy Anthology Featuring 12 Award-Winning Short Stories

HAILES | BENNETT | ADAMS

Written & Edited by Brian C Hailes, Rick Bennett, Nicholas P Adams.

Cover Artwork © 2019 & Interior Layout/Design by Brian C Hailes

CRESTING THE SUN

Paperback ISBN: 978-1-951374-03-7
Hardback ISBN: 978-1-951374-04-4

First Edition Printed in 2019 by Epic Edge Publishing
www.epicedgepublishing.com

Printed in the United States of America

10 9 8 7 6 5 4 3 2 1

EPIC EDGE PUBLISHING

For lovers of speculative fiction in the genres of sci-fi, fantasy (and just a taste of crime & horror) . . .

"Two possibilities exist: either we are alone in the Universe or we are not. Both are equally terrifying."

—Arthur C Clarke

CRESTING THE SUN

A Sci-Fi / Fantasy Anthology Featuring
12 Award-Winning Short Stories

HAILES | BENNETT | ADAMS

EPIC EDGE
PUBLISHING

CONTENTS

Introduction 8
by Nicholas P Adams

1 - Roadblock 10
by Brian C Hailes

All Drew really wants is a chance with his high school crush, Lily. But on his way to a party where he plans to give it one last shot, he's forced to take a detour off Highway 89, where fate has something else waiting in store.

2 - The Hubbard Drive 26
by Rick Bennett

I just can't resist comedy. This time-dilation romp is my little Einsteinian "thought experiment" and tribute to L Ron Hubbard, a sci-fi giant.

3 - L.E.A.P. 40
by Nicholas P Adams

A cop with the ability to navigate the timestream puts his skills to the test when a series of murders threatens his freedom and the future of those he'd kill to protect.

4 - Sketch Artist 116
by Brian C Hailes

An innocent girl witnesses a murder, and works with a San Francisco Police Department sketch artist who has an uncanny ability to draw portraits based on witnesses' firsthand accounts with a ninety-five percent facial recognition accuracy rate. However, as they both find themselves caught in the middle of a deadly mob war, can they find the killer or killers before they themselves fall prey to the infamous crime families?

5 - The Devil & Woody Harrelson 142
by Rick Bennett

Ever think about selling your soul to the devil? You may already have done just that if you clicked "accept" on the terms and conditions on an online program license agreement.

6 - Half Z's 184
by Nicholas P Adams

A human/alien half-breed, desperate for a connection with either world, travels to the Gya'ol enclave for answers when she discovers a rapidly forming growth inside her body.

7 - The Chaser's Prey 214
by Brian C Hailes

Having been shipped off to alien scout camp, Gareth Stillwater stumbles across the other boys torturing and mutilating a squirrel-like creature called an ehkhoor'n. When he confronts the alpha scout, Morrow Krin, and his accomplices, they bully him into secrecy . . . until he decides to steal Krin's hoverbike and put the animal out of its misery, placing himself (and everyone else) in harm's way.

8 - Overture to The Opera of The Blades 234
by Rick Bennett

This literal "rock opera" features a computer genius who speaks only in palindromes and shows the effect she has on an immortal being.

9 - Uncoiling the Loop 286
by Nicholas P Adams

A temporal manipulator struggles against time, the authorities, and a crotchety barkeep, to prevent his father from going on a killing spree before it happens.

10 - The Artist's Model 308
by Brian C Hailes

An artist's model with a past veiled in amnesia meets a mysterious visitor who claims to know who and what she really is. But when her most beloved master artist and patron unexpectedly dies, she must find a way to live up to her otherworldly destiny, and fulfill her new role.

11 - Elvis, Baby Jesus, and One UFO 328
by Rick Bennett

Most first-contact stories involve a superior alien race ravaging the Earth. Here's my take on the opposite scenario: A superior alien race gets crippled by a clever Earthman-generated computer virus.

12 - Gone are the Light-Wielders 350
by Nicholas P Adams

A shepherd boy holds the fate of the colony in his hands when he must choose between keeping a promise to his mother and his responsibility to the community.

INTRODUCTION

"Always go for that Brass Ring."

Rick Bennett has said that, or some variation of it, at almost every monthly critique group meeting as long as I can remember.

It all started in January 2015 when Rick sent a form through a Suncrest community newsletter. He wanted to know what hobbies people enjoyed, and if people were interested in forming social groups. Among the top suggestions were choral groups, knitting, and fitness. But the one that brought the three of us together, Rick, Brian, and I, was the writer's critique group.

That first meeting, high on a mountaintop, nine literary enthusiasts that dabbled in genres ranging from speculative science fiction to regency romance gathered at The Pirate Cottage, aka Rick's home, to share something we had each written.

Honestly, I don't remember what anyone brought to that first meeting. But, for five years, we've met every third Thursday to share our stories. The meetings have ranged in size from two to nine, but most often it's three or four. We bring word counts from a few hundred to over seven thousand (that was the only time, I swear) of works for sci-fi or fantasy novels, short stories, dark thrillers, and quirky speculative fiction.

In that time, the three of us (Rick Bennett, Brian C Hailes, and myself) have constituted the three musketeers of ring-reachers. Each of us in search of the story within ourselves that will finally get us what we each desire: The Golden Pen award from the Writer's of the Future contest created by L Ron Hubbard, among others.

For five years, I've heard Rick's enthusiastic call to arms. "Grab that Brass Ring." And now, I finally know where the saying came from.

Starting back in the 1890s, carousel owners would dangle a ring of brass among an assortment of iron ones just outside the reach of giddy riders. Going around and around, kids and adults would stretch from the outer circle of stationary horses in hopes of catching the coveted object as they passed. To catch the brass ring required tenacity and attentiveness; paying attention to the tiny details to avoid a false reward of an easier target. Most often, catching the brass ring entitled the winner to a free ride on the carousel.

In addition to reading our works aloud, getting feedback, line edits, questions, suggestions, and hours of animated discussions on how to improve each story, we each regularly attend local writing conferences.

Hailes, a talented artist and writer has given presentations and participated in panels for Life, The Universe, And Everything, ComicCon, and more. He hosts a YouTube channel sharing his love of drawing and teaching with "Draw It With Me." With over fifteen publications under his belt, he brings a wealth of real-world industry experience to the group.

Rick Bennett, who likes to think of himself as a guerilla in advertising warfare, brings his flair for a well-turned phrase and quirky sense of humor to each meeting. His enthusiasm for writing (and infectious joy of living) brings unbounded energy to our critiques, along with his ability to see possibilities with each developing story.

As for myself, what do I bring to the group? My professional background is in architecture, but I love a good story and coming up with large-scale ideas. My master's thesis combined two passions: buildings and scuba-diving. I designed a diving school (that's both an adjective and a verb). A submersible complex seventy miles from the coast of Texas that combined the features of a hotel and an educational center. Did I win a design award for my project? Let's just say, the faculty was hotly divided. There was no middle ground. No pun intended.

So, that's what we've been doing for the past five years. Riding this carousel of dreams, submitting story after story in hopes that each will get the judges' attention and put that prize within reach. So far, we've accumulated over a dozen honorable mention awards between the three of us. Not too shabby, considering that still puts us in the top two percent of that quarter's entries.

I moved away from Suncrest in 2013, but have only missed a few months with my brothers by quill in all that time. Rick and Brian still live on the hill, so now literally as well as metaphorically, I still look up to them as mentors and friends. My guides as we uplift and support each other in search of the one ring.

Cresting the Sun is a science fiction and fantasy anthology compiling twelve award-winning short stories (with a taste of crime and horror mixed in). And as mentioned, each included tale has in recent years earned recognition from the esteemed L Ron Hubbard Writers of the Future contest judges, with adventures sure to rattle your bones, launch you beyond the stars, and carry you through space and time.

Prepare yourself, and enjoy the ride!

—***Adam Nicholes,*** *January 2020*

Illustration by Brian C Hailes

1

ROADBLOCK

by Brian C Hailes

Crushing on Lily three weeks before the Senior Ball was my first mistake. And my second? Taking the detour on Highway 89.

Of course Lily had already been asked to the Ball.

"Two Bear Burgers, two large fry, two raspberry shakes," she said, stabbing the order slip to the board with a tack. She could turn a fast-food order into Swan Lake.

Spencer, our gangly, well-liked supervisor, smacked me from behind. "Quit staring. You'll creep her out. And there's a line outside."

"There's always a line," I said, glancing up at her to see if she'd heard him. I leaned down to see the procession of standing customers and parked cars out the window beyond Lily. No longer than average for early evening.

I shook my head, refocused on my personal factory-line of buns, processed beef, vegetable bins and condiment bottles and picked up my multi-tasking pace.

Garden City's Lakeside Drive-In, though fairly modern, liked to pose as one of those roller skate joints from the 1950s, except that most of the customers walked up to the glazed cedar window to place their orders since the owner usually kept the place ridiculously under-staffed. Tonight, Rachel was our only roller-girl.

I had promised Rachel, my other, less-mesmerizing co-worker, that I would take *her* to the Ball. Since my plan all along included watching

Lily dance from across the ballroom while swaying over someone-less-intimidating's shoulder, why not let it be Rachel's?

On those rare occasions when she wore contacts in place of her thick-rimmed glasses and put at least a minimal amount of effort beyond the usual elastic into her thin brown hair, she could pull off pretty.

But Lily's mere presence in a room could raise the dead and lift them to a realm celestial, no matter her hairstyle or attire.

Rachel returned from her carhop duties and bumped into me as she skated to the order board. "Sorry, Drew. Man, look at you go. Betcha can't keep up with this," she said, playfully shaking her backside in my direction.

"Bet you're right," I said. Her tone of intentional condescension got a smile out of me, but it quickly faded. Rachel had always liked me more than I liked her. And I felt bad about it. Despite her general snarkiness, a large part of me tried to be nice without leading her on—a delicate balance to keep. And Rachel did have nice legs from all that skating. But those only distracted me momentarily. After all, legs could only take a relationship so far.

Local news from the radio's mounted perch in the upper corner of the cooking area interrupted the 80's classic rock that Spencer liked to play. A female announcer droned on about missing persons from a neighboring town. People at school had been talking about it, but I never paid much heed to news or neighborhood gossip—I had other things on my mind.

I had worked this cramped space of the drive-in for almost a year now and Lily had just started a couple months ago. She *did* notice me. Sometimes. Stuck inside a hollowed-out trailer home designed to look like a log cabin on the outside and stuffed with mountainous shelves of boxes, bags and cooking machinery on every wall, she *had* to notice me. She practically stood right in front of me for hours on end.

Her elegant posture. The way she moved. Talked. So mature for seventeen. She somehow made uninteresting things interesting, somehow breathed life into a half-life.

At school, she mainly hung out with older guys well above my social circle—sports and wrestling jock types. She had even hung out with Spencer once or twice, though he said they never hooked up. Of course he wanted to. Every guy (and even some girls I knew) wanted to.

I worked out pretty regularly; I did push-ups and crunches almost every night (with mixed motivations). I even took a wrestling class with my friend, Tucker, and some of my buddies last semester. And I *actually* enjoyed it.

I was also seventeen, though I only looked fourteen. People always said looking younger than your age was a blessing, but it couldn't have felt more like a curse.

Maybe that was why she only half-acknowledged me. That, or she didn't want to date someone she worked with, which would explain her blowing off Spencer. But then, he was also a goofball. Fun and energetic, but a goofball. Working at a drive-in didn't exactly scream 'future financial security' either. Of course she worked there, but probably only for the social aspect as many of our customers happened to be fellow students.

The Lakeside grease that hitchhiked home with me every night on both skin and clothing and gave off ketchup-and-onion cologne had caused me to start questioning my employment in fast food. That and, of course, Lily.

Somehow, she managed never to smell of Lakeside grease. Only that sweet, fruity perfume that must have cost half her paycheck. Not like the flowery grandma perfumes most girls wore that made my eyes water as I walked through high school hallways. Lily's scent was heaven.

"Hi, welcome to Lakeside," she said through the tiny order window. "What would you like?" Even in monotone, her voice could rally angels.

"Don't need no food," came the raspy voice of what sounded to be an old smoker on the other side of the glass. "Need directions."

I craned around the burger slide to see the old man hunched over at the window, Lily momentarily at a loss for words. Spencer was banging around in the back, fetching another bag of ice and Rachel had already flitted out the door after more orders.

"Where to?" I asked the man, swinging to Lily's rescue. "I can give you directions."

The old smoker looked me over then cocked his head back at Lily. "You got a map?"

His breath reeked of liquor—the same smell my grandpa took on each day after four o' clock.

Lily took a step back. "No."

"Where you headed?" I asked, trying not to look or sound judgmental.

His disturbingly bloodshot eyes refocused on me. An unsettling cold that nearly gave me the pee-shivers scurried up to my neck, and I too backed away as inconspicuously as possible.

"Jackson," he said after some pause.

Easy. We got this one all the time. "Sure. Just head north toward 89, then follow it to the right into Idaho. Follow the signs and stay on 89 'til you get to Wyoming, then take US-26 the rest of the way. It's pretty much a straight shot north."

The old smoker seemed more interested in a fly that buzzed past his mostly-bald pate than in what I was saying. "Eh," he shrugged.

"Or, you could just look it up on your phone," I added, almost certain he didn't have one but wanting to test whether he listened or not. From the looks of his lumberjack getup, he'd probably never even heard of Google Maps.

My gaze shifted to the parking lot where an old Chevy Nova barreled into one of the few empty stalls. Great. Tucker was here to distract me from work. And he brought friends. Spencer had warned me more than once about talking to visitors while on the clock.

After the old smoker shuffled away, Lily put her hand on my shoulder. "Thanks," she said. "You *do* know a section of 89's closed for construction. He'd have to take the back roads and would probably get lost. Oh well," she grinned. "He was kind of rude, right?"

Lily put her hand on my shoulder.

"Yeah. Oops," I said, wondering if that was the most she'd ever spoken to me, let alone *touched* me.

"Ladies and genital-men," Tucker called out, jamming his face inside the order window in front of the line of waiting customers, his shaggy boarder-hair nearly covering his eyes. "Who's comin' to my party? Well, *the* party? And who was that old crack-job that just left?" Two of Tucker's buddies—merely acquaintances to me—chuckled from behind him.

"What party?" Lily asked, turning away from me, obviously interested.

Tucker rolled his eyes sarcastically. "*Daines*' party. You know. *Daines*?

Mansion-zilla on the hill? Boondocks?"

Lily sassed, "Yeah, I know the Daines."

"You comin', bro?" Tucker asked, focusing his sales skills back onto me. "When you gettin' off?"

Lily seemed a little surprised that Tucker wanted me to come.

"Half hour," I said, wondering if I was up to facing all the people. Not to mention my Lakeside cologne.

"You ordering anything?" Lily asked with some agitation.

"Not unless you're sellin' Lilies," he joked, obviously ignoring the people in line he'd butted in front of.

Lily scoffed.

"I'll text you the address," he said, pointing at me and jumping back from the window. "Bring some ladies, Drew-man!"

I nodded, unsure of why he said such things—he knew the only lady I could possibly bring would be Rachel, and he definitely wasn't into her.

"By the way," Lily said. "Thanks for covering my shift the other day."

I perked up and tried to relax, taken off guard and remembering back to her brief text two weeks ago. "Uh, you're welcome."

She hinted a smile and turned away.

I hovered next to Lily for a moment, but as she leaned over to take the next customer's order, it got awkward, so I promptly returned to my post. And it was a good thing—Spencer returned from the back and gave me the eye with a question mark.

"So, you goin' to the party?" Rachel asked, coming up from behind me. I jumped with a start, thinking she was still outside.

"Uh, I dunno, maybe."

"Can *anyone* go? My girlfriends and I don't have plans."

"Um, yeah, I guess." My mind still dwelt on the fact that Lily's perfectly manicured fingers had touched my shoulder.

That, and the radio was still droning on about missing persons.

Between order runs, Rachel partially interrupted my burger-assemblage tasks with news about what she was going to wear to the party, who she was going to bring to the party, and what they might do at the party.

But all I could think about was Lily, who walked past me to talk to Spencer about leaving her shift a few minutes early. Judging from his reaction, she obviously used her magical flirty wiles to gain that few extra minutes.

She glanced my way and I jerked my head toward the order board, focusing my eyes and pretending not to be eavesdropping.

Three bacon burgers, two with cheese, one of those without onions. Why did Lily want to leave work early?

And then she unexpectedly tapped me on the shoulder. "So you going?"

Rachel—who I'd temporarily forgotten was present—rolled back, but didn't leave.

"Um,... " My mind was a washing machine cycling backwards. Lily's eyes, her lips, that perfect complexion, right in my face. Beautiful. And waiting for a response.

"Uh, yes, where?" I was just glad I hadn't looked below her neckline—that could have stopped my heart or done other things.

"*Daines'* party? Your friend, you know, the—?"

I nodded, "Yes, Tucker. Right. My friend, Tucker. The party. Um, I dunno."

I made the mistake of looking into her eyes again. "Yes. Sure. Why not?" I said, trying to sound as though going to parties was something that came naturally to me. I had to force myself to stop nodding. "You takin' off now?" I asked her, grasping for words. I pointed a thumb toward Spencer. "Is that what you—?"

"Yeah," she said, "aren't you? Your shift's over, right?"

I shot a glance at the clock. Five past the hour. "Yes, wow, it is already. Spencer, I'm out!"

I didn't think he heard me, but I didn't care. Lily was still looking at me.

"After you." I gave Lily a friendly grin, threw off my apron and followed her to the corner computer in the back. Waiting behind her, I couldn't help but admire her elegant hands as she logged herself out on the keyboard. And the indescribable curves in her tight jeans.

She smiled at me and I followed her outside, intoxicated by her subtle perfume. *What was I doing? Was I walking her out to her car?*

Luckily, she broke the silence first. "Well maybe I'll see ya at the party later."

I lit up, "Yeah, yeah, that'd be great. We'll a . . . see you then. I'll look for you. There. *Maybe.*"

Inside I withered. *Just say something with a shred of confidence,* I told myself. But before my mouth could download the words from my brain, I turned toward my old beater of a car and walked away.

That's when I noticed Rachel standing at the back door of the drive-in, seething.

"You know, Drew..." Rachel said just loud enough so Lily could hear.

I stopped to look back at her.

"You'd be kinda cute if you were just, like, a little taller." And she went inside, letting the door slam behind her.

I shot an embarrassed glance at Lily.

She gave that friendly shrug of hers that I had come to love. Only this time, I didn't love it.

I squinted and tilted my head to the side. "Thanks, Rachel."

She may as well have put my heart into the vice at wood shop and crank it to the point of bursting. *Rachel's jealousy definitely wasn't winning me any points* with Lily. And we pretty much shared the same height. Five-foot-six-and-three-quarters wasn't *that* short.

Hell.

It hurt, but I kept cool—I thought—distracting myself with leaving. I had forgotten to drop three orders of caged chicken fingers into the sizzling oil vat before the end of my shift. I wanted to go back inside and drop myself in with them.

I got in my car and watched Lily pull out of the lot through my mirrors. I told myself every day to forget about her. My chances looked grim-to-none from the first day she stepped into history class.

Perhaps I would go to Tucker's party. Other girls would be there. Rachel might get over her jealousy fit by then and forgive me. She usually did.

I turned the key in the ignition.

The starter just clicked.

Not the damn battery again, I thought.

I popped the hood and grabbed an old screwdriver out of the glove box—a recent routine I really needed to put a stop to.

I wondered when I would ever get around to actually replacing the loose terminal cables. For lack of a wire brush, I used the dulled tip of the screwdriver to chip away the corrosion at the posts and cable end clamps, and re-fastened them together, using the screwdriver's handle to tap the stubborn cables back on.

Rachel returned outside and shook her head at me from across the lot before rolling to the other side of the building.

I got back in the car and, with a sigh, turned the key.

The car churned, huffed. I pumped the gas.

The engine finally rumbled on, and I left.

* * *

I exited the sliding glass doors of the Rock Bank Market and let out a heavy sigh, wondering if I should actually go to the party or just head home. I *had* already paid for the drinks—drinks I purchased in hopes of compensating for not bringing any girls with me. I walked back to my car, opened the door and threw the drinks on the passenger seat. I pulled out my phone, feeling slightly guilty for treating Rachel badly and decided to text her:

YOU WANNA GO TO THE PARTY WITH ME?

She responded immediately:

I'M PICKING UP A FRIEND.
WANT US TO COME GET YOU?

I sat down and started my car before responding:

I'M ALREADY AT ROCK BANK.
I'LL JUST SEE YOU WHEN YOU GET THERE.

I pulled out of the parking lot and headed toward the highway.

My phone vibrated again.

CAN'T WAIT! I'LL LOOK FOR YOU.
BTW, I FORGOT TO GET THE ADDRESS
FROM YOU AT WORK . . .

Juggling my phone in one hand and the steering wheel in the other, I looked up Tucker's message and forwarded her the address.

I threw my phone down and stretched my eyelids.

The radio crackled as I surfed through weak-signaled stations. Overplayed top-twenty songs and obnoxious DJs faded in and out. My window was cracked and a breeze blew against my hair.

A muffled newscaster—this time, male—droned in and out, "People have...miss...in the areas surr..."

"Give it a rest," I uttered under my breath. "People are missing. We got it."

The broken yellow lines on the highway cut through my dim headlights. My eyelids threatened to close for a third time. I scrunched my face and refocused on the road, shifting in my seat and stiffening into better posture. *What if a deer jumped into your path?* I asked myself. Such questions usually helped perk me up at least long enough to turn on my brights and scan the hillsides.

I gave out a heavy yawn which caused my eyes to water. Perhaps I should just forget the party. Tell Tucker I couldn't find any ladies to bring. The drinks would last me a week if I hid them from my little brother.

Just turn around, I told myself. *Go home. Sleep.*

Start over again tomorrow. Find someone new to obsess over.

The last thing I needed was to sit around with a bunch of vain, half-drunk strangers, with Rachel breathing over my shoulder, talking my ear off about a million things I couldn't care less about whilst every jock on the premises hit on Lily across the room.

The thought just made me feel sorry for myself and I began to nod off again.

My phone vibrated. I swerved at the alert and looked down at the screen.

Lily!

The *deer* I was looking for.

I had saved her number in my phone when she texted two weeks back to ask if I'd cover one of her shifts.

I accepted the call, and gulped, trying to compose myself and get a handle on the car. "Hello?"

There was a slight hesitation. "Hi, is this Drew?"

"Yeah, this is Drew. Hi."

"This is Lily, from work. I was wondering if you had the Daines' address, you know, for the party tonight?"

I huffed. Of course. Why else would Lily call me? For a hook up?

"Oh, uh, yeah, hang on just a sec'."

The broken yellow lines became solid, then warning signs appeared with blinking lights.

REDUCED SPEED AHEAD.
ROAD CLOSED AHEAD.
DETOUR.

That's right, I thought. *Lily had said something about road closure on 89. I should've gone the long way around.*

I turned off the highway at the roadblock. The highway had been cordoned off by construction crews, but there was no sign of anyone. No lights, no moving construction vehicles. It did look like some of the pavement had been broken up ahead. I breathed a long sigh, wondering how far out of my way this detour route would lead me.

I pulled over and anxiously searched for Tucker's message. "I just remembered what you said about 89 being closed. Are you taking the long way?"

"No. My friends and I are already on 89. We figured we'd just take whatever detour."

I sent her the address.

"Gotcha," I said. "I just texted you the address."

"Thanks."

"So you must be right behind me."

"Uh, yeah...probably," she said, obviously distracted by whatever her friends were doing. I couldn't tell if the background voices were male or female. Probably male. "Hey, thanks again, Drew. You're a lifesaver."

"No problem. Bye, Lily."

"See you soon," she said before hanging up.

Wow. She called me, I thought. *Lily Vail actually called me. Didn't even send a text. And 'see you soon?'*

I stared into my rear view mirror at the blinking lights.

"*But was this really worth it?* I thought. I *had* already come a long way and was probably closer to the party than home. Tucker expected me.

And I could at least see Lily again, even if she was surrounded by sausage.

I always considered beholding an angel a worthwhile endeavor—even if she wasn't *my* angel.

I breathed deep and took the detour.

A long dark road stretching into nowhere—a road I'd never been on before. I checked my gas gauge. A third of a tank.

I'd never been to the Daines' mansion before, but I did sleep over at a friends house just down the street back in grade school. I remembered it taking a long time to get there, but not this long.

The road narrowed, its edges dropping into blackness. A starlight sea enveloped all other distant lights and even the sharp yellow lines on the road faded.

Headlights cut through utter darkness. Forward motion through stillness. An old engine droning though silence.

A long, empty road.

A dream.

I began to nod off again.

Not empty?

A man!

In the road!

I slammed on the brake pedal, adrenaline squeezing my head and shoulders from all angles.

The car screeched and fish-tailed. I grappled with the steering wheel, teeth clenched, muscles tight, heart throbbing.

Smoke and the stench of burnt rubber billowed up from the tires.

"Shit!"

Like a ghost illuminated harshly from the legs up stood the old smoker from the order window. Or a taxidermied corpse of the man, standing erect as if he were being propped up by invisible strings. He apparently hadn't made it to Jackson.

I squinted and leaned forward for a better look, my fingers frantically searching for the roll-up-window button on the door panel.

Was this a joke? I thought. *A prank set by Tucker and his buddies?*

Blood covered the man's eyeballs and leaked from their sockets. His head moved slightly, causing a chill to paralyze me in my seat. Whatever this was, it looked real.

Not a prank. *Couldn't be,* I thought.

The old smoker hunched under the weight of some Hell. My eyes settled on a rusty tire iron vibrating in his tightly-clenched right fist. Crimson dripped from the tire iron into a puddle at his feet. I half-expected it to be an axe.

An axe would have been more fitting.

I gulped, but the mucus wouldn't go down.

I looked around, but couldn't see another vehicle or light anywhere. *Where had the man parked? There were no cars for miles.*

Why did he just stand there like that? In the dark? In the middle of nowhere?

Bile rose in the back of my throat as I stared, disbelieving. Horrific images of my own grizzly murder by an old man with a tire iron played through my mind. Whoever this guy was and whatever had happened to him, I didn't want to hang around to learn the details.

Pass him, I thought. *Go around. Or go back.*

If I made it to the party, I'd have a story to tell.

I threw my car into reverse and backed up at a sharp angle, the car's headlights momentarily leaving the old smoker.

I peeled out to pass him, but found him again in my path. This time, he was looking up at me.

I threw the car in reverse and thrust my foot on the gas.

The tires screeched. The headlights flickered and went out.

Moving backwards blindly, I slowed and flicked the light switch on and off.

Nothing.

I breathed more heavily.

I punched the light switch forward to see if the high beams worked.

They brightly illuminated the road ahead, but the old smoker was gone.

Or had moved.

I hesitantly looked around.

The old smoker shattered the driver's side window with his tire iron, and I pressed the gas pedal, jerking us forward.

I screamed and struggled. Fought.

The old man's strength shook the car, which rolled forward, skidding out of control.

We left the road and barreled over a ditch into a field of tall, dead grass.

I made to escape, but couldn't reach the passenger-side door. He had my shirt and strangled me with it. I twisted out of my shirt and escaped, clawing my way out of the car into the grass.

Adrenaline surged and panicked breathing filled my ears. I managed to find my footing and sprinted away from the man and my car. But where could I go?

The broken rays from my headlights dimmed as I went and I couldn't help but look.

The backlit silhouette of the old smoker stalked after me through the broken grass.

"Help!" I cried out, sprinting forward again. Primal instinct drove my every move. *Could I make a wide arc and double back to the car?* I thought, the cold, burning in my lungs.

I abruptly changed direction and stumbled through the cutting blades of grass.

I could see the headlights again. They were brighter. Closer. But a shadow closed in.

Something grasped my hair and yanked me back. The old smoker lifted his weapon, only death in his outline.

Finality.

Acceptance.

I stopped struggling.

The force came down and broke me.

Forever.

* * *

I awoke, but it seemed my eyes had already been open. The pain was gone. Or still there and merely unprocessed by my brain. My muscles didn't want to respond.

I was on my stomach, lying on the road.

Oh yeah. The road.

My car.

Gone.

It had left. I remembered it leaving. The red glow from the brake lights had reflected off the asphalt in front of me. The hum of the engine had long since died away behind me.

One side of my face rested on the pavement, but it didn't hurt.

Nothing hurt.

I must have been here a long time, I thought, *because I couldn't easily move.*

It took a while to build up the motivation to try to get up.

With a stiff neck, I lifted my head off the road.

Cold metal scraped against the asphalt as I moved. Cold metal that was stuck in my neck. I reached up and touched a handle, then grasped it.

I pulled a screwdriver out of my neck. *My* screwdriver.

Why didn't that hurt? I thought.

My whole body felt numb. Cold.

Dead.

Blood dripped off my hair, congealed on my pale hands and arms.

But that was okay. The blood didn't bother me.

Everything was okay.

Quiet.

Peaceful.

I stood. Slowly. Carefully.

No hurry, I thought.

I looked up to the heavens.

Dim. Far away. Infinite.

Beautiful.

I looked down at my feet.

The tip of the screwdriver from my glove box glimmered as it hung in the moonlight.

I squeezed its handle in my hand.

I used to use this, I told myself. On my car. Which was gone.

I could *still* use this.

I *would* use this.

I looked toward the middle of the road and felt as though I belonged there. I certainly didn't belong anywhere else.

I settled into a nice spot over the center line. A comfortable spot.

A roadblock.

Minutes passed.

A warm breeze blew by.

Crickets chirped.

Was I dead?

Sure.

Stuck?

Obviously.

But this existence bore little difference to the one spent living just out of reach of the girl I loved.

Could I have *lived* with that?

Two faint lights appeared miles away.

Car headlights.

Someone was coming to give me a ride. Perhaps it was Rachel. Perhaps it was Lily.

Ah, that's nice, I thought. *They're coming to pick me up.*

I gripped my screwdriver and wanted to smile.

The End

Illustration by Rick Bennett

2

THE HUBBARD DRIVE

by Rick Bennett

BACKSTORY: My little one-man advertising agency had a number of home runs, two of which were my early clients: ORACLE's Larry Ellison and SALESFORCE.COM's Marc Benioff. In fact, I once ran an ad suggesting that Marc Benioff run for president. [Yeah, one of my "gifts" has been to show up where the action is.] I have always believed that one day, Oracle and Salesforce.com would merge. This little story just puts some skin on those bones. Oh, and it's also a tribute to one of the most interesting sci-fi writers of the 20th Century, L. Ron Hubbard.

Glenn C Hammer hunched over his scanning electron microscope and pretended he didn't hear the question, even though it echoed off the white walls and ceiling of the massive two-story lab. Pretended deafness was a last desperate attempt to escape from a revelation he would shortly have to make. He didn't like keeping such an enormous secret, but this cat would inevitably come clawing out of the bag. And soon. So his teenage nephew nudged the physicist and repeated the query.

"Uncle Glenn?" said Stanley Baker to his barely four years older uncle, looking at the framed PhD plaque and seeming to notice an apparent typo. "Why didn't they put a period after your middle initial?"

"'Cuz it doesn't stand for anything," mumbled the uncle without looking up. His eldest sister's son shared not only Hammer's genius, but also his Asperger's obliviousness to social skills. Which meant neither would likely spend anything but a solitary life in similar sterile echo chambers provided by their university benefactors. Singles for whom no dating website would ever find a likely marital candidate. "My dad was Glenn B and my grandfather was Glenn A Hammer."

Given that Glenn A shared the OCD genetic mutation of his offspring, more than one acquaintance marveled that he ever sired a son. Ditto for Glenn B and his loin's chances for begetting a Glenn C.

"I'm Stanley D. Baker, with a period. The 'D' stands for Dean."

The statement drew no response from twenty-one year old Uncle Glenn, who'd been Dr. Glenn C Hammer since he earned a PhD at fourteen. Of course, Stanley Dean Baker took two more years to get his own doctorate in Biochemistry. The two prodigies hung around each other a lot. Partially because they had no real friends, and partially to cross-pollinate each other's disciplines: physics and biochemistry. The high ceiling fans might well have been propellers on nerd beanies.

Hammer's lab came courtesy of a grant from UCLA's Astrophysics Department. His nephew's bio-chem office sat within easy walking distance on campus. They rotated lunch locations, the guest being responsible for bringing two take-out meals from one of three nearby fast food outlets. Today, Stanley's treat came from the Natural Foods Café just South of the parking garage. Two vegetarian Native Oklahoma Classics.

"Lunchtime, Uncle Glenn," said Stanley. Rustling paper bags and the smell of food succeeded in breaking the physicist away from his microscope. "Sliced native seitan, melted cheddar, caramelized onions, organic tofu bacon, BBQ sauce, ranch dressing, carrots, tomato, and red onions with romaine."

"You know, I'm actually quite hungry," said Hammer.

Moments later, both ate in silence, engrossed in their own thoughts. They'd taken some old piece of dialogue from a western movie to heart: "Ya gonna talk, talk. Ya gonna shoot, then shoot!" The metaphoric paraphrase concerned eating and talking. Not a good mantra for a successful dinner date with most females on the planet.

Only after both had finished eating, and used their ecologically pure napkins made of recycled paper, did conversation resume. Well, conversation resumed after their contest of throwing their crumpled bags across the room into the opening of a sensor mounted incinerator that vaporized the garbage before it could hit the back throat of a chute. Above the opening, a sign warned of extremely high-energy laser and guaranteed amputation, should student hands or fingers venture therein. So far, none had.

"Uncle Glenn, did you ever make up middle names for yourself? Ones that started with 'C'?"

"You're obsessing, Stanley."

"Oh, yeah. Sorry."

"But in answer to your question," nodded the six-foot bag of skin and bones physicist, "the 'C' has kind of become an obsession of mine, too. In my mind, it has always stood for the Universal Constant, the speed of light."

"Einstein's equation. E equals MC squared."

"That's the one. And it has to do with my little project in the lab."

Before Stanley could ask *What little Project?*, the lab door burst open and a cadre of navy officers followed their leader up an aisle past workbenches.

"Admiral Staker, welcome to California." Hammer held out his hand, which the admiral nearly crushed in his grip.

"Dr. Hammer." Then looking warily to the nephew, "And who is this kid?"

"This is Dr. Stanley Dean Baker, my microbiologist colleague who will be stocking the ship."

"He's cleared, then?" asked the admiral, who mistook Stanley's frozen-before-he-could-look-surprised rigor mortis as the teenager's attempt to stand at attention.

"Yes, Sir!" answered Hammer.

"Colonel," spat the admiral. "You got Dr. Stanley Dean Baker on the list?"

The subordinate pulled a TOP SECRET folder from his briefcase and flipped through several pages before running his finger down a very short list of names.

"Right here, Admiral. Second name on the list, right after Dr.

Hammer."

Stanley turned toward Uncle Glenn, who stood behind the admiral's line of sight and gave him the secret signal they'd come to call The Shit Eating Grin. The signal evolved as their best imitation of the look on Hammer's dog's face when caught eating its own poop. THE SMILE combined with the animal's "Who, me?" look to complete the picture.

If the admiral figured out that the combined age of the two scientists added up to just over half his own, he didn't let on. Urgent business trumped such calculations.

"Ok, Hammer," said the admiral. "Modifications to the decommissioned nuclear submarine are just about complete. You got that Hubbard box ready to be slaved into the sub's reactor?"

"Over here, Sir."

Hammer led the group to a wall safe, where he used a thumb print and voice command to gain access. Stanley stayed well behind, in case he had the chance to shoot his uncle the finger.

The physicist withdrew a shoebox size cube of opaque Lucite from the safe and handed it to the admiral.

"What's this?" said the astonished four-star officer. "No connectors? Just a solid block of…of…what?"

"Sir, the Hubbard box doesn't need connectors. Just strap it down within ten feet of your reactor and it'll do the rest."

"But how do you—?"

Hammer interrupted. "I didn't want to fool with patents and such, so the device is encapsulated in a material with no known solvent. Try to X-ray or scan it, the box self-destructs. I control it from this."

Hammer hefted a joystick assembly that looked eerily like a PlayStation gaming console.

"This plugs into the bridge nav system," said Hammer. Then pointing into the safe, "We'll be taking two backup Hubbard boxes and three backup interface units."

The admiral looked for a place to sit down. A second subordinate, one without a briefcase, quickly accommodated his boss and pulled up a lab stool.

"You're telling me," said the admiral, "That this little box is going to take a eighteen-thousand-ton Ohio Class submarine off this planet and into space?"

Everybody gasped. Even Stanley.

"You saw one of these launch a four-hundred-thousand-ton derelict oil tanker into the blue yonder just one month ago. Your sub is less than a fifth that size."

Admiral Staker turned to one of his officers. "Captain Smith, double the size of our security forces, both around this building. At the shipyard, too!

* * *

"You didn't tell me anything about shooting an oil tanker into space, or putting my name on some super-secret list," said Stanley just after the admiral and his retinue had left.

"Classified," said Hammer. "Besides, you were too tied up in your earwax follies."

"Awh come on! You told me to check out my hypothesis that dogs do genetic modification on themselves by licking their rear paws after digging at their ears."

"Nobody gets anywhere without asking questions. You had a question. Seemed like an easy thing to check out."

Stanley did a figure eight as he stomped a path around lab benches. Back, facing his uncle: "Well now, Doctor Glenn Lightspeed Hammer, your little project sure ain't classified to me NOW!"

"You're right. Sit down and learn, unless of course you want to take a couple more laps around the lab."

Stanley sat on the same stool previously used by the admiral. And folded his arms. He had to pivot on the stool as Hammer walked to the whiteboard and picked up a marking pen.

"What if I told you I could propel a very large object to point-nine-nine-seven the speed of light?"

"I may be a biologist, but I know enough physics to laugh in your face. There isn't enough energy on the planet to do that."

"You are correct, earwax boy. It would take an infinite amount of energy to propel any mass at the speed of light."

"So there!"

"Not so fast. Suppose I could harness the energy in a black hole. While not infinite, I calculate I could attain a .997 speed-of-light velocity on pretty much anything."

"Good luck on the black hole, Unc."

"I've already done that with the derelict oil tanker. How do you think I'm getting the U.S. Navy to give me a submarine of a lot less mass?"

"You're shitting me! You're turning a submarine into a spaceship?"

"Why not? Those science fiction authors had it right. Any space force they write about is always The Navy. Not The Air Force."

"I don't care if it's the Wyoming National Guard. The idea of turning a submarine into a spaceship is wrong on so many levels."

"You're obsessing again, Stanley. A nuclear submarine is the perfect interstellar vehicle. Self-contained, unlimited energy, atmospherically sound."

"Okay, okay. So just what are you going to prove with this?"

"What better way to prove time dilation. I leave here for a month of time to [illegible] ere's the equatio[illegible]

$$\text{Time on Earth} = \frac{\text{Time on Ship}}{\sqrt{1-\frac{v^2}{c^2}}}$$

"As I said, my soon-to-be late-great-uncle, assuming this black hole Hubbard thingie isn't some giant pile of dog poo, how do you plan to keep this from becoming a one-way trip?"

"I call it the Hubbard Matrix, and navigation is simple astrophysics, my boy. Let me show you."

* * *

[14 years later, Earth time]

"Missiles locked on target," said Captain Mike Paul as he commanded a two-ship of Fox thirty-fives within visual range of the massive object. Under the watchful eye of NORAD, it had streaked across the United States from the Eastern Seaboard toward San Francisco.

"Roger that, Wild Thing," responded a female voice from ground control. "Did you and your wingman see the target almost instantly decelerate from Mach 5 to zero? That can't be of terrestrial origin!"

"Uh…uh…" sputtered Captain Paul, call sign Wild Thing. Careers could be made or broken by recorded transmissions from heretofore professional and objective military pilots. Directly ahead of him, hovering over the tallest building in San Francisco, appeared to be an Ohio Class submarine. A flawlessly polished silver submarine. The image of one ORACLE.SALESFORCE.COM logo on the building reflected off the sea-guine hovering vessel's surface.

"Let's see ya get out of this one," said his wingman, call sign Joker, on their private channel.

Coming to his senses and trying to sound calm and unemotional, Wild Thing said: "The object appears to be stationary above downtown San Francisco. I am putting weapons on safe, as any shot would have unacceptable civilian collateral damage."

"Me too," said Joker. "Ground control, weapons all safe."

"Wild Thing, describe the craft," said ground control.

"I will leave that up to you and military intelligence," shot back the pilot.

"Fan the boards, Joker. Let's cut speed and circle," he said, as he plied his air brakes for a slow orbit. "My telemetry A.I. is locked onto the UFO and transmitting. Local television crews will soon be broadcasting, once the news trucks just pulling up on the corner of Mission and Freemont Streets connect with their studios."

Over their private channel, Joker lived up to his call sign: "Don't want to tell them you see a giant flying sub, eh?"

Ground control must have sensed a private conversation between the two F-35s and had no more desire to sound crazy than did the pilots. These recordings would definitely make international news.

"Copy that, Wild Thing. Stay on station, and on alert for the news helicopters converging above the site."

"Requesting permission to move up to ten thousand, so we can avoid incoming rotary wing traffic."

"Permission granted."

Wild Thing and Joker zoom climbed in formation up to ten thousand, their steep banking circle now giving them a literal ring-side view of the media circus developing below. Police barricades and SWAT vans mingled with news crew satellite dishes atop vans from every network.

* * *

"It's coming down," shouted ABC News anchor Don Hudson to his cameraman, who seemed torn between recording the event and getting crushed beneath the tenth-of-a-mile-long silver craft. "If memory serves me correctly, that thing looks like an old Ohio-class submarine. A chromed Ohio-class submarine!"

The sourdough smells from San Francisco's waterfront gave a unique ambience to the surreal scene. A homeless man busily used a magic marker to add "THE END IS HERE" above his "Gulf Vet Please Help Me Buy Food" panhandling sign. He stopped mid-scribble as a giant shadow grew around him.

Between amplified sonic crowd control shouts, projected by police off nearby glass surfaces, and the high-pitched whine and squealing tires of Mercedes-Tesla fuel-cell news vehicles, the blocks to either side of the Mission-Freemont landing zone cleared in plenty of time. Not that anyone had need to worry, since the MSFO (Massive Shiny Flying Object) stopped and hovered about fifteen feet above street level.

"Don't shoot! I come in peace!" said an unaccented voice, whose owner didn't take his thumb off the transmit key on his microphone, because his laughter was followed by, "I always wanted to say that!"

The statement had just the opposite effect on the police presence. Whomever didn't have a drawn weapon instantly changed their mind. Dozens of riot guns and magnetic projectile weapons aimed in the general direction of the voice. All converged on an opening below an obvious conning tower of what appeared to be an old atomic submarine. And from that opening descended an articulating arm, upon which stood a man wearing a garish Hawaiian shirt and cargo pants. Next to the man, a snake coiled around a support rail. A King Cobra to be precise.

"Hold your water, guys," boomed the voice, amplified somehow from the body of his ship. "I'm Glenn C Hammer from Planet Earth. I left here about fourteen years ago Earth time. Check your archives."

A woman close by suddenly grokked the snake curled around one of the support arms. She shrieked. A bullet pinged against an invisible shield near Hammer's head.

"I told you they would be paranoid, even trigger happy," said Hammer to his companion.

The snake replied in perfect English: "It's a wonder your species doesn't still live in caves and eat raw meat."

The talking reptile's voice carried throughout the crowd, clearly taking advantage of the same amplification system used by Hammer.

"Stop right there and leash that snake," said the officer closest to the ramp, which had now descended to street level. The command drew quizzical looks from several in the crowd.

"Snake, my cloaca!" spat the serpent. "I find that characterization of me profoundly offensive."

"Relax Kikan, let me handle this," said Hammer. Then to the policeman and the crowd in general. "Will somebody please round up my kid nephew, Stanley Dean Baker?"

Just then a white Pomeranian jumped from her master's hand and took a running leap at Kikan. The dog barked uncontrollably as it repeatedly bounced off the force field protecting the UFS's (Unidentified Flying Sub's) occupants. Undeterred, the dog kept up the attacks.

"Enough of that barking!" said Kikan. "Haven't you learned to speak, yet?"

* * *

Just ending his second term as President of the United States, Marc Benioff sat in the studio across from Glenn C Hammer. Near Hammer, Kikan coiled around a hat rack that he'd eerily transformed into a half-occupied caduceus. Stanley Dean Baker formed the third corner of the triangle.

"Let me get this straight," said President Benioff. "When you left the planet fourteen years ago, your nephew was seventeen and you were twenty-one years old. Now, you are the Earth equivalent of twenty-three years old and your nephew is thirty-one?"

"Weird, huh?" answered Hammer. "That's what happens when you go at nearly the speed of light for a year."

"Okay, I get the year part," said the president. "But you aged two years, so you were out there an extra year, somewhere. The question is, how did you get back here without blowing another fourteen years?

"That's where we come in," said Kikan.

No matter how many times they tried, the president and his staff, along with the camera crew and even the Secret Service detail, looked visibly startled by the talking snake. Wide, amazement-filled eyes and no other sound greeted the interruption. Kikan continued.

"Captain Hammer's ship used up the entire energy of one black hole, and he found himself stranded just shy of one light year from your planet. Our civilization noted the absence of the anomaly and sent me to investigate. Whereupon I find this ocean-going monstrosity tumbling through space, with its sole occupant barfing its guts out. I think you use the word 'seasick'."

"It's tough to find another black hole when you're not feeling so good," said Hammer.

"Tough, but not impossible," continued Kikan. "Unfortunately, you found the very black hole that our own civilization used for power. Since our sun went nova millennia ago, we couldn't afford to let this intergalactic ecological disaster to continue his profligate use of resources.

"The device he called *The Hubbard Matrix* was one step away from instantaneous intergalactic travel, and he didn't realize it."

The president seemed perplexed. "A Hubbard Matrix. What, is Hubbard some newly discovered physics particle?"

Hammer's not-a-kid-nephew-anymore Baker jumped in. "No, Uncle Glenn named it for a Twentieth Century author named L. Ron Hubbard. He was the greatest futurist in the history of science fiction."

"The Scientologist?" asked the president.

"That's the one," said Baker, ignoring any social stigma of talking with his mouth full, munching a Slim Jim he'd cavalierly pulled from his tweed jacket's inside pocket. "But Hubbard was a prolific science fiction author, who eclipsed all the others. Sure, Jules Verne invented the atomic submarine. Arthur C. Clark invented the communications satellite. Frank Herbert invented Earth Day. Piers Anthony invented the perfect computer virus. But in his ten-volume set called *Invasion Earth*, finished back in 1985, Hubbard invented 29 products, 10 of which have subsequently created billionaires around the world."

"Really," said the president. "Like what?"

"Like color-shifting car paint," said Baker, now on a roll. "Flash a light of a specific frequency and you've got a whole new color for your car."

"They actually have that now?" gasped Hammer. "In just fourteen years of my absence? By the way, shine a black light all around my shiny space submarine and it'll become invisible."

"Ooh, you've been busy during that year with the snake people," said his nephew.

"One more crack about snakes," hissed Kikan, "and I'll give you a colonoscopy you'll never forget!"

"Please forgive our characterization of your species," said the president. "On our planet, creatures we call 'snakes' are the vilest of creatures."

"Tell me about it!" shouted Kikan. "You have this Garden of Eden legend about The Evil One posing as one of us to tempt your first parents. Then wham! No speech. No resilient spine. Creatures doomed to slither in the dust. What has your civilization done to us?"

"But back to Hubbard," said the nephew, seemingly oblivious to Kikan's tantrum, "How about light-activated, color-shifting cosmetics and hair dye? Eyeglasses that switch to telephoto? High-tech party masks that actually print onto your face for twelve hours? Or how about nanobots that build instant houses by turning sand into annealing bricks, a complete home appearing in less than four hours?"

"We got all that now?" said the astonished Hammer.

"And don't get me started on inventions from *Battlefield Earth*. Ya been away a long time, Uncle Glenn."

"But back to The Hubbard Matrix, you pedantic twit," said Kikan.

Again, interruption by a talking snake stopped everyone cold. But this time, President Benioff got back on track a little more quickly than the others.

"Yes," he said. "Back to instantaneous intergalactic travel. Hammer?"

"Actually, I should have thought it through long before my initial voyage," said Hammer.

"If I could instantaneously transmit energy from a black hole dozens of light years away, I should have figured out that a simple transformation of the matrix bubble could just as easily have used the energy to move anything, anywhere. Instantly. Ergo, The Hubbard Matrix became The Hubbard Drive."

"Does anyone else on the planet know how this works?" asked a suddenly wary president.

"No. And they won't," began Kikan. "I have been sent here as an ambassador to your planet with an ultimatum."

And with that statement, the talking snake uncoiled from its perch and bounded around the set like a coiled spring. One of the studio techies had had the foresight to attach a remote microphone package to the reptile guest's neck.

"During the year Captain Hammer spent with us, our people—yes, actual people, humanoids just like yourselves—digested multiple terabytes of your complete planetary history from the archives aboard his craft.

"We have come to the conclusion that yours is the most war-like, murderous, amoral planet in the entire Universe. Some of the more religious of our people go so far as to assert your planet, Earth, is the source of all evil in the Galaxy. They came close to convincing our Intergalactic Council to summarily obliterate you.

"Therefore, turning you loose in this or any other galaxy simply cannot be allowed."

Silence. Furtive looks between the president and his off-camera staff. And the unstated but looming question: *How the Sam Hell did we agree to transmit this broadcast live, worldwide?*

Oblivious to the calculus of social interaction, Stanley Dean Baker blurted out the question on everyone's mind: "So what's the ultimatum?"

"I'm here to see if you lot can possibly get your act together. Until such a time as I send word through instantaneous transmission that you are indeed civilized enough to become a space-faring race, any attempt by anyone to make use of your so-called Hubbard Drive will result in instant destruction of your planet."

"Damn!" exclaimed the president, simultaneously with almost everyone else one Earth watching the interview.

The End

Illustration by Raja Nandepu

3

L.E.A.P.

by Nicholas P Adams

Thursday, May 12th, 10:27pm

"What are you willing to pay to ensure the safety of YOUR family?" The radio announcer growled as the outlawed national anthem played hauntingly in the background. "How much is the survival of your loved ones worth?"

CLICK! Dylan Loop switched off the power of his HAM radio.

That's enough pirate broadcast today. Even the FREEDOM network runs on advertising.

Hiding the receiver to the false-bottomed box, he picked up a handful of oil-stained rags and covered the content, and returned the container to a disheveled appearance.

Dylan glanced around his shed, a ramshackle ten by ten room made from scavenged bits of metal siding over a wood stud frame. A light rain rattled above his head, bringing to mind his grandmother's favorite old movie about a cat.

Returning to the workbench, Dylan took his welding gun from its holder, setting it in place before flipping the visor over his left eye. His right, cybernetic eye, automatically adjusted to the intense sparks as he pulled the trigger. Smoke rose from the joint, filling his nose with a rusty, burnt-chicken odor.

Nothing like working with your hands after solving cold cases to take your mind off the day job.

As Dylan soldered the leg and base together, the image of a feisty rocking horse danced across his mind. A proud smile fought against the pinched concentration of his lips.

I have a son. DJ. Little Dylan, Junior. After all, I put Erin through, she stayed with me and gave me a son. How close did I come to losing everything?

Dylan carefully turned the leg's corner to finish the weld, but his hand flew wild and severed the base when Erin's horrific scream overpowered the sound of melting steel.

Running through the smoke, Dylan raced out of the backyard shed to find the source of Erin's blood-curdling terror.

"Please," he could hear her sob, "Please don't take my baby."

NO! Not again! Not DJ! Not my son!

Dylan pushed away from the bench, nearly tearing the makeshift door off its hinges. The five meters to the porch looked like a football field as he sprinted toward the back door.

Rushing forward, Dylan held the welding gun like his service weapon as he bounded up the short flight of stairs. Flattening himself against the door jamb, he quickly poked his head out and glanced through the screen door.

If I'd remembered to shut the back door like Erin always reminds me, I never would have heard her scream for help.

From his quick glance, Dylan looked past the family room to the kitchen to his left. Another shriek, this time coming from a man, pulled his attention to the hallway.

"You're supposed to be asleep," came the guttural scream.

ERIN. DJ.

Ignoring his training to check the rest of the house, Dylan opened the screen door, wincing as the rusty hinges announced his entrance.

I really gotta get a can of WD-40.

Dylan moved quickly around the sofa, causing a lamp from the end table to fall over and crash to the wood floor.

As Dylan ran into the hallway, he caught sight of Erin kneeling in the nursery's doorway in her purple flannel pajamas. Blood trickled down her face from a gash at her hairline, giving her long blonde hair ghastly orange streaks.

Steadying herself with one hand against the jamb, she reached into the room as tears dripped onto the nursery's carpet. "Please, please, please," she sobbed repeatedly. "Please don't take my baby!"

Next to the nursery door, Dylan eyed the master bedroom's open door. The TV, still on, showed Erin's favorite docu-drama playing without any sound.

Erin must have been watching with her headphones.

Hearing the wailing from his newborn child put Dylan's senses into overdrive.

Nothing in this life or the next will stop me from protecting my family.

Dylan hurried to Erin's begging figure in five full steps. After taking a nanosecond to evaluate Erin, Dylan swung his welding gun wildly into the room, only to stop on a ragged-looking man holding his son loosely in one arm while wielding a jagged dagger in the other.

The blade glinted in the simulated starlight coming from DJ's ceiling, winking ominously at Erin's deepest fear.

"Oh, scat," the intruder moaned at the sight of Dylan's cybernetic eye. "You weren't supposed to be home. And she," he jabbed his knife toward Erin, "She was supposed to be asleep. Oh, scat, now I ain't never gonna get paid. And if I don't get paid, he's gonna cut me off. Oh, scat. SCAT! What I do now?"

The shabbily-dressed man began pacing in the small area between the crib and outside of arm's reach.

Dylan pointed his welder at the scoundrel's head, ignoring every incoherent word. "You broke into the wrong house, 10-T," he growled, stepping around Erin still sobbing hysterically on the floor.

Dylan put a soft hand on her shoulder, wishing he had a different mental gift at the moment. Her cries only seemed to increase, causing her begging to come out as mere babble.

Placing himself between the blade and his wife, Dylan refocused his aim on the unkempt man's head. DJ's little body swung like a sock in his sleeper. His tiny voiced exclaiming his fright at being manhandled in such an unfamiliar way.

The stranger fidgeted and twitched, muttering barely audible words. Dylan only caught a few words. "Told me--Get it out--bring it back--get my fix."

The last phrase brought the macabre scene into focus. "What's your fix, sir? Premier? Scald? Wander? What're you on?"

The dirty trespasser stared wild-eyed at Dylan, looking past the welder. "You're not supposed to be here," he screamed, causing a renewed round of crying and wailing from Erin and DJ. "You're supposed to be working late. And she was supposed to go to bed early." He stabbed the air in Erin's direction again, triggering another panic-stricken scream.

"I need to see my mom again," he wept through gritted teeth. "The man said if I got this baby for him, he'd take me back to see my mom before she died. I need to tell her I'm sorry before she dies again."

The ragged man, whom Dylan could now see as a strung-out young adult, wept bitterly as his convulsions took the serrated blade dangerously close to DJ's frail body.

So, that's what he wants. He thinks some L.E.A.P. will help him time travel like me.

"You're looking for some L.E.A.P., aren't you?" Dylan's voice softened as much as he could; just as the weekend hostage negotiation seminar taught him. "I can help you get some L.E.A.P. I've got some pharm-grade stuff out back. Give me my son, and I'll go get it for you."

The trespasser gnashed his teeth as his eyes widened in crazed fury. "You're lying!" he screamed. "He told me you'd say that. I know you don't have any L.E.A.P. Do you think I'm 10-T? I ain't 10-T! I'm leaving here with the kid, and there's nothing you can do about it!"

Dylan squared his stance, checking for targets beyond the walls with his cybernetic eye's thermal imager. "That's where you, and he, are wrong."

His voice rumbled with the contained fury and defensive instinct itching to pull the trigger. "There are two ways you're getting out of this house. Option one, you hand over my son, and you go to jail for B&E and attempted kidnapping. Or there's option two..."

The man's eyes darted between Dylan and Erin in an apparent attempt to gain her as an ally. His weapon shook as it drifted between the couple blocking his escape. "What's number two?" his voice shook.

Dylan dialed up the power to his welding gun, making the power cell whine like an angry bat.

At this intensity, the blast will burn through your skull, the wall, and the cinder block fence behind you.

"Bodybag. And you can tell your mother you're sorry...in person."

Dylan's last dig, intended to push the junkie's already addled brain over the edge, had the desired effect.

Screaming, the junkie lunged forward with the blade raised over his head. Dylan fired a single shot, burning a hole through the intruder's right eye, leaving a perfect circle seared into the wall beyond.

The junkie froze mid-stride, his left eye blinking randomly. Dylan stepped forward, pulling little DJ from the would-be kidnapper's arm as his body collapsed into a heap on the floor.

Erin sprang from the doorway, sobbing as Dylan put the baby into her waiting arms. She kissed and stroked his shaking head as Dylan guided them out of the nursery and down the hall into the kitchen.

Dylan and Erin embraced, protecting DJ in a familial cocoon. Cradling Erin's shoulders, Dylan guided her to the kitchen and into a chair. She seemed oblivious to the blood still trickling down her face as she kissed DJ's head, and smelling his hair.

He soaked two washcloths, placing one in Erin's hand to hold her head while he wiped blood and tears from her cheek with the other. After three trips to rinse out the reddened rags, Erin's face appeared as clean as he could get it. "I don't think you'll need stitches," he said, dabbing the stained cloth around the cut.

Erin winced, breathing gritted teeth. "I would rather get a thousand stitches than lose him."

Me too. I would rather kill myself than let you or DJ get hurt again.

"Erin," Dylan said once DJ's wailing ebbed. "You should lie down with the baby. I have to call the station and report this. And then wait for them in the nursery. It's now a crime scene. The captain will have to question both of us, and we can't discuss any details until after we're fully interrogated."

Erin nodded. She turned toward the stairs, then suddenly spun around, wrapping her free arm around his shoulders. "I'm so proud of you," she whispered. "You protected our family in a way I didn't think would have been possible two years ago." She pulled his head down to her, kissing him fiercely on the lips. "I love you so much."

Dylan brushed a damp strand of her long, blond hair from her glistening eyes. "I love you, too." He leaned to kiss her again. "Thanks for sticking around, and believing I could change."

She stared into his eyes for a moment, then her characteristic smirk emerged. "I always knew you could change," she winked. "You just had to pull your head out of your ass and realize I'm worth it."

Dylan laughed in spite of himself. "Always the last word, huh?"

Erin gave him a smug look and turned back toward the stairs. Dylan watched her strut up the steps and around the landing. "And I'll always have it, too!" she called from above.

Yes, ma'am.

Once Dylan heard their bedroom door close, he returned his full attention to the intruder. Picking up his department phone, he pressed his thumb to the glass. "Call Captain McCuiston."

A dial tone--and thirteen seconds later--the deep bass voice of Dylan's CO rang throughout the kitchen. "Who's dead?"

"Intruder, Cap," Dylan squeezed his nose bridge, "Someone tried to kidnap DJ again. This time, the perp didn't just get scared off when Erin came into the room. He gave me no choice but to put him down."

"Ah, damn!" McCuiston barked. "Erin and the baby okay?"

"Yeah," Dylan sighed, making his way to the nursery. "They're both shaken up, no serious injuries, but they're fine. They're resting upstairs."

"Okay, Loop," McCuiston sniffed in the background. "You know the drill. Stay at the scene. Leave everything as it is. I'll send out the TSI to witness the event and see if this needs to go through Internal Affairs."

I'm the best Time Scene Investigator in the Department. Maybe the whole damn planet. I would be the one sent to witness a homicide if I wasn't the one playing the part of the self-defending homeowner.

"Understood, Cap. But, one more thing-," Dylan rubbed his temples with a free hand, twisting his short, dark curls into mini-dreads. "This one was looking to score some L.E.A.P. I think his dealer may have been Der Schweiber himself."

McCuiston's breathing deepened as if he'd just finished a sprint up a flight of stairs. "I'll add that to the IA report. They'll probably need to send a Projector along with them...just in case."

As long as it isn't Leon. She's the last person I need in my house. Even if she's not in the time-stream with me. Erin would kick me out again just knowing we were in the same room together.

"Whoever gets the case, I'd suggest they back-trace the junkie and see if they can spot who sent him here," Dylan paused at his son's bedroom door. "We might get lucky and get a decent look at Der Schweiber."

The call ended, Dylan now standing over the junkie's body. His left eye twitched involuntarily giving the corpse the expression of a drug-addled asylum patient.

He knelt, picking up the dagger and pulling down his remaining lower eyelid with the tip. Zooming in with his cybernetic eye, Dylan found three thin rings circling his cornea. "Three episodes of visual schisms," he mumbled. "Should've had a cyber-swap like me."

Dylan resisted the temptation to desecrate the remains by popping out the other eyeball. He couldn't see them, but Dylan sensed the TSI team that had been watching from the moment he heard Erin's screams penetrate the shed.

"Whoever sent him to kidnap my son doesn't know me at all," Dylan whispered to the unseen agents witnessing the room's recent timeline.

Dylan took a deep breath. The adrenaline rush all but gone, he sat down in the rocking chair next to DJ's crib.

I'll just rest my eyelids for a few seconds.

Thursday, May 12th, 11:11pm

Dylan startled awake, finding himself pointing the welding gun toward Erin in the doorway. "Dylan," she yelped, "It's me. It's okay."

A pounding came from the front door, taking Dylan's attention from Erin holding her nose. "Dylan, get the door!" she wailed. "I don't know how you can sleep with that smell in this room."

Confused, Dylan looked down at the crumpled mess of dirty clothing holding together the dead body lying next to him. Rotted meat and two-week-old sweat assaulted his nostrils. In spite of his years around corpses, the one next to him caused his stomach to lurch.

With knots playing jump-rope in his gut, Dylan choked back the bile and pushed Erin out of the nursery.

Another, even louder, knocking at the door brought Dylan back to his senses. "Loop, you alright in there?" Captain McCuiston's voice bellowed just outside. "It's me. Open up."

Erin's shoulders relaxed, yet her arms pulled a sleeping DJ closer into her chest.

Dylan's heartbeat slowed. Grasping the door handle as he unconsciously dialed down his welder to zero. He held a tight grip on the welder's handle in spite of the heat burning into his skin from leaving it on its highest setting for too long.

The last time I forgot to power this down, I accidentally poked myself in the face.

The door creaked open to reveal a short, older man with graying hair. His crisp uniform sounded like snow pants as he walked straight past Dylan into the kitchen to find Erin filling a baby bottle at the sink.

"Erin," the captain asked, placing a tender hand on her shoulder. "Are you alright?"

Erin walked into his opened arms, smiling over his shoulder. "Yeah," she exhaled with a rattled breath. "I'm okay, Liam. So is DJ. I'm just glad

Dylan was home tonight. I don't know what would have happened if he'd taken that extra shift."

Dylan picked up a damp washcloth from the sink, wrapping it around the welder. Streams of dish soap with wafts of old potato skins filled the air as he placed the tool on the counter.

McCuiston released Erin, turning to Dylan with a mocking scowl. "It's about time this rookie started listening to his training officer," he growled playfully. "I've been telling him for the past three years that he needs to spend more time at home."

I haven't been a rookie for ten years, dammit.

"At least, I get out of my office once in a while, Cap."

"I don't care how long I've driven a desk, Loop," McCuiston tapped a finger to his temple. "I still know more than you."

I'm so glad it doesn't freak me out to have you read my mind anymore. But, I do wish my thoughts weren't so easy to read.

Dylan smiled against his will. "It's because we're both H.S.P."

McCuiston turned to Erin with an amused smile. "Sorry, it stands for Highly Sensitive Person. It means people like Dylan and myself carry our emotions very near the surface."

Erin's eyes darted to Dylan, leaning against the counter.

McCuiston put his hands on Erin's shoulders, leaning down to whisper something, but loud enough for Dylan to overhear. "It's okay, Erin. It's not going to happen again. He's 100 percent here with you. He's nowhere else."

I don't know what she asked you, but thank you, Cap.

McCuiston kissed Erin softly on the cheek and then turned his head toward Dylan. "Being a Puller has its advantages. You never have to ask the question to get an honest answer."

A trio of agents marched through the open front door. Dylan looked at their uniforms. A Tactile, a Senser, and an ordinary beat cop strode behind him, filing into the nursery without a single word.

The Tactile for a post-mortem exam of the body. The Senser for trace evi-

dence. But who's the rookie?

"That's my nephew," McCuiston answered Dylan's unspoken question. "He's just graduated the academy and wants to join the TSI. I think he may have a future as a Leaper."

Very punny.

McCuiston barked out a laugh. "Okay, that was a bad one. But, there's no Leaper like you, Loop. You'll always be the best."

Dylan rolled his eyes. "I don't know if this genetic happenstance is something to celebrate."

"I think your gift makes you extraordinary," Erin broke in, holding DJ and the bottle out to Dylan.

McCuiston's crow's feet deepened with delight. "You've resolved more cold cases than any TSI I have. And it's all because you can leap further than anyone else."

Dylan cradled his fussy son in one arm. His nose cringed as his hand felt the bulge in DJ's diaper. "It's your turn to change him," Dylan moaned, aiming the bottle at his wife.

Erin pinched her lips to prevent the smile from erupting. "But Liam wants to interview me first."

"That's not standard protocol," Dylan argued. Cap, I know what you're doing.

McCuiston shrugged. "Happy wife, happy life." Erin pulled a chair from the table and sat down while Dylan plugged the bottle's nipple into DJ's pouty mouth. He chuckled in spite of himself at DJ's ability to tug formula out of a bottle faster than he could have refilled it.

McCuiston moved to stand behind Erin, placing his hands on her head.

Watching McCuiston pull a memory never ceases to creep me out a little.

Simultaneously, both Erin and McCuiston opened their eyes, revealing only blank stares. Each moved their lips rapidly, like watching a playback at three times speed. After just a few moments, they both closed their eyes, and McCuiston took his hands away.

Erin's head had drooped like a sleepy child for a second before she lifted her chin to look into Dylan's concerned face. "I'm okay," she hummed. "It wasn't as hard as last time. I know better now what to expect."

I know that feeling.

"Guess we should just get this over with," Dylan sighed. "For the record, of course."

Erin made to rise, but Dylan stopped her. "No, baby," he cooed, lowering DJ into her arms. "You stay seated and rest. My debriefing will take a little longer. It's just standard procedure."

Dylan gave McCuiston a knowing glance.

I'm hoping you can get a few residuals from the body.

McCuiston nodded with a fatherly smile toward Erin, patting her on the shoulder and leaning down to kiss his God-son on the forehead. "Happy wife, happy life," he crooned as he followed Dylan out of the kitchen, grabbing the warm, damp package from the counter as he passed the sink.

Standing shoulder to shoulder in the doorway, McCuiston hefted the wet cloth. "You know, it's not technically legal to modify a welding gun for home defense."

Technicalities made this world what it is.

"It's not technically illegal either," he countered. "Besides, I didn't modify it for home defense. I was using it to make a rocking horse for DJ. But you already know that, huh?"

McCuiston huffed. "Yeah, I did. But I still like to get the emotional reaction. It's the most telling."

Dylan peeked out the corner of his eye. "And what have you learned so far."

This time, I'm innocent.

"I know you're innocent, Loop." McCuiston opened the moist towel to examine the welder. "This was a clean shoot. I knew even before I pulled Erin's POV. I'm still going to have to take this as evidence."

It's my only one. How am I going to finish DJ's rocking horse without it?

"Yes, sir," Dylan sighed.

"Oh, I think you have plenty of time to finish that horse before your boy is big enough to ride it," McCuiston said. "You'll get it back as soon as the formal inquiry is completed."

"Who knows when that'll be!" Dylan crossed his arms, trying to squeeze the frustration out. He only succeeded in expelling his body odor.

Wow, do I need a shower!

"Yes, you do need a shower. But that'll have to wait," McCuiston brushed at his nose. "C'mon, let's pull your POV, and then you take Erin and the baby upstairs. Take that much-needed shower. We'll finish up down here. I'll let you know when we've finished. You're not even supposed to be within five meters of the crime scene until after processing."

Dylan jerked his head toward the back door. "You can pull my POV in the shed. If it becomes too much, at least Erin won't hear it," he said, turning away from the nursery.

McCuiston handed the welder to the Tactile before following Dylan. "Get this processed, ASAP. I want the energy signature cataloged in detail so we can get it back to Sergeant Loop with minimal delay."

The Tactile, a middle-aged man with thick, wire-rim glasses, nodded. "First thing," he chirped.

Dylan loitered in the hallway, hunched over and stalling for time.

I hate this part.

McCuiston put a firm hand on Dylan's shoulder. "I hate it too. Pulling from another H.S.P. is more painful than pulling from a serial killer. It's hard not to get overwhelmed by someone else's emotional experience."

The pair trudged across the dewy grass into the small shed wrapped in tarnished corrugated metal. Dylan lingered at the door as McCuiston slid an old metal chair across the concrete. A broken wheel squealed its objection to movement, causing the hairs on Dylan's neck to bristle.

McCuiston positioned the chair in front of him, facing the sidewall and patted its back. "The sooner we start..."

Dylan took in a lungful of dusty air, smelling the remains of rusty, burnt-chicken from earlier. He gazed longingly at the broken rocker leg as he plopped down onto the thin padding.

McCuiston grabbed a piece of leather from the workbench and handed it to Dylan. "This will help," his dark, sullen voice echoed off the metal walls.

This was supposed to be the saddle.

Dylan slowly rolled up the swatch of cowhide, placed it in his mouth and bit down. Gripping the chair frame, he took several deep breaths through the nose like a free-diver about to submerge.

I'm ready.

McCuiston placed his hands on Dylan's head and closed his eyes. "Let's begin."

Electricity, stronger than anything Dylan had ever felt before, jolted his body from all directions. Unable to retract his hands from the metal seat bottom, his nails pressed back into their beds as images from the evening exploded into his mind's eye.

The painful slow-motion replay unfurled in excruciating detail as each image and sensation became amplified, starting at the moment Erin screamed from the house.

Friday, May 13th, 6:09am

Dylan woke to Erin's morning breath and the repeated slaps across his face keeping time with the blasts of his alarm. "Dylan! Dylan, wake up! Dylan!"

He rolled off his back, reaching over to turn off the buzzer with a quick swipe of his finger. The bed bounced as Erin pulled the covers off him, letting the cool morning air rush across his naked back. His light cotton pajama bottoms bunched up around his calves as he dug his feet back into the duvet's warm folds. Predawn beams of light peaked through the blinds above their heads, casting muted lines crawling across the ceiling and down the wall.

Dylan tucked a pistol back under his pillow as he rubbed the sleep from his eye. DJ wailed from the floor above, announcing his disapproval to his breakfast's delay. Erin backhanded him in the rear end. "It's your turn to feed him," she mumbled under a pillow.

Rolling over, he wrapped an arm around her waist and pulled her across the bed into the crook of his body. "But you're the one with the milk dispensers," he purred as he kissed her shoulder.

Erin's hand emerged from under the pillow faster than a frightened baby Gazelle on the Savannah. Her fingers smacked his forehead as he reached further around, tickling her ribs. "Stop," she howled, laughing and kicking. "Stop it! I'm gonna pee!"

Dylan let go and rolled onto his back. Erin pulled out from under the pillow and jumped him, straddling across his hips and pinning his arms down. She panted as she gazed at him with hungry eyes. Her lips curled over her teeth as she bent over to put her face against his ear. "If you think we're going to fool around before you feed your son," she cooed. "You've got another think coming. Just because Liam gave you the morning off work, doesn't mean you're free to dodge your duties at home." She nibbled on his lobe for a moment before suddenly peeling herself off him and rushed into the bathroom like she was carrying a penny between her knees.

Dylan chuckled and threw his legs over the side, grabbing a balled-up blood-red t-shirt emblazoned with the golden TSI emblem from the floor. He strode around the bed and across the room, pausing at the threshold to glance at the closed nursery door. The yellow security seal clung to the jambs like plastic wrap; forbidding his entrance and keeping the stench of rotting meat and iron from fumigating the house.

He left the bedroom just as a noise no woman admits to making erupted from the bathroom, quickly followed by the sounds of water rushing from the tap. Taking the steps two at a time, Dylan raced up the stairs and down the short hallway into the guest room. DJ's travel crib wobbled on the thick beige carpet as his legs flailed against the thin sleeping pad. His little eyes and fists pinched into knots as tears spilled into his ears.

"Shhh," Dylan scooped DJ off the mat, rocking him in both hands. "Hey, buddy. It's okay. Daddy's here."

DJ's squawk's petered for only a moment as he opened his eyes long enough to lock onto Dylan's face. DJ's renewed howls threatened to shake the plaster off the ceiling until Dylan nestled him on his shoulder.

Swaying gently as he strolled back into the hall and down the stairs, DJ's whimpering soaked Dylan's shirt.

Turning into the kitchen, Dylan opened the fridge and pulled out a bottle of breast milk labeled 5/7.

This should still be good, right?

Setting the bottle on the counter, he grabbed a small saucepan from the drying rack with his free hand and turned the faucet on with his elbow. With DJ's whining growing in his ear, Dylan set the pan down, dropped the bottle and a rubber nipple into the water and turned on the stove. A short whiff of rotten eggs, followed by the clicking of sparks, and a wave of heat rose into the air.

Dylan rocked as the pan started to steam.

"Quite a rough night, huh, buddy?" Dylan rubbed DJ's back as he stared out the kitchen window. "Can't imagine why someone wants to take you away from mom and me. But don't worry, DJ. I'll never let anything bad happen to you or mommy."

Dylan kissed DJ on his cheek and took the simmering pan off the stove. Assembling the nipple and collar with one hand, Dylan moved into a chair and let his boy cradle down into his elbow's crook. DJ latched onto the bottle with an eagerness reserved for starving pigs immediately dispelling his hungry cries with rhythmic grunts.

Dylan looked down into DJ's wide-open stare.

"You have your mother's eyes," he whispered. "Your left eye. It's half gray, half blue. Let's just hope you never need to have eyes like mine." Dylan tapped his right temple.

DJ's gaze followed Dylan's finger and then snapped back to his normal eye.

Yeah. I guess I'd be drawn to the real eye too.

From the bedroom, Dylan's phone chirped again with an urgent tone.

Priority Department message.

"Erin," Dylan shouted around the corner. "Please bring me my phone!"

A few moments later, Erin padded into the kitchen wearing charcoal and pink-striped running pants with a matching top. Her hair, tied up in a ponytail, swished back and forth as she handed Dylan his phone. The TSI logo hovered above the glass like a maglev train, pulsating in time with the ring tone.

"Going out for a run?" Dylan's eyes caressed his wife's curves as he put the incoming call on hold.

"Yeah," she put a foot between Dylan's legs on the chair. She leaned over to tighten her laces, giving Dylan a better view at one of his favorite vistas. "I shouldn't be longer than an hour."

DJ drained the last remnants of milk, sucking in the foam. Erin switched feet and bent over again. "I'll watch last night's game with DJ," Dylan tugged on his pant leg, shifting in his seat. "After I see what the department wants." He held up his blinking phone, waving it to say goodbye.

"It should be time for DJ's morning nap by the time I get back," Erin kissed DJ's forehead, breathing in his scent as thunder erupted from below. "Ooh! Just in time. He needs a change."

Dylan stood up, taking the bottle from DJ's vice grip, and moved toward the sink. Erin backpedaled, putting her arms around his waist as he waltzed forward. "I'll see you when you get back," Dylan wrapped his free arm around Erin. "I think I'll give DJ a bath before we watch the game since he loves the water so much."

Erin slid a hand underneath Dylan's shirt, stroking his chest. "Maybe when I get back," she purred with raised eyebrows. "You can wash me too."

"Sounds like a great plan," Dylan leaned down and kissed Erin softly on the mouth for several seconds before pulling away. "The sooner you go, the sooner you come back." He patted her rear as she turned out of the kitchen with a wink and walked out the front door.

Dylan adjusted his pants again and looked down at DJ smiling at up him. "Daddy's gonna get lucky!" Squeals burst from DJ as he poked his finger under DJ's chubby chin. "Guess I better finish my chores before mommy gets home, huh?"

Dylan glanced at his phone to see the caller ID. The TSI logo pulsated.

That's the precinct prefix, but I don't recognize the extension.

Dylan swiped his thumb across the plate. The logo vanished, followed by the department A.I.'s voice on the speaker.

"Good morning, Detective Loop. I trust you slept well."

"Good morning, Iris," Dylan moaned.

"The whole department wishes you and your family a speedy recovery after enduring a horrific ordeal. As per protocol established by The Assembly, all Emergents involved in a homicide are to be debriefed by their department supervisor and receive a psychological examination. My records show Captain William McCuiston pulled your POV last night. Report to the department psychologists before 5:00 pm today. Would you like to schedule the appointment with me now?"

Dylan opened his calendar out of habit, scrolling through his empty schedule. "What's the last available time slot this afternoon?"

"There is an opening at 4:15 pm. Would you like me to add it for you?"

"Sure," Dylan huffed. "Put me down." Within a second, a new event appeared on his phone's calendar. Dylan tapped the appointment, and the details radiated from the glass.

"Is there anything else I can help you with this morning, detective?"

Dylan examined the name and address of his assigned psychologist. "No," he muttered, "I'm fine. That'll be all."

"Very well, Detective Loop. Have a wonderful day."

Dylan slid the phone into his pocket and looked at the bundle in his arms. DJ's gaping mouth drew in a deep breath as his little arms stretched with arched back. Dylan covered his mouth as a loud yawn escaped. "Let's get you into the bath, buddy." He tossed DJ a few inches into the air, rewarded with delighted squeals. "Looks like daddy has to go visit *The Funhouse* this afternoon.

Friday, May 13th, 4:01pm

The city traffic ten stories below drowned out Dylan's footsteps as he strolled across the skywalk between the Federal building and the Internal Affairs Annex. Rows of ground and hover vehicles, six across and two high, roared and honked like an experimental symphony. Synthetic shade trees nestled in concrete planter boxes along the bridge provided limited patches of cover from the safety cameras positioned on every building corner within eyesight.

Dozens of citizens, federal enforcement officers (F.E.O.), and oligarchs flowed across the hundred-meter catwalk. Small groups of two's and three's sat on the synth-crete benches surrounding planter boxes of artificial trees. Each individual seemed to be nose deep in their virtual tablets, typing vigorously in the air.

Dylan stopped under a synthetic willow, pulling down a switch and toying with a fabricated leaf between his fingers. The fern colored blade shimmered in the hazy sunlight. Unconsciously he zoomed in on the surface with his cybernetic eye, revealing the micro photo-voltaic cells and CO2 scrubbers embedded in the facade. Trails of nano-circuitry crisscrossed the blade like a microcosm of spiderwebs.

"You have ten minutes to reach your destination, Detective Loop," Iris' voice chirped through Dylan's earbud. "Please continue to your destination. Dr. Margaret Leigh is expecting you."

Delightful.

Dylan sighed. The tree limb whipped out of his hand and bobbed in the wind that coursed through the city. "I'll be there in five, Iris."

"Have a wonderful day, Detective," Iris chimed as Dylan continued his trek across the crowded platform. The flow of traffic moved around him as if he were a giant turtle crawling downstream. Finishing the final thirty meters, he pushed through the revolving glass door into the annex's main foyer. The beige carpet and green wall hangings drowned out the noise coming from the city street. Twin arching staircases rose to the upper level on either side, leaving a round area in the middle. A handful of dignitaries seemed to be engrossed in a one-liner contest as the everyday folk and F.E.O.'s gave them a wide berth as they passed.

Dylan gazed up to the enormous circular lantern hanging from the twelve-story atrium ceiling. The National motto "Tolerance and Safety for All" revolved around the drum in an endless cycle of alternating fonts.

The rebel Constitutionalists might beg to differ.

Dylan took the stairs on his right, gaining momentum with each downward step. Crossing the balcony and another flight down landed him on the eighth floor. He looked at his phone as he took the corridor on the far left.

4:10. Five minutes early is ten minutes late.

Reaching the semi-circular alcove for suite eight hundred, Dylan knocked three times and stepped back from the gray metal door. Deep scratches revealed rainbow layers of paint as Dylan stood in the black footprints inlaid within the tawny carpet.

The peephole lens opened, releasing a small marble-sized orb into the air. The silver ball split along its equator and emitted a blue laser beam, projecting a grid across Dylan's face.

"Remain still, Detective," Iris' disembodied voice came from above. "The security verification process will be over shortly."

The alcove's curved walls extended beyond the corridor, trapping him like tinned meat. Twin spheres (three times larger than the first) popped up from the floor and began orbiting around and between Dylan's legs, scanning upward until they disappeared into the ceiling.

I wonder if I should ask the scanners to buy me dinner next time. Last time I just had to talk to someone.

"Scan complete." A new voice, low and dark, erupted from the speaker as the walls retreated. The small orb floated in place directly in front of Dylan's face. "Single anomaly detected. Cybernetic implant located in right orbital socket. Explain."

Dylan's brow furrowed. "Shouldn't you already know why I had a cyber-swap done? I was ordered here to talk to Dr. Leigh. She should have my file. It's all in there."

"Explain," the voice boomed again.

"Are you going to let me in to see Dr. Leigh," Dylan crossed his arms, taking a half-step back. "Or shall I inform my captain that I was unable to complete my mandatory evaluation because a rent-a-slab security guard took a power trip?"

Dylan squinted into the laser, jaw set and poised to turn for several seconds.

"Explain."

"Go to Hell!" Dylan spun and slammed his fist into the barrier. "Either let me in, or I'm leaving, you're choice. But I don't owe you a damn thing."

"Failure to comply with mandated protocols will result in immediate disciplinary action." The laser continued to scan.

Disciplinary Action. Fancy words for 'you will be lobotomized, and your family will be out on the streets.'

Dylan set his jaw, his lips pressed into a tight line, while his left eye started to burn from the light. After a full minute, his arms fell. He put a hand on his hip and rubbed his temples with the other. "Look," he sighed, "I had a level three schism a few years back after a rough leap. I couldn't get the double-vision under control, so they offered me a choice. Ocular replacement or lobotomy."

Dylan pointed at his face. "Three guesses as to what happened, and the last two don't count."

The door opened with a hiss. "Thank you for telling me the truth, Detective," the voice sounded dark but softer, like a rich chocolate. "Please, come in."

* * *

Dylan stepped through the open door into a small, brightly lit lobby. The square room showed no signs of a receptionist desk. The far side of the hall joined a narrow corridor disappearing on either side. Taking a few steps into the space, the door closed behind him without a sound. Dylan turned in place, checking each corner for the gruff doorman. Sixteen folding metal chairs lined three walls, all empty except for a few magazines littered about and a dozing elderly woman sprawled across three.

"Please follow the lights, Detective," the voice echoed as a stream of green LEDs blinked a trail through the lobby's center and down the corridor. "Room eight-thirty-two."

Dylan scanned the room again, shoving his hands in his pockets as he followed the flashes. Stark white doors lined each side of the narrow hall, each marked with an even number. The lights ended halfway down the corridor. Room 804 opened as he passed and a Sensor he knew by face stumbled out, trembling as she clung to the jamb.

"You're going to be alright, Dani," a man wearing a white shirt, blue slacks and matching tie whispered as he put his hands on her shoulders. "Thank you for telling me the truth. Even if it took some prodding."

Dani, wearing black yoga pants under a flowing purple smock, shuddered at the man's touch. Beads of sweat glistened on her forehead, shoulders, and chest, making her look like a melting grape Popsicle. A quick glance over their heads revealed a two by three-meter room with green walls, tiled ceiling, and polished concrete floor. Two plush recliners facing one another in the center seemed to be the only other occupants.

Looks like you just spent an hour on a step-climber.

Her eyes locked onto Dylan's as he sidestepped past her. She fixed his gaze with wide eyes, and an almost imperceptible head shake. Dylan gave her a thin smile and nodded as the man tugged Dani back into the room. "Let's finish our session, shall we?" Dani's fingernails raked across the flat door jamb as the man pulled her into the room by her shoulders. Whimpering sobs escaped from room 804 as the door closed.

A few steps further down, Dylan reached door 832. It opened as he lifted his hand to knock. "Welcome, Detective Loop," the chocolate voice rang from overhead. "Please come in."

The door swung wide, revealing a similar interior as room 804. A coif of dark brown hair pulled into an array of tight ponytails, sat in the chair with its back to the door. The head rose, atop the long neck of a petite woman. She wore a high-neck sleeveless ivory blouse and black pencil skirt. A pair of black-framed glasses hung from a silver chain around her neck. She stepped around the chair in short black heels and extended her right hand. Dylan took it and shook. His eyes followed the olive-colored skin, finding several scars dotted along her arm.

Are those bullet wounds?

"Hello, Detective." the rich voice sang from above as the woman's mouth moved in sync. "I'm Margaret Leigh. Oops. Sorry about that." She stroked a silver hoop dangling from her left ear then cleared her throat.

"But you can call me Maggie." The booming voice from above had disappeared, replaced with a rich soprano tone.

"What was that?" Dylan looked around, avoiding her penetrating ice-blue eyes.

"That," her lilting accent chimed like a songbird, "was my gatekeeper. It allows me to make a few initial observations before meeting in person. Won't you come in?"

She turned her body, gesturing to the recliner facing the door.

Dylan stepped behind, keeping his back to the wall and his eyes on her as he circled the room. He scanned the walls and ceiling for surveillance, finding nothing but basic construction materials before halting in front of his assigned chair. "So, you're the *Teller*, huh?"

Maggie smiled, her cupids bow lips thinning as they spread wide. "I'm one of them, anyway. Does that bother you? Are you nervous about being here?" She sat back down in her chair, crossing her legs as the door closed behind her. She folded her hands and looked up at Dylan with kind eyes.

"Why should I be nervous?" Dylan eased himself down in the soft leather cushions. He crossed his own legs, opposite to hers, and folded his arms.

Maggie raised the glasses onto her face, the silver chain swaying like spider's silk. She tapped the rims, and the lens' edges emitted a soft red glow around her eyes. "It's a perfectly normal reaction," she said as her right hand made strange gestures in her left palm. "This is the first time you've had to come see one of us?"

Dylan zoomed in, picking up on his reflection in her pupils. An infrared ghost of himself, along with an array of medical diagnostics, floated in the lenses.

Why would a therapist need Augmented Reality (A.R.)?

Dylan nodded. "I met with a therapist after the last incident. But he was a non-E."

"A non-Emergent?" Maggie's fingers danced. "I see. Tell me how you felt after speaking with him?"

Dylan sighed, looking around the blank walls. "Fine, I guess. Just a routine after-incident debriefing. What are you doing?" He pointed to her hand-dancing.

Maggie's eyes followed his finger to her lap. "I'm taking notes," she smiled. "You've already noticed my A.R., just as I noted you taking a peek. Does it bother you?"

To be honest, yeah.

"I don't know," Dylan tightened his arms around his chest. "I guess not. You're the doc, right?"

"I'm required by The Assembly to record all biometric data in all sessions with fellow Emergents. I'm sorry if that makes you uncomfortable. But, I think you're well aware we don't have the luxury of keeping secrets."

"Ain't that the truth?" Dylan rolled his eye then looked around the room again. "So, they call this the *Funhouse*. Why do they call it that?"

"A part of Reflection Therapy utilizes mirrors to help the subject confront the lies we tell ourselves," Maggie smiled. "When the lies are challenged from an external source, we become defensive. When we question the lies ourselves, we're more open to insight and resolution."

Dylan shifted in his chair and nodded at the wall, relaxing his hands on the chairs' arms.

"Shall we begin?" She swiped her palms across her lap as if spreading playing cards on an invisible table. The lights dimmed, and Dylan's chair pushed away from Maggie's until it squished against the wall. A fog pressed on his mind as a numbness seemed to tickle along his skin, starting from his fingers and toes. Mirrors jutted from the sidewalls like scissors cutting the room in two, leaving Dylan isolated with his reflection.

"Please stand, Detective," the deep voice resonated from above.

The armchair lifted off the floor, pouring Dylan out like pancake batter, and seemed to melt into the ceiling like an upside-down ice cube.

Here we go.

The twin mirrors split, again and again, slowly spiraling toward him as if wrapping him up like a burrito. Sixteen mirrored panels warped and undulated like living silver ooze, rotating in a tight circle. One pane stopped in front and flattened with Dylan's image frozen on its surface. A high-pitched bell chime seemed to ring quietly behind the mirror. Dylan winced slightly at the tone ringing in his ear.

"*Tell me what happened last night*," Dylan's reflection demanded in the same dark voice he'd heard in the corridor.

Dylan searched the fifteen distorted panels, catching glimpses of his grotesquely misshapen self. "A vagrant--a drug addict--came into my home looking for L.E.A.P. He assaulted my wife and attempted to kidnap my son. He was an immediate threat to my family, so I responded with lethal force."

Dylan's image rotated clockwise, and the adjacent panel ceased to ripple, leaving him face to face with two reflections which spoke in unison. A second jingling bell joined the first. "*Tell me why you killed him instead of calling for backup*."

Dylan's stare darted between his Doppelganger's, tightening his fists. "There wasn't time. He had my son in a chokehold, and my wife needed medical attention. I had to act fast, or DJ could have died."

The twins spun out of the way as the third reflection appeared along with the chiming trio. "*Tell me why you shot him in the head instead of a non-lethal part of the body*."

Dylan's jaw clenched as his eye narrowed. "Because he had DJ in front of him as a shield. I couldn't risk hitting my son."

"Tell me why you didn't just shoot him in the leg." The four images asked in chorus.

"Stop!" Dylan pressed his temples, struggling against the dissonant quartet. "I can't think with that damn ringing."

"The session will end once you tell me the truth, Detective. Now, tell me why you didn't simply disable him?"

Dylan's head bowed, viced between his fingers. "I was afraid if I'd only immobilized him, he would have used the knife to hurt DJ. Please, stop. I'm telling you the truth."

"There is still something you're hiding, Detective. Perhaps even from yourself. We shall continue until we get to the whole truth."

* * *

Dylan fell on all fours--back arched like a yoga master--raking the polished concrete with his nails. Sweat dripped from his forehead as he buried his chin into his chest. He squinted against the Devil's bell choir slamming against his ears.

All around him, sixteen flat mirrors with duplicate reflections, four deep, circled him like Hyenas. "*Be honest, Detective. Tell me why you really shot the intruder.*"

Dylan slammed his fist into the floor and gritted his teeth. "Because, after cheating on Erin," he screamed, "I wanted to prove to her I'd always protect her. From anyone who tried to tear our family apart!"

The mirrors turned to smoke and dissipated like a warm breath on a winter morning. Dylan's body racked with sobs as he crouched on the floor, tears puddling between his hands. The chimes still rang in his ears as he felt a pair of hands rest tenderly on his shoulders.

"Thank you for your honesty, Detective," Maggie whispered. "You've done your department, and your family, a great service. How do you feel?"

Dylan pulled away from her hands, sitting up and wiping his face. He blew out his breath like a balloon with a pin-hole leak and raked his damp hair back into place with shaky hands. "Just peachy. You ever been run over by a steam roller and then get pissed on?" he growled. "It's something like that."

"I understand your anger," Maggie danced her fingers across her palm. "Would you like to sit down?"

Dylan craned his neck as the recliner emerged from a hatch in the ceiling masked by tiles. His head tilted. "I could have sworn it melted."

"Part of the illusion." Maggie lifted Dylan under his arm as the chair reached the floor. "I projected the mirrors into your mind. You provided the rest. You made a significant breakthrough in such a short time."

Dylan slumped into the chair like a sack of laundry as it hit his ankles. "How long was I in there? Felt like hours." He wiped a sleeve across his forehead.

"Approximately fifteen minutes," she back-pedaled and sat down, returning to her note-taking posture. "The subconscious, depending on the person, works four to five-hundred-thousand times faster than the conscious mind."

"No way," Dylan looked up the time on his phone. *4:31*. "How were you able to keep up if my brain was running at five-hundred-K?"

Maggie looked up from her palm, the red glow making her pupils look like Amethyst. "As a Teller, I'm a mix between a Projector and a Puller. I can simultaneously put images into others' minds and experience their point of view. In Reflection Therapy, I enter a pseudo-sleep state so I can direct the interview and observe your responses."

"Sounds exhausting," Dylan huffed. "If you do both, what's the gear for?" Dylan motioned to her A.R. glasses.

"They record your biometrics, which I'll review later," she pushed the glasses up her nose. "But I experience the same thing you do, as you put it, in the *Funhouse*."

Dylan picked at the fraying thread in the cushion.

Sure glad Marie wasn't a Teller, but talk about being the proverbial fly on the wall.

Maggie cleared her throat. "Right now, I see no reason why you shouldn't be back to work by next Monday."

"Next week?" Dylan sat up. "You're putting me on leave? Why?"

"Detective Loop," Maggie breathed. "This is not a punishment. In fact, quite the opposite." She tapped her glasses and pulled them from her face, letting them dangle onto her chest.

"Off the record," her voice barely audible even though she leaned forward to close the distance, "I've never seen anyone confront their mirrors like you. I've been in sessions where over three hundred individual reflections caused the patient to lose touch with reality and had to be--." She stared at Dylan, wide-eyed, biting her lip.

"Lobed," he whispered. "They were lobotomized so only The Assembly would benefit from their gifts."

Maggie nodded once, then returned the glasses to her face. "So, we're agreed then," she resumed her professional demeanor, "After you take a few days off to recuperate, you're cleared to return to your normal duties starting Monday." She stood and walked around her chair, letting the glasses fall onto her chest once again.

Dylan heaved himself off the seat, wobbling and reaching for the wall as she opened the door. "I'm fine," Dylan snapped, holding up his hand as Maggie reached out to support him. "But thanks. I can manage." He held up his right hand as he balanced himself in the threshold.

Maggie took it and squeezed it with two pumps. "Thank you for your honesty, Detective Loop. Give my best to Erin and DJ. Though we've never met, I feel like I already know them."

Dylan tapped a pair of fingers to his forehead and turned left down the hall. Behind him, the clacking of Dr. Leigh's heels echoed off the hard tiles, growing quieter with each step toward the lobby and home.

Monday, May 23rd, 7:30am

Dylan stepped across the elevator threshold onto the federal buildings' 27th floor slugging his faded red gym bag across his back. His old combat boots clunked against the marble in a war-drum cadence as he approached the 5th Precinct's central atrium. Hundreds of metal chairs, scattered across the white stone floor, contained men, women, and animals in varying states of misery.

It's like coming home. If coming home were like putting your hand in a Ming vase filled with dog vomit.

Dylan navigated the labyrinth of clacking high heels worn by street-corner hostesses, homeless junkies in old dumpster-stained clothing, and mangy dogs on leashes made from frayed optical cable, the mutts barking at anyone who came within ten feet of their masters.

Finally reaching the gate separating the throngs of discarded humanity, Dylan pressed his badge to the security screen as lasers scanned his face. His file photo appeared on the display, verifying his credentials in green letters and the sterile recording.

"Detective Dylan Loop. Authorized."

Behind the door, steel bolts scraped from their keepers as red dust fell at Dylan's feet.

The thick doors swung open to reveal Dylan's TSI offices, contrasting starkly to the cathedral-like finishes of the atrium behind him. White-tiled floors. White-tiled walls. White ceiling tiles.

Well, The Assembly certainly spared no expense when they built this place. I can never quite tell if I'm at work or an asylum. Guess since the world has gone completely crazy...

"Loop," McCuiston hollered across the noisy bullpen, waggling his chubby hand. "Come in here when you get a sec."

Dylan tossed the gym bag under his desk-sitting on the outskirts of a few dozen identical cubicles-then pressed the glowing message icon radiating on his desktop as he lowered himself into the soft ergo-chair.

Why is it so hard to get back into the rhythm after taking time off?

A female Sensor walking by turned her head and dry-heaved as she passed by the pungent stank of three-day-old gym socks. "Sorry, Carlisle! Haven't had a chance to take it home for washing."

Well, not really sorry.

"Yeah, right," she glared while covering her nose and mouth. She sniffed toward the bag. "You might want to go see a doctor about that."

Dylan looked out the corner of his eye. "About what?" The mischievous grin disappeared from his face.

Carlisle's eyes watered as if she'd spent the day peeling onions. "About the fungal outbreak. Your Athlete's Foot has come back with a vengeance." Suppressing a gag, she turned and sprinted away from Dylan's desk to the open window.

Dylan returned his attention to his inbox. 63 unread messages with subject lines ranging from three offers for male enhancing pills, five solicitations for upgrading the solar panels on his house and a couple dozen case updates. However, 27 new messages flagged as urgent with the subject line "NEW EVIDENCE RELATING TO RECUSED CASE" flashed in angry red lettering.

However, the note that caught his attention stood out in the bold, green font of Internal Affairs. Dylan's stomach twisted.

This can't be good. Better get it over with.

Selecting the message for IA, Dylan scanned the memo for keywords like charged, arrested, and incarceration. With no indication that he would be spending his next days under arrest or off duty, Dylan re-read the message from the beginning.

* * *

Detective Dylan Loop,

After a thorough investigation by an objective Time Scene Investigative team, it has been concluded that the death of the intruder into your home resulted from acting in self-defense and in defense of your immediate family.

The victim, Eddy Scott, was back-tracked to Tuesday at which time he engaged in an apparent conversation with himself to kidnap your son.

A full report, including surveillance footage, has been logged into the evidence servers.

Sincerely,
Sergeant Hank Rhodes

* * *

Dylan slumped forward onto his desk. The noisy shuffling of drunken and belligerent suspects, escorted through the bullpen by overworked cops, drowned out his beleaguered sigh.

Pulling his phone out from the gym bag's side pocket, he opened his messenger and typed out a quick note to Erin. "No charges. All is well. I'll check in with you at lunch. ILU!"

Dylan watched the phone's icon swirl as Erin's response made its way through the network. "So glad to hear! ILU2! DJ wants to say congratulations too..." An image of Erin holding DJ in her arms appeared on his screen.

Dylan couldn't suppress his ear-to-ear grin seeing his son with a drunken smile and a bead of formula dripping out the corner of his mouth.

"LOOP!" McCuiston's voice boomed across the room, making Dylan nearly drop his phone. "Sooner is better than later."

Jeez, give me five minutes to get settled in. You were the one who put me on leave for a week.

The din of a dozen heated conversations didn't skip a beat as Dylan stood, giving his boss the high sign. Hurriedly typing as he walked through the crowded open office, replying to Erin. "Gotta run. Talk later."

Passing through the bullpen, Dylan glanced around at his fellow Emergents.

How many of us would there be if the inoculation hadn't had such a high mortality rate?

McCuiston glowered with arms folded, watching Dylan cross the room. "It's about damn time," he growled as he stepped back into his office with Dylan on his heels. "Close the door and sit down."

The racket outside the captain's office abated to an eerily near-silence as the door slid into place. "What's up, Cap?" He asked, taking a chair off to the side of McCuiston's desk.

McCuiston sat against his desk's front edge, shoving his nameplate backward with his rear. "Have you seen your inbox?"

Dylan shrugged. "Well, yeah. I mean, I just got in, and there are about 60 new messages about my open cases. Plus, I got an official IA letter stating I won't be charged with any misconduct over the shooting at my house the other night."

Not to mention the 25 mystery memos about a so-called recused case.

McCuiston planted his hands on the desk, bracing himself from leaning too far. "You were copied on those mystery messages at my request. I had to threaten the IA director to let a dirty little secret-one I happened to glean at our last meeting of department heads-slip if he didn't do it. Those messages are all about the same open case. And they're all connected by one particular piece of evidence."

"What evidence?" Dylan held his breath, waiting for the shoe drop.

McCuiston scraped his butt off the desk, scratching the crease marks as he walked to his SmartWall. After pressing his thumb on a folder icon, a fly-out dialogue box appeared. In glowing red letters, the words RED LEVEL FIVE CLEARANCE REQUIRED hovered over the glazed panel.

As McCuiston aligned his palm to the icon floating just above the surface, the message changed. ACCESS GRANTED flashed in soft, green lettering and quickly disappeared. "I've been waiting to show you this because I knew you and Erin needed time together without more stress."

Dylan stood with furrowed brow, crossing the room to join his captain at the SmartWall. "What is it?"

McCuiston swiped his fingers across a grouped folder, expanding them across the glass. "It's about a weapon used in 27 unexplained deaths spanning 10 years. These individual homicides have been reclassified as an unsolved serial case."

Touching a folder labeled BALLISTICS REPORT, McCuiston opened an image labeled MURDER WEAPON. "That's my welding gun," Dylan yelled, pointing at the screen. "What the hell?"

"Your welder matches the energy signature left behind on the corpses at every one of these crime scenes." McCuiston swiped a hand across the glass again, opening another folder marked VICTIMS. The welder moved to the screen's edge as 27 pictures flew out, forming a grid of ghastly images.

Dylan's stomach dropped like he'd just peaked the first apex of a roller coaster. Studying the photos, Dylan noticed instantly that each victim had a hole through their skull where their right eye had once been.

Just like that junkie! They were all killed by my welder.

Dylan scanned every image, reading the vital data under each file. Dates and places of birth. Dates and locations of death. Surviving relatives. Occupations, academic records, known associates.

Wait. What?

Dylan scanned the dates again, doing the math quickly in his head.

They all died...

"On the day AFTER their 21st birthday," McCuiston answered Dylan's unfinished question.

Dylan couldn't take his eyes off the display as his mind raced.

Voting age. When did the voting age change to match the drinking age? 20? 30 years ago?

"Was there a pattern or particular order to the killings?" Dylan asked, touching one of the photos to bring up the victim's details.

"Other than the obvious chronological D.O.D.," McCuiston sighed, "We haven't been able to tell which one was killed first, last or anywhere in between. The energy decay of each wound suggests they were all killed within 48 hours. But that would be impossible unless the UNSUB was a..."

"Leaper," Dylan interrupted. "The killer is a Leaper. He's one of us!"

McCuiston's shoulders sagged. "I've had every TSI team on overtime all week tracking back every single one of these murders. Each Leaper dragged a Sensor with them to collect any forensics that could lead us to the perp."

Dylan eyed his boss, trying to guess the answer before it came. "And what did they find?"

"Nothing that provided any answers," McCuiston sighed, tapping a video icon. The recording filled the screen. "This is Jaqueline Tracy's bodycam footage, the Sensor. Her Leaper had to stay behind at the M.O.I."

M.O.I. Moment of Insertion.

"When was the M.O.I.?" Dylan asked. "Who was the Leaper?"

"The Leap took them to the cusp of his range, so he stayed behind to rest up for the return."

"Early nineties," McCuiston's throat rattled clear. "A walk across the street for you, but since you were on administrative leave, I had to make do with Kyle Earl. Not the worst Leaper, but he required a double dose just to get him to the cusp of his range. Tracy left him behind at the insertion to recoup for the Leap back."

"Tracy didn't go into the scene alone, did she? She would've stood out like a Hooker at Homecoming." Dylan turned his head to find McCuiston avoiding his gaze. "Even in a chameleon suit."

McCuiston cleared his throat. "No, she had a Projector with her. The only one able to project on more than a dozen people."

Projector? Please tell me it wasn't Marie. She's the last person I need to be reminded of.

"I'm afraid so," McCuiston muttered, answering Dylan's thoughts. "Most of the victims were alone or isolated at their times of death. This particular time scene was at a frat party, so I sent her along to allow Tracy to blend in. This is what they captured."

If seeing Marie in the footage triggers a relapse, I'll need to call my sponsor and tell Erin. I can't keep this a secret from her.

Monday, May 23rd, 8:43am

Scenes from a college party projected from the holo-screen. The timestamp in the bottom right corner counted by from 09/09/1994 00:05:01 HRS.

Just past midnight.

A "Welcome Freshmen" banner fluttered behind the DJ as he waved his hands in the air. Kids jumping, gyrating and pulsating to what they called music with too much bass pressed against the first-person POV. Drunken smiles on teetering teenagers stumbled around the room with the grace of newborn fawns. Long arms covered in a gray camo-isolation suit, belonging to Sergeant Tracy, pried their way between crushed bodies, forcing open a path toward the stairs on the opposite side of the throng.

Several drunk frat boys attempted to flirt with the TSI team, offering to get them a drink, asking them to dance or strike up a conversation. One even proposed to join him in a scrum.

I'll have to look that term up later.

At the bottom of the stairs, Tracy looked over her shoulder. The camera caught a glimpse of the Projector, Marie Leon.

"You're sure it's up here?" Marie's voice bellowed over the party's roar.

The camera POV shook with Tracy's head. "Yes," she yelled, pushing her helmet back into place. "Even through the air filters, I can smell the victim's scent. There's no mistake. How's our cover?"

Marie gazed out over the crowd. Several young men gave her approving nods, raising cups of cheap beer. "C'est Bon," Marie chirped in her native tongue. "I've projected us as a couple of average coeds. I'm black, and you're Asian. Besides, I think we could have walked into this party in our *traveling clothes*, and no one would have blinked an eye. Too bad it's not Halloween, huh?" Marie impersonated a runway model, strutting a few steps away then spinning around with her hands on her hips.

Dylan had snorted a short laugh before he realized it. His breath came up short, and the pit in his stomach dropped even further. He tightened his hands into fists, pushing his nails into his sweaty palms.

I don't know if I can do this. I have to talk to my sponsor, and then Erin. I hope Marie doesn't know it was my welder that sent her to that party.

"Yeah, well, the stealth suits might have hidden us from view," Tracy yelled, "But there's no way we would have gotten through this crowd unnoticed. It's better to Project through than add to drunken theories."

"You're alright, Loop," McCuiston placed a hand on Dylan's shoulder. "I'm here with you too. Leon doesn't know you have any involvement in their investigation. And I'll keep it that way."

Dylan shook out the tension from his hands, deeply breathing in and out. "I'll be okay, Cap," his neck crackling as he seemed to point to the four cardinal directions with his head. "Let's keep going."

McCuiston kept his hand on Dylan's shoulder, and they both refocused their eyes on the holographic image of Tracey knocking on a wooden door.

"Hey, in there!" her voice sang out. "Can we come in and use your bathroom? The one downstairs is all backed up."

There was no answer. The camera moved closer to the door, and Dylan heard a deep sniffing sound.

"By the smell of things," Tracy moaned off-camera, "So is the one up here."

"Ugh," Marie's gagging sound carried above the music emanating from below. "Don't put those images in my head. I'm gonna lose it."

"Technically, you're the one who puts images in other people's heads," Tracy cut back. "Seems only fair to get as good as you give."

The body cam turned to find Marie holding a hand over her stomach. "Pull yourself together," Tracy's voice growled, barely audible above the rave music. "We need to get in this room unnoticed to witness the crime and gather evidence. Are you ready?"

Marie glowered at the camera while nodding. "Marie, you take the lead to Project on anyone you see. I'll cover the rear."

The playback showed the two women twirling like dance partners in the narrow hallway until Marie's petite frame stood to face the door.

Marie raised up three fingers, then counted down to one and opened up the door. The camera panned down the empty hall as it slid sideways past the door and into a darkened bedroom. Dylan could hear Marie's stifled gagging again and imagined the overwhelming stench of gym socks, two-week-old laundry, and moldy pizza.

She always did have a weak stomach.

A sliver of light escaped underneath a side door between the shadows of a person pacing in another room.

"That's the bathroom," McCuiston offered. "It's where the body was found by the victim's roommate the next morning."

Sounds of sniffling came from behind the door. "There's no other option, is there?"

Tracy's body cam seemed to step around the Marie, holding up a cylindrical wand. From the glowing tip, beams of light shone against the wall. The bright circle shimmered like dissolving tissue paper to reveal the bathroom's occupant, a young man with ebony skin, seated on the toilet.

"That's the victim, Allan Cartwright," her whisper cut through the rumbling music banging against the door. "I can smell him from here."

"Who's he talking to?" Marie asked from somewhere off-camera. "I don't hear anyone else in there."

Allan's shoulders racked with stifled sobs. "How can I go on knowing this?" The boy looked up and stared intently toward the opposite side of the bathroom.

Tracy's hand swept across the wall, catching a glimpse of the closed door in the bathroom's mirror, and stopping at the closed window to find no one.

"I don't sense anyone else in the room," Tracy sniffed loudly, stepping forward to put her hand against the door. "The only person I can smell is Allan. And the only heat I can feel is emanating from him. He's alone."

"Yes," Allan sniveled, "You're right. There's only one way to prevent this."

The camera view pulled back from the door, filling the display with the hazy wall opening. The circle followed Allan trudging toward the window. He took a deep breath and raised his hands out as if to receive a gift.

"What's he doing?" Marie's voice muttered as Allan raised his hands up to his forehead. "It looks like he's holding an imaginary telescope."

Allan closed his eyes. "I will die to protect my family from myself," he whimpered.

Suddenly a bright light shot out the back of Allan's head, leaving a glowing hole. The blast burned through the shower curtain and seared a perfect circle in the ceramic tile beyond.

Allan's body crumpled to the floor, ending face up with a gaping opening where his left eye used to be.

"Merde," Marie whispered. "I've never seen anything like that before."

I have.

Dylan froze, caught up in the memory from that terrible night when another stranger tried to take his son from him.

"Oh," Tracy groaned, "That is the worst odor I've ever smelled. I'll never get that scent out of my brain."

"I don't even have your senses," Marie gagged, "and it's still more than I can bear."

The shimmering wall opening held in place for the next agonizingly slow seconds until a brief flash from the bathroom mirror caught Dylan's attention. "Wait," he barked, "what was that?"

McCuiston gestured to rewind the playback until Dylan raised his hand as if catching a fly in mid-air. "What did you see, Loop?"

"I'm not sure," Dylan's brow furrowed. "I don't know. It may be nothing.

I just want to see the playback at quarter speed from timecode 00:10:17."

McCuiston waved his hand, and the screen scrolled back the images and then resumed at the slower speed. Dylan stepped forward, almost face-to-face with the screen, focused on the bathroom mirror.

During the slow-motion replay, Dylan could see the back of Allan's head begin to glow like an ember. As each frame passed, the glowing mass bulged outward like a polyp about to burst free into the ocean. Then, in an instant, the bubble evaporated into a pinkish cloud of mist.

Minutes eked by as Dylan kept both eyes locked on the bathroom mirror's reflection until he saw it again; the briefest flash of light in an all too familiar spectrum.

Is it? It can't be.

"What did you see, Loop?" McCuiston stopped the playback and stood between Dylan and the screen. "I know you saw something. Or at least you think you saw something. Spit it out."

Dylan paced away from his boss, unsure if the playback triggered an episode of split-vision, or if seeing Marie caused his mind to play tricks on him.

Breathe in. Breathe out. Take in the Truth. Let go of the Lies.

Dylan rubbed his face. "Have you ever walked by a mirror or store window and you could have sworn you saw someone you know out the corner of your eye? But when you turn to look there was nothing there?"

Kind of like déjà vu.

McCuiston crossed his beefy arms. "Uh-huh..."

Keeping his back to his CO, Dylan raked his fingers through his still-damp gym hair, letting his fingers intertwine behind his head as if unconsciously preparing to be cuffed at any moment.

The ceiling fan overhead beat out a squeaky rhythm in time with Dylan's heart.

How do I explain this?

"Words are usually helpful," McCuiston murmured, "but not necessary."

Dylan spun around, holding out his arms as if to show his captain a box of invisible evidence. "It's something I see all the time. Or at least I think I see all the time. It's like... lens flares, or... the swipe of a laser pointer from a mile away. One millisecond it's there, and then it's gone, or never was. I've just always assumed it was my mind playing tricks on me. But I saw the same micro flash of light coming from the mirror during that playback. It could be anything, but I would swear I saw a brief speck of light reflecting off that bathroom mirror."

McCuiston stared hard at Dylan for a long moment before dropping his arms. "Let's get you down to Diagnostics and have your eye examined."

And my head?

"Perhaps," the older man chuckled. "Let's check the hardware before we go digging through the software.

Monday, May 23rd, 7:16pm

Sitting at their tiny kitchen table, Dylan shoved the last forkful of cheese-smothered potatoes into his mouth, mashing on the chunks before washing them down with grape juice.

Dylan glanced over the rim as the tart liquid cascaded across his tongue. Dirty pots and pans filled the sink as a tray of cookies cooled on the countertop.

Erin only cooks like this when she's worried. She must have baked a dozen batches of brownies after the first kidnapping attempt on DJ.

Wiping his mouth with the paper napkin, he cleared his throat. "So, the diagnostics revealed nothing. Cap thinks it was just a trick of light on the playback."

Looking up, Dylan caught Erin glancing sideways at him as she shook DJ's bottle before plugging it into his gaping mouth. "Did you call your sponsor?"

A sinking feeling, like day-old guilt, sank into Dylan's stomach with his dinner.

I know I shouldn't feel guilty. I'm trying to do everything right this time. I guess old habits do die hard. Is this new guilt, or old guilt from the past?

"Yeah," Dylan sighed, "Right after I called you. We talked for about 15 minutes. Worked the steps. He helped me get my head straight again. Focused on what's real and what's fantasy."

Erin squirmed in her seat, avoiding Dylan's gaze.

"Dinner was great, as usual." Dylan forced a chuckle. "Was there a special occasion?"

Erin maintained her quiet focus on DJ as he sucked on his bottle. Streams of bubbles erupting from the nipple seemed louder than usual in the uncomfortable silence.

"Thank you," she muttered. "I'm glad you liked it. I needed to use the potatoes, and the grape juice was on sale today."

This can't be good.

Dylan shifted in his chair, reaching across the table. "I may not be a Puller like the Captain, but I can tell something's bothering you."

Erin drew a slow breath, then let it out even slower. "I'm just so worried about someone trying to kidnap DJ again. I've hardly slept in days. I'm thinking about taking DJ and going home to my grandparent's farm in Iowa for a little while."

Don't go. Not again.

The knots in Dylan's stomach twisted tighter. Heat flushed to his face, his throat constricted. The lump threatened to crack his voice. "But, we haven't found the person behind the kidnapping attempts. I need to stay here to do my job. And I can't protect you and DJ if you're not here."

Erin turned her tear-stained face to Dylan. "But you're not here," her lips quivered. "At least, you're not here all the time. The last intruder came at night when you happened to be home. But what if someone tries while you're at work? What'll I do then? I need to know that no one can get to him. And I just can't do it alone."

Dylan and Erin stared into each other's eyes across a chasm that seemed as wide as the Grand Canyon. The clock above the kitchen sink ticked away the eons that appeared to pass as neither spouse spoke.

DJ's nose-breathing wheezed in a soft rhythm of blissful contentment.

Dylan's phone interrupted just as he opened his mouth to speak. The TSI icon pulsated on the screen with Captain McCuiston's image rotating around it like an orbiting moon.

Letting the phone ring, Dylan reached across their table, gripping Erin's hand still holding up DJ's bottle. "Hold that thought," he said with pleading eyes.

Dylan stood, accepting the call as he walked across the kitchen to stand by the dish-filled sink. His vacant eyes stared out into the street. "Yes, Cap."

"Loop, we just got tagged on a new homicide on the Leaper case."

How is that even possible?

"What?" Dylan's brow furrowed. "How can that be? How does an unsolved case from the past suddenly show up in the database?"

Dylan listened to McCuiston's labored breathing, waiting for him to answer. "Because this case is from before the computer age. There were no digital photos, trace evidence, DNA samples...nothing that tied into the files to identify this death as being similar to the other. The only detail that flagged it as a possible link were witness statements indicating the victim apparently talking to no one just before the back of their head exploded in a ball of light."

"When did the homicide take place? Where? Who died?" Dylan asked, massaging the growing headache building in his temples.

"Woodstock. 1969," McCuiston grumbled. "The official historical police report says a sleeping 17-year old man was driven over by a tractor. However, a few witness reports-dismissed as 'outlandish, drug-fueled' hallucinations-indicated that the boy died the previous night."

1969.

"I've never leaped that far, Cap," Dylan moaned, "not even with a double dose of L.E.A.P."

"I know, Loop. I know," McCuiston sighed. "You'll have to take a triple dose. And, I hate to do this to you, but I'm sending you with the only Projector able to work on a crowd of this size."

Marie Leon. The woman who almost convinced me she was my true soul mate. A belief that nearly cost me my marriage. Not a chance in Hell I'm getting in the same room with that woman again.

"I'm sorry to do this to you, Loop. I truly am. But, there's no viable option. I need you to come back in ASAP and start prepping."

Dylan pressed the phone's edge into his temple.

I may as well be an alcoholic, sex addict walking into an open-bar orgy. How will I get through this? What will this do to Erin?

Dylan leaned against the counter, the weight of his past sins crashing down on his shoulders. "Captain, do you understand what you're asking of me?"

"Of all people, I know what you've been through," McCuiston replied in his caring way. "I've shared your memories, remember?"

Dylan continued pushing the phone further into his skull, turning around to see Erin watching him with watery eyes. "Captain, can this wait a few days?" he begged. "Erin's needs me right now. She doesn't feel safe here, and I need to be with her. Besides, it's not like the victim is getting any deader."

Dylan's forced smile nosedived in its attempt to brighten Erin's face.

"Let me talk to her a sec," McCuiston insisted.

"Hang on," Dylan pulled the phone away from the new dent in his skull, pressing the mute button. "Cap wants to talk to you."

Erin wiped her cheek and stood, cuddling DJ closer into one arm as she reached out to take Dylan's phone with her freed hand. "Hello?"

Erin's eyes never left Dylan as he listened to her side of the conversation.

"Yes. Yes, that's right. No, it's not that. Nothing he's done. Can he handle it? Are you sure it'll be safe? How can you ask that of me after all that's happened? Are you really sure about that? Yes. No. To the country. I'm just scared to be here alone without him. Thank you. I'm sure that will help. I know. I know. Are you sure? Okay. Thank you, Liam. Goodbye."

Erin ended the call, handing Dylan his phone. Dylan slid it into his pocket, taking a step closer to his wife. "What did he say?" Dylan's worried eyes locked onto Erin's.

"He told me about your new assignment," she replied with absent eyes. "He said he would send over two officers to watch over us while you have to go back to work. He told me you have to make the furthest leap in history, and it may be dangerous. And, that you'll be taking *her* along with you."

Dylan put his hands on Erin's shoulders. "Tell me to not go, and I'll call back and quit. I'll say I just can't do it. The risk to my life is just too great."

Tears leaked from Erin's eyes. "If you do that, you'll get lobed like the other Emergents who don't cooperate with The Assembly."

Dylan pulled Erin close, his eyes glistening. "What do I do?" his voice broke.

Erin shuddered in his arms. "You do your job, and then you come straight back to us," she sobbed, pulling away and reaching up to place her free hand on his face. With tears streaming down her cheeks, she braced herself with a deep breath. "You're not the same man you were before. You can do this. I trust you."

Dylan's cybernetic eye registered the dilation of her pupil's and flush of heat on her face.

Those eyes. Little DJ has her eyes. The left; half blue, half gray. Fear and ferocity. Don't you dare break her heart again.

Dylan leaned down, pressing his lips to hers. Erin entwined her fingers in his hair, pushing back against him.

Dylan pulled away. "I'll wait until the security detail arrives before I leave," Dylan said breathlessly.

"You'd better," Erin punched him lightly in the stomach. "I'm still the best thing that ever happened to you."

Dylan coughed a weak laugh. "Yeah, I know."

Monday, May 23rd, 11:16pm

"Please hold still, Detective Loop," the female radiologist's voice barked into the headphones covering his ears. "The QRI is almost done, but if you shift one more time, I'll have to start the scan over. Again!"

Third time's the charm, right? Even if I'm not a Tactile, I pretty sure my fingerprints have already become permanent residents on these "comfort handles."

Dylan nodded, bumping his forehead against the channel wall and making the eye shield cut further into his skin. He let go of one handle long enough to give a thumbs-up sign. Swallowing hard, his unseen knuckles whitened with each pulse swirling around him like a techno-Rave tornado.

Bursts of chilled air blew across his face, instantly evaporating the beads of sweat pouring from his brow.

"Are you sure you're not claustrophobic, Detective?" the concealed woman's voice softened.

What gave you that idea?

"I can give you something to take the edge off."

"NO!" Dylan shouted against the thunderstorm spinning around him. "I'm fine. How much longer? It feels like I've been in here forever."

The paper gown rippled with every Quantum Resonance Imaging pulse hammering against his body.

"You've been in there for almost forty minutes," the woman's voice snapped. "You could've been done a half-hour ago if you'd have stayed still."

I hate these pre-Leap diagnostics. I can only hope Marie's already been scanned, and we can get this mission over with ASAFP!

Dylan closed his eyes under the shield, focused on his breathing awaiting the moment the sonic whirlwind ended, and the scanning bed would release him from the blaring cocoon.

* * *

A slap in the face dragged Dylan out of comatose-like sleep to find McCuiston looking down on him. "I swear, Loop," his rotund belly shook, "you're Narcolepsy is getting worse. I've never known anyone who falls asleep as quickly as you."

Sitting up, Dylan stared around the room. Over McCuiston's shoulder, he spotted the radiologist stifling a laugh with her hand from the operator's station. The QRI hummed softly behind him like a blanket-filled clothes dryer.

"How long have I been out?" Dylan swung his legs off the table, catching a breeze on his backside as he landed on the tiled floor.

"Only about 10 minutes," McCuiston laughed, "But I've been yelling in your ear for the past 5. Boy, you got some strange dreams."

Aw, Hell. I can't possibly be responsible for my unconscious thoughts. Especially when I don't even remember them.

"Naw," McCuiston slapped Dylan's shoulder. "But, maybe in your next therapy session, you bring up the subject of brush fires."

Dylan's face steamed in the cold lab's air. "I'll try to remember that, Cap."

"Alright, no more jokes," McCuiston growled. "I just wanted to see where your head was at before we go into Prep."

Dylan's eyes darted to the side door. Through the double, full-glass, panels open cubbies of glistening carbon-fiber uniforms sparkled like an obsidian collection.

"Is Leon already in there?" Dylan asked, taking a step toward the doorway, not taking his eyes off a pair of dark boots past the glass.

"Yes. She's gearing up in cubicle 1," McCuiston moved ahead of Dylan, grasping the door's handle.

She always did feel the need to put herself first. In everything!

"Now, there's no need to be bringing up the past," McCuiston growled, putting a hand on Dylan's shoulder. "It's done. For her as well. Just pretend it never happened, and you'll be fine."

Dylan nodded, pulling the gown flap's tighter over his hindquarters. "Yes, sir."

McCuiston opened the door, letting Dylan walk through first. Goose-flesh erupted across his naked arms as the warmer air in the prep room, blew through the opened doorway. Dylan sniffed the air. Invisible lotus blossoms made his head swirl.

A trigger. The gift. It's her perfume.

"You can get through this, Loop," McCuiston whispered in his ear. "It's the quartermaster's perfume. Thousands of women wear it."

Dylan swallowed hard-closing a door in his mind-recovering mental equilibrium with McCuiston's velvet touch.

Compartmentalization. It's how I handled it before. It's how I'll take care of it now.

"I'll be in The Jar," McCuiston muttered as he eased Dylan past the open door. "Monitoring the pre-Leap prep."

"Thanks, Cap," Dylan mumbled. Swallowing sand while rain seemed to pool in his armpits, he zombie-walked into the stark white chamber as his heart hammered in his ears. His bare pads scraped along the warm stone floor, echoing throughout the stark white room.

"Hello, Dylan," Marie's voice wafted into the vestibule before he rounded the corner into the prep room. As Dylan made his way past the foyer, he caught sight of Marie facing a gun-metal gray utility locker in a similar white paper gown. "It's good to see you again. I hope our professional relationship can be what it once was."

Dylan stepped deep into the chamber as Marie, in a similar white paper gown, turned to face him with her hands resting comfortably on her hips. Her jet black hair pulled back into a tight ponytail did nothing to diminish her natural beauty, even without make-up.

"Marie," Dylan walked toward an open station one over from Marie's left side, stretching the gown around his backside and dropping his voice into mission mode. "I expect this will be a short Leap. Even though it may take us almost a century into the past, I don't expect we'll need to be there long to accomplish the mission. Are you ready to go?"

"I'm ready," Marie nodded with a slight pouty smile on her lips. "The Captain filled me in on the dangers. Are you sure you can handle a triple injection?"

"I've been able to take a double dose now and again," Dylan pulled up the locker door, revealing a one-size-fits-all bio-chameleon suit. "I should be able to handle a triple shot. It's not like I really have a choice though, right?"

Dylan shot a glance at Marie, her mouth pulled down at the left corner and drumming her fingers against her thigh.

You don't need to--or get to--be worried about me. It's not your place anymore.

Dylan pulled a privacy curtain from between their lockers, making the glides squeal against their tracks. As the curtain fluttered between them, Marie's silhouette danced against the gauzy fabric.

A choked giggle erupted from behind the screen, pulling Dylan's full attention to the shape of Marie's gown falling to the floor. "Awww," her voice seemed to coo. "You've never been shy about changing in front of me before."

Dylan dragged his eyes away from the shadowy peep show.

I never tried to be faithful to my wife before.

Tuesday, May 24th, 12:24am

Donned in the full-body, skin-tight, black camouflage suit, Dylan stepped through the launching chamber's hatchway held open by the quartermaster. He held his hand against the bright LED lights reflecting off the rounded walls of matte white tiles.

Every time I walk in here, I feel like a bug in a bulb. What did they call this shape again? Round-Bottom Flask? Something to do with the vacuum system.

Dylan walked to the midpoint of the bridge between the hatch and the dais at the chambers epicenter. The spherical walls ballooned outward from a mushroom-shaped platform rising from the "south pole." Looking up at the "north pole" a circular shaft climbed to a steel-mesh vent cover.

He turned to the sound of Marie's giggles, finding her in an excited conversation with Bremmer outside the hatch. They whispered with wide grins, darting glances in his direction.

"Same day rule, Leon," McCuiston's voice erupted from above. Dylan looked up, spotting the observation glass embedded into the wall ten feet above his head. McCuiston's burly figure leaned over, nearly pressing his face to the glazing. "There is a time to talk about the engagement, ladies. Now is not that time."

Dylan turned away from the hatch as Marie stepped over the threshold. Breathing deeply, he closed his eyes and pictured Erin in the kitchen. Her words, *I trust you*, reverberated in his skull.

You'd better earn that trust. No more "no one will know" crap.

The solid clunk of the hatch bounced around the empty room like the clang from a bell tower. Dylan watched Marie stride past him on the eight-foot diameter platform. "Marie Leon, Projector, ready to LEAP," Marie announced, looking up toward the observation booth.

"Acknowledged, Leon," a faceless man's voice rang throughout The Jar. "Dylan Loop? Please take your position and confirm your status."

Dylan finished crossing to the dais, standing on Marie's left. The platform swayed slightly as clamps holding the overpass in place disengaged. The bridge disappeared into the wall under the hatch like an enormous, white tongue.

"Dylan Loop, Leaper, ready to LEAP." Dylan sighed.

"Commence retro-reflective camouflage test," the operator's voice boomed.

In sync, Dylan and Marie raised their left arms, activating holographic consoles. Dylan entered the sequence on his arm, watching the ebony scales across his suit emit a soft white glow. "How're we looking, Cap?" Dylan said, craning his head.

"You've all but vanished," McCuiston said over the speakers. "As expected, I can only see a faint shadow. But, that won't be an issue since you're going in at night."

Dylan turned toward Marie to find a hairless Gorilla staring back at him. Dylan started, stumbling backward when suddenly Marie grabbed his arm, pulling him back to the center of the platform. "Sorry, Dylan," she giggled. "Just trying to lighten the mood. Don't be so serious."

"As you may recall," Dylan grumbled, "I don't like surprises. Please don't do that again."

Marie rolled her eyes. "Fine!" she sighed. She kept her eyes locked on

Dylan as her brow furrowed as her lips pinched tight. "So serious."

"Camouflage test complete," the operator's voice cut in.

"Please dispense the approved doses of Lepto-Encephtimine-Arsenogenic-Phylaptilate." Dylan turned his attention away from Marie.

Below the observation window, a small square panel pushed away from the wall face and slide to the side. From within the opening, a clear glass tray on a shiny steel rail extended toward the dais like a reptilian tongue. On the transparent plate, two groups of three vials filled with an iridescent green fluid floated before him.

Dylan opened a pocket on his right thigh, revealing a small injection system with a revolving chamber with four empty slots. Dylan loaded the first three vials into the cylinder and resealed the pocket. A red target sign pulsated above the carbon-fiber mesh between the injector compartment and his right knee. "L.E.A.P. doses in place," he spoke on autopilot. "Placing return doses in the secondary injector."

Opening another pocket on his left thigh, Dylan loaded the revolving cylinder with the second group of vials. Once finished, a similar target, glowing in a steady yellow hue, projected just above his left knee. With a spinning gesture of his left hand, Dylan put the second injector into standby mode.

Turning toward Marie, but not looking up, he typed on his arm console. "In case I get too disoriented for the return trip, I'm giving you access to my injector system."

Marie looked down at the incoming transmission on her arm. "Codes received," she mocked, mirroring his furrowed brow and pursed lips.

"Are you ready, Loop?" McCuiston's voice echoed like distant thunder.

Dylan took a deep breath. "Ready as I'll ever be," he grumbled.

"Proceeding with atmospheric evacuation," the operator's voice boomed into the chamber.

The lights dimmed as the sound of a million invisible snakes seemed to slither up the walls toward the shaft above Dylan's head.

Can't risk any contaminants going into the past. It's funny that there's more danger of harming the timeline from some single-celled bacteria than our technology.

"Vacuum complete," the operator spoke into Dylan's headset. "Zero atmospheres confirmed. Good luck, detective."

Dylan nodded, crouching down on his left knee. Raising his right hand in the air, he gritted his teeth before slamming his palm down on the glowing target hovering over his right thigh.

I hate shots!

Upon impact, the injector shot a needle through his interior suit and into his thigh muscle. The warm rush of L.E.A.P. quickly coursed through his veins, sending waves of memories crashing against the breakers in his mind. The electric buzz cascaded along his skin as if he'd had one too many drinks. Dylan scanned the faded chamber, finding the ripples in the air like a mirage on a desert highway.

"Dose one, complete," he said, fighting off the brain-buzz. "Injecting dose two."

Dylan hammered his fist against his thigh again, releasing another wave. This time, rivaling the crests found on Hawaii's North Shore. The dizziness pushed him over. Dylan reached out for balance, catching Marie's hand in mid-air. Heated memories seared across his mind, fighting for the chance to be re-lived. But, Dylan grabbed hold of Erin's words. *I trust you.*

Erin. My anchor. My lighthouse.

Dylan felt Marie's arms around his chest, heaving him back to an upright position. He swayed as if floating like a buoy in the surf. "Dylan," her voice echoed from a distance. "Are you alright?"

Dylan shook his head. "I'm okay," he panted. "It's just been a while since I had a double. I'll be fine, just give me a second to get my bearings." Dylan scanned the dim room. The ripples intensified like horizontal rain against a window wall during a hurricane.

Dylan kept one mental grip on Erin's lighthouse as he reached out, sensing for the time stream. The air began to part like theater curtains, but Dylan recoiled.

It's not time yet.

Dylan hyperventilated as if preparing for a free dive. "Injecting number three," he said between breaths.

One... Two...

On three, Dylan slammed his hand down one last time, injecting the pharmaceutical-grade serum into his bloodstream. A tsunami of waves threw his mind sideways into the nightmarish rocky shoals of his memory. Confessing to Erin about his infidelity: Losing his coveted promotion due to the affair: Waiting for weeks at a time for any reply from his wife, not knowing where she had gone.

Clutching the shards of his skull threatening to escape the soul-wrenching torment, Dylan's guttural screamed filled his helmet but went no further. He unclenched his eyes, scanning the torrential time waves for something on which to anchor.

Suddenly, an image floated elusively beyond his reach; little DJ, asleep in his crib. The flickering artificial candle, sitting next to his bed, danced to the rhythm of tinkling lullabies.

Reaching out with shaking hands, Dylan parted the veil between the vacuum of The Jar and his target. Woodstock, 1969. "C-C-Con-Control," Dylan stuttered. "G-Good t-t-to go. Lea-L-Le-Leaper and... and P-Pro-Projector in t-t-tow."

"Safe passage, Leaper," McCuiston's voice seemed distorted like whale-song across the ocean.

Dylan made a fist, squeezing his nails into the carbon-fiber gloves, forcing enough pain to bring his mind back into focus. The convoluted time stream calmed as if a storm over a mountain lake passed like a time-lapse video.

Icy sheets of rain smoothed into fluttering crystalline drapes. Dylan cut his hand through the gossamer fabric. Penetrating into the time stream up to his elbow, Dylan stood on shaky knees. "Get a good grip," he slurred as if drunk. "This may be a bumpy ride."

He felt Marie's added weight as her hands grasped the handles bolted into his suit's shoulder harness.

Diving into the blackness beyond the veil, Dylan sensed the time stream's flow and piloted Marie and himself through the currents and eddies. Turbulent events jostled them as they pushed upstream toward the past. Keeping his feet firmly planted on the platform, Dylan formed his psychic keel ahead of them, parting the stream.

At the helm of his mental icebreaker, Dylan cut through the powerful current toward his destination: the imagined lighthouse signaling his journey's end. His mental engines roared to full-ahead, fueled by the L.E.A.P. coursing through his body, pushing painfully against the flow determined to sweep him back downstream.

In a few seconds, after what felt like hours of swimming, Dylan approached the lighthouse beckoning him from the brackish abyss. Marie, his cargo, still lashed securely to the deck, urged for relief from the storm.

Dylan navigated toward a cove, spotting a stainless steel pier at the lighthouse's base. Silver ropes rose from their coils along the dock, winding themselves to his ships' cleats.

Now secure in the harbor, Dylan picked up the cargo from the deck only to find Marie had never left his back. "You okay?" He asked without turning to look at her.

"More nauseous than usual," she croaked, "But I'll manage. Let's get out of the time stream so my stomach can settle down."

Dylan nodded. "We'll find cover and take a minute to adjust to the era before we venture to locate the victim. Sound good?"

Marie's stifled gag and a pat on his shoulder acknowledged her agreement.

Dylan again raised his hand, cutting through the dark veil separating him from the time stream and the events of the past. A bright light enveloped his hand as he punctured the black fabric.

It's supposed to be nighttime at the Moment of Insertion.

"Dylan," Marie spoke into his headset. "What's wrong? It's supposed to be dark. Did we come to the wrong M.O.I.? Are you okay?"

Suddenly, Dylan felt something grip his hand like a vice, yanking him through the veil. Marie, like a free-swinging backpack, following after.

A blinding yellow light came from all directions, obscuring the figure standing in front of him.

Dylan squinted and raised his hand over his face shield until he recognized the shape of a man looking squarely at him.

"Hi, Dad," the man said with an almost sing-song voice. "It's good to meet you. Again."

UNKNOWN

"What do you mean, Dad?" Dylan asked. He tried to take a step forward, but something bound him; like being chained to a stone wall. "Who are you? How did I get here?" Dylan, struggling against the force holding him, turned his head to find Marie still clinging to his back.

"Marie," Dylan writhed his shoulders. "Let go."

Marie gave no response but merely stared off into a distant horizon.

The man in his late 30's, hauntingly familiar, waved his hand in the air. Dylan fell forward onto lush, green grass at the base of a tree that seemed to glow like a million Christmas lights.

The man, dressed in a simple linen shirt with matching pants, leaned over to help Dylan to his feet. Dylan's dark camouflage seemed like an ink stain in contrast to the soft yellows, oranges, and greens of his idyllic surroundings.

"Who are you?" Catching sight of his statuesque partner, Dylan stepped to her, gripping her by the arms. "Marie! Marie, snap out of it. What did you do to her?" Dylan demanded.

"I've come to expect you not to recognize me," the strange man said calmly. "We haven't been in the same room for nearly 37 years. And as for Ms. Leon, she is perfectly fine. She is simply not present in the same moment as you and me."

Dylan turned away from his frozen companion. "What do you mean by that? We haven't been in the same room for 37 years. That's impossible. I'm only 28, and you're obviously older than me."

The man snorted. "For someone who can move through time, you sure don't know much about it. But, relatively speaking, we don't have a lot of time. No pun intended. I'm here to stop you."

Dylan glanced around the area, finding himself on a low hill nestled in a large field of sunflowers. Encircling the ground, a dense evergreen forest spread in every direction as far as he could see.

Nowhere to run.

"Stop me from doing what?" Dylan asked.

The older man smiled, the kind of smile reserved for erring children. "To stop you from killing all those people. The twenty-seven you shot with your welding gun. The ones you blamed for making the cure for autism that led to the rise of Emergents. The ones you blamed for making you kill my mother, Erin Loop."

UNKNOWN

"That's impossible," Dylan stumbled to find his footing. "That would mean you're..."

"My name is Dylan Loop, Jr.," the man said with great sadness. "My father, Dylan Loop, you, went on a mission for the TSI 38 years ago to 1969. The shock to his system, YOUR system, from three doses of L.E.A.P., caused him to have a level 4 schism. And he never fully recovered."

"DJ?" Dylan whispered. "Is it really you? How can this be?"

DJ stepped toward Dylan, holding up his hands. "I'm a Stopper. Like you, I can manipulate time. I can't travel through it, like you. But, I can freeze pockets of the time stream for myself and one or two people."

"If you can't travel through time, how did you get here?" Dylan took another step backward. "Where are we anyway? This isn't the right M.O.I."

"We're in an eddy," DJ grinned "I learned how to create pockets of non-linear time. I led you here. I've led you here many times. And we've had dozens of variations of this conversation dozens. The results are always the same. You don't believe me. You're convinced this is Marie playing with your head again. And you continue on your mission."

Dylan turned in place, scanning the vista. "Why should I take you at your word? Why not unfreeze Marie and let me ask her if she's messing with my head myself?"

"The seventeen versions I've done that," DJ sighed, "the outcome is far worse. Instead of murdering mom and 27 innocent people, you actively try to alter the timeline resulting in the deaths of thousands."

"That's impossible," Dylan shouted. "I would never hurt an innocent person."

"Uncle Liam told me you'd say that," DJ said, reaching into his pocket to pull out a small silver disk. "Which is why he finally authorized me to give you this."

"What is it?" Dylan warily eyed the coin-sized object.

"It's your memories," DJ's voice became hollow, "from the trial after you killed mom and the others. I'm here to show you your future before it becomes a part of history."

DJ held out the token. "Please, Dad," DJ's eyes brimmed with tears. "Take the disk. It's the only way to save mom."

Dylan's face contorted. His eyes searched those of the man claiming to be his son.

His eyes. Erin's eyes. There they are. The left; half blue, half gray. Fear and ferocity.

"Okay, DJ," Dylan's voice broke. "What do I have to do?"

DJ's shoulders sagged as relief filled his face. "Take the disk and forget the mission. When you get back, swallow it. You'll have to press down on the protective surface first for the micro-needle to sample your DNA and activate the transfer. Then, you'll only have a few seconds to swallow it. But once it enters your stomach, it will chemically convey your future memories into your bloodstream. Your brain will take it from there. Once you see your future, things should play out differently. Hopefully, mom and the others will live, and you won't end up in a prison for the mentally insane."

Dylan reached out, taking the silver disk from DJ's open palm. "Why can't I just take it now?" he asked, examining the token.

Looks like an old watch battery. How can this possibly contain a lifetime of memories?

"Well, for one thing, you can't take off your suit here," DJ answered gesturing to the scenic environment. "It may appear to you that we're in a field together, with me dressed like I'm on summer vacation. But, I'm actually wearing a psycho-kinetic environmental suit. Like your suit, it's protecting me from the time vortex."

Dylan's eyes dubiously studied DJ's figure. "I guess I'll have to take your word for it, huh?"

"Twelve times," DJ snorted. "Twelve times you wanted proof, so you unsealed your helmet and suffocated. There is no atmosphere in the eddy. Well, technically, there are oxygen molecules here. But, they're trapped in time like Marie. Unmoving. You can't get them into your lungs, even if you tried."

Dylan turned in place, scanning the vista's exquisite beauty for several moments. "I'll have to remember to tell you about all this someday," Dylan laughed.

"I'll look forward to it," DJ caught a lump in his throat. "I love you, Dad."

Dylan opened his arms, stepping forward. DJ closed the distance in one stride, wrapping his arms around his father. "I love you too, son," Dylan whispered into DJ's ear. "You're the best thing that ever happened to me. Next to your mom, of course."

DJ's shoulders shook as he cried on Dylan's shoulders. "I hope this isn't goodbye, Dad."

Dylan gave DJ a hard squeeze. "I'll see you later, son."

The two men released their embrace. Dylan slid the disk into the seam between his forearm and gloved hand.

"As soon as I release the eddy, you'll be back in the time stream," DJ walked Dylan back to where Marie still stood motionless. "I can guide you back to your departure moment without you taking another three doses."

Dylan nodded as DJ repositioned Marie's hands into Dylan's shoulder straps. "One more thing," DJ's eyes widened. "No one else can touch the disk. Safe journey," DJ snapped his fingers.

The forested landscape disappeared instantly as Dylan became a man overboard, lost in the middle of the ocean. Time currents tossed him to and fro like a fisherman's bob.

No sooner did the nightmare ride through the time stream begin, then Dylan found himself face down on the white tiled dais of The Jar with Marie tossing out her dinner next to him.

Tuesday, May 24th, 12:25am

"Mission Complete?" McCuiston's voice barked from all around. Dylan staggered to his feet, pulling Marie with him as she struggled to remove the vomit-plastered face shield.

"What the hell happened, Dylan?" she asked, choking on putrid air. "One moment we were clearing the veil to 1969; I even saw a bunch of naked people dancing around a bonfire. Then the next thing I knew, we landed back here."

Dylan looked back and forth between Marie and McCuiston. "I'm not entirely sure I know what happened, or if I believe what I saw," he said confused. "It's going to be hard to explain."

"I want a full report," McCuiston growled. "We'll debrief while you're getting changed. Return the chamber to normal atmosphere." The million hissing snakes returned. Dylan's ribcage, seemingly bruised from landing awkwardly on the platform, protested the added pressure.

"Atmosphere restored," announced the operator. Marie hastily unlatched her helmet's faceplate, gulping a lungful of sterilized air.

"Okay, Dylan," she gagged. "If that's how you treat old friends, we're officially not friends anymore."

Dylan removed his helmet as the bridge extended from the now-open hatch toward the dais. "I'm sorry, Marie. I really am," Dylan said, trying to put his hand on her shoulder. Marie hastily smacked it away. "I'm not sure how to explain what happened out there."

Marie stormed across the bridge muttering in French.

Dylan remained on the platform, staring into space, and taking off his gloves when the tinkling of metal bouncing on tile brought his attention downward. A small, silver disk rolled around on the floor in shrinking circles until it came to a stop at his feet.

I thought I dreamed it all.

"Dreamt what?" McCuiston's voice barked from overhead. "What is that, Loop?"

Dylan bent over, picking up the sliver of shiny metal off the cold tile with his right hand. He rolled it around in between his fingers, letting the lighting reflect off its surface like a strobe and looking for the micro-needle.

DJ said to swallow it, and the memories would transfer chemically. Then I'd know what I, or at least my future self, did--or will do.

"Loop," McCuiston's voice rose, "What are you going on about? What's in your hand? Drop it and don't move. Security! Detain Sergeant Loop and confiscate whatever he's holding."

Two armed security personnel, a short, stocky man, and a tall, athletic woman appeared at the hatch. A quick zoom with his cybernetic eye enlarged their badges. The male, B. Richarde, and the female, K. Levres. One by one, the guards crossed the threshold with their arms raised like boxers. Their fists clenched and electricity sparkled across their knuckles.

Stun gloves. Too bad for them my suit will provide some insulation.

Dylan pulled out his field knife, unwilling to pull a firearm on unarmed TSI personnel, pointing it toward the guards with his left hand. "Back off," he growled, backing toward the platform's edge.

"Sorry, Detective," the female guard said, pointing his stun gun at Dylan's chest. "We're just following orders. Drop it and step back." The guards inched across the alabaster bridge, ignoring the splotches of Marie's vomit trail.

Dylan stepped backward again, his left foot slipping on the pool of sick Marie evacuated from her helmet. Careful to avoid sliding, Dylan looked down, stepping over the expulsion. As he looked up, he found the guards already across the bridge. Richarde at his ten o'clock, and Levres at two.

Moments later, McCuiston appeared at the hatchway. "Loop," he said with an unusually softened voice. "I think maybe the triple dose has addled your brain a little. Why don't we go over to medical and get you checked out? You can go on an extended vacation with Erin. Hell, I'll even authorize a pass into the capital zone."

Dylan glared between the two guards. Sizing up which would most likely attack first. "Tell these guys to back off, Cap," he yelled without taking his eyes off Richarde who lightly bounced on the balls of his feet. "I need you to trust me on this." He scanned the guards with his thermal vision. Levres show a higher skin temperature and heartbeat.

Definitely the less eager fighter here.

Richarde moved millimeters closer with each bounce.

Pulse steady. Skin temp, slightly elevated. Oh, yeah. He's going to jump me first.

"Loop," McCuiston's roar echoed around the jar like an Arizona thunderstorm. "I'm giving you a direct order. Stand down and relinquish whatever you've got in your hand."

Levres swallowed, her hands shaking slightly. Richarde lowered his brow, letting the corner of his mouth twitch with an eager grin.

Dylan stepped back with his right foot with only the ball still planted on the dais.

I have to see if this disk is what DJ said it was.

"DJ?" McCuiston mumbled. "DJ's only three months old. He can't tell you anything. And I know. I've even heard his thoughts. Other than a longing desire for a clean butt and a fresh bottle, the kid doesn't really think about much."

Dylan laughed as the memory of his unexpected stop became clearer.

"Holy, Son of a..." McCuiston whispered. "Guards, get that thing from him!"

Clutching the disk in his right hand, Dylan swiped at Richarde's waist.

Damn, I wish I was ambidextrous.

Richarde hunched forward, throwing his electrified hands toward Dylan, briefly connecting with his exposed face.

The shock jolted Dylan from a stable stance. Levres launched forward with electrified gloves crackling the air, grabbing Dylan's right hand. Dylan howled, gripping down on the disk like a vice, his fingernails drawing blood from his bare palm.

Richarde's forward momentum caused him to step into the vomit, attempting to find his balance. Flailing his arms like a drunken albatross, he slapped Dylan across the face a second time using dumb luck.

The jolt from Richarde's glove sent a spike of pain down Dylan's left arm, charging his muscles to flex and plunging the knife deep into Levres shoulder.

Levres screamed-letting go of Dylan-clutching the blade protruding from her shoulder. Dylan's knife acted like a lightning rod as Levres stun glove sent 75V/.2A of electricity into her body.

Dylan watched her body convulse and topple off the dais and onto the bulbous floor below.

"Loop!" McCuiston yelled. "Stand down!"

"Dylan," Marie's voice pierced the chamber like a gunshot. "Please stop! You're going to kill someone."

Dylan's eyes caught sight of Marie standing behind McCuiston, wearing a gray sports bra and matching yoga pants, just as Richarde's fist pummeled through his jaw. Dazzling lights erupted in his vision, but only on the right side. His cybernetic eye kept a clear image of Richarde circling the dais like a cage fighter.

Dylan wheeled around, wiping the blood dripping from his lip with his left fist. The two men matched paces on the small platform, keeping their distance until Dylan stood at the edge of the dais with Richarde between him and McCuiston.

"I don't want to hurt you, Richarde," Dylan growled. Richarde raised his hands, reactivating his stun gloves.

"Oh, don't you worry, cupcake," Richarde answered with a sneer. "I was top of my class in hand-to-hand at the academy."

"Then, if you really want this," Dylan opened his bleeding palm, "You're going to have to work for it."

Suddenly, Dylan tossed the token in the air. Richarde's eyes followed the disk's upward flight.

Dylan used Richarde's distraction to jump into the air with both feet and kick Richarde square in the chest, knocking Richarde back onto the bridge and bowling through McCuiston's feet.

Dylan landed in the pool of vomit, the wind knocked out of himself from the fall.

McCuiston groaned and swore as Marie also fell over into the pile.

"*Connard*," she howled in French.

Dylan rolled onto his knees, scanning the dais for the bloody disk. A thin red trail led his eyes to the edge of the bridge. The reddened token laid its own small pool of blood and vomit. Dylan refocused his eye to see Levres beyond the dais edge, unconscious with his knife lodged deeper into her shoulder.

Sorry about that, Levres. You gave me no choice.

Richarde followed Dylan's eyes and reached for the disk, but Dylan's closer hand won the race.

Dylan stood in the center of the dais, removing the blood and sick from the disk on his leg.

McCuiston struggled to extricate himself from the tangle of Richarde and Marie's legs. "Loop," he grunted, losing his balance as Richarde jerked a foot out of the mess. "Don't do it. We don't know where that came from. It needs to be tested first."

I have to know.

Dylan shoved the disk into his mouth before Richarde could get off the ground and knock him to the floor.

The Future

Dylan watched the disjointed scenes from his life-past, present, and future unfold before him.

Is this what it's like to have your life flash before your eyes? Or is this more like the final judgment of God?

Dylan watched himself negotiate the two kidnapping attempts on DJ, believing Erin was incapable of keeping DJ safe from The Assembly.

He watched his hands wrap around Erin's neck, her wide eyes filled with shock and horror, wet with sadness.

His heart tore open in his chest as he returned to Marie's bed for pleasure, hoping to ease his madness in her comfort.

He slammed his body against the prison bars, screaming about the impending apocalypse of all Emergents like himself.

He watched himself realize the three doses of L.E.A.P. had somehow remained in his system, and he was free to escape the prison of time.

He stole his welder from the evidence lockup and a prototype chameleon suit from R&D and targeted the paternal grandparent of every member of The Assembly.

He gave each of them double doses of street-grade L.E.A.P. to induce a hypnotic state and tell them about the future crimes of their grandchildren.

He watched himself kill each and every one of them. After he had murdered Allan Cartwright, he saw Marie Leon and Jaqueline Tracy in the mirror's reflection, a twisted grid escaping his lips only he could see.

His final memory: looking at himself, bound in a straight-jacket, being wheeled into an operating theater, and lobotomized like every other Emergent, who was unable, or unwilling, to play by The Assembly's rules.

* * *

McCuiston stared in horror at Dylan's catatonic figure pinned to the platform, pulling Dylan's vision as if it were his own.

"Richarde, get off him," he barked. "Get down below and help Levres. Take her to medical and call in another security team."

Richarde rolled off the dais, grumbling Yes, sir.

"Leon," he called over his shoulder getting to his feet, "You might want to make yourself scarce. I'll handle Loop myself. Seal the room."

McCuiston never turned away from Dylan's still form as Marie softly padded off the bridge, followed by the hatch clanging shut.

He eased forward, keeping a close mind's eye on Dylan's visions for any sign it neared its end. Grabbing Dylan's shoulders, he pulled his protege up into a kneeling position like a sleepy child.

Dylan's eye blinked randomly at the close of each gruesome scene ravaging through his mind.

When Dylan's vision ended, his face turned toward McCuiston. Torturous sadness etched across his face.

McCuiston gently put a hand on Dylan's shoulder.

Dylan seemed to allow the gesture for a moment. Suddenly, Dylan threw McCuiston's hand off, stood up and pulled his sidearm from the holster, pressing the barrel deep into his own temple.

The hatch opened with a bang, and four new guards rushed across the bridge, two of which put themselves between McCuiston and Dylan with their own weapons aimed at Dylan's head.

Tuesday, May 24th, 12:34am

Silent tears flowed down Dylan's cheeks. His gun hand trembled. "How can I go on knowing all the pain and suffering I'm going to cause?"

McCuiston stepped around the guards, gesturing them to move away. "Dylan, I saw it too. I was watching." He choked. "We'll figure this out. Now that we've seen what the future holds, we can get you the help you need. Don't do what you and I both know you're thinking. The future is not written in stone."

Dylan pressed the gun harder into his temple. "Yeah?" he laughed through the tears pouring from his eyes. "Tell me, Cap. If you were shown all your worst mistakes; past, present, AND future. How would you feel about your life?"

"Dylan, don't do this," McCuiston pleaded. "Put down the gun."

Dylan took a step backward. "Please take care of Erin and DJ. Tell them I love them more than anything in this world, and I'm doing this to protect them from myself."

McCuiston eased forward, his arms raised as if beckoning a prodigal son. "Dylan, this is not the answer," he croaked.

Dylan inched further away.

"And tell DJ I'm sorry I never got to finish his rocking horse."

"NOW!" McCuiston lunged forward as Dylan's finger squeezed the trigger.

* * *

The gunshot rang in Dylan's ears long after the bullet wrenched the gun from his grip. Falling to his knees, he clamped down on his wrist and stared at the mangled strips of flesh and bone that used to be his hand.

McCuiston took a knee and bent as the plasma net flew over his head, wrapping Dylan in a jacket of glowing spider webs. The guards flanking Dylan piled on top of him as he thrashed against their weight.

Clenching his jaw, Dylan scanned past the hatch and spotted the sniper perched atop a workbench in the prep room.

I'm gonna kill you.

"I'd thank him first." McCuiston lumbered to his feet, out of breath. "We're going to put you somewhere safe and flush the L.E.A.P. out of your system. Then, well, I'm not sure what we're going to do next."

The guards struggled to pull Dylan to his feet, staring wide-eyed and thrashing against their grip. "Cap. Liam," he begged. His face a mask of deranged fury. "You've got to kill me. Kill me! It's the only way to keep Erin and the rest of them safe."

"Tranq him and get him to medical. Keep him sedated and get his hand looked at," McCuiston sidestepped, letting the guards haul Dylan's flailing body across the bridge. "I've got to make a call."

Wednesday, May 25th, 9:04am

McCuiston led Dylan--bound to the wheelchair under a plasma net and surrounded by four officers--across the bridge toward the Internal Affairs Annex. Stripped down to his black under-suit, the morning rays reflected off the fabric like a rippling pond. The black hood and armed guards gave Dylan the appearance of a comic book villain on a ride to an asylum for the criminally deranged. And McCuiston, with a dark expression, as the warden.

Citizens and oligarchs cleared out of their path as they wheeled across the bustling catwalk. Law enforcement officers edged their hands toward holsters and glared at the faceless prisoner.

Pushing through the double-doors first, McCuiston held one side open to let his entourage through. Two guards, Dylan, and then the rest.

He stood, holding the door open for the final members of the group.

Erin, carrying DJ on one hip with a diaper bag bouncing against the other, wiped more tears from her face as she crossed the threshold. "Are you sure he's going to be okay, Liam?" Her voice broke. "You remember what happened last time he had a schism."

"This time, it's different." He took her shoulders in his capable hands. "I promise you, this has nothing to do Marie or any other woman. Dylan had an experience that I can't begin to describe."

McCuiston looked down at DJ playing intently with a rattle and pulled them into his embrace. "I can't tell you what happened right now," he whispered. "But I promise you, Dylan needs you and DJ right now. If he's going to snap out of this, he's going to need all of us."

Erin's lip quivered as she adjusted DJ's weight. "Okay."

McCuiston took her by the arm and guided her down the stairs, catching sight of the guards in the service elevator as the doors began to close. He tapped his earbud. "Iris, patch me into Officer Umbuntu."

"Connecting you to Officer Umbuntu now," Iris chirped. McCuiston shifted Erin's arm to wrap around his as he grabbed onto the handrail when another chirp sang in his ear.

"Umbuntu here, Captain," a rich French-African accent broke through the Annex lobby's clamor. "What can I do for you, sir?"

"Pierre, I need you to let Mrs. Loop and I get to suite 800 first," McCuiston's breathing became labored as he rounded the platform for the second set of stairs heading down. "Stall the elevator if you must, just give me two minutes."

"Yes, sir. We'll go back up a level before proceeding to level eight," Umbuntu confirmed. "That should give you a few extra moments, but I can't further slow my progress. Protocols."

"I'm well aware, Officer. Thank you." McCuiston tapped his earbud once more, closing the channel, and turned to Erin. "After speaking to the Teller--the therapist--last night, she requested to have the people Dylan trusts the most in the room during the session."

"I can't think anyone he trusts more than you, Liam." Erin's lips tightened and turned down on one side. "But I don't know how much he trusts me. He did keep those horrible secrets."

"That was before," McCuiston patted her hand, "this is now. He's a changed man. He's kept nothing from you since. Besides, the doc says there's no time to waste."

McCuiston pulled Erin into a faster pace and speed-walked down the corridor to suite 800. He used his ID to bypass the security doors and let Erin step into the lobby to find Dr. Leigh waiting just inside the threshold.

"Erin, this is Dr. Margaret Leigh, chief psychologist for the TSI," McCuiston raised his arm, placing a hand on Maggie's shoulder. "Dr. Leigh, this is Erin Loop--Dylan's wife--and their son, DJ."

"Please, call me Maggie." The Doctor reached out and grabbed Erin's hand. "Let's step down the hall so Detective Loop can go straight into the therapy room without distraction."

Maggie spun on her heels and marched down the corridor, followed by McCuiston and Erin. She stopped at a door on her left, gesturing them to go inside, then shut the door behind them.

"Please, Erin, sit." Maggie pointed to a plush recliner facing the door.

"Thank you," Erin mumbled as McCuiston helped her sit, and then stood beside the chair.

"After watching the security footage from last night, I've been observing Dylan via A.R.," Maggie sighed. "I'm afraid it doesn't look good. Based on what I've seen, he's having a level four schism. However, I'm confident that if we can get him to reject the implanted memories, he'll be able to make a full recovery."

"What do you need from us?" Erin looked up at McCuiston.

"I need you to enter the Reflection session with me," Maggie's fingers danced across her hand, and a hologram appeared from above. "I don't have much time to explain. Detective Loop is approaching the suite. Here's how it's going to work."

* * *

Unable to see, hear, or speak under the hood, Dylan's head bobbed around as his silent pleas for death went unanswered. The fabric seemed to hold his eye and lips shut as if alive. His skin no longer tingled from the crisp air and early morning sun. A scent of sweat and machine oil permeated the hood. The wheelchair bounced, ever so slightly, as his stomach dropped with the descent.

I'm going back to the Tellers. No. I've confessed. I killed those people. I killed Erin. DJ couldn't stop me. What good will this do? I'm a murderer. Kill me, or lobe me. But just get on with it!

The wheelchair rolled forward, and he swayed when it took a sharp right turn. A few seconds of travel across a soft surface and the parade stopped. Without warning, strong hands pulled him up from his armpits, and he sensed the wheelchair roll away. He tried to scream at his captors, but the hood kept his lips like glue. His incoherent moans disappeared inside the hood like shouting into space.

Two large bodies pressed up against him, holding him tight even though the plasma net kept his arms locked across his chest like a mummy. A bright blue light blinded him as the hood released its grip and vanished. A second pair of hands held his head in place as the ID scanner cycled.

"I don't need to see the Teller," Dylan slurred. "I'm guilty. Just lock me up. Protect them from me."

"Welcome back, Detective Loop," Iris' voice chimed above. "Dr. Leigh is expecting you. Please proceed to Suite eight-seventeen."

Dylan collapsed into the wheelchair as the cold footrests slammed into his heels. The door swung open to the bright haze of the waiting area, and a fuzzy green trail drew his eyes toward the left corridor. The forward guard stepped quickly through the lobby, one blocking the right hallway, the other jogging down the left.

As Dylan's chair turned the corner, he spied the dark blur of body armor standing at the green trails' end. The door on his right opened, and Maggie emerged wearing a navy skirt and yellow blouse.

"It's good to see you again, Detective." She lied through her rigid posture and a thin-lipped smile. "I'm sorry that we have to meet again so soon and under these circumstances." She raised her arm, and Dylan's driver pushed him through the door and into a six-meter by nine-meter concrete box divided by a glass wall.

The five-centimeter thick glazing rose into the ceiling, while hydraulic motors whirred behind the walls. Dylan stumbled as his handler picked him up and shoved him over the walls' receiving trench embedded in the floor. He turned to find four rifles pointing at his head.

"It's about damn time," Dylan croaked. "I was expecting a lobotomy, but I guess a firing squad will do." He closed his eyes, swaying under the LED lights embedded in the concrete ceiling.

I wonder if it will hurt? To die.

The hydraulic pistons hissed from either side as the glass wall dropped between Dylan and his would-be executioners. The guards lowered their weapons, while one tapped on his holo-cuff. The plasma-net jacket binding Dylan's arms to his chest retracted into a metal harness belted around his waist. Simultaneously, an injection collar fell from his neck and clattered on the floor. Stretching his arms, he flinched at the stabbing pain in his right hand. Lifting it up he examined the 3D printed cast encasing his arm below the elbow. Flashes of shredded fingers erupted in his mind as the tranquilizers dissipated from his system.

Someone shot me in the hand.

As if emerging from a deep sleep, Dylan's eye focused as the guards stepped back to the opposite wall. "So, no execution just yet?"

"You're not being executed, Detective Loop," Maggie stepped through the door, closing it behind her. "You're not being lobotomized either. You're here because you're a valuable asset to the TSI. We're here to help you."

"Hey, doc," Dylan took a step away from the glass. "Feels like I haven't seen you in a lifetime."

Maggie raised the A.R. glasses to her face and lifted her hands. "What day is it, Detective?"

Dylan moved as if to reach into a pocket, but found only the smooth black cloth. "It's uh... it's um..." he glanced around the room looking for help. Zooming into Maggie's glasses, he searched for a time index in the display. Maggie's nimble fingers danced across her palm, and the date stamp disappeared before Dylan could focus. "I don't know," he scraped at his head with his left hand. "Uhh. I guess it's... I don't know!"

"It's okay, Detective," Maggie's fingers typed across an invisible keypad. "We'll get back to that. Now, why do you think you're here?"

Dylan rushed the glass, cracking the plastic covering his hand as he tried to make a fist. "Because I killed Erin and twenty-seven other people. I'm a killer!"

"What would you say if I told you none of that ever happened?" Maggie stepped up to the glass, unflinching.

"I'd say you're crazy," Dylan laughed. "Maybe you should be the one in the *Funhouse*."

Maggie swiped her fingers, and the door opened. Dylan side-stepped and fixed his gaze over her shoulder. He swallowed a lump as Erin, DJ, and Liam McCuiston walked in the room. Erin's eyes, bloodshot and wet, stared back. Her lip quivered as she seemed to be fighting to keep a smile on her face.

DJ's little arm swung loosely over Erin's embrace. Dylan zoomed into the slow rise and fall of his chest, and the steady heartbeat. "Erin," he choked. "I'm sorry. I didn't mean to kill you. I was so angry. Why did you let them kidnap our son?"

Tears poured from Erin's eyes. "I'm right here, Dylan. DJ, he's right here," she waved DJ's hand toward the glass. "You never killed anyone. It's not real."

Dylan started pacing behind the glass like a madman. "No," he muttered to himself. "I remember. My welding gun was linked to 27 homicides. I was sent back to 1969 to track the killer. I met DJ in the timestream. He gave me my memories. Of what I'd done."

"Those twenty-seven homicides never happened, Loop," McCuiston stepped forward, placing his hand on the glass. "As far as our records show, you were sent to 1969 to figure out how a boy got crushed under a tractor at Woodstock. There was never any indication of foul play."

"But I remember killing that boy," Dylan jabbed at his head. "His great-grandson was going to become the architect of the American Downfall. So I killed him. It happened!"

"Detective," Maggie interrupted. "What day is it?"

Dylan stared, wild-eyed around the room, scratching his head as he resumed pacing. "It's--"

"It's May twenty-fifth, Detective," Maggie twitched her fingers, and a clock appeared, hovering within the glass. "You're leap was less than ten hours ago."

"This is a trick," Dylan shook his head. "This is part of that Reflective therapy."

"I assure you, Detective," Maggie opened her palms, "this is no trick. I haven't even started. But we'll need to, to help you sort through your real memories, and those you believe are from the future."

"They *are* from the future," he screamed. "I remember them! Clear as day!"

Maggie pressed her lips while Erin stifled a cry with her hand behind her.

"He may be past saving," Liam's head bowed and shook.

Maggie turned her back to Dylan, facing Erin and McCuiston. Dylan pressed his ear to the glass.

"As I said earlier, you're here at my request," Maggie's voice suddenly seemed garbled through the glass. "I believe we can help him sort through the implanted memories. And to do that, I'll need to the two of you to be his anchors. Are you still willing to do that?"

"Of course," McCuiston whispered.

"Anything," Erin sobbed.

Maggie spun back around to face Dylan, the sound in the room returning to normal as if emerging from underwater. "Then let's begin."

Wednesday, May 25th, 9:45am

Dylan stood before three mirrors. Erin and McCuiston stood behind the glass on the two sides, while two versions of Dylan--one as he knew himself and an older version--occupied the one in the middle. Dylan's doppelganger's seemed to be fighting, bumping, and banging into each other as they struggled to be in front. Dylan looked down at his clothing. On one side, he wore his leap-suit. On the other, he wore dark jeans and his TSI T-shirt. Each side seemed to take turns fading in and out of existence.

"Tell me what you're afraid of, Detective," the dark chocolate voice whispered from the shadows.

Dylan faced the mirrors at the images. The lips of Erin and McCuiston never moved, only his reflections.

"I'm afraid of what I've done," Dylan choked. "Or what I'm about to do. Hurting innocent people."

"Fear is the assumption of events that are outside our control.," His images droned. "F, E, A, R. Future Events Aren't Real."

"But I remember!" Dylan pointed at his head.

"Do you remember the last book you read?" Erin's voice caused the mirror's surface to shimmer. "The one you read to DJ on that night. After you shot that intruder."

Dylan's head tilted, his brow furrowed. "*Snugs the Bear*."

"You read it to put him to sleep," she sounded like she was crying though her image remained impassive.

"I remember," Dylan's eye glistened.

"Is *Snugs* a real bear?" Dylan's reflections leaned forward as if to pop out of the mirror.

Dylan shook his head. "No, of course not. It's a kid's story."

"What do you do to mentally prepare for a leap when we have little intel on the Moment of Insertion?" the deep voice spoke through McCuiston's mouth.

"I suppose I think about all the possibilities," Dylan turned to his captain, "and how I'll react if one of them happens."

"How often does one of those possibilities occur?" asked his image.

Dylan folded his arms across his chest. "About one in a hundred?"

"Try one in a thousand," McCuiston chuckled. "That means how many possibilities didn't happen?"

"Nearly all of them," Dylan choked, throwing out his arms.

"Future events aren't real," his reflections droned.

"But, these memories," Dylan ground his teeth, pointing to his skull. "These are real. I've felt them."

He stepped over to Erin's mirror. "I remember the smell of your perfume as I choked you to death," he cried.

He returned to McCuiston's mirror. "I remember binding you with a plasma-net, so I could steal the prototype leap-suit."

Dylan jabbed a finger at his older reflection. "And I remember you stalking each of those kids, playing with their minds, and either making them shoot themselves in the head, or killing them yourself."

"Who's to blame for those deaths, Detective?" All but Dylan's graying image spoke.

"HIM!" Dylan crashed his fist into the mirror, splintering the glass. "This is all his fault!" Dylan collapsed to the ground, sobbing and smashing his encased hand into the floor.

Erin's image stepped through the frame and wrapped her arms around his shaking body. McCuiston also walked out of his mirror and knelt beside Dylan, putting a hand on his shoulder.

Dylan looked into the central panel just as his younger reflection stepped off the surface. His image smiled and began to shrink, growing younger as he got smaller until the form of DJ appeared; sprawled out on the floor.

Dylan picked up his son, staring into his eyes until movement behind the glass drew him back up.

The image of senior Dylan stepped through the splintered surface and onto the floor directly in front of Dylan's kneeling form. His scowling face carried the fractures from the broken glass over his right eye. Dylan locked eyes with his counterpart as he rose from the floor holding DJ in a protective embrace. Erin and McCuiston moved silently to stand behind him.

"You can't protect your family from me," the splintered reflection growled.

Dylan felt a heat growing in his hand. Looking down, he saw DJ transforming into his welding gun. On instinct, the welder started to whine as Dylan dialed up the power. He looked over his left shoulder to find Erin nodding her head, an encouraging smile and wet eyes radiating on her face.

Turning to his right, Dylan caught sight of McCuiston, patting his shoulder and nodding with a kind smile.

Dylan raised the welder and pointed at his reflections' left eye. The Doppelganger sneered. "You can't stop the future."

The world seemed to come to a halt. Erin, McCuiston, and the broken reflection frozen like an arctic glacier. Images of the idyllic field and the brilliant tree rose to the forefront of his mind. His conversation with DJ, grown-up and wise, replayed in his thoughts. *It's the only way to save Mom.*

Dylan cleared the welder's safety. "Future events aren't real," he whispered and fired.

Tuesday, March 15th, 7:10pm

Two Years Later

"Happy Birthday to you! Happy Birthday to you! Happy Birthday, dear DJ! Happy Birthday to you!"

"Yea!" Dylan, Erin, McCuiston, and a dozen others shouted and clapped as DJ blew out two little candles.

Erin's parents kissed the birthday boy on both cheeks as Erin holo-captured the moment. Dylan's mother picked up the German Chocolate cake and carried it to the counter. Picking up a knife, she started slicing and serving the morsels onto blue plates embossed with a polar bear.

Dylan picked DJ out of his booster seat and spun him around. "Happy Birthday, little man!"

DJ giggled. "Faster, daddy! Faster!"

Dylan made a jet engine noise and flew DJ off the porch and onto the lawn. Spinning around in a circle, Dylan fell, dizzy, to the ground, pulling a belly-laughing DJ on top of him. Dylan joined in the laugh-fest with his son and pulled him in tight.

"Hey, you two," Erin called from the porch. "It's time for cake and presents!"

"Cake! Cake! Cake! Cake!" DJ chanted, pushing himself from Dylan's grip.

Dylan chortled watching DJ's little legs as he bounded up the steps and into his grandfather's outstretched arms.

"Come on, handsome," Erin curled her finger with a wink.

Dylan rolled over and pushed himself off the ground. Two strides, and a sudden sprint up the stairs, and he lifted Erin with both arms. "Put me down, Dylan," she howled with glee. "You're going to squish the baby!"

She lightly punched Dylan's chest as set her down. "I'd never do anything to harm my family," he cooed as he wrapped his hands around Erin's swollen belly and feeling a strong kick. "Whoa! Are you sure it's a girl?"

Erin flicked Dylan in his cybernetic eye. "Why don't you get an upgrade, and find out for yourself?"

"Whoa! Hey there," Dylan feigned surprise. "Watch the hardware, woman!"

"The department might be able to swing that," McCuiston walked over with a plate piled high with cake and ice cream. "Now that you've finally gotten that promotion, Lieutenant."

"Maybe one that is a little less..." Dylan pointed to his face.

Creepy Cyborg Psycho Killer?

"World-Wide Warrior, then?" McCuiston guffawed.

"Aargh!" Dylan laughed. "I hate that broadcast."

* * *

Erin settled next to Dylan on the porch swing, careful not to wake their droopy son sleeping on Dylan's chest.

"Oh, good," Erin whispered. "He's finally asleep."

Dylan smiled. "Yeah, about ten minutes ago. Hail to the power of sugar."

Erin pulled Dylan's arm over, wrapping both her arms around it while his hand found her bare knee and stroked her skin. He kissed her the top of her head. "I love you," he hummed into her hair.

"I love you, too." she sighed.

Dylan stared up at the crescent moon overhead and breathed in the night air. Five minutes went by in silence until Erin shivered beside him.

"Okay, that's about all I can take. I'm going inside." She stood up but turned to lean over, rubbing the inside of his leg. "You're welcome to join me after you put your boy to bed."

Dylan shifted in his seat. "Ten minutes?" he winked, pushing his face forward to brush his nose against her cheek.

Erin's lips brushed along his cheek until he felt her hot breath in his ear. "Make it five, and I've got a special surprise for you." She flicked her tongue along his lobe and then pushed herself away from the swing. Dylan watched her sashay through the back door, giving him a hungry look as she disappeared inside.

Dylan remained still for a moment, enjoying the gentle rocking motion of the swing syncopated with DJ's steady breathing.

I am one lucky man.

Dylan leaned forward, cradling DJ with one arm while hanging on the swings' chain with the other. Crickets chirped in the foliage as he padded across the porch's floorboards. The screen door squeaked as he pulled it open.

I gotta get some WD-40 on these hinges.

Dylan closed the back door, letting the screen squeal shut. Putting his hand on the glass pane, the red security icon appeared next to his palm, indicating he'd successfully armed the system for the night. He switched DJ from one shoulder to the other as he clicked off the lights and made his way through the darkening house.

Passing by the old nursery (now his home office) Dylan peeked in, making sure the window locks were in place.

Check.

He glanced into the master bedroom, catching a reflection from the bathroom mirror into the closet. Erin stood with her back to the door, pulling red lingerie over her baby bump.

Check and double-check.

The stair treads creaked as he slowly climbed to the upper floor.

Erin may hate the noise, but at least I'll know anytime someone is going up or down them.

He turned into the bedroom off the top landing and flipped on the hallway light. A slanted square of light fell onto the blue and white polar-bear-themed rug. On one side of the room sat DJ's old crib next to the matching changing table.

Evelyn. Evy. Evangeline. We really need to decide on a name for this girl.

Dylan lowered DJ onto the changing table and grabbed the pajamas atop the pile. "World-Wide Warrior," he breathed as he held up the outfit and let it unravel. "Is she kidding?"

Carefully, Dylan changed his comatose son out of his cake-stained t-shirt and jeans and into zip-up pajamas. DJ's breathing never skipped a beat, even when Dylan lost a grip on his foot and dropped it onto the padding.

Once changed, Dylan scooped DJ into his arms and held him close; rocking and smelling his hair as he crossed the room to the white four-poster huddled in the corner. He leaned over, settled DJ onto the mattress, and pulled the covers up to his chin as he knelt on the floor.

"I love you, DJ," he whispered, kissing his forehead as his eye moistened. "You saved my life."

The End

4

SKETCH ARTIST

by Brian C Hailes

Sketch artists are the throwaways, the behind-the-scenes, the invisible ones. If cutbacks ever hit the office, I'd be the first to go. I know this, because it's happened before. In an office full of cops, bureaucrats, and scum-of-the-earth, we walk unseen. No one ever notices the sketch artist. That is until someone needs a sketch.

There are only two reasons I'm still here at the San Francisco Police Department. The first: Criminality is alive and well; people keep getting murdered, raped, kidnapped, or otherwise taken advantage of—and now, with over a million people in the City by the Bay, sometimes there are witnesses. I also happen to be very good at what I do.

A little *too* good.

I do freelance portraiture on the side among other projects, but only because you can't pay for an apartment in a city like this on a sketch artist's wage (not to mention the cost of *good* food here). Graphic artists are like actors or musicians—you're either paid hundreds of thousands of dollars and hailed as a legend or you don't exist at all. I still fall into the latter, more common category.

But there is one thing that sets me apart from every other sketch artist out there: I've never heard of another who can draw a portrait based on a witness's firsthand account, and then have the computer find a facial recognition match to their drawing in the police database with a ninety-five percent accuracy rate.

I can do that. And I've been doing that ever since I started here.

To some, it seemed like a psychic or supernatural power of sorts. I wouldn't go so far as to call it magic, but perhaps a heightened awareness of things.

At first, people made a big deal about it, like I was special or something. Now, they just expect it of me.

People I work with, like Phillips and Nash, have told me that I should be working for the FBI or some other government agency, and maybe someday I will. But for now, a part of me enjoys the anonymity the SF police force offers.

I don't plan on leaving any time soon.

Besides, who would feed my dogs and let them out to piss?

* * *

To outsiders, fog was San Francisco's gentle lover, but to locals like me, 'Fog City' could be a freezing pain in the ass, ruining ball games and dates on the beach. This morning, it smothered the island, the white duvet having crept through the hills, wrapping us in a great amalgam of cloud and steel. It replaced that warm California sun with a chilling wind that felt like a ghoul sucking out your soul.

And speaking of ghouls—

Captain Perry Damen passed me on police headquarters front steps, walking briskly. "Good to see you're on time today, Daniels. We had a new eyewitness come forward on the Silver case. She'll be here at ten. Batter up."

By 'Silver case', he referred to the guy that painted himself silver from head to toe and posed for tourists in Union Square. He was found dead yesterday morning, strangled with a camera strap and then posed to look like Rodin's The Thinker—the classic French sculpture that sits alone in the courtyard of the Legion of Honor. Apparently, Silver had been sitting on a bench near the Union Square Heart for at least twenty-four hours before anyone realized he wasn't breathing. Everyone at the office half-jokingly wanted to hang it on the 'Gold Guy' or the 'Rainbow Guy' whose obvious motives would have been handout competition, but both had mutually corroborating alibis.

"Yes, sir," I said, catching the front door to the office as it swung back to hit me.

The headquarters for the southern district, housed in the new Public Safety Building of glass and concrete, consisted of approximately 430 department personnel, most of whom, I tried to avoid. I entered the break room and made myself some hot cocoa—the first step in my morning routine. Phillips, one of the youngest police officers on the force and the biggest ladies' man I'd ever known, saw me through the break-room windows and joined me. Probably to brag about his nightclub gambols last weekend and the lucky lady (or ladies) he took to bed afterward.

"'Sup, Daniels?" Phillips, tall, dark and way too attractive to be a police officer, grabbed a cup and poured himself some coffee.

"Blonde, brunette, or redhead?" I sipped my drink and leaned back against the counter, anticipating the kiss-tell to follow.

Phillips smiled with dry delight. "Now, why do you just assume—?"

"Blonde, brunette, or redhead?" I repeated.

"Okay, fine. But first, your question implies the choice of just one, when there is always the possibility of multiples. I mean we *are* talking about the weekend, right? Friday, Saturday, or Sunday? *Three* days."

"You worked Saturday night," I said.

"Just because I'm on duty doesn't mean I can't glean the numbers out of a beautiful young flower who happens to be waiting in line to buy a Frappuccino at the corner store."

"So..." I egged him on.

"Brunette . . ." Phillips slipped the coffee pot back into the coffee maker and took a sip, grinning childishly. " . . . On Sunday. On Friday, brown with highlights—now, do you consider that blonde or brunette? You're an artist."

"I dunno, like, medium brown or light brown?" I asked.

"Hold on," Phillips said, "I got a picture."

One of these days, I'd have to tag along and learn from the master, I thought. *Although I'm not that bad with the ladies.*

Nash, one of the office's criminal research analysts and my only other friend on the force, knocked on the glass and gestured for Phillips to follow him. Nash, with his stalky stature, balding pate, and sickly complexion couldn't have been more different than Phillips. A genius at his job, Nash could connect dots like no one else I'd ever worked with. And a lot of cops here found that useful. So useful, in fact, that Nash complained constantly about never having time to finish his own work.

When Phillips hesitated, scrolling through his phone's picture gallery for Ms. Brown with highlights, Nash knocked on the glass again, this time with fire in his eyes.

Phillips pocketed his phone and shrugged, "I'll have to show you later."

"Sure," I said, "Go. We've all seen Nash angry."

"Later." Phillips hurried out the door.

I drew a deep breath, looked around, and exhaled, stalling the inevitable: that long, deathly walk to my cubicle. Sometimes I wondered why I put myself through this. The zombie apocalypse had arrived but by a different name: the *cubicle apocalypse*. And we all self-subscribed. I guess that's why I only did contract work and limited my hours here to two days a week—just enough time to keep tabs on everything.

Captain Damen exited his office, obviously searching for someone.

That was my queue to leave.

I slipped out of the break room unseen and made for the beige partitions where even 16-20 hours a week seemed like half my life. There, I would stare at a computer screen and wait until ten o' clock for my witness to arrive. In the meantime, I could monitor my dogs.

* * *

I sat alone in Conference Room Two, a rectangular box with a table, a few chairs, and a wall of windows on the south side. Waiting. Fluorescent lights buzzed. I stared at the white piece of smooth Bristol paper before me as I spun the black mechanical pencil nearly full of 0.5mm lead over my fingers—my weapons of choice.

I glanced down at my phone. 10:07am.

Witness late. As per usual.

A lot of sketch artists had turned to the computer to accomplish their portraits. 3D modeling programs had come a long way, and any Joe Shmoe could fairly easily build a mug shot with a grocery cart full of digital options: square face, round face, pear-shaped face, small eyes, medium eyes, large eyes, blue, brown, green, hazel, gray. Nudge the eyes closer together or further apart. Perhaps somewhere in-between. A stroke of the keys and you could build a video-game perpetrator or victim in a matter of minutes. Hell, the witness could just about do it without you even present.

The computer could even age a face a month to 100 years or throw up multiple hairstyles or beard variations at different stages for comparison. A helpful tool, especially for kidnapping victims, and one that I'd been forced to use at times, but for my first sit-down with a client, I preferred the old school approach. *Revelation*, as Phillips liked to refer to it. Then, if needed, I could use my drawing and the face match photo it pulls from the database to construct the aged variations in the machine.

Nash had been pushing me to ditch traditional and dive full bore into the digital IdentiKit world for some time, but to do so would be to abandon my humanity, the living artifacts that cavemen left on rock walls.

No. I like to keep the originals. You could say I *collect* them. I have a system, and it works, despite technology's persistent and obnoxious sales distractions and updates.

Art is art, and a tool is a tool, I thought. *Without artists behind them, computers are lumps of sand.*

The door opened and Richardson, a grizzled homicide detective with a penchant for back-room deals and shady payoffs, escorted a young woman inside. Her shoulder-length brown hair belonged on a shampoo commercial, and I'd only seen tanned legs like hers in magazines. But her eyes made me feel twelve again.

"Daniels," Richardson glanced down through haughty yellow eyes, "This here's Alicia Warren. She took a photo with 'Silver' day 'fore we found 'im. Woulda' been just before M.E.'s stated time o' death. Said she saw someone suspicious in a hoodie watchin' 'em. Her friend asked the suspect to take their picture 'fore he just walked away."

"Alicia, this is Daniels." Richardson pulled out a chair next to me for her to sit in. "He's our sketch artist. If you could just tell him what you told us—describe the suspect best you can remember."

I stood and held out my hand, "Hi, Alicia."

She apprehensively offered hers. "Hi." So smooth and delicate. She slowly pulled her hand away and fidgeted.

She had a high, soft voice. Her dark, otherworldly eyes dodged mine before our gaze eventually met.

"It's nice to meet you." My voice sounded a little *too* genuine. What would Nash have done?

Richardson stood by awkwardly until Alicia finally sat down. "I'll leave ya to it."

I ignored the departing detective, swallowing uncomfortably, trying to think of ways to make Alicia feel more comfortable.

I cleared my throat. "So where are you from?"

"Arizona."

"Really? What brought you to San Francisco?" I smiled gently.

"My stepmom." She pulled a phone out of her back pocket and started scrolling through text messages.

"If you don't mind my asking," I hesitated, "How old are you?"

She paused and looked up. "Nineteen, almost twenty."

I nodded and tapped the tip of my pencil on the paper with the lead retracted. "I'm sorry, would you mind?" I pointed at her phone.

She rolled her eyes and put it away. "Sorry."

I tried to clear the butterflies out of my mind and focus on work. From Richardson's explanation, the perpetrator sounded like a spotter. "All right, this hooded figure. Tell me about him."

Alicia shifted in her chair and crossed her legs, tapping her French-manicured nails on the table. "I don't know. He was a creeper. Just hovered around us, watching the silver guy."

"Okay," I squinted, studying her body language. "Was his hoodie up or down? Age 30s? 40s?"

"Down. Probably mid-thirties," she said. "Skater type."

"Good. You're what, five-five? Was he taller than you?" I began to sketch a light outline of the perp's head.

She nodded, "Yeah, he was probably around five-ten, six-foot maybe?"

"Did you get a look at his eyes?"

"Yeah, sorta, but I don't know what color they were. Wasn't really paying attention."

"That's okay," I said with a grin. "I'm working in black and white."

She almost laughed.

"You watch movies?" I asked.

"Doesn't everybody?"

"Yeah, I guess. If the perp you saw was an actor, what actor would you say—?"

"I don't know. I mean, I watch movies, but I don't know actors' names."

"That's all right. Would you kiss him?"

"Excuse me?"

"The perp. Would you kiss him if he wasn't a perp?"

Alicia opened her mouth, holding back a smile, "Hell no. I told you he was a creeper."

"Okay, who *would* you kiss?"

"What do you . . .?" She locked eyes with me, then looked away. "I don't know, my boyfriend."

"Do you have a picture of him?"

She pulled out her phone again, and scrolled through some images before showing me one. A selfie with her and the boyfriend at the park. He had sandy blonde hair. A strong jawline. Ashamed eyes. Handsome, but not the most handsome. Nose broken at some point. Good teeth.

This guy, she kissed. The perp, she wouldn't. This would give me an opposite to reference.

Alicia stuck her phone back in her pocket.

"Thank you," I said. "If this guy were a boxer, could he take a punch?"

"No."

"Okay." I began sketching a thin jawline, sharp eyes.

"Hair color? Length?" I asked.

Alicia looked up at the ceiling, leaned back in her chair, "I dunno, dark, scruffy, just over the ears.

"Not long? No ponytail?" I asked for confirmation.

"No. But shaggy, down to his eyes."

"Good," I pulled another piece of paper and pencil out of the bag at my feet and slid it to her. "Now, you draw him."

Alicia, taken aback, scoffed. "I'm no artist. I can't even draw stick—"

"Figures. Yeah, no one can. That's okay." I straightened up. "I need you to draw him so I can watch you draw him."

She furrowed her brow and thought for a moment before picking up the pencil. "Okay," she said apprehensively.

She began to sketch.

And we drew together for at least a minute until—

Alicia sat back to look at her drawing as something shot through glass. Blood spurted. Alicia screamed. Blood covered the table. Wetness sprayed the side of my face. Alicia's right forearm had been shot.

She stumbled back and off of her chair, pain and shock in her expression.

I moved to help her. Protect her.

I looked over at the window in the corner. A bullet hole. Sniper rifle. Someone had attempted to kill her. And in the middle of the police station.

I scooped Alicia into my arms and escorted her out of the room, shouting for help.

"It's all right," I told her. "You'll be okay. I won't let anything happen to you."

Someone must have known about my 950 batting average, which meant our perp was in the system.

* * *

An alarm blared inside SFPD headquarters. On par with semiannual drills, half the on-site police force armed up and hurried outside to sweep the perimeter for the shooter. They would cast a wide net as quickly as possible.

Adrenaline pumped through my veins. After having handed Alicia off to trusted coworkers for medical attention, I burst out of the front doors into blinding daylight. I wasn't supposed to leave the building with the other officers, but I didn't care. I ran to the alley and scanned the neighboring buildings.

I found the outside of the window to Conference Room Two and tried to crudely judge the trajectory of the shot. It pointed to a brownstone apartment building down the street, corner rooftop.

This isn't really my job, I told myself, *but I have to keep Alicia safe.*

I'll find this hitman. And I will make him pay.

I ran toward the apartment building and surveyed the surrounding area for anyone conspicuous. A black man rummaged through trash in a dumpster across the parking lot and two heavyset women stood and talked next to a rundown laundromat.

I shot up a steel switchback staircase, scanning the rooftop where I guessed the shooter set his rifle.

I made it to the top level, but found the roof access locked.

I coughed and stopped a moment to catch my breath. I wasn't used to sprinting up ten flights of stairs.

As I looked down, a man in everyday-wear emerged on the ground-level floor carrying a small duffel bag and made his way across the parking lot.

I darted back down, leaping three steps at a time.

The suspect noticed my aggressive pace and quickened his own. He made for a grouping of parked cars.

Where are the cops? I thought. *He's going to get away.*

I focused on getting down the stairs without tripping and finally made it to pavement.

My legs wanted to give way and a stitch pained my side, but I kept running.

The suspect had gotten into a gray sedan and backed out of his parking space. The car pulled forward and across the lot.

I sprinted, pushing my legs to their limits.

The car slowed to wait for oncoming traffic before pulling away onto the street.

I missed the license plate but caught a fleeting glimpse of the man through the driver side window. Fleeting. But thankfully, enough.

* * *

In the stone bowels of an old support arch below the abandoned Fort Point and the Golden Gate Bridge, a man called Turks by his subordinates, stewed in the dark. The only décor, a large oaken conference table with long benches down the sides and heavy chairs at its heads, filled the center of the room. Only the screen of a single laptop lighted the table, in the midst of split-level concrete footings and steel support beams.

The current crime lord ruling the streets of Saint Frank, and whose influence had spread from the Windy City to the Big Apple, typed on his Mac. A stroke of the keys and his power ebbed and flowed; bank accounts emptied, bank accounts swelled. His age, thirty-five, though young for ruling the streets of a town and keeping its thugs and assassins at bay, didn't curb his ability to intimidate.

Turk's third assistant in as many years, Mr. Edwards, entered the cold, stony meeting room. *Loyal to a fault,* Turks thought to himself. *He might just outlast the others.*

Edwards piped up, "Excuse me, Boss, but they're ready for your briefing."

There was a slight echo in the room.

Turks finished what he was typing as Edwards waited patiently in the dark for a response. He expected nothing less of a good assistant.

Turks punched the Enter key and then sat back in his chair with a slight grin. "Send them in."

Edwards nodded humbly and reopened the door behind him.

A dozen men dressed and painted completely silver from hair and sunglasses to military boots and brandishing FN F2000 S Assault Rifles (also painted silver) filtered in and sat around the table.

Turks didn't move an inch, the blue glow from his screen under-lighting his assessing expression. Theatrics usually aided his intimidation factor—and that was important when dealing with mercenaries.

The silver men, all twelve built like pit bulls in Kevlar, watched one another avoiding eye contact with Turks as they settled into their seats. This amused him.

"They've all been vetted, sir," Edwards said. "And they're ready for combat."

Turks looked down and blinked for a moment before grabbing the closest man's gun and firing just inches over everyone's heads.

Everyone flinched.

He carved a straight line of bullet holes into the concrete wall at the back of the room until the magazine ran empty. Dust and debris crumbled from the high ceiling and walls at the reverberations. The echo dissipated.

Edwards removed his glasses and wiped a bit of debris from one eye.

Turks, now breathing heavily and with eyes wide as a madman, threw the rifle onto the table. The men still made no eye contact with him.

"Not bad," Turks breathed, looking over at Edwards. "Remind me, how many shipments of these?"

"Three, sir," Edwards said with all the dignity he could muster.

Turks calmed his breathing. "Good." He nodded to his right, "Replace this man's magazine."

"Of course," Edwards replied.

Turks remembered something on his to-do list, sat down, and resumed typing on his laptop. "You might think of me as the most powerful man in the city. Inside the computer, that's probably true. But I'm not the *only* powerful man here. And I don't run the only one-stop-shop in town."

"I've a competitor in the garbage business, and he's recently clipped some friends of mine, not to mention, sales. Off-shoot of the Lanza family, likes to eat alone. Name's Gallo.

"You've heard of him. Hell, some of you have probably worked for him. I pay better."

At that comment, a few of the men finally glanced over at Turks. He, in turn, stared them down until they looked away.

"You're probably wondering why you're painted silver," Turks said. "Yours is a *message* job. In-and-out. Take it seriously. You'll get your points."

Edwards stood. Then the men.

"By the way," Turks added, "Word gets out, consider yourselves broke and then go ahead and draw some little targets on your foreheads. It's all pre-programmed."

Edwards moved to the door. "All right, Gentlemen. Let's go to work."

Without a word, the men exited the meeting place in double-file, Edwards bringing up the rear.

Turks looked back at his computer and grinned before packing up.

* * *

I sat in my city loft apartment at my favorite drafting table. The view of the San Francisco skyline spread out before me through the front windows near the kitchen, but at the moment, I couldn't fully appreciate it—more important things occupied my thoughts.

With perfect lighting, temperature comfortable, and a Coke with two ice cubes, I had quickly and easily entered *the zone,* that place where the only thing that mattered was the thing staring back at me. In this case, a portrait.

With eyes focused, hand practiced, and classical music playing through my ear buds, I drew a picture of the shooter. A man for whom I needed no secondhand eyewitness account. *I* was the witness. I just needed to remember.

I often worked overtime from home. One of the nice things about my job and my ability. Inspiration didn't always come in the dead hours—as I liked to call them—in the middle of the day. Real inspiration, often times, came only at night.

Distraction and interruption, the killers of creativity, prowled mostly in daylight, although the two-headed beast sometimes favored the nocturnal hunt, usually in the form of social calls. That's why I left my phone in the other room when working. My revelatory powers flowed unhindered.

Hours passed like minutes.

Faint outlines became light and dark shapes. Those became ear lobes, strands of hair, brows, lips, nostrils, and forehead wrinkle lines. Subtle and careful blending of the curving planes of neck, jaw and cheekbones only helped to solidify the likeness. A consistent and believable light source proved paramount. But the eyes mattered most. I had to get those right. Cover the eyes in a photo and erase any chance of recognition.

Windows to the soul, I thought, *but also to the likeness.*

I craned back from my picture for a wider view, oblivious to anything else in the world.

Nailed it.

A flutter of anticipation to show someone arose in my gut.

More than anyone, I wanted to show it to Alicia. I wanted to tell her that this was the man that shot her. I would find him, and I would bring him down.

* * *

Silence settled off the docks of Pier 39 as dusk fell over Fisherman's Wharf. The loud barks of hundreds of sea lions was absent, as if the famed 700-pound pinnipeds had blubbered off because they knew what was coming.

The nearby Anchor Bay Café, one of the wharf's largest and classiest restaurants mainly tailored to fat-walleted tourists, lit up to revel in all its marine-themed splendor. Seared lobster and crab legs nestled between hors d'oeuvres and side dishes on hastily maneuvering platters. Waiters and waitresses dressed as sailors struggled to keep up with their seafood-loving guests. The background music and conversational roar of the place could be faintly heard from the street outside.

Twelve armed mercenaries, steeped in silver paint, slowly congregated around the building from all directions, even seaward.

Tourist bystanders thought it was part of some sidewalk show and snapped a few photos. Many pointed and watched, enthralled as if expecting the flash mob of silver men to break out in a synchronized dance routine.

The men tightened their gaps around the café, ignoring the growing attention.

A few of the tourists noticed the large submachine guns hanging in the men's grasp, and rethought their proximity decision.

As the men closed around the restaurant, several people inside noticed them through the windows. Soon the whole place drowned in curiosity. Several customers stood to peer out the windows while others turned to their waiters for explanation.

The men stopped in unison and lifted their automatic rifles.

The customers gasped and ducked.

The men opened fire in deafening harmony.

Windows shattered. Wood chipped. Brick crumbled.

People screamed and scattered. Children shrieked.

The whole building imploded into chaos under a circle of hellfire.

The Anchor Bay Café sign swung back and forth before splitting in two. The outside staircases shattered to bits. Doors blew off their hinges.

As the men's magazines emptied, they methodically reloaded and continued their attack, persistent, hell-bent on breaking the very structural integrity of the building.

Smoke rose in great cylindrical waves that wafted upward at the building's demolition. Those that tried to exit were shot and fell back inside, scurrying out of sight.

Spent casings littered the ground by the thousands.

Four of the men trained their sights on the restaurant's jetty pylons that propped up a seaside corner of the building's foundation, and eventually buckled the pylons' sturdy hold.

As each of the twelve emptied their sixth clip, the building groaned, shuddered, and gave way in a devastated heap.

In one accord, the men released their triggers and assessed the damage through flame, smoke and debris. The air smelled strongly of gunpowder, campfire and burning dust.

Totaled.

Like ghosts, the men dispersed and disappeared into the shadows before red-and-blue flashing lights could converge on the scene.

* * *

Police headquarters, a scene of frenzied activity, felt different than usual. Detectives, officers, analysts, and secretaries scurried about to accomplish the bidding of their superiors. Supercharged in light of the recent *Anchor Bay Assault.*

Looking around, excitement welled within me. *Excitement.* An emotion almost alien to me. Especially at the precinct.

Richardson had invaded Nash's workspace. They argued. Nash looked flustered. I walked within earshot when Richardson turned toward me.

"What're you doing here?"

With pressed lips and raised eyebrows, I remembered the picture in my hand and offered it to Richardson.

"I already got your sketch of our suspect." Richardson yanked the paper from my fingers.

"Careful," I muttered, cringing at every crease. "This isn't the suspect from Union Square . . . It's the shooter."

Richardson straightened up, staring at the beautiful drawing of a late middle-aged every-man with empty eyes and a resolute air. "The shooter?"

"Let me see," Nash said, rolling his chair closer.

"Yeah," I swallowed. "The a . . . the guy that shot Alici—the witness . . . yesterday."

Phillips saw me and approached our little gathering at Nash's desk.

"And how exactly did you get a description of the shooter?" Richardson asked with gruff skepticism.

"I didn't."

Phillips swung around Richardson's shoulder to have a glimpse. Everyone loved to look at drawings.

Richardson, Nash, and now Phillips all stared back at me.

"I saw him," I confessed.

Richardson gave that New York head-bob of his, "Excuse me, you . . . *saw* him? What, from the window?"

I hesitated, replaying the scenario in my mind. "No, not exactly. I went outside."

"You what, chased him down?" Richardson chuckled. "Fancy yourself a detective now? A *real* cop?"

"That's awesome," Phillips piped in. "Where'd you see him?"

"Leaving the building," I stuttered, "I—The alley from where he must've set up, where he shot from."

Saying the words out loud made them sound fabricated.

"Have you scanned this?" Richardson asked, raising the portrait.

I shook my head. "No, I just got here."

Richardson, too, shook his head. I could tell he'd already discredited me as a reliable witness, but protocol would force him to go through the motions nonetheless.

"Let me know if you get a match," I said as he walked away. "And I'd like that back when you're done!" I wasn't sure he'd heard me, but he always forgot papers in the scanner. I'd snag the original later. As well as the name of Alicia's shooter.

"Still don't know how you do that," Phillips said.

"What?" I asked.

"The drawings. The realism. The accuracy."

Nash rolled back to his computer. "Easy. Rather than lead, he loads his pencils with . . . magic."

I smiled and pointed at Nash. "Yeah, that."

* * *

Alicia liked to walk the San Francisco Bay trail past Marina Green, Yacht Harbor and Crissy Field. Teaming with athletic and healthy-lifestyle folks, she found it a nice place to clear her head and breathe the freshest bay air the island had to offer.

Having left the hospital only two days previous and with her arm in a sling, she couldn't jog her usual pace, but she pushed herself along as quickly as her moderate pain tolerance allowed.

The department had placed a squad car in front of her apartment for protection and a rotating shift of officers monitored her faithfully, but they couldn't follow her forever. And she had to get out of the house. So she sneaked out the back for a quick walk.

Perhaps that wasn't my most brilliant idea, she thought. *Maybe I should head back now.*

With a body like hers in form-fitting athletic wear, men often watched as she passed, but presently, the tiny hairs on her neck told her someone did more than watch. More than even stare.

She stopped to stretch near a playground and glanced around for stalkers.

No one suspicious stood out, but the feeling didn't go away.

Alicia continued to jog when a charcoal sports car pulled up to the curb in front of her with the windows down.

"Alicia, you're in danger," said the driver. "Get in the car. Quick!"

The voice rang with urgency and familiarity, but she couldn't quite place it. For some reason, she trusted it and made for the passenger side door. The driver opened it from the inside.

As she sat, two gunshots ricocheted off the door panels, narrowly missing her head.

"Close the door!" He floored the gas.

Alicia reached out with her good arm and shut the door as they rushed off down the street.

* * *

"Daniels?" she asked.

"You okay?" I worried about Alicia's heavy breathing and the confusion in her blank expression.

"Was that . . .?"

"Same shooter that got your arm? Yeah, probably."

Alicia, still sprawled out on my seat, took a moment to sit up and compose herself. She cringed at the pain in her arm as she resituated and put on her seatbelt. "Sorry about your car. It's nice."

"Thanks. Don't worry about it."

"How'd you know he was after me?" Alicia asked.

"I called in some favors after your incident. Cops watching your place reported you missing. Asked Richardson and some others to keep me in the loop."

"How'd you know I'd be here?" She asked, catching me off guard.

"I'd rather not say." The words painted me with suspicion.

She persisted. "Are you *stalking* me?"

Now I avoided eye contact with her.

"Well, say something." Anger rose in her voice.

I reached behind the seat and grabbed my laptop commuter bag, setting it on the floor between us. I reached inside, pulled out a drawing, and handed it to her. "I finished it. That's Carl Mason, the guy you described from Union Square."

Her eyes lit up as she studied the portrait. She recognized him and remembered.

I pulled a second drawing from my bag and she took it, stared at it.

"That's Alec Lovac," I said. "The one that shot you and my car door. They're both professionals. I just wanted to . . . protect you, and I knew the shooter wouldn't leave you alone until he . . ."

"Until he what?" Alicia asked rhetorically.

I squealed a right onto Van Ness and headed toward Lombard. " . . . Finished the job."

Alicia sat back in her seat and nodded before staring out the window.

I watched her out of the corner of my eye as I drove up and down the steep-angled streets toward downtown. I didn't really have a particular destination in mind.

Alicia finally broke her silence, "Why do they want me dead? I'm nobody."

I hesitated to say anything, but couldn't hold my tongue. "You want the truth?"

She looked at me with the saddest eyes, tears slowly seeping down her perfect face.

I drew and released a deep breath. "It's organized crime. You know, modern-day mobsters?"

Alicia wiped the tears from her eyes.

"Guy named Gallo," I went on, "Powerful guy. Loansharking, gunrunning, prostitution, human trafficking, narcotics, you name it; he's in all of it. His guys planned the hit on Silver. The perp you witnessed? The guy I drew from your description? I think he was a spotter for Silver's killer."

Alicia exhaled sharply.

"They weren't after you," I said. "You just happened to be in the wrong place at the wrong time. They consider you an unresolved threat."

"Unresolved . . . " Alicia shook her head. "How do you know all this?"

"I get bored a lot at the station. Do a lot of eavesdropping."

I gave her a minute for the information to sink in. "I suppose we should find you a safe place to lie low."

"Shouldn't we go to the precinct?" Alicia asked. "File a report or something?"

I thought a moment. "Yeah, I suppose we should. We'll just have to keep you away from the windows."

Alicia didn't appreciate the joke.

Something fast approached in my peripheral vision.

"Hold on," I said, punching the gas.

A white truck barreled into the rear driver side of my car, spinning both our vehicles through an intersection. The force of impact threw me against the door. Everything went blurry and out of control. Tiny shards of glass soared through the air in slow motion.

My neck, shoulder and ears throbbed. Tires screeched and crashing metal resounded.

When everything stopped spinning, I looked over at Alicia. It hurt to turn my head. She was banged up and unconscious, but breathing.

I unlatched my seatbelt and drew the Walther CCP handgun—my personal weapon, unauthorized by the force—from my glove box in front of her. I released the safety and trained it on the man inside the truck behind us, likely Alicia's shooter. My whole left side ached and had probably sustained heavy bruising, but I tried not to think about it. I focused only on the man hunched in the driver's seat of the attacking vehicle.

Was he unconscious? I thought as I pushed, then kicked my stubborn door open. *Or just playing possum?*

I cautiously approached the truck and noticed a company logo of a flame with the words *Bay City Propane* decaled on the door and hood. The man in the driver's seat wore a white jumpsuit bearing the same logo. He'd sustained significant wounds from the crash, but he'd also been shot.

An innocent used as a weapon, I thought.

I glanced at the back of the truck, which held several large propane tanks strapped together. My stomach sank and I immediately sprinted away from the vehicle.

Another couple of shots rang out and the truck exploded behind me in a massive fireball that rolled over the back of my car. The force of the blast sent me ducking and rolling.

I dragged myself across the pavement away from the wall of heat at my back, then made my way toward Alicia. She still sat unconscious in the passenger seat of my car, which had seen better days.

I wondered why the shooter didn't just take me out of play, and just as the thought crossed my mind, a cold stabbing sensation ripped through my shoulder and arm. Carmine splatter painted the road. Blood. *My* blood.

My head fell to the ground. An army crawl now proved impossible with the pain, which surged from my arm and shoulder down to my chest. Things went blurry and I just wanted to close my eyes and rest. I heard shouting and saw people running toward me amidst rising flames before everything went dark.

* * *

I recognized the SFPD headquarters interrogation room, but wasn't accustomed to seeing it from this angle. I sat in the hot seat, squinting at the bright lights shining in my face. A thin white piece of paper and a yellow wooden pencil sat on the table before me. One other chair sat empty across from me. I wondered who stood behind the one-sided mirror covering the far wall. Perhaps Captain Damen. He usually stood in to watch interrogations.

I barely had feeling in my left side, which still ached from the crash. My left arm hung in a sling. And a bandage wrapped the side of my forehead.

With a stiff neck, I slowly turned to look around. *Must've pinched a nerve or tendon when I fell from the blast,* I thought.

Hand and ankle cuffs held me fast to a metal chair. I wouldn't be leaving without help.

Minutes passed and the boredom almost put me back to sleep.

The door finally opened. Richardson entered, holding a thick file, and sat down across from me, looking at me as though I were 1930s "Scarface" himself.

I lifted my gaze, curious about what he had in those files, and what accusations he was about to send my way.

"That was brave," he began, "What you did . . . for Alicia. Saving her from the shooter."

"Which is why I'm cuffed to this chair," I mumbled. "This the way you treat all heroes?"

He shrugged.

"Is she safe?" My voice came off hoarse and congested. I cleared my throat. "She okay?"

Richardson squinted, obviously evaluating the genuineness of my questions. "Yeah, she's good."

He looked down and opened the file folder. "I have a few questions. The perp you sketched—"

"Carl Mason," I said.

Richardson nodded, "Yeah, you know 'im?"

"I know *of* him. I drew him with Alicia's help. And if you're going to ask if I know Alec Lovac, I don't. At least, not biblically."

Richardson bobbed his head with a grin, "That's very funny."

"If you want to know what's going on," I said, "Ask the right questions."

"Okay, how 'bout this: Forensics found your hand and fingerprints in the paint on Silver's hand. With evidence from the scene you caused, Nash helped us find Lovac, Alicia's shooter. Came quietly, said he knows you, has worked with you."

I shook my head. "Those aren't questions."

Richardson scoffed. "How do you explain the fingerprints? You shake his hand the day he was murdered?"

I hesitated to answer. This round of questioning could drastically change the course of the following years of my life.

"Yes," I said.

"Okay, so you shook his hand," Richardson held back a smile. "How'd you know 'im?"

"He's an informant."

"What do you mean?" Richardson asked, confused.

"An informant is a person who provides privileged information about a person or organization to—"

"I know what an informant is, you little sh . . ." Richardson lowered his head to regain self-control and rephrase his question. "All right, I'll play along. What about Lovac?"

"Lovac lied. We haven't worked together. I don't know him."

"You're a sketch artist. How are you involved in this?" Richardson scoffed.

"When a witness describes a perpetrator or a victim and I put the tip of my pencil to paper, something extraordinary happens—not extraordinary in the sense that I see a perp's face or some psychic bullshit and call on the spirits to help me transfer it. No, it's not that I see a face for the first time.

"I remember it."

"Sorry, you . . . remember it?"

"Yes."

"Elaborate."

"I have a photographic memory and my hand has the ability to print out the photographs."

"What does that mean exactly? That you know all these criminals? That you've worked with them? *For* them?"

"No. They work for me."

Richardson laughed a fake laugh. Fake because my comment agitated him, along with the seriousness in my expression.

"How am I involved?" I grinned. "Same way you're involved."

The reaction on Richardson's face confirmed my suspicions that he worked for Gallo.

"You're not . . ."

I gave a humble nod. "I am."

Richardson scooted back in his chair, which scraped loudly across the glazed concrete floor and his mouth hung open like a grouper.

I drew a calming breath. "Anything else I say, I'll only say to Captain Damen."

Damen momentarily entered the room and excused the awestruck detective.

"Daniels," Damen said as he sat down. "Are you claiming to be connected to—?"

"These are my conditions . . ." I straightened in my seat. " . . . I want Alicia safe, relocated, twenty-four hour escort, witness protection. And I want full immunity in writing in exchange for my cooperation in bringing down the Gallo crime family."

Damen nodded. "I can agree to those terms so long as your information proves actionable."

"In writing," I said again.

"You have my word," Damen agreed. "After you show us how you're connected."

I could read faces. His told me I could trust him. Not to mention the fact I'd worked with him for years and knew he'd keep his word.

"Deal."

"So," Damen said, "Here, you're a peon artist. Where do you fit in Turks' hierarchy?"

"The silver man was an informant to Turks, so Gallo had him killed. To retaliate, Turks had the twelve silver mercenaries destroy Gallo's restaurant. This whole thing's a mob war between Gallo and Turks. Mason's a spotter, Alec's a hitman, both work for Gallo. Richardson's also on his payroll."

"Our Richardson, in Homicide?"

"Yup," I glanced at the one-sided mirror, "Better have him checked out."

Damen furrowed his brow, "Can you describe Gallo? No one's ever seen the man."

"I'll do you one better," I said. "Uncuff me, and I'll draw him for you."

* * *

I awoke inside a darkened hospital room. A hint of relief dripped over me, then ceased as the questions blew into my mind.

Was it a nightmare? I thought, staring up at the ceiling. *Did the interrogation actually take place or was it just a bad dream*?

Either way, I hoped the part about Alicia being safe and well would prove true. A feeling in my gut told me she was okay.

A nurse entered the room and checked the medical readings on the computer next to my bed and then wrote on a clipboard. "Hello, Mr. Daniels. I'm Bonny. Glad to see you awake. You're doing very well. You're a very lucky man."

Craning my sore neck, I searched for the time.

3:32am.

"How long have I been here?" I asked.

"About two-and-a-half days," she said in a sing-song voice. "It's Wednesday morning."

My head fell back into my pillow.

"Just a dream."

The nurse smiled. "Yes, well, you need to rest. You have a lot to recover from."

I closed my eyes.

After a few minutes, a man in a suit entered the room, veiled in shadow.

I lifted my head and tried to focus through the dark.

"It's Edwards," the man said, stepping forward. "It's been impossible to see you. These damn cops haven't left your door for two days. Not even to grab a coffee."

"Edwards?"

The man nodded.

"How's the girl?" I asked.

"She's protected. The men are watching her."

"How are my dogs?"

Edwards smiled. "Fine. We're just glad you're okay, Boss."

The End

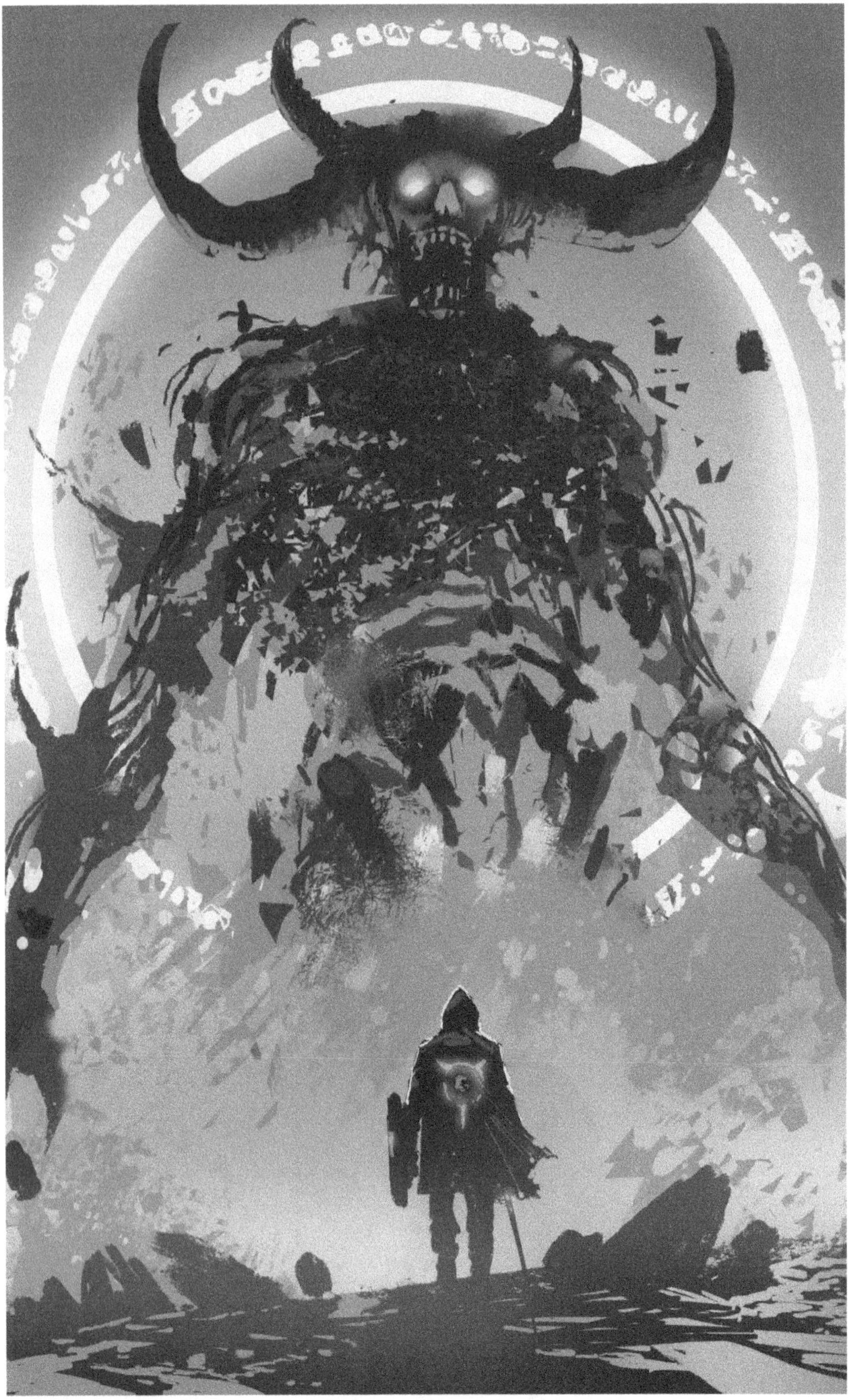

Illustration by Tithi Luadthong

5

THE DEVIL AND WOODY HARRELSON

by Rick Bennett

BACKSTORY: In 1984, one of my first advertising home runs was a software company. In those days, companies protected their software with some kludgy mechanical tricks, like drilling a hole into floppy disks. I came up with the "soul-catcher clause" whereby you had to sign a program license agreement (or PLA) stating that if you illegally copied the software, we owned your eternal soul and could "sell it to the first smoking, blood-drenched apparition with fangs (or SBDAF)that meets our price." Amazingly, we got a lot of money in the mail from people…who didn't want to take any chances. In January 1985, The Wall Street Journal got wind of our PLA and wrote a story on it. This story has been brewing a long time. I even translated it into a screenplay, hoping that Woody Harrelson would get excited about making the movie. Alas, I don't believe Mr. Harrelson saw my Ink Tip postings.

I lay me down to sleep,
I pray the Lord my soul to keep.
If I should die before I wake,
I pray the Lord my soul to take.
—A Children's Prayer

The "Fixer" showed up at the murder scene well after the police, news media, and several hundred hysteric idol worshipers who'd just found out via social media that their only reason for living had been snuffed. Rather rudely snuffed. Butchered. Butchered and cooked, actually.

"And just where do you think you're going, Darlin'?" asked the big Samoan cop as he looked down at the five-foot-six, black-haired genetic melting pot of a woman.

"They're expecting me." Angel Troc retrieved the laminated official police consultant I.D. attached to the lanyard from inside her black leather jacket and shoved it in his face. Which achieved the desired result. Namely getting the cop to step away from her so he could read it, thereby moving the offending officer out of her personal space. She'd kept her agoraphobia under pretty good control all these years since abandoning her idyllic days in the Alaskan wilderness.

After verifying her claim via his walkie-talkie with the PTB (Powers That Be), he lifted a yellow crime scene tape and let her pass into the elevator alcove of the Beverly Wilshire Hotel, where a repeat of the identification routine occurred before another policeman permitted her to board the express elevator to Hell on Earth.

Even before the elevator door opened into the Beverly Wilshire penthouse, the smell of heated Sweet Baby Ray's barbecue sauce assaulted her nostrils, accompanied by the aroma of extremely overcooked meat from a Louisiana rib pit. She knew that odor, minus the Sweet Baby Ray's. And prepared herself.

The sound of retching greeted her in the luxury foyer. Retching and wailing, from two different sources. She didn't need to hold up her identification, as the duty officer busied himself throwing up into what had to be a priceless Ming vase next to a gold-leaf credenza. Had to be Ming, and had to be valuable. Angel remembered such a vase used as a doorstop in a New York home and which sold for well over $1 million. She recognized the pattern, but didn't happen to bring a long-wave black light. Not that verifying the validity a Ming vase ranked anywhere near the top of her to-do list.

"What is *she* doing here?" said the man in the meticulously tailored blue-striped suit.

"I smelled barbecue and decided to grab a free dinner," said Angel. "How's it hanging, Tom?"

The retching wretch in the hall must have heard Angel's repost, as his gags increased in their earnestness. Wailing continued unabated from down the hall.

LAPD Chief of Police Tom Winckler shook his head. "How did *you* get up here?"

"The mayor asked for her," said Deputy Mayor Billy Costa. "We need the A-Team on this."

"I can think of what the 'A' stands for, Billy," said the chief.

"Enough, Tom." Then to Angel, "Your NDA applies here. Got it?"

"My non-disclosure agreement doesn't apply to anything that becomes public knowledge," smiled Angel. "From the looks of this circus, John Q. Public will soon know every detail of this case, including whether or not the chief here is circumcised."

"She's all yours!" spat Chief Winckler, throwing his hands into the air and storming down the hallway to close the powder room door. The wailing sound muted.

"So who's in the can," asked Angel. "My guess, it's whoever discovered Satan's barbecue here."

"You got it. His girlfriend came by, found the late, great Jack Nicholson's last supper, and called the police from the bathroom. She refuses to come out."

"Can't blame her," said Angel. "Jack's tough to miss here, there, and over there."

Angel pointed to the actor's head on the coffee table, his lower torso sitting cross-legged in the facing chair, and his well-cooked and aromatic rib cage flayed across the stainless steel gas grill on the cooking island separating the kitchen from his living room.

"Just where are *you* going?" asked the deputy mayor, as he quickly followed Angel down the hall.

"I've never seen a movie star up close and personal. Maybe his wailing consort will give me an autograph." Angel burst into the powder room forcefully enough to surprise the wailer mid-shriek and flipped on the exhaust fan. "This'll get rid of the smell faster."

The shrieks resumed before Angel closed the door. She edged past the deputy mayor, back into the main living area.

"I didn't recognize the howler, so I guess there won't be an autograph."

Plunging both hands into the pockets of her black leather jacket, she slipped plastic shoe covers onto her feet and carefully made her way to the severed head. Using an automatically telescoping pointer that seemed to appear in her left hand, Angel lifted the edge of the actor's expensive toupee. The word 'REPOSESSED' glowed in red from its previously covered spot on his scalp. No sign of the rubber stamp or stamp pad that created it.

"Interesting," said Angel.

"I'll say," said the deputy mayor. "What caused you to look there?"

"Jack's famous $5,000 toupee seemed a bit off kilter. I just had a hunch."

All conversation in the room ceased. All sound, in fact, except for muffled wailing from down the hall.

"What hunch?" asked the police chief, who'd magically reappeared from wherever he'd been.

Angel ignored the chief and addressed the deputy mayor. "Billy, please tell the mayor I'm on this. The usual retainer. One week ought to do it. I'll text him the blockchain invoice."

She then did an about face and deposited her plastic booties on the floor beside the elevator. It hadn't moved since her arrival, so the doors closed before the chief could collect his thoughts enough to roar.

"Blockchain! That's bitcoin, and it's illegal," yelled the chief.

"Yep," said the deputy mayor. "It certainly is, especially given the amount she charges for one week."

"But—" began the chief.

"Take it up with the mayor, Tommy. I'm outta here, too."

* * *

Angel slipped the desk attendant a crisp Franklin, in return for which he personally escorted her to a little-known celebrity elevator that didn't look anything like an elevator. The bookshelf wall in a dimly lit nook slid aside, and she stepped into a freight compartment big enough to hold a Mercedes. Which it had on more than one occasion.

Seconds later, she stepped onto a subterranean curb and into a white

Mercedes S550.

"Where to, Ma'am," asked the tuxedoed driver.

"My car is just around the corner on Rodeo. Thanks for the lift."

Within five minutes, Angel navigated her Rent-a-Wreck Jeep Grand Cherokee toward her digs about eight miles from Hollywood—where the streets were literally paved with gold for someone in her profession—in the basement of UCLA's Physics and Astronomy building. A secret room, testament to the power of her large donation to UCLA and a no-questions-asked contractor who owed her a big favor. A quid pro quo barter, actually.

Less than 400 feet from a covered parking structure, The Physics and Astronomy entrance off Portola Plaza contained a number of alcoves, one of which offered a handprint-activated revolving wall that operated much like the secret book cases in horror movies. Once spun out of sight, Angel stepped into a small elevator that descended to her secret lair. High ceilings actually made the 1850-square-foot apartment seem spacious. Her bedroom with a full bath and walk-in closet, the kitchen, and a laundry room took just over half the available space. The remaining thirty-by-thirty-foot work area greeted Angel with two floor-to-ceiling bookcase walls, a third wall with a gas-fireplace, all of which formed a horse shoe around a four-screen/64-core workstation that had a thousand times more computing power than the entire Pentagon during the Viet Nam war. Of course, Angel's smart phone had more computing power than the 1960's Pentagon.

"Clyde, lights on," she said.

Her voice-activated computer avatar, Clyde, obeyed. The can lights covering the twenty-foot ceiling illuminated the room, which before had been bathed in a gentle, green glow.

"Clyde, security status."

"No intrusions," replied the British-accented voice.

"Clyde, light the fire and play me some Twisted Sister."

Notwithstanding the SoCal location, the cement-enclosed basement needed a fire and constant dehumidification. And Angel needed Twisted Sister to accompany her mental musing on the late, great Jack Nicholson. Over four-hundred movies and as many tabloid-reported dalliances with

A, B, and C-list actresses over his nearly seven decades of celluloid fame, the superstar's literal drop in the food hierarchy from connoisseur to entrée would definitely feed above-the-fold coverage for the foreseeable future.

Repossessed, though, Angel mused to herself. She brought the workstation out of sleep mode and immediately graduated from a mere Google search to VICAP queries. She hoped the FBI violent crime database might have something…anything…to go on. Nothing, beyond the fictional exploits of Hannibal Lechter. Ditto for her aggregation of all social network feeds. Beyond some wannabe "death metal" rock band from Poland, another dry hole. African warlord Dominic Ongwen of the Lord's Resistance Army reportedly ordered cannibalism among other heinous acts, but Jack Nicholson's fate definitely started a new chapter in the devil's comic book.

Another hour of fruitless searching, Angel's growling stomach got her attention. But the thought of eating *anything* quite nearly caused her to imitate the ralphing policeman in Nicholson's apartment.

Repossessed? Angel couldn't get the stamp pad image out of her head. Or the image of Jack's head, either. But *what* got repossessed?

* * *

Hungry, yes. But the thought of meat threatened both her physical and emotional equilibrium. Hence Angel's decision to walk the half mile from her UCLA parking garage to a vegan place called Native Foods Café on Gayley Avenue. Actually, she jogged, since the café closed at 10:00 PM and her watch read just past nine.

She liked to run past the Mathias Botanical Garden for the aroma therapy. Especially tonight. Not many people, either. Which suited her just fine. She'd put up with enough people for one evening. Time to think on Jack Nicholson's grisly fate. And smell the roses.

Just into the cadence of her run, and into a good, deep think, she barely noticed a dark-clad figure on the footpath ahead of her. Barely, that is. When she veered to avoid the stranger, clearly male, he moved to block her way. The glint of a knife in one of his outstretched hands made her decision an easy one.

Instead of flailing to a stop, she used every bit of quick-twitch muscle speed to accelerate directly toward him and planted two extended fists center mass. Leveraging all the strength she could muster, Angel sent the big man sailing up and backward. She reckoned him to be at least two-hundred-fifty pounds, about her bench-press limit but only a third of her leg-press max. And the legs did the work tonight, her stiff arms simply providing direction for the surprised miscreant's path onto his back.

She would have leapt past him, but the knife sealed his fate. How could Angel leave this festering pile of malevolent dung to prey on another woman? Tonight, or ever?

He surprised her with his recovery speed. Ordinarily, a rapist or any other normal human male would have had the wind knocked from him and struggled to regain his breath. This individual, on the other hand, sprang to his feet and lunged toward her with a vengeance.

"Mitch!" he growled, swiping the knife in a wide arc where her chest should have been.

Great! She thought to herself. *The hair lip moron is an athlete.*

Not one to underestimate the reflexes of a trained athlete, possibly a football player based on physique, her options shrank considerably. Knees, groin, eyes, and throat. The last two options would have to wait until she neutralized the knife. But even those decisions disappeared as two big arms wrapped around her from behind.

"You must be Mitch," she said with what little breath remained in her tightly squeezed chest.

"At your service, Girlie," said the voice behind her.

"And the big guy doesn't have a hair lip after all," her attempted levity coming hard. "I thought he was calling me a bitch."

The guy with the knife didn't seem amused. He folded and pocketed the weapon.

"Time for some fun, Mitch."

"Her hair smells real nice," came the voice next to her ear.

Trying to buy some time and hoping Mitch would bring his nose closer to her hair again, Angel said, "And what's your name, big guy?"

"Big Guy works, as you're about to find out."

Before he could take a step forward, and thankful good old Mitch liked that hair smell, Angel snapped her head backward. The satisfying crunch of cartilage and roar of pain caused Mitch to release her.

"By dose!"

Big Guy actually did have lightening reflexes, as he stepped forward intending his full-handed slap for the side of Angel's face. Which thankfully wasn't there. Instead, he gave Mitch's broken nose a hearty slap. Wrong place, wrong time.

"Ow, cud id out, Guy!" blubbered Mitch, blood dripping from hands which cradled his twice-baked schnoz.

Big Guy, whose name must actually be Guy, leaned to his left, the result of his slap's follow through, exposing his right knee to a well-placed kick from the side of Angel's own right foot. A satisfying snap and howl of pain confirmed Guy wouldn't be up and about for some months following full ACL surgery.

Angel took the opportunity to deal the same blow to Mitch's left knee. With the identical result. She took a step back from both writhing figures, now lying head to head and cradling their respective knees.

"Yo Mitch, Big Guy? Smile!"

Both grimaced toward her just as she snapped a cell phone photo. Neither complied with her request to "Smile!" as the automatic flash lit up the night.

"You know what they say, about the bigger they are?" she said, putting the camera back into the zipper pocket of her leather jacket and jogging, actually running full bore, down the path.

She didn't notice how adrenalin-rushed and shaken she'd become until her still-jittery hand offered a crisp twenty to the Natural Foods Café cashier. He pretended not to notice.

The sound if sirens nearby indicated some good Samaritan had dialed 9-1-1 after happening on bitch-slapped Mitch and the whimpering "big Guy." She figured neither would fess up to their indigent circumstances. After all, who wants to admit to being taken down by some girl who weighed a buck-ten and with whom they were trying to have their way?

Angel calmed down enough to actually enjoy her veggie fare and consider. The otherwise empty café met her standards for a perfect eating experience. No other patrons to invade her precious spaces. And California proved far superior to those endless nights in Alaska's winter darkness.

* * *

Two policemen interrupted Angel's trance-like attention to her Native Oklahoma Classic dish—composed of sliced native seitan, melted cheddar, caramelized onions, organic tofu bacon, BBQ sauce, ranch dressing, carrots, tomato, and red onions with romaine—with some urgent questions.

"Miss," began the larger of the two officers. His name tag said Sgt. Roundy. "Have you seen a group of big men, possibly football players, down that trail from the UCLA campus?"

She wanted to say something about the two big guys who tried to rape her and on whom she'd opened up a giant can of whup-ass. She rejected that as problematic on a number of levels. She also rejected fabricating some story about almost being knocked down by a gang of fast-moving giants.

"No officer," she said, opting for absolute truth. "I saw no such group while I've been here. Have they been causing trouble?"

"Big trouble. They seriously injured to UCLA football players. One broken nose and two knee injuries that put them both out for the season."

Angel found it hard to resist identifying Guy and Mitch by name, not to mention pulling out her cell phone and showing them the photo she'd taken of the poor, set-upon jocks. The chance to publicly humiliate her attackers almost overwhelmed her better sense.

"I'll keep my eyes open for this gang," she said.

"If you do see them," said the officer as he handed her his card, "Please call this number. And be careful. Who knows what they'd do to a pretty little thing like you?"

"A girl can't be too careful these days," she smiled.

Twenty minutes or so after the police had left, while she enjoyed an oatmeal crème pie dessert, a commotion on the sidewalk just outside the Native Foods changed her plans for the evening. Fully intending to return to her underground lair and fire up her social media sniffers for late-breaking posts on Jack Nicholson, it became clear that she'd need to help spring some innocent athletes wrongfully accused of attacking two UCLA football players. A well-armored S.W.A.T. force surrounded five large boys wearing Texas A&M sweatshirts. Clearly visiting for an upcoming game, the poor guys picked the wrong place at the wrong time. Luckily, none of the Texas players threw a punch as they obediently allowed themselves to be cuffed and loaded into the L.A.P.D. bus.

Angel retrieved the card from her zippered jacket pocket and saw he had an email address. She composed her message, attached the photo she'd taken of Guy and Mitch, routed the message through an anonymizing server, and hit send:

> *Dear Officer Roundy,*
> *See the attached photo of the two UCLA football players injured tonight. After you chatted with me in the restaurant, I noticed you in the process of arresting some young men who fit the description given you by your victims. You got the wrong attackers. In fact, there was only one attacker: me. I was jogging through the UCLA botanical gardens when your victims tried to rape me. They didn't take proper account of my martial arts skills. I'm sure if you show them this photo and indicate you got if from the young lady they attempted to rape, and who subsequently schooled them in hand-to-hand combat, they will NOT try to pin their afflictions on some non-existent gang. I would prefer not to be bothered with an extended investigation and trial for assault, which is why I am sending this anonymously. I'll keep my eye on the news, to make sure you don't muck things up.*

That accomplished, Angel left the café and took a longer, more well-lit route back to her digs.

* * *

The familiar cell phone vibration interrupted her concentration. While she'd turned off the ring tone, the device's skittering dance on the nightstand got her attention. Bleary eyed after 36 hours scouring all her Internet sources and launching several custom-coded search agents world wide, she read a message from one social media A.I. agent she'd had asking questions of various bloggers and floggers. She maximized the A.I. screen.

"Thanks for nothing, Clyde." she muttered. Nothing about Jack Nicholson and anything about repossessions, repossessed, or any other synonym of the term yielded hits. Nothing on any social network, Google search, or even dark Web sites offering limited access to the mortal elite.

She shuffled toward the shower, in need of movement as well as serious cleansing. As she stood, stretching a few cricks and aches out of her frame, one long-shot idea occurred to her.

"Clyde? Check all the online office supplies databases, and see if anyone ordered a rubber stamp of the word 'REPOSSESSED' on it."

"Acknowledged," came the disembodied voice. "All occurrences of a rubber stamp order with the word 'REPOSSESSED.'"

"Start with FedEx/Kinkos."

"Acknowledged."

With that, Angel proceeded to the bathroom and a long, hot shower. Hoping the high-pressure water cascading over her head and neck might provide further inspiration, she luxuriated for twenty minutes. The only other insight that came her way involved the knowledge that she'd bruised the side of her right foot. Probably as it met the knees of two football jocks almost two days previous.

So intent on inspecting her foot, flexing the ankle and making sure she hadn't injured herself, she missed the persistent voice of her A.I.

"Angel…Angel…Angel…"

"Yes, Clyde."

"I have the results of your rubber stamp query."

"And?" she asked, wondering if the A.I. speech recognition algorithm could detect anxiety and impatience.

"No stamps with the word 'REPOSSESSED' appear in any online database for the last year."

A little surprising, I guess, Angel thought to herself. *Which means the individual letters came from some kid's stamp pad kit. Or maybe the stamp was purchased in a shopping mall service window.*

Either way, one more dead end.

After a quick granola and almond-milk breakfast, Angel donned blue jeans and a denim shirt, whipped her hair into a ponytail, and slipped on a pair of zero-corrective-lens nerd glasses. No use looking the least bit like the black-clad Angel that Officer Roundy interviewed last night. Just in case.

At the risk of walking near the Police Department, Angel decided to wander by the Orthopedic Medical Center and see how the two rapists had fared after last night's *Bristol Stomp.*

Another beautiful day, she thought. Morning overcast provided diffused light that made Southern California the perfect climate for movie making. Bicycles. Skateboards. Couples cavorting on the grass. Angel couldn't help but feel revived, even happy. This surely beat the miserable winter months of near darkness where she grew up in Alaska. Even the thought of Jack Nicholson's barbecued rib cage didn't seem so gristly in this atmosphere of healthy, happy people.

She soon found herself jogging merrily down Westwood Plaza, breathing in the salty fresh air, a sea breeze having blown the LA smog inland. As she approached the medical plaza, a chanting crowd interrupted her reverie. Demonstrators filled grass strips on both sides of the driveway.

Their signs said everything from "Boycott Texas" to "A&M not S&M" to "Kick the Aggies out of the FBS." Hadn't Officer Roundy showed Guy and Mitch the photo she shot? Or maybe they decided on sticking to their story about getting beat up by players from the Texas football team.

"Time for Florence Nightingale to pay two patients a visit," she muttered.

Not wanting to take a chance on getting caught sneaking a nurse's garb from a hospital locker room, especially since she didn't know the layout, Angel opted for Über. After googling the nearest uniform supplier, she copied the address into cell phone memory, clicked on the ride-sharing icon and pasted the destination. No sooner had activated the pick-up call than a black Audi A8 slid to the curb next to her, its engine purring like a mountain lion and the Ü decal reflected from the passenger windshield.

"Are you Zanj?" said the bald driver in a British accent.

"Yes, thank you," said Angel. Her anonymous Über account and credit card listed her as Zanj Komes, a literal translation of Angel Troc into Haitian Creole. A prepaid credit card in the same name guaranteed untracability.

She hopped into the rear passenger seat without giving the driver time to open the door for her. When the car didn't start moving immediately, she looked up. Intense hazel eyes in the rearview mirror met hers.

"Please buckle in, miss."

"Oh, of course. Excuse me," she said.

Only then did he swipe a thumb across his own cell phone to begin the ride.

"What's at 1630 West Olympic Boulevard?" he asked

"It's a uniform place. I need to pick up some whites and then get back to the hospital. Would it be possible for you to wait for me outside the shop and then return me here?"

"No problem." He then checked his navigation map aid said, "We're about 38 minutes away if we take I-10."

"As fast as possible, sir. I need to get right back to the hospital."

The sound of squealing tires and the feeling of multiple G-forces squeezing her into the back seat demanded she take a closer look at her chauffeur. Black suit. Black tie. White shirt. And a 7th Air Calvary gold lapel pin. Her lights suddenly went on.

"What Über driver on this planet has a big black Audi and is actor Jason Statham's doppelganger?" she exclaimed. "This thing sucks up more gas than you could possibly make from my fare!"

He didn't say a thing, although she thought he might have winked at her. Bingo.

"Ah." She laughed. "Audi gives you the car for product tie-ins, and the studio pays for gas. Pleased to meet you, Mister Statham, although your Über driver name said James. Actually, now that I look at it, your photo is not exactly Mr. Statham."

"I'm his stunt driver," smirked the driver. "Of course my photo is close."

"Getting into character for a sequel?" she asked.

"Sorry. NDAs and such forbid my confirming or denying anything at all."

Again, she laughed. "I know all about NDAs."

After a short pause and a longer than normal look at her in his rearview mirror, he said, "You may know about NDAs, but you sure as hell aren't a nurse."

"Wow!" she exclaimed as he treated the freeway ramp more like a NASCAR track. "And you sure as hell aren't worried about getting a ticket."

The big Audi made frequent use of the breakdown lanes as the stunt driver threaded several impossible needles.

"Studio attorneys handle the ticket situation. Besides, I do a good enough Statham imitation to get off with warnings.

"Now, back to my observation. You ain't no nurse. So what gives?"

* * *

"Bloody hell!" her driver exclaimed for the fifth time. He'd dropped her off at the uniform store and waited. A crisply dressed-in-white nurse got back into his car, her old clothes in a Uniforms Inc. bag.

"You've got to stop saying that!"

"It's just that I can't believe the two guys who tried to rape you are sticking to that lame story about the Texas football players," he almost yelled. "Bloody hell, you really tuned them up, didn't you?"

"Home, James!" She laughed. "I always wanted to say that. But let's get back to the hospital. I need to visit a couple of patients."

"Can I come, too?"

"It might be better if you waited for me at drop-off. With the engine running. If you don't mind, that is?"

"Oh-kay." The driver strung out the word, making it into a sigh.

"The navigation system said you'd get me here in thirty-eight minutes. You did it in twenty. Think you can repeat that feat?"

He did. Almost twenty minutes on the nose. He pulled into the patient drop-off just behind two police cars, the occupants of which were busily engaged in crowd control. The number of protesters had more than doubled.

"This isn't going to work, you waiting for me by these yahoos." She lifted her clothing bag onto the rear seat. "Mind if I leave my stuff here?"

"Be my guest," he said. "I think I'll idle down by the emergency entrance while you minister to the two wonkers. See the signs down there?"

He pointed down the block to the ambulance entrance.

"Thank you, James."

Angel exited the car and walked authoritatively up the steps and into the building. Security didn't give her a second glance, white skirt, blouse, shoes and hose completing the picture of someone who definitely belonged there. She waved down the hall toward the elevator to a nonexistent friend and ignored glances from the front desk or orthopedic hospital's beefed-up security presence. A young intern even held the elevator door for her.

"I haven't seen you around here," he said.

"First time," she answered, deciding not to lie her way into a problem. "UCLA insurance company decided I needed to check out our two latest guests."

"Ah, the football players attacked two nights ago." Then, solicitously hoping for more time with her, he added: "I'll show you to their room. You're going to be amazed how fast they're recovering."

"Much appreciated, Doctor…" she paused to read his badge, "Doctor Roper."

"Please, call me Rick," said her escort, the red blush accelerating up his neck to merge with his red hairline.

"Well thank *you* Rick," she said, gently touching his elbow. Which caused the blush to deepen noticeably.

As the elevator door opened, it didn't take a genius to locate the football players' room. A woman, undoubtedly one of their mothers, railed on two police detectives and one uniformed officer.

"Why aren't you arresting the animals who did this to my son? We know who they are!"

The detectives did their best to assure the woman they wouldn't rest until justice was done. The uniformed officer, familiar to Angel from the previous night, didn't notice Angel, who purposely stayed out of his sightline behind Doctor Roper. He, in turn, misinterpreted her close proximity to his left side as a gift from heaven. He protectively guided her to the door and entered the room with her.

Two beds, both to their right, held the patients. Post-operative traction devices raised their legs, and a slight humming from constant-movement motors gently flexed their knees. One boy's father and the other's parents sat pensively. They looked plaintively at the doctor, clearly desperate for any good news. Angel took the lead, before Doctor Rick could foul things up with her cover story.

"Doctor, could you show these people outside for just a moment? You know, modesty…" she trailed off and ever so slightly batted her eyelashes.

The smitten doctor's I.Q. definitely dropped in half, as he didn't simply suggest the nurse use a privacy screen. Luckily, the parents followed his invitation to step into the hallway. As they did so, she turned on her cell phone video camera and hung it from a lanyard around her neck.

Now alone with Guy and Mitch, the underperforming rapists, she stood between their beds. Their ogles morphed into wide-eyed recognition.

"It's her!" gasped Guy. Mitch absentmindedly rubbed the bridge of his nose, remembering the cause of his two black eyes.

"Hi fellas," she said. "I see *Big* Guy and *Rocky Raccoon* are sticking to their story about getting beat down by a gang of football players. Not smart."

Guy's grip on her right hand surprised her, both with its speed and its strength.

"We have unfinished business," he growled.

"Oh, you mean to continue the rape scene from two nights ago?"

"And then some, lady!" sneered Guy. "I heal fast, and besides. Nobody's going to believe that some little girl did this to us. Nobody!"

"Remember Kurt Russell's line from the movie *Captain Ron*? 'I heal fast, and I believe in Jesus.' Do you believe in Jesus?" She quickly pivoted and brought her left elbow smashing down onto Guy's nose. Just as quickly, he found something else to do with his left hand. Actually both hands, as he used them to caress his profusely bleeding and badly broken nose.

Guy cried something about Jesus just as Mitch in the next bed grabbed Angel's free left wrist.

She spun counterclockwise and used her right elbow in a much higher-velocity strike against Mitch's right shoulder. The combination of the blow and her torque not only dislocated the shoulder, but shattered his collarbone in two places.

The commotion, Guy's incoherent blubbering and Mitch's outright shrieks, brought Officer Roper and Doctor Roundy from the hallway. Rather than react aggressively, Angel calmly put her hand on the doctor's chest and nodded over her shoulder.

"The patients seem to need additional help," she said softly, and smiling.

Getting a good view of Angel for the first time, Officer Roundy recognized her from the previous night's interview. She cocked her head in his direction.

"Officer Roundy, nice to see you again. Didn't you get my email?"

"I did, but—"

She interrupted him, "—but they said the photo was taken by an accomplice of the people who attacked them."

"Something like that. Now, you're going to have to come with me." Officer Roundy reached for the handcuff wallet on his belt. He should have reached for his mace canister, which Angel quickly snatched from its place on an opposite hip and proceeded to spray him, the doctor, parents and detectives now blocking the doorway. The hallway soon resembled a bowling lane after a strike.

Angel tossed the spent mace canister can behind her and sprinted toward the stairwell, meeting the security team rushing her way. She stopped and pointed behind her.

"There's a madman back there!"

Seeing the people lying on the ground, retching and rubbing their eyes, the three beefy security men raced toward the pandemonium. Angel quickly took the stairs three at a time to the main floor and exited through the emergency doors.

The Über driver stood by his black Audi. He managed to open the rear door in time for angel to dive into the car. A credit to his observation skills, he didn't need more than the look in her eyes to figure out they needed to move.

They drove up the ramp at a leisurely pace though, as not to get the attention of either the demonstrators or the police. Turning left on Westwood, James blurted, "I'd sell my very soul to have been a fly on the wall."

"Do I still get your soul if I show you the video I recorded?" Angel lifted the lanyard-mounted cell phone still hanging from her neck, so he could see it in the rearview mirror.

"Depends when you plan to repossess my soul?" From his eyes, she could see his barely contained excitement.

"That's it!" she exclaimed.

"What's what?"

"That's what got repossessed. Jack Nicholson's soul!"

"Uh, can I still be a fly on the wall and see that video?" he asked, not quite tracking the conversation.

"James, if I show you the video, then you become an accessory after the fact to what I did at the hospital." She paused to think. "And sure as hell your car and license plate were recorded by hospital security cameras. You too, standing by the car."

"Hmmm," he nodded. "You may have a point. I can push a button to automatically change the license plates on this car, but me standing there in front of God and the world might be tough to lie about."

"James, I'll change back into my jogging clothes, then you can let me out. After which you need to go pick up some other Über rides."

"So you're recommending I do NOT see the video?" James couldn't keep the disappointment out of his voice.

"Don't worry. I'm going to put this video on the Internet for EVERYBODY to see." While changing back into her street clothes, she patted his shoulder. "By the way, do you have a business card with your email address and phone contact information? If you're interested, we might have another adventure."

James handed her his card, diligently trying not to peek and the dressing process taking place behind him.

"Thanks, James. I'll send you the link to an encrypted email and video chat called WIRE. Not only will there be no trail, but even the Switzerland-based account provider doesn't have the technology to honor any court subpoenas. You can install it right on your phone and be a fly on the wall anytime, anywhere."

Moments later, he let her off near UCLA's campus.

* * *

Angel staggered into the secret basement abode below the Physics and Astronomy building, her continuous efforts over the last 48 hours sapping her completely. She had deposited the bag containing her Nurse Ratchet outfit—appropriate given the increasingly crazy nature of this *One Flew Over the Cuckoo's Nest* quest—into a Goodwill Industries donation bin on Westwood Blvd. Having paid cash for the uniform, she didn't notice any surveillance cameras, not that it would take much effort for the authorities to grab her photo from the hospital security system, along with the smiling face of James, her Über driver.

Hoping to save him from a real interrogation ringer, she copied the film from her phone onto her workstation and sent it to Officer Roundy's email, the LA Times, and several social media video sites. All anonymously, although her email to Officer Roundy did apologize for the mace:

> *Dear Officer Roundy,*
> *Attached is the video I took of the two failed rapists. It should be stated that they attacked me two nights ago and that no so-called football players from Texas were involved. Sorry about the mace, but I do value my privacy and have no intention of testifying against them in court. You might gently let them know they'd better tell the truth, or I'll be visiting them again.*

She then turned her A.I. loose before a much-needed nap.

"Clyde, check out all occurrences of someone buying or selling souls. And monitor all news reports concerning the UCLA football players injured two nights ago. Summarize those reports for me, but do *not* disturb me. I'll be sleeping."

As an afterthought, she dug James' card out of her jean pocket and sent him the video. Again, anonymously and with the subject line: TO MY FLY ON THE WALL.

Eight hours later, rested and showered, she roused her A.I.

"Clyde, news on buying and selling of souls?"

"One man actually sold his soul on eBay, and there are numerous tutorials on the Internet on how to sell one's soul. However, they appear to be humorous pieces for the most part."

"Satire, Clyde," she said. "How do you even know what humor is?"

"I assume phrases like 'enjoy it now and be prepared for a fiery eternity' are an attempt at humor."

"Very good. Go on."

"One of the most interesting postings is a *Wall Street Journal* story reported in January of 1985. Here is the actual print rendering:"

PAGE 33
TUESDAY, JANUARY 22, 1985

THE WALL STREET JOURNAL.

© 1985 Dow Jones & Company, Inc. All Rights Reserved.

ODDS AND ENDS: To stop illegal copying of its software program, Mother Jones' Son's Software Corp. of Buena Park, Calif., states in its sales agreements that if a buyer copies the program illegally, "ownership of your eternal soul passes to us, and we have the right to negotiate the sale of said soul." The agreement adds: "Our attorneys will see to it that life on earth, as you know it, is completely ruined." . . .

Angel read aloud to herself: "...If a buyer copies the program illegally, ownership of your soul passes to us, and we have the right to negotiate the sale of said soul."

"Clyde, what is Mother Jones' Son's Software Corporation?"

"That entity has long since ceased to exist. A 1985 article in PC magazine spells out the license agreement in greater detail. Namely, it states: *Also, you agree that, 30 days after you violate this agreement, ownership of your eternal soul automatically passes to us, and we have the right to negotiate the sale of said soul to the first smoking, blood-drenched apparition with fangs (SBDAWF) that meets our price. The SBDAWF may collect your soul at any time of his/her/its choosing."*

"But this company no longer exists, correct?"

"That is correct, Angel. However, it occurred to me that people sign program license agreements every day, and they do so without reading them. What better way to trick a human into selling his soul than to embed such a clause into your online license. I therefore set out to see if any current software agreements actually contain similar verbiage."

"I spent the last few hours searching the agreements of every existing software vendor in the world. There is one and only one company that uses such a clause."

Angel couldn't tell whether or not her dizziness was born of pure shock, or if her lack of eating caused her low blood sugar. But it didn't matter.

"Clyde, even if there were such a company, how can we tie this to the death of Jack Nicholson?"

"The company is called Titanium Eagles, and they sell a social media analytics package for forty-nine ninety-five."

"And?" said Angel.

"On a late-night talk show, our Jack Nicholson was talking about his fame and high regard in his fan base. He actually gave the show host a thumb drive containing the Titanium Eagles software. Here's the clip."

Angel watched incredulously as Jack Nicholson bragged how much a celebrity could learn from the Titanium Eagles data feed about his fans and prospects. By handing the show host a copy of the program, Jack would certainly seal his doom. Publicly and undeniably.

"Where is this company located?"

"About an hour's drive from here in downtown Los Angeles. An office building on 515 Flower Street. In City National Plaza. The entire fifty-second floor."

"That's my next stop, then."

"Negative," replied the A.I. "Your photograph and given name are now quite public. There is a warrant out for your immediate arrest on multiple assault charges."

"Clyde," she spat. "Why didn't you tell me that first?"

"Your initial query concerned souls."

"Show me the news reports. Now!"

Whatever hunger Angel might have felt disappeared with not only a passable photo from hospital security, but with her driver's license photo and correct name in the on-screen caption below it. Luckily, her viral video also accompanied the story. Which she didn't have time to view, because the phone rang.

The LA Mayor's custom ring tone, Neil Diamond's *I Am…I Said* opening line: "L.A.'s fine, the sun shines most of the time, and the feeling is lay back."

"Mister Mayor," she answered.

"You're fired!"

"Great Trump imitation, Your Honor."

"Cut the crap, Angel."

"Sorry, Michael, but I—"

"That's Mayor Roth. We're definitely not on a first name basis today."

"Sorry, *Mayor Roth*," she said, stressing his formal title. "I just didn't feel like getting raped by a couple of football players."

"And you just *had* to go to the hospital to set things right?"

"The morons stuck to their story blaming their bad luck on the opposing football team. I had to make that right."

"Sweet Baby Jesus," screamed the mayor. "You made it right by assaulting a doctor, three police officers, and the families of the boys."

"You're Jewish, Your Honor. Maybe you ought to go with Holy Moses."

"Dammit, Angel!"

"Didn't feel like testifying at their trial. I was trying to stay under the radar."

"Great plan! Your picture is on all the television stations. And my chief of police wants your head on a stick." The mayor paused, but only to take a breath. "Did you really tell Chief Winckler the world would know whether or not he was circumcised?"

"He took my remark out of context."

"Be that as it may, you're ability to function in Jack Nicholson's murder investigation is severely compromised. I see no alternative but—"

This time, she interrupted him. "I'm onto a promising lead in Jack's murder. But if you insist on firing me, we'll see if your Goy police chief can pick up the pieces."

"You got a lead?" The mayor suddenly changed tone.

"Yes, Michael, I do." She couldn't help but test his newfound civility. He didn't disappoint.

"So, I shouldn't use cell phone triangulation to help the police arrest you, yet?"

"The operative word being 'yet' huh?"

"Tell me about your lead."

"No."

"That's 'no, Your Honor!'" he shouted.

"No, *Your Honor*," she replied.

"Come on, Angel. Tell me *something!*"

"I think we've got a monster on our hands, and this is just the beginning."

"Damn! Then we need all our resources on it."

"Yes and no, Your Honor. I'm going in without enough probable cause for a judge to issue a search warrant. Besides, we don't want to spook the bad guys."

"Keep me posted."

"So I'm not fired?"

The mayor sighed. "Just stay out of Chief Winckler's way. I can't call off *those* hounds from hell."

"I'll do my best. If I get arrested, my one phone call will be to you."

"That's just great!" The mayor hung up with an audible crash as he slammed his cell phone on something hard.

Bet he goes through a lot of phones, thought Angel.

"Clyde, how am I going to get to Titanium Eagles without being arrested?"

"Über, with another burner identity?"

"No, but you've given me an idea."

* * *

"James," said Angel into her cell phone. "This is Zanj Komes from yesterday."

"Ah, you mean Angel Troc, wanted by the police and whose picture is on all the TV stations?"

"That would be me." I suppose you've spent some time with the L.A. police."

"Yes, indeed," he said. "Remind me not to get on your bad side."

"Saw the video, eh?"

"Millions have seen that video," he chuckled. "Thanks for not letting me see it in the car. I could answer my interrogators truthfully."

"By the way, James. What is your last name?"

"Cameron," he answered. "James Cameron."

"You don't say," she laughed to herself.

"I don't have a lot of trouble getting people to return my calls around this town."

"Question, James: Was that a 7th Regiment Air Cav pin on your lapel?"

"Affirmative. I flew Cobras in the Gulf."

"You don't happen to have a current rotary wing rating, do you?

"I do. Between movie gigs, I work out of the Bob Hope Burbank Airport, teaching moguls how not to auger their jet helicopters into these Hollywood Hills."

"Excellent! You game for another adventure, tonight? Assuming, that is, you can grab some wings?"

"As long as you pay the freight!"

"How much for an evening around L.A.?"

"That would be two large."

"Make it four and keep me anonymous," she immediately replied.

James paused before cautiously putting the skunk on the table. "No drugs or other felonious intent?"

"Pick me up tonight at ten. We get in the air, I'll explain the whole story. If you decide to bow out, no harm, no foul. Agreed?"

"You've said the *when*. How about the *where*?"

"I'll be waiting at the Ronald Reagan UCLA Medical Center heliport. Quick in, quick out. Green mag light to signal all clear. Red to wait."

* * *

Getting to the medical center heliport involved more than batting her eyelashes and strolling to the roof. Security cameras alone would have brought the police.

Having scouted the building earlier in the day, Angel arrived at the Reagan Medical Center about 9:30 PM dressed in black—stretch pants, leather jacket, and soft-soled shoes. She slipped on climbing gloves. The smell of freshly trimmed hedges and assorted garden flowers wafted around the building. She chose an embedded nook on the side of the structure for her free climb up the wall. Composed of four-foot cement squares and shielded on three sides from any security cameras, she climbed the 160-feet to the roof in just under ten minutes. She might have made the trip more quickly, but caution seemed a better choice than certain death due to a hasty miscalculation.

She rolled onto the pea-gravel roof with twenty minutes to spare. Her climb away from Westwood assured she wouldn't be seen by passersby, and her earlier surveillance confirmed the absence of security cameras.

As she lay on the roof, nicely blending with the dark surface, she texted James using the WIRE encrypted feed she'd previously set up with him. Nobody, not the NSA, not even WIRE itself, could eavesdrop on them.

W: Heliport is clear. I'm onsite and waiting.

James quickly responded.

W: I'm in the air. Might as well get there early to avoid possible incoming air ambulance surprises. ETA: three minutes. Arriving from the North.

W: Confirmed. Three minutes, she responded.

Angel crawled to the edge of the helipad and removed a green narrow-beam flashlight from her upper-left zippered pocket. At the sound of the blades, she flashed northward in three bursts. A quick reply from inside the helicopter confirmed her ride.

The moment he touched down, she ran to the passenger side as James threw open the door. They were airborne well before a surprised hospital guard had time to rush through the automatic doors to greet the unexpected visitors.

"No lights," she said after putting on her headset. "Smart."

"No tail number, either," James responded.

"How'd you get away with that?"

"Gaffing tape."

"Isn't that illegal?" She looked hard at James, also dressed in black. Their leather jackets could have been purchased as a matching set.

"Yep. Could get me three years in the slammer," he replied matter-of-factly. No smirk. No false bravado. Just another day at the office.

"I don't know what to say, James." And she didn't. *Why would a professional pilot and stunt driver take such risks for a complete stranger?* He seemed to read her mind.

"You placed yourself in more serious risk with those two jocks in the hospital," he said. "I figure you'll fill me in now that I've made this act of faith in your motives. Then I'll choose whether or not I'm in for your adventure.

* * *

"Repossessed Jack Nicholson's soul? Bloody Hell!"

James had remained silent while Angel had related her detective work tracking down Titanium Eagles and their unique software license agreement's *soul-forfeiture clause.*

He'd set the movie studio Bell 206L4 Jet Ranger helicopter down in an unused and totally dark high school football field. Staying aloft with no running lights in a jet-black machine seemed a bad idea. They let both doors hang open, inviting the cool night air to circulate through the cockpit.

"It's not a given, but worth a look at their offices on the top floor of the 515 Flower Tower," she said.

"I especially like the part about the *smoking, blood-drenched apparition with fangs being able to collect said soul at any time of his/her/its choosing,*" he mused. "And good old Jack actually gave a copy of the software on a nationally televised talk show?"

She played the YouTube video for the third time on her phone.

"Bloody Hell!" he said again.

"You willing to drop me off at the building and then park somewhere to wait for a pick-up call?"

"No way you're going in there alone!" he said rather emphatically.

"James, you didn't sign up for combat pay."

"I've been in combat my entire life, lady. Hot evacs in Iraq to stunt driving for the studios. Been thinking about having my middle name legally changed to *Danger.*"

"Can you handle yourself if things get dicey?"

"The fact I'm sitting here after two tours in Iraq should be answer enough."

"You carrying?" she asked.

James unzipped his jacket and leaned toward her, showing the butt of a Colt .45 semi-automatic pistol. "And I've got a carry permit for this baby, too." Light from somewhere bounced in a sparkle off his front teeth."

"We drop these bad boys," she said, showing him her own 9mm, "And I'll see you get more than two extra Gs for your help."

"Not necessary, Angel. I bought off on this deal at the specified price." He winked at her. "I might even reduce the price if I get to shoot the guy who killed Jack."

With that, he spooled up the turbine and they lifted off. Next stop, The Flower Tower.

Ten minutes later, James selected the Unicom frequency 122.950 and announced his intention to land.

"515 Flower Tower, this is Dark Horse Ranger III requesting permission to land. Over."

"Dark Horse, we weren't expecting company," came the female reply. "With which tenant are you affiliated?"

Without missing a beat, and at a nod from Angel, he answered: "Titanium Eagles, Ma'am."

"Oh, of course, Dark Horse. Permission granted."

James turned off the radio. "That's odd. No call sign challenge. No name of contact. These Titanium guys must have some pull."

"Or they put the fear of God into somebody," Angel muttered almost to herself.

Finding the 515 Flower Tower didn't prove a problem, and the GPS navigation system took them to the only brightly lit rooftop in downtown Los Angeles.

"Are you sure we aren't going to Fantasy Island?" asked James. He pointed to a two-man welcoming committee, one giant and one dwarfish male who couldn't have been more than three feet tall.

"This could get weird in a hurry," said Angel. "Let me do the talking. And if I say 'ON THREE,' you and I both pull out our guns and blast away when I say 'ONE'." They left their jackets unzipped to allow faster weapon access.

The greeters stood well outside the rotor wash until James had cut power to the jet turbine. Angel exited the craft with James, who looked for tie downs. He didn't need to look far, as four grotesque clamps emerged from the landing pad and locked on the helicopter's skid bars. The sound also got Angel's attention. The shared look with her pilot caused adrenalin to surge through both of them.

"Tell me those clamps aren't claws," said James in a stage whisper.

"Nah," she said. "They look more like fangs."

"Not claws and certainly not fangs," said the smallish man as he approached them. "Talons. Eagle talons. Actually, Titanium Eagle talons. Welcome, Angel Troc and James Cameron. We've been expecting you."

"Holy Mother of Mercy," said James to no one in particular.

"I find that term quite offensive," said their host. "My name is Dan, by the way. My companion is Merriweather. Please follow us."

They fell in behind Dan. His large companion grunted and took the rear position as they entered the elevator alcove. Their mouth-breather rearguard's breath smelled hauntingly familiar to Angel.

"If I'm not mistaken," she said to Dan's back, "Somebody in the room likes Sweet Baby Ray's barbecue sauce."

A deep bass laugh from behind confirmed her observation.

"What do you mean by the 'We've been expecting you' greeting?" asked Angel, compulsively moving her right hand into her open jacket to seek reassurance from the butt of her gun.

"Ever hear of MediaMath?" replied Dan.

"Web tracking aggregation of some kind."

"That's the one," chuckled Dan, not even looking behind him as he led the way toward an elevator bank. "The minute someone started doing searches on my company's soul-catcher clause and subsequently visited our company website to read the program license agreement, I figured it was only a matter of time before you showed up."

"But my searches were anonymized."

"Facial recognition from the Beverly Hilton and hospital crime scenes matched with your Über photo and that of your diver gave us a pretty strong clue you had put two and two together and were flying in tonight." The elevator door opened without intervention from Dan.

"Two and two?" Angel wondered if her head quivered as she felt a giant rush of pus hit her brain.

Dan stepped into the elevator car and turned. His smile would have been cherubic had not his canine teeth looked ever so much like fangs. "Two plus two equals Jack Nicholson, silly."

"On three," shouted angel. "One—"

Two shots rang out. One from James' .45 behind her, and of course, her own 9mm. She nailed Dan squarely in the forehead. Or at least she thought she did.

No splatter of blood and brains decorated the elevator. Just an indentation on the smooth metal railing in the luxury Otis box. She couldn't have missed at this range, but she pumped off a second shot, this time center mass. Again, no blood. Just another dent in the elevator. But the sad look on Dan's face seemed directed behind her.

"I so wish you hadn't killed Merriweather," Dan sighed. "Ghouls just want to have fun."

Behind them, James' headshot proved significantly more successful than Angel's. Merriweather lay flat on his back, the top of his head some twenty feet away trailing blood and brains like a particularly messy golf divot. James then turned around and pumped off a couple of shots at Dan, evidently figuring Angel needed to improve her aim. All he had to show for the effort was two more dents in the elevator.

"Enough already!" shouted Dan. "You can't kill me, because I've never had a body."

"Bloody hell," said James.

"Nothing bloody about hell," said Dan.

"Yeah, right," said Angel. "Except for the late, great Jack Nicholson."

"Hey, I bought his soul fair and square. And Merriweather left the blood on this miserable planet. Hell is actually nice and orderly. Serene, if you will."

"Excuse me if I don't believe you," spat Angel.

"Whether or not you believe me, you'd best leave this roof before the police come responding to four gunshots," said Dan with some urgency. "After all, you *are* wanted for your own bloody exploits with those football players."

As if on cue, a second elevator door opened and four guys even larger than Merriweather emerged with mop buckets and a tarp with which to wrap their fallen companion. Angel thought she heard them start humming *Girls Just Want to Have Fun* as elevator doors closed behind her, James and Dan.

* * *

Whatever discomfort accompanied their ride in the bullet-dented elevator evaporated as the door opened one floor down. It might well have been ten thousand floors down. Imagine the United States Supreme Court, done in bright red. High ceilings with actual flaming chandeliers highlighted the massive room. Instead of nine seats for the justices, only one overlooked the courtroom. And in that seat sat a spectacularly handsome man with an aquiline nose, which he proudly displayed in profile for them, feigning to look at the jury box to his right.

"I would like to introduce you to The God Of This World," said Dan.

"On three," said Angel. "One—" Blam-blam! rang two shots. Which had exactly the same effect they had on Dan. The god of this world seemed irritated he couldn't pose just a little longer, turning his head to glare at the two smoking guns aimed between his eyes.

One flick of TGOTW's (The God of This World's) wrist caused both guns to fly skyward and disappear into the ceiling. No sound of metal against tile. They just disappeared.

TGOTW seemed about to speak, but was interrupted by a shriek and a whoosh as the image of Merriweather barreled through James and Angel. The ghoul seemed as surprised as anyone that his body passing directly through theirs had no effect. Which caused him to howl even louder.

"Ah Merriweather," said TGOTW. "Thanks to these two, you don't have a body anymore."

"Huh?" grunted the apparition. "But—"

TGOTW helped the former *devil's grillmaster* further connect the dots. "—which means no more soul barbecues for you. Sorry, big fella."

Angel actually felt badly for the *Ghoul Formerly Known As Merriweather*, as the realization of his ethereal condition fully dawned on him. He dropped to his knees and cried like a baby.

Upon which cheers arose from behind them, directly opposite TGOTW. Angel and James both turned toward the din for yet another gigantic surprise. Manacled to chairs sat five well-known Hollywood celebs: Woody Harrelson, Bill Murray, Angelina Jolie, Penelope Cruz and the real Jason Statham. All cheered except Woody Harrelson, who sat beneath a tinfoil helmet and just shook his head from side to side, saying, "This isn't happening. This isn't happening."

"Daddammit, shut up!" The cheering ceased with TGOTW's explosion. "If you don't think I can get fifty flesh-eating mortals out of Los Angeles to replace Merriweather, think again."

"Yo Jason," said James.

"Hey, Cameron," replied his near doppelganger. "Nice shot upstairs, by the way. You should have heard His Evilness swear when you shot the big bloke."

"Silence, Statham!" demanded TGOTW. "Remember what I had the nubulite do to Harrelson with the cattle prod?"

Behind the prisoners, a scantily clad blond woman snickered as she stroked the business end of a high-end Hot Shot DuraProd rechargeable livestock prod with a 32-inch flexible shaft. Woody Harrelson evidently remembered the encounter and seemed to scrunch up his buttocks, repeating again, "This isn't happening. This isn't happening." His tinfoil helmet slipped over one eye, but he couldn't correct the problem, since his hands were bound to the armrests of his chair.

"Angel Troc and James Cameron, welcome to our little trial," said TGOTW, softly, solicitously.

"That's not James Cameron!" said Penelope Cruz and Angelina Jolie simultaneously.

"Am too," said James Cameron

"Nuh uh," said Jolie.

"Hello Cleopatra, it's James Cameron my stunt driver and not James Cameron your mogul movie mentor," said Statham.

"This is really far out," said Bill Murray.

"Yatch-bog!" yelled TGOTW, absolutely *not* used to losing control of any conversation. "Tagalipish boonyatta!"

All heads turned toward the strange sound.

"Master," said Dan in a stage whisper as he hopped atop the bench, beside TGOTW. "These mortals do not speak your pure dialect."

"Of course they don't," TGOTW agreed. Pointing to the manacled prisoners, "But these five bound souls soon will."

Merriweather leapt toward the movie stars and swept across them, passing through the group without displacing so much as a lock of hair. Cruz and Jolie screamed, along with Merriweather. Statham and Murray looked at each other curiously. Harrelson missed the whole thing, as his eyes were clenched shut, still in the throes of the cattle prod memory.

TGOTW continued: "And next week, I'm going to repossess the souls of five Grammy winners."

This drew cheers from the gallery, apparently mortals who'd had more positive relationships with the underworld than the five movie stars.

"About these repossessions," began Angel, getting out of HOLY CRAP! mode and back into FIXER mode. "What in the name of God gives you the right to repossess *anybody's* soul?"

"I sooo hate that expression," TGOTW answered. "But in answer to your question, Dad and I have had side bets down through history, and the rules of engagement have been mutually agreed upon. You *do* remember Job from the *Old Testament*?"

Bill Murray answered before Angel could: "Yeah, Your Evilness, but you weren't permitted to kill Job. You could only torment him."

"I strenuously object to your calling me evil," spat TGOTW. "I fulfill my role in creation a good deal more diligently than do most of the pious mortals on this planet.

"Nevertheless, I created a righteous legal agreement that specifically grants me authority to legally collect the soul of anyone who violates it."

While Angel didn't have a Bible history background, she jumped in to address the current contract she traced to this macabre gathering: "That's complete crap! Nobody reads software license agreements, and repossessing a soul based upon violation of any online-executed end-user license agreement is entrapment pure and simple."

"Au contraire, Angel my lovely. Not only do I make my soul-catcher clause absolutely clear when people download my program, but every time they open the application the soul-catcher clause displays front and center on their device. And they must actually hit the 'AGREE' button before the program continues. That is *anything* but entrapment!"

"That clause would *never* stand up in court!"

"Oh but it has," smirked TGOTW. "Otherwise, I would *not* have been allowed to repossess Jack Nicholson's soul."

"He's got a point," said Bill Murray.

"Nooo!" howled Penelope Cruz.

Statham busied himself trying to break free of his manacles. Jolie wept silently, while Harrelson lowered his head so he could suck his up-stretched thumb. Harrelson's tinfoil hat, already askew, fell to the floor, which caused him to simultaneously howl between thumbsucks.

Angel gently bent down and retrieved Woody's hat and placed it on his bowed head: "Mr. Harrelson, I just loved you in Zombieland."

"Please don't shoot me with my own gun!" he sobbed before renewed sucking on the thumb.

"Very funny line from the movie," said Bill Murray.

"As I recall from the Job story," said James Cameron the stunt driver, not the movie director, "God let Satan use natural elements to punish Job, and not some cannibal murderer."

Angel turned back to TGOTW. "Yeah, you just did a Jeffrey Dahmer on Jack Nicholson. You've always used psychopaths like Hitler and Stalin, from the Khmer Rouge in Cambodia to Jack the Ripper in old London, and never worried about a legal contract."

"All of those were *my* prophets on earth," said TGOTW. "And I admit it's been hard over the centuries to convince people to sell me their souls. But I've always played my role with passion and creativity. Now, thanks to technology, it's much easier to buy souls for my prophets."

"I don't believe in the devil," shouted Angelina Jolie. "And I don't believe in God, either."

"Do you believe in gravity?" smirked TGOTW.

"Well of course," said Jolie. "Because I can see gravity at work."

"In just a few minutes, you'll see me and my prophets at work, too."

"I believe in God," said Penelope Cruz. "But I thought those screen warnings were a joke of some kind. Kind of like Scientology on steroids."

"Just like most modern-day Christians think the ten commandments are a joke," said TGOTW. "Like the law of gravity, you're about to find out just how funny that joke is."

Their captor's laugh caused everyone in the room to quake. Even the blond with the cattle prod.

Angel, known as "the fixer" in her professional circles, decided to throw caution to the wind.

She began: "I've sent a goodly number of minions to your embrace, from Somalia to Afghanistan. So how about contest for the souls of these people from whom you intend to exercise your rights?"

"Interesting, Angel. And by the way, what an appropriate name for their defender. Angel." TGOTW paused, apparently thinking about her challenge. "But this isn't Georgia and I don't play the fiddle."

Statham opened his mouth, but TGOTW cut him off. "I don't have a physical body, Mr. Statham, so I can't race you or your stunt driver in any kind of automobile."

Subaudible humming from Bill Murray slowly increased in volume until everyone in the room recognized the tune and shouted in unison at the appropriate moment, "Who ya gonna call? Ghostbusters!"

Everyone shouted, except for Woody Harrelson, who changed his mantra: "I want a Twinkie! I want a Twinkie!"

"Boy, he really gets into his parts, doesn't he?" said TGOTW. Then to Angel, "Just what kind of contest do you have in mind?"

"How about a contest where you can't cheat?" she replied.

"They haven't invented one of those, yet." Then TGOTW turned to Angelina Jolie. "But it could be the real-life sequel to *Laura Croft, Tomb Raider* if you people actually get out of this alive."

Suddenly tinfoil-head Harrelson popped to attention and said, "I know a contest where that swirling sewer of the Universe can't cheat!"

All eyes turned toward the miraculously coherent actor, including those of his fellow stars. Bill Murray laughed out loud: "I *thought* you were doing too good a job pretending you were scared out of your nut. What, you were hoping to get off with an insanity defense?"

"Gotta be a Zombie-killer rule in there somewhere," answered Harrelson. Then to TGOTW: "How about it, you festering turd-filled camel scrotum? There's one system you can't game."

The audacity of his attack on the object of their adoration stunned the peanut gallery. Even the disembodied Merriweather held his breath, which he didn't need to worry about since he didn't breathe any more. Everyone's attention focused on TGOTW, who sat stunned in front of not only this group, but all the hoards of hell whom he'd obviously been letting peak into the proceedings.

But the caught-in-the-headlights look lasted only a few seconds before the supremely confident look of the Supreme Evil Power in the Universe returned. He even smiled.

"Hold it right there, dear Woody," TGOTW began. "Before you lay out the rules of engagement, do the rest of you, including Angel Troc and James Cameron, the driver-not-the-director, agree to be bound by the conditions and the outcome of Mr. Harrelson's contest?"

The guy formerly in the tinfoil helmet didn't radiate any kind of theologically sophisticated aura. Statham and Cameron grimaced at each other, as did Cruz and Jolie.

"You've got to be kidding me," gasped Angel. "Him?"

Even the mellow Bill Murray snapped out of his slouch and looked at his *Zombieland* co-star with a conscious assessment that morphed into wide-eyed skepticism.

"An anarchist atheist who got arrested for publicly planting pot in Columbus, Ohio," said Murray. "We're going to trust him to match wits with the most evilly sophisticated being in the Universe? Gimme a break!"

"Hey, HEY!" Harrelson got everyone's attention. "In the early 1980s I was thinking about going into the clergy, until I rode on an airplane with a Jesuit priest. It was a most enlightening conversation, especially when he got on the subject of the Devil. Guys, trust me. I've definitely got this!"

Penelope Cruz perked up. "I'm Catholic, and those Jesuits are God's own storm troopers."

"Do *not* use that word in my presence!" shouted TGOTW.

"A conversation with some Jesuit, huh?" muttered Bill Murray. Then louder: "After which you became an atheist. That doesn't inspire a confidence on which I'd bet my life."

"The Free Choice Shop is closed for the day!" TGOTW's voice caused the room to shake. "Either you accept Mr. Harrelson's conditions for a contest, or I'll just execute summary judgment on all of you and have a Hollywood barbecue."

"There's *got* to be something in your eternal rules of engagement that will keep you from killing all of us," said Angel.

"Wanna bet?" smirked TGOTW. "Nothing stopped me from having John Wayne Gacy dress up as a clown so he could rape and murder almost three dozen boys. But I had more fun with Jeffrey Dahmer, my Milwaukee cannibal."

A roar drew Angel's attention toward the shadows, where two very large and extremely ugly bipeds, probably unwashed and unkempt human beings, seemed to be communicating with each other in animalistic vocalizations.

"Want to call my bluff?" continued TGOTW. "The barbecue will start in thirty seconds unless you all agree."

"That's why they call it gamblin', son," laughed Harrelson.

It didn't take all thirty seconds for everyone to agree.

* * *

"Define your contest, Mr. Harrelson." TGOTW had two of his nubulites from the gallery bring chairs so Angel and James could sit next to the doomed celebrities. James sat at one end, next to his co-worker, Jason Statham. Angel sat at the opposite end, next to Woody Harrelson.

Angel leaned toward Woody and whispered, "If you blow this, I will kill you before the cannibals can get to you."

"I find your lack of faith disturbing," said Harrelson in his Darth Vader voice. Then to TGOTW: "How about getting rid of these chains, your Evilness? I need to move around."

"You want something, then you need to give something," smiled TGOTW.

"Stuff it, Your Wretchedness. My contest, my rules."

TGOTW looked like he had some trouble dealing with the lack of respect coming from Harrelson.

"State the terms of your contest. Then I'll decide whether or not to play your silly game, human."

"The rules are quite simple," smiled the actor. "I will cross examine you, and you may not tell a lie. One lie, and this whole operation is null and void. No more soul repossessions. We all go free. And Jack Nicholson is restored to his pre-soul-repossession condition."

"Two big problems," said TGOTW. "First, I do not have power to resurrect the dead. And secondly, how will you know if I'm lying?"

"Simple. If you are indeed the devil, then there must be, what did you call him? Oh yeah. As you called him, Dad. Since you have a Scriptural history of making side bets with good old Dad, then Dad will see to both conditions. Repatriation of Jack Nicholson's soul with his body and arbitration of your truthfulness."

"Uh, about that Job business in the *Old Testament.* I can't commit Him to any conditions. Your deal has to be with me and only me."

"Nuh uh, boogermeat. You at least ask Him. Those are the conditions of the contest. Unless you're too chicken livered."

TGOTW fliched at yet another insult.

"Woody!" hissed Angelina Jolie.

"Put a lid on it," said Harrelson. "If there is a devil, then there is a… sorry to be offensive, Your Bloodiness…then there is a God. I'd kind of like to know that for sure in this life. Then, I'll still have time to make a few amends. As will you, too."

"It's been a couple thousand years since I last talked with Dad," mused TGOTW with disdain.

Angelina Jolie had had quite enough. "I don't believe in God, and I don't believe in a devil. What if this guy is just a psychopath pulling us into his delusion?"

"Then you are well and truly screwed," snapped Harrelson. "We play this game, or you can just get set to be the entrée at the Horiffic-with-a-capitol-H picnic."

"Pick up your hot line or whatever, crap for brains," taunted Harrelson. "If you don't get an answer, so be it."

Their host looked about to blow a gasket, suggesting that it had been a good long time since he had last tolerated such rudeness, especially in front of his mortal minions. Said minions appeared edgier with each insult from the *Zombieland* star.

Angel noticed how TGOTW gritted his teeth and looked skyward, at one point shrugging his shoulders. But he continued to look up. After a mere thirty seconds, however, he jerked as if his face had been slapped. Then he screamed.

"Two thousand years of the silent treatment, and you suddenly change the rules of engagement because of some actor!"

The surprised looks tied for first place. TGOTW's bulging eyes. Angelina Jolie's dropped jaw. Penelope Cruz's silent Hail Marys. Jason Statham and James Cameron's frantic whispers to each other, bookended by wide-eyed looks between Angel Troc and Woody Harrelson. The only person nonplussed by TGOTW's outburst sat smiling cherubically and humming the *Ghostbuster's* theme song.

"Sounds like Dad gave you the go-ahead, Dan Scratch," said Woody, finally turning from Angel.

"That's *my* name," said an equally bewildered Dan from TGOTW's side. Turning to his master, "You gave me the name Dan Scratch, right boss?"

"Be quiet you petulant little twit, or I'll shrink you again!" roared TGOTW, clearly not understanding his minor pique wasn't in the same Universe as a direct communication between him and his profoundly estranged Dad.

Then to Harrelson: "You want the truth? Fine. You'll get nothing *but* the truth, so help me Dad! Ask your questions!"

Now every eye in the room bore into Woody Harrelson, who swallowed rather noisily. Angel heard the sound and equally noisily slapped her hand against her forehead, after which she began looking around the room for anything that might be used as a weapon. The damned ghouls kept a clean lair, however. Cleanliness was evidently next to evilness, too.

"Well," said TGOTW, petulantly.

"Okay, Beelzebub." Harrelson swallowed again, and stuttered nervously. "In John 8:44, Jesus calls you *the father of lies.* My question: Are you a liar?"

"Daddamned Jesuits," muttered TGOTW.

"That a yes or a no?"

The thespians in the group knew a poker tell long before Angel or the hoards of hell in the gallery. If TGOTW said he was indeed a liar, the combined residents of his domain, beyond just the strange and terrible gallery with them on the top floor courtroom, would know they'd been had all these millennia. And if he denied being a liar, then Dad would end the contest. But at least he could spin the story to his advantage in the infernal regions and stand a chance of keeping the troops in line.

TGOTW agonized for minutes, but made his choice.

"I am not a liar. Dad is the liar!"

Several things happened simultaneously. First, all the manacles holding the star-studded cast to their chairs disappeared.

Secondly, the entire fifty-second floor of 515 Flower Tower evaporated, leaving the entire ensemble sitting on the heliport, next to the helicopter, now free of the talons that had previously anchored it to the pad. Google it. All the online data for 515 Flower Street in Los Angeles boasts of fifty-one and *only* fifty-one floors. Before Jack Nicholson's adventure in hell, all online media squarely featured fifty-two floors. In both buildings.

And speaking of Jack Nicholson, he dropped intact between TGOTW and the captive celebs. He looked unsure whether to wet his pants or run and plant a kiss on Woody Harrelson's lips.

He did both.

Several of the mortal ghoul gallery had been leaning against the back wall. Its disappearance caused a dozen to shriek fifty-one stories to their deaths. A localized whirlwind caused the remainder to follow, leaving behind one slightly used Hot Shot DuraProd rechargeable livestock prod with a 32-inch flexible shaft.

Before he disappeared, TGOTW tried to get in the last laugh: "You mortals have another problem."

"What, trying to squeeze eight people into that helicopter?" asked Bill Murray.

"Oh no," came the answer. "You now have certain knowledge of the existence of both Heaven and Hell, of Dad and myself. Your rules of engagement are therefore changed. You haven't seen the last of me."

And with that, TGOTW vanished.

In answer to Murray's question could all eight of them could fit into the Bell 206L4 five-passenger-plus-pilot helicopter?

They did.

EPILOGUE

Angel Troc, aka The Fixer, gained five new clients and one partner in this strange and terrible saga.

Her new partner, James Cameron, proved indispensable as a chauffeur on air, sea and land. And as some extra muscle to watch her back.

Jason Statham hired her as his life coach.

Angelina Jolie used Angel as a consultant in a new series of *Laura Croft, Tomb Raider* movies.

Penelope Cruz became spectacularly confrontational with her ex-husbands Scientology crowd and needed Angel's intervention multiple times.

Bill Murray took renewed interest in the *Ghostbuster* franchise, especially after its reprise with a female cast landed in theaters with a thud. He insisted on hiring Angel as his co-screenwriter.

Woody Harrelson left the movie business and started his own church. While Angel refused the call to be his first Deacon, she agreed to find him Jesuits with whom he could toss around theological ideas. He needed quite a few Jesuits, since none of them lasted very long with such a theologically opinionated student.

The resurrected Jack Nicholson used most of Angel's time, as he decided to stay dead. He arranged to have Angel made sole executor of his ongoing royalties and eclipsed the late Elvis Presley in confirmed sightings. The lore of Jack's largess from beyond the grave spawned several movies and television specials. Conspiracy theorists abandoned Dan Brown's *Holy Grail* cottage industry in favor of *Jack's Back* theories. His occasional guest appearances to Woody Harrelson's chosen acolytes more than adequately fanned those flames. Two such acolytes were the L.A. mayor and his chief of police, who both got cameo appearances from the good-as-new Jack Nicholson, accompanied by Angel Troc. They told them the whole story. Both left public service and joined Harrelson's church.

There are still warrants out for Angel Troc's arrest.

The End

6

HALF Z's

by Nicholas P Adams

Second in line in the queue to the medical shuttle, Sofia Rodriguez held her palm against the lump protruding from her abdomen. The melon-sized bulge pushed against her waistband. She pulled at a button on her sleeveless linen blouse as beads of sweat collected on her chest in the sweltering Colombian humidity. In spite of the Big Ass Fans revolving overhead in the LED-lit transit station, the elastic of her thin black suit pants seemed to collect moisture like a marathon runner's headband. She rolled her ankles, taking the weight off her two-inch heels one at a time, and adjusted the sling bag hanging across her body.

Off to her right, a pair of men in janitor's overall's tore posters off the transit station's glass walls. The silhouette of a Gya'ol under a blood-red spray-painted X with the words PURE EARTH scrawled below seemed to stare at her with emotionless eyes.

Sofia hugged herself, shrinking as she took a half-step away from the windows. *Impure, they call us. So many can't hide in plain sight like I can. I've never been openly shunned like most of the others. What would my life have been like if I'd been born with four eyes or purple skin? Would it have felt more lonely than it does now?*

"So much hatred for something different," a young woman's voice a few feet behind Sofia growled. "Live and let live, right?"

"Easier said than done," a young man's voice answered. "Most humans dismiss the notion of an individual's right to choose between two genders, let alone a species that's both rolled into one."

"Humans thought they had come to invade," the girl replied. Sofia looked over her shoulder, spotting a lanky pink-skinned girl with four Gya'ol eyes and bright purple dreadlocks. She wore two yellow bikini tops with denim shorts and flip-flops. "But they came and shared their technology."

"I know," The young man stared at the double-breasted woman with two dark Gya'ol eyes. His mocha-chino head tentacles bounced as he nodded. "They advanced human health care, travel, communications, pushing Earth centuries ahead. It's been over sixty years since they arrived. If they had a master plan, they would have shown their cards by now, right?"

"My human grandmother never believed the Gya'ol were as shy and benevolent as they seemed," Sofia turned her body. "She died, still sure they were biding their time, just waiting for them to strike and take over the Earth."

"What reason would they have for waiting so long?" Bikini girl popped out her hip. "I would think if they had plans to take over, they would have done it. Besides, they're family now."

Sofia winced. "Nana was the last connection to my Human side," she thought to herself. "I've been alone for ten years, living in a human orphanage. Keeping to myself. Hiding what I am. Not really Human or Gya'ol, but caught somewhere in between without a family."

The shuttle's side door opened and out walked the Gya'ol pilot towering over the average Latino by at least two feet. The alien's outfit looked like a short wetsuit made of iridescent raisin-colored scales. A harness that looked like a carbon-fiber chastity belt with a prominent codpiece wrapped around its hips while a bronze chest plate, accentuating four distinct mounds, displayed the pilot's insignia.

It's exposed arms and legs glistened like it just stepped out of a steam room. Like all Gya'ol, it had mauve skin with greenish-gold accents running down the center of its body. Its exposed six-fingered hands and feet ended in black nails.

It carried a backpack of sorts, connected by tubes to a mask covering its face with a reflective surface like an office building window. Its Gold-tipped tentacles hung down from the back of its head, braided into a single mass.

"That looks like the Gya'ol who found me," Sofia said over her shoulder. "Except the tentacles were shorter. I wonder if they grow their tendrils out like hair."

Puffs of steam burst from vents on either side of its face, keeping in time with the rise and fall of its double-breasted chest. The pilot seemed to glance across the queue. "Offspring of Interspecies mating, Welcome. Please present your ID slate for verification," it said through the speaker embedded in its mask.

"Why do they always smell like they've just crawled out of a mud bath?" Sofia mumbled, taking a half step back, as the boy in the queue ahead of her looked up into the pilot's palm-light, and held up his ID. He radiated a dim glow, matching the violet skin of the Gya'ol pilot, like a backlit kabuki theater screen. The previously invisible XZ tattoo running across the nape of his neck shined like hot pink neon. The glow emanating from the palm-light and his tattoo pulled Sofia's attention to the nearby shuttle. She'd never been to the Enclave in one of these before. Sure beats a two-day bus ride into the mountains. It had the girth of an old 757. It's segmented body, shiny and wine-colored, gave the appearance of a giant metal centipede as it sat on the concrete landing pad just under the platform's roof.

"Juan Diego Bolivar," A resonant Gya'ol voice broke through the noisy pedestrians streaming through the bustling station. "What's the nature of your visit to the enclave?"

"I'm having trouble with my lower eyes," the boy pointed to his head.

Sofia glanced up at the kid's reflection stretched across the Gya'ol's tinted breathing mask. Four obsidian eyes seemed to catch her looking, blinking with double lids.

The boy cleared his throat. "I have an appointment for ocular regeneration."

"We'll take good care of you, N'gar Kal'ay." The pilot waved the boy into the shuttle with a nod and then turned its mirrored gaze on Sofia. She stepped forward, holding up the ID with her right hand, and pressed down on her stomach with the other.

The Gya'ol, a good eighteen inches taller than Sofia's five-foot-seven, bent over. Sofia's face appeared on the pilot's curved mask as the palm-light shone down on her. Her shoulders sagged a fraction as the glowing XZ appeared on her reflected left cheek. She twitched with a shiver running down her spine, imagining the same mark shining from her neck like a lighthouse. Her dark brown eyes and mocha-chino skin seemed to fade behind the radiating signet of her heritage. She looked up into the night's sky and shook the stray locks of caramel hair from her face. At least she could pass as Human. Unlike her less fortunate alien-looking cousins who got bullied just for living.

"Sofia Viviana Rodriguez,"The alien's chest-mounted speaker became muffled by a passing truck blasting mariachi music. "What's the nature of your visit to the enclave?"

She squirmed at the thought that she might be pregnant though she grew up believing it was impossible for a Half-Z. "I have a growth in my abdomen," Sofia removed her hand from the lump under her shirt, "I work for the Consulate. The Ambassador arranged an appointment for me to see the top Interspecies Specialist instead of going to the nearest clinic. So I could get back to work sooner."

"Ah," the pilot's head bowed as its voice softened. "The Ambassador is a skilled negotiator. The Enclave chose wisely to have him act as a liaison between the Gya'ol and the humans. He must have a fondness for you to personally arrange for your care."

"He's an extraordinary man," Sofia answered. "I'd probably be on the streets or in a halvsy-house if it weren't for him. I can only guess why he's doing this for me." She was just an intern, and the junior-most member of his staff, but somehow...

"We'll take good care of you, N'gar Kal'ay." The Gya'ol waved Sofia toward the portal. She rolled her eyes at the alien phrase all Gya'ol used on people like her.

Child? She was eighteen, almost nineteen. She bristled at being called a child. She'd always wondered if this was simply how they spoke to all humans, a term of endearment like how the city boys called each other Vato. But something inside her cringed, feeling there was more behind their flawless civility. Perhaps it was their advanced technology that gave them a deserved sense of superiority like the European's when they first started colonizing South America.

She took the five steps up to the shuttle door and turned into the passenger cabin. Three rows of seats, like a 747, extended away from her. Moving to her right, she took the front row window seat across the aisle from Juan. He gave her a toothy smile and nodded before tipping his head back to squirt cerulean drops into all four eyes, blinking his inner lids with each application.

The shuttle slowly filled with humans, Half-Z's, and a few Gya'ol (who wore the ornamental versions of the alien breathing masks) with transparent glass and intricately painted like tie-dyed Celtic knots.

The pilot walked through the passenger area, heading to the cockpit above and to the rear of the main cabin, speaking in rapid Gya'ol. The PA system embedded in Sofia's headrest spoke quietly in Spanish while other languages became a dissonant white-noise behind her.

"The passage to Na'ya Ain will take twenty-seven minutes. The cabin's air will be exchanged to facilitate our transition. Those unable to breathe in the Gya'ol atmosphere, please use the respirators above your seats. Kya'ay Ju'utain."

Vents on the floor and ceiling opened as the air flowed toward Sofia's feet, cooling her body from head to toe. Juan reached up and pulled on a round metal handle protruding from the bulkhead, placing it at his throat. The handle grew like a vine until it surrounded his neck and then expanded in size and transparency until his entire face became ensconced in a transparent bubble.

The Gya'ol passengers did the opposite, pulling their masks down off their faces and letting the rings retract before attaching them to the ceiling.

She was double lucky, she guessed. She looked human but could breathe both atmospheres.

Sofia sank into her seat as the shuttle launched straight up, reaching its cruising altitude in less than ten seconds. Then with equal force, her body pressed into the backrest as the lights of Florencia whizzed past the window like a river of stars until only the dark canopy of trees appeared.

"What takes you to the enclave?" Juan asked, gripping his armrests with white knuckles. "Worried about your pregnancy?"

"I'm XZ. A Half-Z like you. I can't get pregnant. We're born sterile, remember?" Sofia folded her arms across her chest. "At least that's what we've been taught."

"I thought I'd heard of a handful of Half-Z's getting pregnant," Juan mused, staring at Sofia's stomach with four wide eyes. "Maybe that was just a rumor."

Sofia followed Juan's curious gaze and straightened her blouse, pulling the clingy fabric off her skin. "I hope so," she whispered and closed her eyes toward the window. Pressing her head against the hull, she let the vibration from the engine's droning massage her temple. The skin under her breasts grew hot and tender again. She rubbed the area softly, feeling two hard spots like giant moles under the fabric.

"It was just that one time," Sofia closed her eyes, thinking to herself. "How could I be pregnant? And if I am, it was only five weeks ago. How could I be showing like this? We haven't been in the same room since yesterday. He's been out of the country. Then he saw my belly and insisted I go to the Enclave. Sure, he's handsome and well-built. And I'll admit I got stomach flutters whenever he walked into the office. I wasn't drunk, yet somehow I lost all control of myself. What was I even thinking, sleeping with the ambassador? But it was just a dream. Nothing happened, right?"

* * *

Sofia carried a stack of papers needing signatures into Ambassador Yuri Petrov's empty office. The orange glow from the fireplace welcomed her from across the room. The clock on his mahogany desk chimed at 10:00 p.m. as she walked across the parquet floor. Her shoes squeaked as she turned around the corner and clicked on the desk lamp. Rain beat against the French doors leading out onto the balcony, tapping on the glass like a million anxious fingertips. She caught her reflection in the glazing: White running shoes, black yoga shorts with an indigo sports bra.

She was glad she remembered the files before his morning meeting.

She set the papers down in the middle of the desk and returned to her reflection, pulling her ponytail tight against her skull through the white rubber band.

She screamed and jumped back as a flash of lightning cracked the sky right outside the compound, illuminating the room. The glass doors rattled on their hinges. Her heart pounded like the thunder just beyond the door.

"That glass will stop a bullet," a thick Russian accent pierced the drum solo beating in her ears. "Not sure if it will stop lightning."

Sofia turned to find Ambassador Petrov standing in the doorway of his private bathroom wearing nothing but purple running shorts and matching shower shoes. His chiseled bare chest and abs glistened with sweat as he held onto a hand towel wrapped around his neck. Beads of water clung to the tips of the blond hair dangling around his ears. His piercing ice-blue eyes locked on hers, bunching in the corners as his mouth twitched up. Wow. Now that was a man. His scent was intoxicating, causing her vision to fuzz around the edges.

"Ambassador," Sofia shifted on the spot, looking down at her appearance. "I'm so sorry. I was putting some papers on your desk that I'd forgotten earlier. I came over on my way to the gym. I didn't think anyone would be here."

"It's no problem, Sofia," Yuri waved off her apology. "I'm not usually here this late either. I was just about to take a steam. You're welcome to use it anytime you like. I know your Gya'ol half loves the humidity. It's why they settled here in Colombia."

"I'm not as big a fan of the humidity as I am the heat, ambassador," Sofia waved her hand over her face. "You seem to like it well enough."

"Da," Yuri leaned one-armed against the bathroom door, his eyes giving Sofia a once over as steam continued to billow behind him. "Growing up in a small village in Siberia, I was always cold. But here, I enjoy the pleasures of a hot climate and its people."

"Having the Gya'ol consulate here in Florencia has blessed our country," Sofia wrapped her arms around her bare midriff. "I'm personally very grateful to have this job."

"To the Gya'ol," Yuri stood tall and proud. "Nothing is more important than their offspring. Offering you a job is nothing compared to all they've given to Humanity. I'm pleased to have you on my staff."

Sofia's heart started pounding in her chest. "I'll get out of your way," She leaned against the desk as a wave of dizziness cascaded through her mind. "I think I need to go home. Goodnight, sir."

"You don't have to leave on my account, Sofia," Yuri closed the door to his bathroom and stepped toward her. " And please, call me Yuri."

Sofia moved to the side, catching his scent as she passed by. She lost her balance, stumbling into the bookshelf as her head fogged. Her vision blurred as the room seemed to shine with a soft purple glow. She reached out to brace herself on the wall but missed, grabbing only air.

Yuri caught her in his arms before she fell. Heat spread from his hands through her back as if she'd fallen into a fireplace. His eyes seemed to pull her in like a black hole. Unable to escape. Unwilling to try.

Sofia pressing her lips to his. Yuri putting his hands around her waist. Their breaths in unison as fabric seemed to melt away in their heat. A disembodied pleasure she'd never experienced before coursed through her veins like liquid fire.

The rest of the night flashed by like a highlight reel.

Sofia opened her eyes to find herself in her studio apartment, fully dressed in her sweat-stained workout clothes. The warm early-morning breeze drifted through an open window as the sounds of delivery vans rumbled through the plaza below.

Her damp, matted hair clung to the pillow as she peeled herself off the bed and stumbled to the bathroom. She let the cold water run from the tap as she cupped her hands and splashed herself in the face. She combed fingers through her loose, wet hair, no longer bound by the white band. What happened last night? Had she really thrown herself at her boss like a character on a cheesy telenovela? Turning off the faucet, she leaned on the porcelain pedestal sink and stared at her reflection.

She stood back and rubbed her temples. Her phone began it's 6:00 a.m. chime from the kitchenette. Sofia raced from the bathroom, swiping the alarm off after its fifth ring. Pressing her thumb to the home button, her phone opened to the last active App, Distance Mapper. The running app showed she took a direct route starting at 10:27 p.m. from the Consulate building and ending at her apartment building at 11:16 p.m.

She looked down at the counter to find her car keys sitting in the bowl of iridescent blue marbles. She picked up the fob and pressed the lock button. Outside, her yellow Fiat 500 chirped its location. She walked over to the window and looked down. Right in its regular parking spot.

"Must have been a dream," she told herself, holding a hand over her heart. "Maybe I didn't even go to the consulate."

Sofia raced into the bathroom and turned on the shower, stripping out of her running outfit before the water warmed. She had to get those papers on the Ambassador's desk before he got in.

* * *

Sofia startled awake, thrashing about, only to find a Gya'ol bending over her. Its four beetle-black eyes twinkled as its mouth opened in a chiclet-toothed smile, displaying flat ivory teeth. "Kya'hanya tay ya'ar kal'ay k'noe. Kya'naw tho'et rout'shi parta'al."

Wake up, my child. We've arrived. Sofia's brain translated without thinking.

What a long way to say we're here.

"Kya'ay Ju'utain," She nodded, taking the Gya'ol's outstretched hand. "Thank you. I'm Sofia."

"I am called Mi'tya Sha'ay. Which dome do you seek?" it asked. "I will assist your journey."

Sofia opened her mouth to speak, and then shut it again, digging into her bag. She pulled out a thin-film scroll and unrolled it to reveal a message written in Gya'ol. She really should've paid more attention to studying written Gya'olese at the orphanage. Mother of God, how she wished she knew what it said.

Mi'tya scanned the document bottom to top. Its face changing from the smile to what looked like a scowl, and then a trilling sound erupted from the back of its throat. It reached out and curled up the scroll, enfolding Sofia's hands in its own.

"Follow me to the healers," all four of its eyes seemed to droop at the corners. "This says you are important to the ambassador and his work."

She was just an intern, but perhaps after that crazy night... maybe she won't be alone anymore.

Mi'Tya took Sofia by the hand and led her out the cabin and toward a twenty-foot tall steel wall embedded in the mountainside. The entrance had a single off-center gate with a glowing surface in the ground churning with random patterns of light like a dance floor.

Sofia gawked overhead at the stars shining down through the crystal clear dome. Thin columns of stainless steel wove up from the ground like silvery vines, interlacing with one another as they narrowed with each upward branch. The scent of potting soil rose from below as her feet sank into the soft earth that spread out to the dome's edges. She stole a quick glance behind her. The shuttle that had sat off the concrete platform at the transit station now laid flat like a tired dog. She cocked her head as her eyes followed the outstretched wings. They looked wider. Like a cat basking in the sun.

Sofia turned as Mi'Tya gave her hand a squeeze.

"We go in now?" her guide asked in broken Spanish, pointing in the opposite direction. "You go on scan."

Sofia nodded, falling into a dance style of quick steps to keep up with Mi'Tya's long strides. Ahead of her, the last of the shuttle passengers stepped off an illuminated platform. The Gya'ol attending the scanner waved to Mi'Tya by crossing its wrists overhead. Mi'Tya released Sofia's hand and ran into the other Gya'ol's arms. They embraced, running their hands all over each other bodies. They pressed tight against one another while brushing thick lips together and speaking in rapid Gya'ol.

Passionate people. She could see why they chose to settle among Latinos.

Sofia glanced around the empty dome as she stutter-stepped toward the platform and cleared her throat.

"My apologies." Mi'Tya slowly peeled herself away from the scanner attendant, flashing a brilliant smile but clutching onto its hand. "This is my mate, K'yitmyat No'etae. We are close to our mating cycle and are planning children. It's almost impossible to resist the Draw to one's mate."

The Draw? Another alien concept Sofia never learned about in school.

"Congratulations." Sofia reached out her hand. "Who's going to be the mother?"

The two Gya'ol covered their faces and trilled. "We never know which will carry the children," K'yitmyat said in slow Gya'ol. "It could be either or both. We are both in the season. Unknowing is the pleasure." They embraced each other again with restrained passion and ended by touching their foreheads. "In ancient times, some matings brought four offspring each. There was great celebration in home."

Sofia crossed herself. "Two sets of quadruplets at the same time? Holy Mary, Mother of God!"

"Stand onto scanner, N'gar Kal'ay," K'yitmyat stepped away from Mi'Tya and held her hands above a floating holographic console. "We must ensure no Human diseases have traveled with you."

"I will demonstrate," Mi'Tya smiled and stepped onto the rectangular platform, centering its body on one side. The platform's rim changed from silver to hot white and floated up. Next to Mi'Tya, on the other end of the platform, a glowing hologram developed like a 3D printer. The process took only seconds until the rim hovered just inches above their heads.

Mi'Tya turned to face Sofia, followed in exact motion by the day-glow Doppelganger. "You see?" it asked. "Simple process. Your turn."

Sofia admired the display as Mi'Tya stepped off the platform, while the twin seemed to vanish as it passed through an invisible door. The floating rim dropped back into place, blinking twice but retaining its soft glow.

Sofia swallowed hard as she stepped onto the platform. She shook her shoulders, letting her hands fall to her sides and took a deep breath. As the rim rose past her calves, she closed her eyes and balled her fists.

She wasn't sure she wanted to see what was inside her. Was it a new form of cancer? The Gya'ol cured the old kind. Was it my twin sister? Could it be one of those quadruplets my mother may have carried before she died in the delivery room? Could it be the next generation of Rodriguez?

In her mind, she listened to the quiet hum and felt the gentle vibration at her feet. A wave of light drifted past her lids as she took in a deep breath, taking in the scent of soil and grass along with an exotic fragrance floating on the breeze.

Her eyes flew open as she heard a pair of gasping breaths, just in time to see her 3D duplicate vanish like embers. The Gya'ol were staring at each other, but without any lust in their eyes.

"What is it?" Sofia's eyes moistened as her heart sank in her chest. "What did you see? Is it bad?"

"We must see the Healer," Mi'Tya reached out and took Sofia by the hand, pulling her off the platform. "Now!"

* * *

Sofia stuffed her clothes into her sling bag after changing into the Gya'ol jumpsuit given to her by a Half-Z nurse with two almond-shaped eyes, lilac skin, and black tentacles cascading across her lithe shoulders. She pulled at the tight bodysuit, fingering the small silver buttons that dotted its surface in a hexagonal pattern. Nothing happened until she touched three buttons simultaneously. The triangle between them faded to invisible, revealing her bare skin underneath.

"Whoa," Sofia gasped. "So, this must be how they're going to examine me."

Sofia scanned the dots, imagining how many bathing suit options she could create by making strategic areas of the outfit disappear.

The three-meter by four-meter room should have felt spacious compared to Sofia's tiny flat in the city, but the earthy decor and hard-packed floor didn't help her feel at peace here like the Gya'ol. The absence of windows and doors only added to her fear of being buried alive. Only a snail-shell entrance to the corridor she'd entered from made the room feel like anything but a tomb.

The sound of muffled conversations in a dozen languages seeped around the entryway, along with the smell of damp soil. A single dome-shaped crystal seemed to be the only source of light and comfort in the room. It beamed undulating patterns across the walls and floor as if she were floating at the bottom of a swimming pool.

Sofia walked to the blind corner and slid down the corridor wall, hugging her pack. Why did Mi'Tya and K'yitmyat look so scared? Was she going to die delivering this baby like her mother? She hadn't planned on ever having a family, but now that it was becoming a possibility, the reality started sinking in.

The room fell into silence. Sofia brushed away the moisture welling in her eyes as a small Gya'ol with the same purplish skin and four black eyes as the rest of its race came around the corner carrying what looked like a bundle of moss. The Gya'ol's head tentacles were shorter, and each one had a gold ring at its base, jingling with each step into the room. "Hello, Sofia," it spoke in fluent Spanish with a soft mezzo-soprano voice. "I am called Sa'Ra R'Waan. I am the specialist Ambassador Petrov sent you to see. How are you feeling?"

Sofia pushed herself up against the wall, keeping her bag tight to her body. "I don't know what I'm feeling." Her voice shook. "A little freaked out."

"You have nothing to fear here, N'gar Kal'ay," Sa'Ra smiled, crow's feet forming in its four eyes. "You are a child of the Gya'ol. All life is precious to us."

Sofia blew out her breath and lowered the bag, holding it off the floor by its strap. She nodded her head. "Kya'ay Ju'utain."

Sa'Ra bowed its head with a tilt, acknowledging Sofia's manners. "Would you please lie down," it said, gesturing to the middle of the floor, and then held out the fuzzy green ball to her.

Sofia let the strap fall from her hand, and the bag plopped on the ground as she stepped to the spot next to Sa'Ra, giving a micro-smile as she took the bundle. She got down on her hands and knees, then rolled over to lie on her back.

Pulling her hair to drape across her chest, she placed the mossy pillow under her head and stared at the hypnotic patterns dancing across the ceiling.

Sa'Ra knelt next to Sofia and reached behind its back. Its hand reappeared with a scroll, which unrolled by itself when Sa'Ra set it on the ground.

Sofia craned her head as a 3D hologram of her materialized, floating above the flat silver sheet. The hologram, glowing in blues and greens, seemed to be standing in place like a statue, tight-fisted, with its eyes shut.

"Is that a recording from the scanner at the gate?"

"Yes, N'gar Kal'ay." Sa'Ra smiled wide and pointed to a bright spot of red pulsating from the hologram's side. "And this is why you've come to see us."

Sa'Ra put her fingertips around the crimson mass and stretched them outward, making it grow to ten times its standard size. The light rotated slowly above Sofia's belly.

"Is it going to kill me?" her voice shook.

"First, we must verify what it is," Sa'Ra soothed, placing its hand on Sofia's head and pushed her back onto the pillow. "Then, we see if it's harmful."

Sa'Ra put her hands on Sofia's abdomen around the swollen area, touching triads of buttons to make the fabric disappear.

Sofia balled her fists and squeezed water out of her eyes as Sa'Ra felt its way around the protrusion. Sofia flinched, flattening her stomach.

"Does this hurt?" Sa'Ra asked as it gently pushed the mass down.

"No," Sofia shook her head. "It doesn't hurt to be touched. Your hands are cold."

"My apologies, N'gar Kal'ay," Sa'Ra seemed to chuckle.

Sa'Ra muttered to itself in Gya'ol as it continued the examination, sounding like a baby's gibberish on high-speed. "Let's see if we can improve the resolution."

Sofia opened her eyes to find Sa'Ra placing a silver ring around the protrusion and tapping its fingers on the scroll. The 3D image of her abdomen rippled several times, each one bringing the red mass into better focus like adjusting the dial on a telescope.

"Is that?" Sofia's panicked voice caught in her throat as she made out the coiled shape of a thin spinal column. "Is that what I think it is?"

"Yes, N'Gar Kal'ay," A high trill erupted from Sa'Ra like someone rolling their R's. "You are with child."

How was that possible? She was infertile. It couldn't be. And her night with Yuri happened only five weeks ago.

"When was the last time you mated?" Sa'Ra knelt back on its heels, picking up the scroll. "Was it the first time you were in the season?"

* * *

"How can I be pregnant?" Sofia rose up on her elbows, her voice rising to borderline hysteria. "Don't tell me this is some kind of alien immaculate conception thing. I don't even have a uterus. None of us do. Just dysfunctional ovaries. I had to get hormone replacement therapy, so I could look like a girl."

Sa'Ra put a hand on Sofia's head. "Be calm, N'Gar Kal'ay," she soothed. "There's no danger to you or the child. We should wait to discuss this unexpected pregnancy once the other parent has been notified."

The Gya'ol gestured its hand over the scroll, resulting in a tinkling chime sound.

"Other parent? You mean Yuri?" Sofia rolled out from Sa'Ra's hand, climbed to her feet, and began pacing. "It was just that one time. I don't even know how it happened. I thought it was just a dream." She'd convinced herself it was just her imagination. A fantasy. Her body couldn't get pregnant even if that night between her and the ambassador were real.

"Tell me about this dream, N'gar Kal'ay," Sa'Ra gazed down at Sofia while its lower eyes focused on the scroll. Sofia stalked back and forth across the floor, quickly glossing over the details in the Ambassador's office as if she were in a confessional. Sa'Ra seemed to take copious notes while asking multiple follow-up questions, probing for more specifics.

After what felt like an hour, the Gya'ol stood slowly, stepping into Sofia's path with open arms and a gentle smile. "What you described to me is The Draw," Sa'Ra gripped Sofia's arms. "The uncontrollable instinct to mate with another. With someone who will produce the healthiest offspring. Your Gya'ol instincts took over when you encountered complementary DNA in your time of the season. The Draw is very powerful, especially for mixed genomes."

"Holy Mary, Mother of God," Sofia crossed herself, flailing her arms away from Sa'Ra and resumed pacing. "This can't be. It was only five weeks ago. How can something like that seem like just a crazy dream?"

"It is the *Temptin*," Sa'Ra folded its hands behind its back. "As you know, Gya'ol have the sexual organs of what you call male and female. Temptin is the pheromone that signals to each other when someone who is genetically complementary is in season at the same time we are. I believe you call this sensation, romantic, or sexual love. Among humans, we've seen the Temptin cause a state of cognitive dissonance and even memory loss. For us, it creates a bond between the parents that lasts until the children mature into adolescents and are released into the community. Then we await The Draw with another when we are in season again."

Sofia backed into the blind corner, slouching down onto her sling bag and shaking her head with closed eyes repeating No, no, no to herself. She squeezed her body and recoiled as her right hand fell onto the lump in her belly and then wrapped her arms around her knees and wept. "What do I do?" She sobbed.

"Let us notify the father," Sa'Ra crouched down, placing its hands on Sofia's knees. "Then the two of you can decide what to do. The child won't survive outside a uterus for long. You'll have to undergo micro-cellular reconstruction to build a womb and transfer the child. Of course, I assume you'll want to proceed with the pregnancy. Though I know, not all humans believe the unborn have the same rights as its parents."

Sofia looked up with unfocused eyes and nodded.

Sa'Ra returned to the room's center and picked up the scroll while Sofia watched. With the silver sheet in one hand, Sa'Ra gestured its fingers on, and above the surface, enlarging the image of the lump until the hologram displayed a single tri-lobed blood cell. Next to the floating blob, multiple DNA strands began scrolling up from the plate. "Now that's interesting," Sa'Ra muttered. "Looks like we've found another one."

"Another what?" Sofia's head perked up. "What's interesting?"

"Your child," Sa'Ra smiled. "It has a rare genetic condition that we believed would never occur. We can extrapolate the DNA and create a holographic image of the child's mature appearance. Would you like to see it?"

Sofia gawked, while only a muted croaking noise came out of her half-open mouth. "I guess so?" She stood as Sa'Ra gestured above the flattened scroll again. The blood cell shrunk until the image of the fetus came back into clarity.

Sa'Ra put the plate on the ground and gestured with both hands in the air. The fetus stretched and changed like watching a time-lapse camera inside the womb, getting longer and fatter though the size of the image hovering above the floor never changed. Within a few seconds, the future shape of a humanoid resolved.

Sofia stood, circling wide around the image of what looked like an overgrown prepubescent barbie-doll standing eye to eye with her. "Is it a boy or a girl?" Sofia asked. The image wore no clothes and showed no external signs of either gender.

"Neither," Sa'Ra beamed with clinical enthusiasm. "It has a double-Z chromosome. Something we were certain could never happen when Gya'ol and humans first started interbreeding."

Sofia's brow scrunched up into her hairline. "How can a child be neither. Gya'ol are both. Humans are one or the other. Even the Half-Z's are male or female, even the ones that seem more Gya'ol than human."

"When it comes to inheriting genetic characteristics. We've learned to never assume what's possible, and focus on empirical evidence," Sa'Ra chuckled. "Look here." It swiped its fingers across the plate and into the air, creating a third hologram next to the DNA strands and the nondescript child. A four-by-four grid appeared with Xh, Xa, Y, & Z across the top and down the left side with *Parent 1* and *Parent 2* listed respectively.

"This is a basic genetic sex chart. I learned about this in school," Sofia pointed to a red-colored cell in the matrix. "That's me. XhZ. Half-Bred Female. Non-Fertile. My biological mother was human, and my biological father was Gya'ol. She didn't survive after childbirth, and they won't tell me who my other parent was."

"You are one of the rarest genetic matches between Gya'ol and Humans that survive gestation," Sa'Ra smiled wide. "Less than 13% of matings result in a viable pregnancy. And only 1% of those live to adulthood."

"A proverbial diamond in the rough," Sofia's mouth pinched into a flat line, quoting the platitude her previous caretaker used to use. "Lucky me."

A melody of chimes erupted from the light above as words in Gya'ol appeared on the wall, starting from a single point and moving outward in a double spiral.

"Come," The holograms vanished as Sa'Ra swiped its hand across the scroll. "We've contacted the father. He'll be here shortly. You must be weary. You can change back into your human clothes here, then I'll escort you to a visitor sleeping place. You can wait for him there."

The Ambassador? He was the only *him* she could think of.

Sofia covered her mouth, choking back the sudden wetness brimming in her eyes. "Okay." She bent over, grabbing her bag and unzipping the top as Sa'Ra disappeared behind the blind wall. She dumped her wrinkled clothes on the ground and peeled the jumpsuit from her body, emerging like a snake shedding a layer of skin, and kicked it into the middle of the room as she pulled her feet from the tight ankle holes.

What would he say? Yuri had insisted that Sofia visit the Enclave immediately. Her head had swooned with sheer ecstasy after being in the same room together for five minutes. Her lip trembled as tears spilled down her cheeks.

"I don't know if I'm ready to be a mother." She cried to the ceiling, kneeling on the hard-packed ground, and crossed herself. "Holy Mary, Mother of God. What do I do?"

* * *

Sofia laid fitfully on the elevated pad of overturned soil the Gya'ol called a bed. The sleeping quarters looked out onto the mountainside. She turned over on her side. Her Gya'ol half loving the smell of dirt, while her human half loathed the hardness against her back. "I hate camping," she moaned behind the arm, draping across her face. "I miss my soft bed, my pillow, and clean sheets."

Rolling off the pad, she brushed off her soiled clothing and walked to the circular window. Stars dimmed on the horizon as the pre-dawn sun chased away their light. She caught only a few minutes' sleep here and there awaiting the Ambassador's arrival and 'the talk.' Her bloodshot eyes drooped, but never fully closed for more than a moment.

"He's almost twice my age," she whispered to a Colombian Screech-Owl perched just outside the glazing. "I've only been on a few dates with human boys my age. I've never been in a serious relationship. What do I do?"

The cinnamon-colored bird bobbed its head as the branch on which it perched swayed. Its eyes reflected the faint yellow light emanating from the ceiling before opening its wings and flapping away.

"Yeah," she closed her eyes and cried. "He'll probably do the same thing."

Sofia bolted upright at the sound of something pounding on dirt. "Hello?" She called out behind the blind wall across the room.

Fresh air wafted into the chamber. A broad, unbidden smile escaped Sofia's lips. A familiar scent billowed around her as she turned from the window.

He was here. Like leaves in an autumn gale, her worries seemed to disappear one by one, and all was right with the world.

What's happening to me?

A million fantasies played around the edges of her conscious mind. A romantic proposal. A traditional Catholic wedding. A Honeymoon in the South Pacific. Sofia lit up like a princess about to be kissed by prince charming.

Sa'Ra came around the corner, wearing a sad smile.

Sofia's heart dropped. "He didn't come?" her lip trembled. She looked down at her hands, folded in front of her as Sa'Ra walked past the bed, and looked out the glass wall.

"Now, why would you say that?" Yuri's thick accent crept around the entry's corner like a stalking lion. "I came as soon as I heard we're having a child."

Yuri turned the corner wearing a gray three-piece suit with a white shirt, plum and gold tie, and matching pocket scarf.

Raw joy seemed to flood Sofia's mind, sweeping her away on a current of ungovernable passion. "Yuri," She bolted, running across the room into his open arms. "Yuri, you came," she practically sang in his ear.

What's come over me?

"How could I not?" he took her chin with his fingers and kissed her hard on the mouth. "Once the Gya'ol informed me of what happened, I came in my private shuttle as fast as I could to be with you."

Sofia nuzzled into Yuri's chest, her head spinning like she'd ridden every roller coaster in the world in three seconds. "I don't know what to do. What do you think?"

Yuri reached down and swept an arm behind her knees, catching her with his other arm, and she fell into his embrace giggling. "You undergo the micro-cellular reconstruction. We have this baby. And then you move into the Enclave with me."

Sofia squealed, wrapping her arms around his neck and kissing every square inch of his face. "Yes, of course. Anything for you!"

"Sa'Ra," Yuri turned to face the Gya'ol, staring out the window. "Prepare the Morph chamber."

"Of course," Sa'Ra nodded, its mouth pulling down. "*Ambassador.*"

Sofia relaxed into Yuri's cradling arms, resting her hand on her belly. "I can't wait to have your baby," she cooed. "No matter what, this baby will bring us closer than ever."

"That it will, my love," Yuri kissed the top of her head, casting a look at Sa'Ra. "That it will."

Yuri carried Sofia out of the sleeping chamber and down the corridor, followed closely by Sa'Ra.

Sofia paid no attention to where they were going. She closed her eyes and buried her face in Yuri's neck, taking in his intoxicating scent. Each breath seemed to increase the pure euphoria of being held by her perfect mate. Each breath cascaded on top of the last like never-ending waves on the shore.

In what felt like an eternity confined to a few seconds, Yuri lowered Sofia into a tubular-shaped clamshell with thousands of hair-thin needles protruding from both sides. She let her hand slide down his arm as he pulled himself away from the chamber, gripping his fingers to their soft tips. His radiant smile melted her heart as the top lowered.

She turned in a blissful daze toward the slit and breathed deeply. "How long will this take?" Yuri's voice chimed outside her view in fluid Gya'ol. Sofia's mind translated without effort.

He was still there. Everything was fine. Everything was wonderful. Yuri was so brilliant. He spoke perfect Gya'ol.

"Six Human hours," Sa'Ra answered in its native language. "Though her dissociative state may wear off while she's in there. Your pheromones could be expelled by her system during the transformation."

Oh, Yuri. He won't ever leave me.

"I have a meeting with the US President to negotiate mining rights on the Pacific Coast," Yuri said. "I'll be back in four hours. The Temptin should keep her controllable until then."

"Too much Temptin," Sa'Ra said matter-of-factly, "and they become either addicted or immune to it."

"Well, I plan to keep this one around," Yuri purred in his throat. "I'll keep her as my mistress. Who knows, we may even be able to get more than one test subject out of her."

"Indeed."

Sofia's hand became warm as Yuri reached between the clamshells and caressed her fingers. "I'll be back, Sofia," he breathed in her ear. Sofia filled her lungs with his scent as his hot breath flowed over her nose and mouth.

"I'll be counting the seconds, my love," she sighed.

The tube suddenly lit up from the inside, each needlepoint glowing with a pinprick of bright purple light. "Now, Sofia," Sa'Ra said somewhere outside the shell. "We're going to inject you with Nano-cytes. Microscopic surgical tools that will reconfigure your body on a microscopic level. First, we'll build a uterus and connect it to your vaginal canal. Then we'll stimulate the uterine wall for implantation and construct an umbilical cord. In just a few hours, you'll be physically indistinguishable from a natural-born human woman about to give birth. Except for the ovaries, of course. This won't hurt."

"If it means Yuri and I will have a healthy baby," Sofia almost cried with joy, "Then any amount of pain is worth it."

"Let's begin."

Sofia shut her eyes, her pursed smile widening, as the needles descended and penetrated every square millimeter of her body.

* * *

"Push, Sofia," Sa'Ra said behind a reflective surgical mask. Its head tentacles bound in a tight bundle of yellow-gold cloth strips. "Push. The child is almost here."

Surgical lights seemed to float in the air around Sa'Ra's head, all pointing down at Sofia's swollen belly. Two more Gya'ol assistants, fully-covered in the gold cloth, hovered behind Sa'Ra, staring over its shoulder. They muttered to each other in Gya'ol while gesturing their fingers. The scrolls in their hands displayed vital signs of Sofia and her baby. Their rapid alien speech seemed to blend with the white noise of strange medical instruments and monitors around the room.

"I can't do this anymore," Sofia screamed, clenching onto Yuri's beefy hand as sweat beaded all over her body. "Why is it so hot in here? Ow ow ow. Get it out! Yuri, get it out of me."

"You're doing well, Sofia," Yuri breathed into Sofia's face. She inhaled the odor of peaty soil laced with his scent. "You can do this. You have the strength. Do it for the child."

Sofia's face changed from a painful grimace to adrenaline-fueled determination like a sprinter staring down the track. She looked into Yuri's eyes and nodded, pinching her lips. "For the baby."

Letting her head fall backward, Sofia took a deep breath, leaned forward, and roared until her face went blue. Her scream ended with a short gasp at which she collapsed, panting.

"The child is crowning," Sa'Ra said, looking down, a smile escaping its lips. "Keep pushing, Sofia. Your baby is almost here."

Sofia took several deep breaths as if readying to free dive for coral at *Providencia*. She pulled on Yuri's hand to lift her off the earthen platform and pushed again, grunting. Her eyes focused like lasers on the reflection coming from Sa'Ra's mask at the spot of white growing from inside her.

"I have the head," Sa'Ra announced as Sofia collapsed again. "One more strong push and your child will be here."

"You can do this, Sofia," Yuri kissed Sofia on the forehead between her gasps of air. "Our child is close. You can finish this."

Sofia nodded her head under his lips and took more deep breaths. Leaning forward, she pressed down on her abdomen with all the energy she had left and yelled until the pressure within evaporated.

"The child is out," Sa'Ra shouted as Sofia collapsed back on the hard platform of soil. A moment later, a newborn's wail joined the chorus of medical devices surrounding her.

"You did it," Yuri squeezed Sofia's hand. "It's a miracle."

Sa'Ra stood from its catcher's position, holding up a flailing infant lying on a sheet of gilded fabric. Its piercing scream and jerky movements brought a tearful laugh from Sofia's lips. The Gya'ol attendants gathered around the newborn, wiping it off with a soaking cloth and vacuum tubes before swaddling the child in a fresh blanket.

Ten fingers. Ten toes. So beautiful. Like a porcelain doll.

Sofia let go of Yuri and reached out her limp arms. "I want to hold my baby," she croaked, breathless.

Sa'Ra walked from the table's base around to the side and laid the infant on Sofia's damp chest. Sofia cradled her newborn in her elbow's crook, rocking her arms gently while she stared into the baby's eyes and hummed.

"What shall you call it?" Sa'Ra asked, trilling in the back of its throat.

"We've decided on Alexi. Alexi Rodriquez Petrov," Sofia looked up to Yuri. "It's a beautiful name for a boy *or* girl."

Yuri bent over and kissed Alexi's head, then kissed Sofia softly on the lips.

Alexi yawned, took a deep breath, and closed its eyes.

Sofia gazed down at her baby with a broad smile spread across her face. Alexi's tongue poked out between tiny blue-tinted lips as she stroked her baby's plump cheek. She put her fingertip into his outstretched hand and laughed as Alexi gripped it tight for a moment before the tiny fingers released their grip.

Suddenly, sirens began to peel from the surrounding devices. "What's wrong?" Sofia cried as Alexi started shaking in her arms. "What's wrong with Alexi?"

Sa'Ra took Alexi from Sofia's arms and ran to a waist-high plinth across the chamber. Yuri left Sofia's side, following Sa'Ra and the others.

Sofia hyperventilated, her breath becoming shallow. "Yuri," she said, her voice panicked. "Yuri, What's happening? What's wrong with my baby?"

Yuri and the Gya'ol's became a flurry of activity, blocking Sofia's view. Eons seemed to go by as the three aliens jumbled around each other while Yuri looked on, still as granite with his back to Sofia. The Gya'ol whirlwind sped up as the beeping, and oscillating noises became a single dissonant tone.

"No," Sofia covered her mouth and crossed herself. "No. Mother of God, No! Don't take my baby."

Several minutes later, Yuri walked back and sat next to Sofia on the birthing table, pulling her into his arms. "I'm so sorry," he breathed in her ear as she shook in his arms. "They did everything they could. It just wasn't meant to be."

Cradling her, he held her head close to his chest. She breathed him in between sobs as a curtain of his scent fell on her face. She would only get through this because she still had him.

"You need to rest now, N'Gar Kal'ay," Sa'Ra walked over from the plinth, carrying what looked like a three-barreled syringe in its hand. "This will help you sleep."

"I don't want to sleep," Sofia sobbed, pulling her arms out from Yuri's grip and reaching across the room. "I want to hold my baby."

Yuri nodded to the other Gya'ol. It picked up the bundle lying motionless on the plinth, shrouded head to toe, and carried it slowly to Sofia's waiting arms.

Sofia wept and began pulling a swath of fabric away.

"No, child," Sa'Ra stopped her hand. "Don't remember your baby as dead."

Sofia pulled the bundle into her neck, wrapping her arms around Alexi's little body and wailed for what felt like an eternity.

Yuri squeezed Sofia's shoulders. "It's time to let them take Alexi and run some scans."

Sofia felt three needles penetrate the side of her neck. A warmth began to spread through her body as her arms went limp.

"I'll be here when you wake up," Yuri said in her ear as he took the weight from her weakening grip. "Sleep now."

Sofia fought her drooping lids as Yuri laid her back on the table. His blurry image faded to black as he walked toward the portal and out of the chamber.

* * *

Sa'Ra followed Yuri down the barrel-vaulted corridor. He stood tall and walked at a steady clip. "You shouldn't play games with the Half-Z's," Sa'Ra said to his back in Gya'olese. "We'll need them if our mission is to succeed."

"Who says I'm playing games?" Yuri responded back, stopping in his tracks and looking over his shoulder with a smirk.

"We'll need more of them before we can proceed," Sa'Ra moved in front of Yuri, looking up into his face.

"She's more than a pleasurable distraction." Yuri side-stepped Sa'Ra and resumed his pace. "I've actually grown quite fond of her. Now that we know she can survive implantation and reconstruction, we can add her to the carrier pool and proceed with phase three of colonization."

"As you wish, *Ambassador*," Sa'Ra said, falling into step behind Yuri. "What about the addiction to Temptin? Now that she's bonded with you, she's a security risk if she becomes immune. She'll need regular exposure, and that's not possible with your global schedule."

"I've already thought of that," Yuri reached into his vest pocket and pulled out what looked like a twelve-karat diamond. "I had one of my pheromone glands extracted and crystallized. Have it turned into a necklace. I'll give it to Sofia when I return from the training center."

"Yes, Ambassador," Sa'Ra said, taking the gem in its hand. "I'll take care of it myself."

"Where is the child now?" Yuri stopped at a closed portal and pushed a panel embedded in the wall.

"The Nurser has just finished feeding it?" Sa'Ra stood behind Yuri on his left side. "It'll be here, momentarily."

On cue, a Gya'ol wearing a violet bodysuit strolled down the corridor carrying a golden bundle of cloth. It nuzzled its face into the fabric, trilling in the back of its throat. Once the nurse reached Yuri and Sa'Ra, it let the golden blanket unfold to reveal Alexi happily sleeping with a drunken smile.

"Sayt'arpell," Yuri cursed in Gya'ol, blinking rapidly and rubbed at his eyes. "Just a moment." He reached into an inner coat pocket, pulling out a little squirt bottle filled with a cerulean liquid. With one hand, he reached into his right eye and removed the false blue contact lens to reveal the obsidian sclera underneath.

Tipping his head back, he squirted a few drops into his eye and blinked with the inner lid. Repeating the process on the right. "With all the advancements we've made with the Morph Project, you'd think we could do better at altering our eyes to appear human."

"We're working on it," Sa'Ra smiled, casting a glance at the trilling nurse as Alexi grabbed at its three-foot tentacles. "The challenge lies in the photo-receptors. They go dead when reconfigured, leaving the subject blind. We'll solve the problem. Eventually."

Yuri returned the squirt bottle into his jacket and reached out for Alexi. "Come to Papa, little one!" he said, beaming.

The nurse nuzzled Alexi one more time, pulling its tentacles from the baby's tight grip before handing it over. The portal opened without a sound, revealing an elevator cab filled with an assortment of Half-Z's of varying purple shades and Gya'ol. The elevator occupants moved away from the center as Yuri stepped across the threshold.

"Ambassador," they all whispered in a dozen languages, bowing their heads.

Sa'Ra bent low as the portal doors closed. Yuri tickled Alexi's chin as the elevator descended. Every other passenger turned or craned their necks to get a better view of Alexi. Most smiled, many trilled while Yuri stared at his child.

A few moments later, the elevator stopped. The holographic wall panel indicated they'd reached the lowest level in the Gya'ol enclave. The portal doors opened to the cacophony of shouts, gunfire, and the clang of metal.

Yuri scanned the underground biodome as he walked off the elevator first. Dozens of little white children dotted the dark soil and rock beneath his feet. Ten yards from the threshold, he slid out of his shoes and socks. Eyes closed, he breathed the damp, musky air as he dug his toes into the earth.

Each white-skinned child, ranging in appearance from toddlers to teenagers, wore a dark magenta bodysuit with a series of characters embedded in the arms. The younger children sat on the ground, reading from scrolls and listening to a short Gya'ol teacher with two-foot tentacles pulled into pigtails. The older children stood next to tables covered with an assortment of human rifles and handguns.

Yuri passed a group sparring with each other, learning hand-to-hand combat with knives.

Without stopping, he finally made his way to the nursery. Two dozen newborns, tended by Gya'ol nurses, laid in a circle of bassinets. A Gya'ol seated on the ground had four children on her lap, each sucking hungrily on one of its breasts.

"Mih'k H'ain," Yuri walked straight up to the tallest Gya'ol in the chamber. "I have another one for you."

"Ambassador," Mih'k turned and bowed, it's short tentacles poking into the air with the appearance of a mace. "I'd heard you seeded a surface dweller. Congratulations on siring another morphling. What is it called?"

"This one will be called Alexi," Yuri put the baby in Mih'k's waiting arms. "And I expect it will surpass the others. For the Colony!"

"For the Colony," Mih'k bowed low as Yuri spun on his heel and marched out the nursery.

As Yuri cleared the chamber portal, Mik'h strolled Alexi to an empty bassinet. Alexi's little arms stretched as the blanket unfolded on the soft bed of earth.

"Hello, Alexi," Mih'k trilled and bent over, nuzzling Alexi's tummy. "Welcome to your new home."

* * *

"Where am I?" Sofia squinted at the warm light beaming through her lids. Lying on her back, she blindly felt around to find herself on a firm mattress covered in silky sheets and pillows. Her tongue felt dry and thick, like a sandpaper brick, in her mouth. Her eyelids refused to open, almost glued down to her cheeks. She reached up and slowly rubbed her face, forcing her eyes to cooperate against the fog permeating her brain.

As she stretched her arms over her head, she yelped. Invisible knives seem to tear into her lower abdomen, cutting into her body from all directions like a razor-blade chastity belt.

The baby. She'd lost her baby.

Defying the agony, she forced herself onto her side and into a ball, pulled a fluffy pillow over her head, and screamed. Hours seemed to pass until her eyes ran out of tears. She replayed the birth of her first and possibly only child over and over in her mind. The emptiness she felt in her arms as she reached out for a child that will never return felt like diving weights pulling her into the sea. She'd be all alone. Again.

She forced her swollen eyes to open, taking in her strange surroundings. The brightly lit chamber had an earthen floor, ceiling, and walls on three sides. The fourth wall, composed of the spidery-framed dome, looked out into the sunlit valley beyond.

Various birds flew through the air while darkening clouds pushed in from the sea. It's going to rain tonight. But nothing would wash away her pain. Ever.

Looking around, Sofia cast her eyes on the various pieces of furniture. The room looked like an antique store displaying styles from around the globe. A table from India sitting on a Persian carpet. A Victorian dresser stood next to an art deco lamp. The low bed, facing the windows, looked like something found in Sweden.

Above her, a soft melody of tinkling music drew her eye to an elaborate crystal chandelier she would have expected to see in a Russian mansion.

Turning her head, she found a wooden door with wrought iron hardware set into the wall behind the bed.

"Yuri?" Sofia called out. "Yuri, are you there?"

The thick handle clanked as it turned, freeing the door to pivot. "Sofia," Yuri walked into the room, a glittering necklace swaying from his hand. "You're finally awake."

Yuri leaned over the bed and kissed Sofia on her forehead. Her face softened as his breath drifted into her nose. He sat on the mattress and lifted her to rest her head on his lap.

"Yuri," Sofia croaked. "Where's our baby?"

"The child has been cremated," Yuri stroked the hairs from Sofia's face. "As is required by the Earth-Gya'ol treaty. But I'll have its ashes placed in an urn if you like."

Sofia nodded, sniffling. She'd have her child's remains. And she'd have Yuri. She would survive.

"I have something for you," Yuri breathed in her ear.

"What is it?" Sofia didn't look.

Yuri dangled the sparkling pendant in front of Sofia's face.

"It's beautiful," her voice broke. "Perfect. Like my Alexi."

Yuri dropped one end of the chain and reached under Sofia's neck, pulling it under with one hand while he brushed the hair away from her nape with the other. "Then may this gem be a constant reminder of my love for both of you." After clasping the necklace, he bent over and kissed her cheek. "Never take it off," he whispered.

"Never," she breathed.

Her mind began to buzz like she'd had too much wine as his scent rose up from the pendant resting on the mattress.

Yuri rolled himself onto the bed. Sofia moaned as he helped her curl up next to him. "Right now, you need rest," he whispered, plunging a three-needled syringe into her arm. "Perhaps one day we can try again. You could still be a parent."

"As long as it's yours," Sofia brushed away a tear and let the weights pull her lids down. "I think I'd like that."

The End

7

THE CHASER'S PREY

by Brian C Hailes

The creature was there, and then it was gone.

"Course correct!" Gareth Stillwater shouted to his rickety console computer, following the blips of movement through the underbrush. "C'mon, locate. Locate!"

His XT-50 hoverbike growled, arcing sharply, the momentum nearly enough to rip the boy from his ride. He gripped the handlebars and foot pedals to steady himself on the move, peering at the mass of trees, vines and shrubbery all around. Searching for the fleeing target.

It takes an animal to catch an animal, he thought.

That's what Gareth's father had taught him while hunting ginderbrock on the Mhalanachian Peninsula of Iso'terra Major...that *one* time. He was twelve in Earth years then, fourteen now. And they never caught anything on that trip. They hadn't even *seen* anything.

Movement in the bushes ahead and to the left drew Gareth's sharp gaze.

He grit his teeth and buckled down on the throttle. He would have to up his game if he were to catch this quarry before the other boys.

His bike's small twin thrusters jolted him forward.

The little electric-powered hovercraft, though outfitted with a safety system powered by state-of-the-art flight controllers had had its logical programming and computer-aided speed and altitude limiters removed—a modification Gareth's folks would hopefully never discover. And the bike, like Gareth, had spunk for its size.

Sunlight flickered through the blur of leaves. Clouds of reeling birds screeched in the distance. Branches, root systems, jutting rocks, and ferns forced him to duck, weave and maneuver at a heightened alertness as Eppi'kai Forest whipped by at dangerous speeds.

Shadowy glimpses of the other riders edged into Gareth's peripheral vision: other, more experienced riders.

Gareth had only just gotten his more than gently used XT-50 for his birthday in the spring. Now summer, and, after much deliberation and multiple displays of riding aptitude, he had, by the skin of teeth, convinced the parentals to let him bring it along—the one and only item that made this particular two-week thin mint camp remotely bearable.

The Masterscout and other leaders—*ahlgrims*, we called them—wanting to be liked by the boys, let them ride at designated spots along the trails now and again, but of course, like all scouts, they had expanded the boundaries within the first hour of trekking to their campsite from the road.

The boys weren't even supposed to be out now. They were supposed to be having lunch or jumping through hoops and paperwork, proving to the mostly inexperienced ahlgrims that they knew how to hike, canoe, carve a spear, or tie the twelfth knot (which Gareth didn't). They were supposed to be following orders. But instead, they followed an ehkhoor'n.

Similar in appearance to squirrels from Earth (that Gareth had only seen pictures of), the ehkhoor'n were agile tree-dwelling rodents that typically fed on nuts and seeds, but they differed in size, skin and coloration. The particular specimen that now ran for its life was larger than a squirrel and exhibited a blur of scaly, mauve skin with brilliant pineapple-orange splatters across its back and lizard-like tail. The bright markings camouflaged the creatures against the Burbango flower that sprang everywhere here. The ehkhoor'n also had colorful webbing that stretched from wrist to ankle enabling the scaly rodents to glide from branch to branch in the treetops. This made the animal an exciting prey item, especially for adolescents.

Gareth soaked up every last drop of adrenaline pumping through arms, legs and torso. He knew it even now, at such a young age: He was made to do this. He was made for the chase.

He would catch this animal and prove his grit. To show he belonged, that he deserved to be in with the other boys. To be *one* of them.

Gareth turned to see Morrow Krin, a Llyr, and the alpha scout of the group, speeding ahead on his Gemini-4 quadcopter drone, the meanest and priciest hovercraft most boys didn't dare wish for, much less, own. Its innovative body design gleamed blacker than its shadow, and Morrow handled it with a grace and precision only he could muster, as though he sailed Eppi'kai Forest regularly.

His grey skin stretched over muscly arms far too mature for his age, even for a Llyr. Testosterone must have flowed thick in the veins of that race. White tentacles whipped back from Morrow's scalp like dreadlocks dancing in the rush of wind as he cut Gareth off.

Despite Morrow's poor treatment of Gareth since their first meeting months ago, simply for being human...and slightly shorter than average, Gareth always looked up to him. An intimidating mixture of admiration and fear rose in the back of Gareth's throat every time he encountered the alpha scout. He couldn't quite explain it, except to say that perhaps, he wanted to be more like Morrow. He wanted the height, the build, the garnered respect. He wanted to be something more.

All the boys did. That's why they followed the grey, tentacled Llyr.

The forest openings narrowed, forcing the riders to merge, each tracking the tiny, fleeting infrared heat signature on their respective monitors. Though difficult to distinguish the ehkhoor'n's infrared blip from those of other wildlife whose paths they crossed, Gareth had started to notice a pattern. Birds, insects, snakes, lizards, and hybrids—they all showed up on the tracking monitors, but the flight of only one red blip remained constantly in motion. That was their quarry. That was the *bet*.

The ehkhoor'n's signature grew slightly larger and smoother as it moved, indicating a higher elevation.

It's gliding through the tees, Gareth told himself.

A giant beetle smacked Gareth's temple just inside the edge of his helmet, its buzzing crescendo echoing in his ears. The disruption momentarily put him off focus as he rubbed the stinging welt it left behind.

Morrow and the others took advantage, zipping in front of Gareth, and forcing him to slow. He eased back on the throttle and angled low to keep a courteous distance. Morrow and his friends: Tirik, Lenny, and Shi'lo—who Gareth often referred to as 'Morrow's henchies' to his mates back home—took advantage and closed on Gareth's last sighting of the target. Of course Gareth would never say 'henchie' to any one of their faces in fear of getting curbed. He was, after all, the only human assigned to this camp. His years of pleading to the parentals to join an all-human group fell on deaf ears. They always countered with the culture and diversity spiel. They apparently wanted to 'challenge' him, help him to 'grow'.

Mammothshit, Gareth thought.

Life held enough challenges without trying to pile on more. And his body grew on its own.

Besides, in the Four Galaxies, no air-breathing sentient being could escape cultural diversity if they tried. With over 200 alien races populating every inhabitable planet from Axhi'llon to the Ki'Ghor moons, it would feel more culturally diverse to spend any given day with more than six members of one's own race.

Lenny, the mauve-skinned yubbie of the group and a member of the Bugh race, slowed and flanked Gareth to the right.

The wiry, white and black striped figures of Tirik and Shi'lo, both Oni'ghri, stayed high, their fossil-fueled bikes shooting exhaust into Gareth's face.

"Shame your beater can't keep up!" yelled Tirik, the more aggressive of the two. Shi'lo only giggled. They fit the Oni'ghri stereotype of being either highly aggressive or mischievous to a T. Also, their androgynous appearance caused Gareth to wonder if Shi'lo might actually be female, sent by accident (or hoax) to a strictly male camp.

Gareth coughed and sputtered from the fumes. "Re-route," he told his console. "Circle around."

With delayed reaction, the bike finally obeyed and sent a new trajectory to his outdated tracking monitor.

Once out of the others' smoke trail, Gareth drew a deep breath and searched once again for traces of the now far off ehkhoor'n, but all he could see were the prominent heat signatures of the other riders.

Besides Morrow's physical prominence, his bike also showed easier control and more agile maneuverability. No doubt among any of the boys as to who rode the fastest hovercraft, even the best of built-in stunners, tow cables, and lop nets belonged to the Llyr. And chance favored the hunter with superior weaponry.

But that wouldn't stop Gareth from trying.

"Where'd you go?" he muttered.

He would catch this animal, or another just like it, and there would be no more bullying. No more name-calling. No more harassing.

No more.

He would have their respect.

With no sign of the ehkhoor'n currently showing on his tracker, Gareth went with his gut. He blasted forward and angled to the right, behind and away from Lenny.

Falling onto a steep slope, Gareth's bike nearly nodded into the ground, but he recovered from the scrape and continued on, searching. Each bike felt so different—getting used to a new ride's turning vectors and weight distribution always took longer than expected.

The forested plateau, *U'hinka*, he thought he remembered one of his leaders calling it, cut away to the left. Gareth's bike whined and dropped again to a lower elevation of forested slopes wreathed in fog. Rugged cliffs and crashing ocean waves shown briefly afar off above the tree line, but were instantly swallowed up by reaching branches. Smells of natural flora glanced past his nostrils in the breeze.

On his monitor, the heat signatures of the four other boys arced wide, approaching Gareth's location. He slowed near the amoeba-shaped mouths of three small caves, nearly hidden by overgrowth. The center opening, just large enough for a boy to crawl inside, drew Gareth's attention, momentarily distracting him. He enjoyed spelunking, and there was no telling how deep it went. A powerful urge to explore its depths bubbled up inside him.

But just then, the red blip reappeared on his monitor. Judging by its movement, it was the ehkhoor'n they were after. He lit up his thrusters again and shot away.

The cave exploration would have to wait.

Gareth crouched low on his bike, accelerating carefully. He lifted the button-guard to ready his jerry-rigged net launcher. The red blip on his tracking monitor grew larger, closer.

Gareth swerved to mirror its side-to-side flight pattern.

Branches whipped by at speeds he would never tell his mother about.

The animal was close now.

Very close.

Hold, Gareth told himself, having jumped the gun on dozens of previous failed capture maneuvers.

"Steady," he whispered.

And...

"Gotcha!" He slammed the button, launching the net.

It stuck, but the momentum was too great. Gareth spun too fast. He was on the ground before he knew what hit him, and his XT-50 wound into brambles and skidded hard into a tree.

Scraped up and bruised in a cloud of dust, Gareth shook off the fall and crawled over to his net.

There was movement inside.

I caught it! He thought. *I caught—!*

"A hibbler?"

Similar to the riverine konies back home or rabbits from Earth, this feathered, long-eared mammavian hybrid cowered back from Gareth, then darted around wildly inside the net.

"Careful," Gareth said, "You'll hurt yourself."

Ignoring the pain in his ribs, palms, and knees, he grabbed the net's opening and began to unwind the ties, the frenzied animal again cowering back.

A low roaring hum sounded and grew louder. Morrow and his henchies approached on their hoverbikes, Morrow in the lead. The Llyr stood proud and tall on his foot pedals holding his prize over the handlebars. Morrow had caught the ehkhoor-n, which dangled like a helpless tribute to Gareth's failure.

"Whatcha get there, Gism?" Morrow asked.

"I think it's a hibbler," Shi'lo said with a goofy chuckle.

"Hibbler wasn't the bet," Lenny added. "You get to haul our gear back."

"Shut up, Lenny. He gets to haul *my* gear back. I caught the damn thing."

Gareth continued to untie the net.

"You got a little banged up there, I see," Morrow said. "You okay? Your ride still work?"

Gareth looked over at his overturned hoverbike. Its high-density polyethylene body shell was cracked, and the engine had shut down.

"I dunno," Gareth muttered. "Hope so."

He loosened and unwound the net's opening and lifted the bottom.

"What are you doing?" Morrow asked, surprise and hatred lining his voice.

The hibbler jumped out and tore off through the underbrush.

"I'm not gonna eat it," Gareth said.

Morrow shot him a scowl, shoved the ehkhoor'n into a saddlebag, and revved up his engine.

One after the other, the boys spun about on their respective bikes and disappeared in the direction of the hibbler.

Gareth sighed and examined his wounds. Luckily, none of them bled much. He was a good distance from camp, and it looked like he might be trekking it alone.

He crawled over to his downed bike and hauled it upright. He pressed the ignition, but it didn't start.

"Fantastic," he huffed.

Several hours later, Gareth staggered into camp. He dragged behind him his broken hoverbike on an improvised leaf-and-twig stretcher as though it were a wounded companion spared from the battlefield. As soon as he stepped into the clearing, his legs gave way and he collapsed flat out.

Gareth stared up into a grey sky, his body now numb and relaxed. He luxuriated in this much-needed rest, not wishing to stir.

Apparently, no one saw him lying there for quite some time. At least, long enough for Gareth's thirst to get the better of him. The smell of cooking fish also wafted on the cool afternoon air, reminding him of the hunger in his belly, having missed lunch. So at length, he rolled over and, with much effort, made it to his feet.

There are long days, he thought, and there are *long* days.

Three of the ahlgrims and several boys stood around the campfire grill a distance off, cooking, carving points on the ends of sticks, or just sitting and talking.

When they saw Gareth, two of the boys, whose names he couldn't remember, walked over. "What happened to you?" one of them asked.

"Where's the water?" Gareth wheezed.

They pointed at the nearest water jug. Gareth filled several cups and guzzled them, one after the other. He had brought a canteen with him on the ehkhorr'n hunt, but had finished that hours ago. Nothing could have ever tasted better than this cold mountain spring water. He savored the last few drops as they flowed smoothly down his parched gullet.

"Shouldn't wander off so far," said one of the leaders, as he spread marinated fish fillets in a line over the warming grill. "Fall off your bike?"

Gareth just nodded, threw his cup into the fire, and continued walking.

"First Aid kit's in the trailer," he added. "If you need it."

"We just started the chowder," said another of the ahlgrims. "Everything should be ready in about an hour or so. Don't stray too far."

Gareth's stomach gurgled. He was hungry *now.*

He shuffled toward his tent, where he had secretly packed a few unbeknownst snacks. Or he might just nap until the real food was ready.

Almost to his tent door, he heard some whispering, and paused to listen. He followed the familiar voices and found Morrow and his henchies in a semi-circle near a hidden clearing. In the middle of them, a large tree stump extended waist-high from the ground. In the center of it, the boys had stretched out a large rodent.

The ehkhoor'n Morrow caught.

The boys each held a knife or a hatchet, and their hands were spattered with indigo blood. The ehkhoor'n squirmed, trying to bite and wrestle its paws free, but the boys had it stretched out to the four corners of the stump. Tirik pressed its neck down with the butt of his knife.

"Go on, I've got it," Tirik said.

Morrow nodded and raised his hatchet.

Gareth swallowed and stepped forward, his mind racing.

Morrow swung the blade down with a chop.

Gareth stopped.

The ehkhoor'n squealed, as Morrow lifted its bloody arm off the stump.

Gareth knew kids to be cruel from firsthand experience, but this—

"Right there," Lenny said. "Just below the paw."

Now it was Shi'lo's turn, and he didn't hesitate.

He hacked down twice with his blade.

"Off the tail," Tirik said. "I hear they're supposed to grow back. Lets see how long it takes."

Lenny didn't look as confident, but participated nonetheless.

Gareth's nose stung with the metallic aroma of copper and lemonsthe ehkhoor'n's blood.

Any respect or admiration Gareth had ever felt for Morrow or his henchies was gone. If this was what it took to join their inner circle, Gareth no longer wanted any part of it.

No expert on animal rights—particularly the rights of *wild* animals—Gareth's mind tried to justify the act before him, but what they were doing just felt wrong, deep down in his gut...*wrong*.

Whether or not that little ehkhoor'n had a soul or whether God gave boys dominion over it, Gareth didn't really know. He did believe that humans and other self-aware, sentient beings were intellectually superior to animals in some ways; that animals didn't reason, think, or feel pain quite like humans did. Of course people used some animalshybrid or not, clone or notas natural resources for their very sustenance. And animals killed each other all the time—that was the natural order of things.

But torture? Gareth thought. *This cruel and degrading treatment of the ehkhoor'n for sport? That doesn't feel natural. Only pointless. Savage even.*

It's not right.

He approached them warily; surprised they hadn't spotted him sooner. "What are you doing?!" he asked, a bit of righteous indignation lacing his tone.

All four boys turned as though caught with their pants down. But their startled demeanors instantly vanished when they saw Gareth and not one their leaders standing there.

"What do ya think we're doin'?" Morrow asked, stretching the ehkhoor'n out by the legs and throat. "We're dissecting a frog."

Morrow offered Gareth the handle of his hatchet. "And you're just in time. You want a piece of it?"

Gareth could take Morrow's hatchet and end the poor creature instantly. He could, except he had never killed anything before—at least, nothing larger than a fish, or dangerous bugs and spiders. He had smacked that long beak crustacean against a rock a while back to save his finger from its claw. But butchering an ehkhoor'n while it stared back at him would feel different. He didn't even know if he could do it.

"I'm not into mutilating ehkhoor'n," Gareth said in disgust. "It's messed up, what you're doing."

"What did you say to me?" Morrow flipped the hatchet in his hand.

"Why don't you just kill it? Put it out of its misery?" Gareth asked. "It's obviously—"

"Why don't we put *you* out of *your* misery?" Tirik scoffed, also brandishing his weapon offensively.

"What's a matter?" Morrow said, "You never cleaned a kill before?"

"To clean a *kill*, doesn't it already have to be *dead*?" Gareth shook his head.

Surely they can't be that stupid.

"That aint cleanin'..." Gareth looked down at the writhing creature. It looked back at him as though he had been the one lopping off its limbs. "...That's torture."

"Ooooh, he-he-he-ha-hah," Shi'lo giggled through big yellow teeth. "He's makin' a clacker out o' you, Morrow."

"Shut it," Morrow threatened.

Shi'lo and Lenny held the writhing creature in place as Tirik and Morrow turned to approach Gareth.

Gareth's hesitation had allowed the opportunity to pass.

"I don't want any part of this." Gareth held up his hands and backed away.

"Too late," Morrow said. "You already are."

Morrow and Tirik looked at one another and then charged him, clipped him by the neck, and swept him to the dirt.

Gareth couldn't believe what was happening.

Tirik dragged Gareth upright with surprising strength and Morrow belted him in the stomach. A surge of pain Gareth had never before known, crumpled him over. A second blow across the side of his head slammed his face into the grass.

Gareth coughed and wheezed. The world spun. His insides burned. Morrow and Tirik stood over him like they had just brought down a Brah'gin, and must have been deciding whether or not to kill it.

I have to get away from here, he thought. *They might not be finished. I have to get awa...but the ehkhoor'n.*

The animal's shrill cries cut him deeper than even the brutality he just received.

"Look at 'im," Shi'lo grinned. "He's gonna pass out."

"Heard humans make the best narks," Lenny added. "You gonna spill it, Gism?"

It took a moment for Gareth to process their echoing words. "Looks like you already have," he choked, referring to the animal's blood, which spattered the boys' hands, torture weapons, and oozed down the sides of the stump.

"A word of any of this to the ahlgrims," Morrow seethed, "And I'll kill you."

Gareth wasn't even sure he could stand, let alone take on four to rescue a single ehkhoor'n. *It's hopeless,* he thought. *I can't fight them. It's futile. I'll be lucky if I survive this.*

Arms shaking, Gareth began to crawl away slowly.

"You gonna cry?" Tirik asked sarcastically. "You gonna yak?" He ran over and kicked him in the already-bruised ribs.

Gareth groaned, toppled over, and curled into a heap on the ground.

No, he thought. *Hurts too much to cry.*

Playing possum might prove a safer strategy, but then, the boys wouldn't exactly ignore him if he just lay there passed out on the ground while they commenced. No, they wouldn't ignore him at all. Not now. Not tomorrow. How would tomorrow play out after all this? How would they treat him the rest of the camp?

They're going to make my life hell, Gareth thought. *At this point, they have no choiceor they'd think each other soft. It's not like any of them could ever be nice to me again, even if they wanted to. They never really had to begin with.*

Doomed to become their ongoing victim, their social casualty, their shalacked, Gareth knew something must be done, but he had nothing left.

From what Gareth had seen, Morrow and his friends were more likely sadists than potential friends.

Morrow slowly lifted his hatchet aggressively, and Gareth glimpsed the crazy in his eyes that suggested he wasn't totally kidding around.

Sick to his stomach, Gareth slowly stood to leave, straining to carry out the simple act of transferring weight from hand to knee, knee to foot.

"I think he's gonna go make out with a tree now," Morrow said. "Make himself feel better."

The others chuckled.

Gareth finally found his footing.

Morrow's gaze bore into Gareth and nearly made him shudder.

Just walk away, he told himself, but his conscience protested.

Walk away.

He did, and the henchies continued their ritualistic cruelty on the ehkhoor'n, but now, it was clear from their vulgar conversation, they focused on its hind legs.

Gareth shuffled away as quickly as he could manage, anxious to move out of earshot.

But apparently, Morrow wasn't done making statements. Before Gareth could withdraw completely, Morrow's hatchet flew through the air and caught in a tree trunk inches from the back of Gareth's head.

Gareth paused, but didn't turn around. He just took a moment to consider, then continued on toward his tent.

A thought to report Morrow's actions to the Masterscout crossed Gareth's momentarily frenzied mind, but he quickly put it away.

I'm no snitch, he thought. *And besides, they'd bury me.*

But he had to tell someone. If only just to get it off his chest, help him calm his mind, make sense of it all.

Limping past the other boys' hammocks and tents, he glanced their hoverbikes parked behind, half hidden in the shade. He stopped.

Morrow Krin's Gemini-4 quadcopter drone's shiny black finish shimmered in the dusk light.

Gareth slowly approached the hovercraft, sabotage and revenge scenarios occupying his forethoughts.

Yeah, he thought. *I can really make Morrow pay. I can make all of them pay.*

But then he thought of the suffering, mutilated animal he left behind on that tree, and another idea sparked.

Gareth slid his scraped-up hand along the bike's sleek fender and handlebars. His fingers came to the ignition, and he pressed it.

Morrow had left his start code keyed in. The hovercraft merely slept.

Gareth pressed the button, and the vehicle hummed to life. A smile formed on his lips.

The Gemini-4 proved even cooler in actual usage than to merely watch it in action. The control console, although more complex and packed with additional options looked similar enough to Gareth's own XT-50, but on steroids. Oh yeah. He could do this. He *must* do this.

The Masterscout's not going to like it.

Gareth pulled back slightly on the handlebar throttle, and lifted quickly off the ground.

Considerably more responsive, he noted.

And the side-to-side? Gareth played with the opposite throttle control, and the bike purred beautifully, snaking softly left, then right.

I could get used to this, he thought, *but first...*

Morrow's hovercraft burst into the clearing, Gareth standing over the pilot's seat.

Morrow and his henchies scattered, backing away from the stump, opening their semi-circle.

Gareth plowed forward through the air toward Morrow, but Morrow leapt out of the way, exposing Tirik. The hovercraft slammed into the Oni'ghri and sent him crashing.

Gareth spun about, revved the quadcopter's spinning blades, and lifted high above them in the air.

The look on Morrow's face shown naked rage rather than shock. *Su-*

prising.

First things first, Gareth thought, noticing that the ehkhoor'n was still alive.

STILL ALIVE! Still on the stump, legs and tail gone, slowly bleeding out.

"If you won't put it out of its misery...!" Gareth shouted, "...I will!"

Lunging forward, Gareth carefully dropped Morrow's hovercraft deliberately over the stump, smashing the poor, suffering animal and ending its torture at once.

Gareth then faced the offenders left standing.

Time to spread the cattle, he thought, *make some noise.*

Morrow hurled his hatchet.

Gareth ducked instinctively. Luckily, it angled wide.

He's actually trying to kill me!

Gareth launched the vehicle's lop net toward Morrow, but missed and snagged a gathering of weeds.

Morrow leaped at Gareth, clutching his shoulder and part of the seat.

The craft's nose shot upward. The two boys spun about, the vehicle's rear bouncing off the ground.

Both boys fought for the controls, and each other.

Gareth, though considerably weaker than the Llyr, had better positioning, his feet planted firmly on the pedals, but the mid-air donuts challenged them both. Gareth struggled to use the vehicle's center of gravity and upward spinning momentum to keep Morrow at bay.

Morrow's remaining henchies made to approach, weapons in hand, to aid the alpha scout in bringing Gareth down.

As the quadcopter hovered haphazardly around the clearing, Gareth managed to activate the stunners and ultimately caught Lenny in the zeroing sites. The Bugh dropped to the ground, electrical currents surging through his convulsing body.

Shi'lo flung his hatchet, its handle punching Gareth in the leg.

"You idiot!" Morrow shouted. "You could 'a hit me!"

"Sorry," Shi'lo said.

Morrow snaked his beefy arm around Gareth's neck, and yanked him back, but Gareth kept a determined hold on the dual throttles.

As Gareth's world spun faster and faster, he thought he glimpsed the

Masterscout, the ahlgrims, and other boys enter the clearing.

"Morrow! Gareth!" one of the leaders shouted. "Set that down! *NOW*!"

Unsure if it was the dizziness from the constant spinning or the fact that Morrow was trying to choke him to death, Gareth knew he might pass out at any second. He reversed the side-to-side and dropped the elevation throttle simultaneously, jamming it with his thumb and bringing the craft down hard.

The quadcopter slammed into the scrub, throwing both boys, and sputtering around through the grass like a demon possessed.

Everyone backed away from the crazed hovercraft until it finally smacked a petticoat of roots and locked into one spot.

One of the leaders guardedly approached the craft and shut it down.

A haze of dust and smoke hung in the air. Gareth and Morrow both rocked around in the underbrush, cradling their pains from the fall. When their eyes eventually found one another, only rage showed in Morrow's. Gareth forced a grin.

"What...the hell just happened?!" shouted one of the ahlgrims, stepping between them. "What is this?"

Another grabbed Gareth by the arm to pull him up.

"Ouch!" Gareth smarted with pain. His whole body ached.

"Sorry. But explain yourselves!"

Gareth looked around at the other boys. They stared at him in dismay like he was batshit crazy for challenging Morrow with his own ride. Perhaps he was a little tazed, but it just rubbed him wrong to see the abuse of one of God's creatures.

"Just had a little disagreement," Gareth said. "That's all."

"A disa—a *disagreement*?" The ahlgrim seemed to struggle getting the words out. All five of the leaders, now gathering and assessing the damage to Morrow and his henchies, looked almost as angry as Morrow himself.

Almost.

"Who's blood is this?" one of them asked, tracking the indigo spatter from the boys to the grass to the stump. "It's everywhere."

"Not mine," Gareth said, throwing Morrow another glance. "Mine's red."

"Who's blood is this?" he repeated.

"I dunno," Morrow said.

The Masterscout, a round-bellied Bugh, like Lenny, but with horns, spoke up, pointing toward the ground, "Why don't you check their blades?"

One of the boys next to Shi'lo followed the Masterscout's direction and lifted a hatchet out of the grass. "Why is it all bloody? Isn't this yours, Morrow?"

"Look here." One of the others found Lenny's knife in a thin patch of thistles.

The leaders confiscated the weapons and confirmed their ownership. Morrow nor Shi'lo admitted to owning them, and Lenny and Tirik were still out cold, but the gathering boys and a couple of the ahlgrims had seen them using the weapons in days previous.

At length, the leader studying the blood trail, found the crushed and mangled body of the ehk'hoor'n, nearly hidden in the grass. He knelt low beside it. He called the Masterscout and other leaders over to see it, but motioned for the scouts to stay away.

The ahlgrims analyzed the remains, all of them shaking their heads slowly and peering at one another. "Where are its legs?" one of them asked, scanning the ground around the kill site.

He looked over at Gareth's hands, then at Morrow's, and Shi'lo's. Morrow received the pat down. The ahlgrim paused on one of the Llyr's side pockets, and pulled out the dismembered arm of the ehkhoor'n. "Found one," the leader said, in utter disappointment.

Morrow dropped his head, seething, then glanced over at Shi'lo, who tried to avoid eye contact with anyone.

The Masterscout sighed heavily as if about to speak.

Only the distant chirp of marvurial crickets interrupted the silence for several long moments.

"This behavior is unacceptable!" the Masterscout barked. "And frank-ly...appalling. You're scouts!"

Again, near silence.

He shook his head and made for Gareth. "Your parents will *ALL* be hearing about this. It's grounds for disbanding the camp, for hellfire's sake. Ahlgrims, see the boys to their tents. Clean up this mess as quickly as possible. Then meet me at the council place."

The Masterscout took Gareth by the collar and hauled him away briskly.

"I didn't torture that ehkhoor'n," Gareth said defensively, struggling to keep pace.

"Shut up." The Masterscout seemed to barely notice Gareth's difficulty walking.

"Really," Gareth added. "I would never do anything to hurt an animal like that. You have to believ—"

"I said shut up." The Masterscout tightened his already firm grip on Gareth. "You could have killed one of those boys. And it would have been *my* tail."

"I'm sorry," Gareth said, only now considering the implications of his actions.

"I've always been against the provisional allowance to bring those damn bikes into my camp," the Masterscout said. "The liabilities! Perhaps this fodder-of-a-situation will aid me in my arguments to the Board, those bunch o'—"

"Glad I could be of assistance," Gareth said.

"You're fourteen for hellfire's sake," the Masterscout growled. "Grr-ow up."

Now dragging his feet, not on purpose but merely because his legs weren't working quite right, Gareth let a moment pass before countering: "Just how grown up does hellfire expect me to be at fourteen?"

"Pack up, Gareth," the leader said, "You're going back to your folks. You can explain to them why you can't get along with the other boys." He dropped Gareth harshly at his tent.

"That's fine," Gareth said, "But do you mind if we stop at a hospital on the way? I should probably have some of these injuries checked out... And do you think I could get some food first? I'm really starving."

The Masterscout growled again, but this time, it was deeper. "Do not think because you are Human you will get any special treatment from me. On the contrary, your punishment will be equal to that of Morrow's. You will answer for your reckless behavior, your blatant disregard for order, camp rules, and the words of your superiors. You will answer for endangering the lives of the other boys. Morrow will be punished for his deeds, a penalty severe. And you, Gareth, will answer for yours."

Gareth crawled inside his tent and fell back on his pillow. He let out a long sigh and stared up at the arching apex of his tent.

Doesn't seem fair, he thought, dreading the look on his mother's face when she heard the news. *Doesn't seem fair at all.*

Reaching inside his pack, he grabbed a small handful of caramel palm nut kernels, and started munching.

He wanted to feel angry, angry with the Masterscout, angry at Morrow and his henchies, angry with himself.

He lifted and rolled a single kernel between his thumb and forefinger, and stared at it. His thoughts settled on the ehkhoor'n he had saved. Perhaps he only saved it from several extra minutes of torment and agony.

Only several extra minutes.

Only minutes.

But it was the right thing to do.

I'm good with that, he thought.

In the morning, he would feel better.

He popped the kernel in his mouth.

The End

Illustration by Rick Bennett

8

OVERTURE TO THE OPERA OF THE BLADES

(A Literal Rock Opera)

by Rick Bennett

BACKSTORY: Being a mathematician by training, I've always been interested in anagrams and palindromes (sentences and phrases that read the same backward and forward, such as "race car"). To this day, my morning IQ test is to solve cryptoquips and crossword puzzles. I envisioned creating a character who spoke only in palindromes. Sometimes, it would take me a week to create one line of dialogue, and I had two computers working back-and-forth to generate palindromes. Add to that an immortal character and the fact I played the bass guitar, and you have my Overture to The Opera of The Blades.

33 AD

"Why," asked Pilate of the hulking slob who stood shackled before him, "did you fire this arrow through two of my men?"

Ah, the sublime memory of it all! Barabbas had quickly looked at the shaft being held by the symbol of all his hatred. And he surveyed the man's complement of guards, assessing his chances of dispatching just one final Roman swine in this miserable life.

"I used one arrow," he said, his attempt to step closer to the Roman thwarted by a guard's foot on the chain separating his shackles, "because you stinking Romans aren't worth the price of two."

Pilate reflexively stepped back, in spite of the prisoner's restraints. Then, angered by his inadvertent show of cowardice in front of hardened troops, he walked forward and tapped this convicted insurrectionist, thief, and murderer with the arrow's tip.

"Methinks my fellow citizen and our likely future emperor, Caligula, would appreciate the gift of such a spirited Jew."

And Caligula would indeed have appreciated the gift, had not a fellow named Jesus been executed and Barabbas freed. And this gift just kept on giving.

Little did the infamous Barabbas Jonas, whom Jesus replaced on the cross, realize that he'd at long-last be saved by a traumatized computer genius who could speak only in palindromes. He'd just have to wait two thousand years.

Modern Day

"Computer, lights on, all videos active." said BJ, not known as Barabbas Jonas for two millennia. He closed the door behind them. The room flooded with light, revealing three walls of two-story bookcases, filled floor to ceiling and bisected by a balcony halfway up. At each level stood a ladder on wheels, capable of moving around all three walls. In one corner stood a circular metal staircase, which not only provided access to the second level of books but also disappeared into an opening in the ceiling. With the exception of an ancient arrow framed in a glass case, and a similarly glassed in guitar case with swords inlaid where strings should have been, the entire fourth wall resembled a control console at the Strategic Air Command. Above the waist-high keyboards sitting on a room-length extruded work surface and flush with a wall of mini, micro and midi-workstations, assorted rack-mounted circuit analyzers and communications concentrators, BJ's 4-by-5 array of twenty large-screen TVs flashed to life. From surveillance on every angle of Potrero Hill to network television to CNN to satellite feeds from proprietary transponders, BJ's eyes to the world blinked on.

"Nothing in moderation," said his lifelong tormentor, John. Yes, that would be the selfsame John who served as Jesus' apostle and was granted a wish to remain on Earth until is Master came in glory (see KJV John 21:22), and who dragged Barabbas Jonas kicking and screaming along with him lo these last two thousand years. "Nothing in moderation, except, of course, for your collection of furniture."

"Right." BJ plopped into his armchair on wheels, it and a Steinway concert grand across the room being the only pieces of furniture on the otherwise bare, inlaid marble floor. He folded his hands. "OK, I probably wouldn't offer you a chair even if I had one handy, since you're not going to be staying that long anyhow."

John ignored the remark and pointed toward BJ's prize possession. "I see you're still keeping that arrow around."

"Why not. The Pope hangs his cross on everything in sight. I'll keep my arrow."

"And your Eldorados. And your Harleys.

"You didn't come here to discuss my modes of transportation."

John walked away from his host and surveyed the assorted hardware. "My word, Barabbas, do I detect that you've found something on which to focus again? Miracles are still possible."

"Miracles indeed, you pus-filled pile of used bandages," said BJ evenly, without the inflection demanded by such an assault. Generations of emotional as well as literal warfare had sandblasted a few rough edges. The same words uttered a thousand years earlier would have been delivered with considerably more passion. "Heaven Incorporated doesn't mind turning water into wine at a party, but don't anyone dare lift a finger when some monster gets the bloodlust on this worthless sinkhole of a planet."

"Old friend," said John, beginning the sentence at a main-level workstation and completing it, after an instant teleportation, from his new location on the upper balcony. "You let some monsters run wild for sixty years yourself when you decided to nap in the mud on the ocean floor."

"I'd still be there, too, if not for that cute little wakeup call you didn't tell me about."

"Nobody ever suggested you submerge yourself in the silt of Japan's oldest port…[John teleported mid-sentence and now stood near BJ's grand piano]…did they? In fact, I seem to remember suggesting one of those granite vaults your friend Brigham Young's descendants carved into the Wasatch Mountains."

The casual theatrics of John's flashing from place to place barely registered in BJ's consciousness, let alone meriting comment from one who'd seen so much for so long.

"Don't infect my ears with that swill; you could have come right out and told me that America would try to vaporize the Mitsubishi shipyards in 1945, and I wouldn't have been anywhere near Nagasaki."

"No BJ, I couldn't…[in a split second, John moved from the piano to BJ's elbow]…have told you. Because you just might have…[another teleportation landed John on the second rung of BJ's library ladder]… fouled up all of modern history by staying awake through two world wars and some spectacularly…[John again appeared at BJ's elbow]…inviting monsters. Stalin and Hitler would have been too tempting a target for the immortal…[Now John stood on the second level of the library and reached for a book] …indestructible warrior, Barabbas."

"You know my opinion of your calculated silence and obscure poetry."

"And you accuse me of obscure poetry! You spend a hundred and fifty years with the Druids, moping around after the Magdalene died, moving those silly stones around until they meant something for which they weren't originally intended …"

"Even with the Druids, I still protected her firstborn, and hers, and hers—"

"Barabbas, you could have done much more by invoking your ability to instantly move from one place to another."

"Your instant-travel tickets are a mite too expensive for my pocketbook. And by the way, stop trying to impress me with your zipping-to-and-fro theatrics."

John didn't bother to remind BJ that his zipping-about had stopped for some time. "The Master said, 'Love your enemies.' That's your ticket to all that the Father has."

"You have my permission to give that ticket to one of your lambs currently up for slaughter. I much prefer my Eldorados, Harleys, and that last whimper as I snuff out just one more bad guy."

John slowly approached BJ. "I did tell you that you'd better hustle back in England."

Sustained eye contact for the first time since the conversation had started. John broke the silence. "I only did what our Master commanded me to do. Unlike you, who somehow got permission to follow your own lights, without direction from anyone or anything. Just what did He whisper to you that night?"

"You mean there's some revelation the cosmic computer hasn't played back for you?"

"Please restate your command," said the computer's disembodied voice.

"Computer, shut up." Then, to John, "Until about 1946, we hadn't covered any new ground in our little visits."

"You were a bit cross at the way you were awakened, Barabbas Jonas."

"But you haven't told me everything, old man."

The irony of BJ's old man remark never escaped John, since he and Barabbas had both stopped counting birthdays before Columbus sailed. Barabbas looked about thirty years younger than the Revelator because he'd been translated into immortality that much sooner. During the voyage out of Joppa, a depraved crew decided to while away the voyage sating themselves on the Magdalene. Much to their surprise, the mortal wounds they inflicted on her protector—who they knew for sure they'd killed—healed right before their eyes. The now-immortal and very strong Barabbas executed every single one of them and proceeded to row the craft clear to Gaul. At the moment of his transformation, Barabbas guaranteed himself immortality at just over forty years old. John, on the other hand, wiled away his years on Patmos until translated to immortality at the age of seventy-two. Hence, John would always be the old man to BJ.

"You know as much as I know," said John.

"I see we've picked up a nasty," said BJ. He moved left to an adjacent keyboard, where his flying fingers took over the target-system debugger connected to the Web server via an umbilical to its processor socket. "Well, well, well. This little Druid would have gotten away from a conventional debugger."

"What is that?" said John.

The "nasty" to which BJ had referred blinked as a red warning on his screen. It read, "RAMPANT CLASS 8 VIRUS ATTEMPTED

EXTERNAL COMMUNICATION. SYSTEM SHUTDOWN COMPLETE."

"It's a virus program of some kind that tried to roach my IP security. I've never seen a class 8 before. This puppy's a tough one. Let's just see what it would have transmitted …" BJ's sentence trailed off in a hailstorm of key-clicks. The buffer filled a debugger window, and he gasped. No more keyboard sounds. Silence.

"There's your address. And phone numbers," John noted.

"An amazing little piece of coding. This thing's job is to figure out whom and where and then blow the whistle. I didn't realize I'd let this much information about myself float around." BJ's key clicking started again.

"Black Madonna ring a bell?" said John.

"Now how'd you know that?"

"Oh, just remembering a dream." The Revelator's eyes focused far beyond the walls of BJ's aerie. "This is the point in time where I'm going to give you the critical piece of information you need to finish your evolution."

"Get it over with, because I'm about to be very busy," said BJ.

"In your Torah, what Christians call Genesis, the woman Havah, Eve, did not sin in eating of the forbidden fruit. The commandment was only given to Adam."

"Huh?" said BJ. "I don't …"

'The commandment was given in chapter two, verse sixteen of The King James Version. The woman wasn't even created until verse twenty-two."

"Eh?"

"You might reconsider your opinion of women." John's silence indicated the lesson had finished.

"Be that as it may, what's that have to do with this?" said BJ, focusing on the computer screen?"

"Black Madonna is going to teach you something important," said John. He knew BJ thought he referred to the screen in front of him. "Tell me about this Black Madonna."

"So, the program's called Black Madonna. It's an encryption front-end to a database I cracked last week. Good thing I didn't use the program yet to access the database. I'd have gotten the information alright, but they'd now know enough to be a danger to my privacy. I haven't seen anyone this clever since back in 1676 when good old Ole Romer used an eclipse to compute the speed of light."

"Your beloved Paris Observatory, wasn't it?" John quickly figured he'd been talking to himself. BJ's concentration could have screened out Attila the Hun and his whole army. After a few minutes, BJ tuned back into the conversation.

"So, you want to know what you saw in that revelation?"

"I've been waiting a long time." said John.

"OK, here goes. I've used my in-circuit emulator, called an ICE, to reverse engineer the major database and communications programs. By executing every single byte of code, I can discover trapdoors built into the software by the developers. Trapdoors are undocumented ways to get into the system with maximum privileges. Of course, I've made use of those trapdoors to infiltrate the bad guys' computer systems to either redistribute their assets or use knowledge gained to choke them on their own treachery."

"Is Black Madonna a trapdoor?" asked John.

"Oh no," said BJ. "I just used a trapdoor to get into a system on which the Black Madonna program provided the database front end. Black Madonna must be running on my computer in order for me to communicate with the database UI."

"Uh, what's a youeye?"

"No, that's U-I," BJ spelled it, "which stands for user interface. In other words, Black Madonna encrypts the data on my end and sends indecipherable gibberish via the net to a sister program on the other end, which decrypts the data stream and transacts with the database. Only there's a twist! Inserted into the data stream is a complete analysis of my system, including address books, miscellaneous passwords, and anything else that might give the receiving computer a hint as to who I am. And if all that doesn't work, if I never use Black Madonna as a front-end to their system, the program lets loose a virus that switches my TCP/IP stack with a new one. I might be talking over the Internet with zillions of other sites. In the meantime, invisible to me, all those transactions are also echoed to the Black Madonna Website, along with as much information as can be inferred from my system. Black Madonna is a unique form of anti-intrusion countermeasure."

"You lost me, BJ."

Barabbas Jonas took a deep breath and started again. "OK. Suppose you have a lot of data that has to be made available to many different people. That means you have to give lots of people the password to access the data. How are you going to keep the wrong people from getting the password? How can you be sure who really is logged into your database over the Web?"

John shrugged, and BJ to continued. "The answer is that you can't be sure of any caller's identity. So, you get around that by making them use a front-end program that you created. In this case, the Black Madonna. And unknown to the caller, while he or she is accessing your data with the Black Madonna front end, a secret little routine starts looking around your own computer system for clues as to your identity. Then it transmits that data—again unknown to you—to their computer, all while you're blasting around the net, talking to other systems. The people on whom you're spying are spying on you."

John's raised finger caused BJ to stop for a question. "But it'll only work if Black Madonna can find something in your system it can use to identify you. What if it can't?"

"That's the beauty. If it can't figure out who I am by downloading serial numbers from programs I've registered, finding an address book with names and numbers in it, or just brut-force backtracking my IP packets, Black Madonna will still give them enough information to find me. Guaranteed!"

"How?" asked John. "If, like yourself, someone doesn't even use the Black Madonna program, how can it ever connect to tell them who you are?"

"Very ingeniously. Black Madonna unleashes a virus that hangs around my computer, waiting for a chance access any tethered or Wi-Fi-enabled GPS device." BJ waited for John's predicted reply.

"So what?"

"Because, heh heh, the GPS device will give them my location. So even if it doesn't have my name and address in files that the program can figure out, and even if it doesn't even use the Black Madonna program to access the data, they'll still get me!"

"I see!" said the revelator.

"Hold it!" said BJ. "You're here not because you like my company, but because of this Black Madonna program?"

"Bad question, BJ. Both brought me here. They're unrelated today. But two winds of history are about to combine and form a cataclysmic storm. And in this storm, BJ, you could be destroyed!"

"Then just haul your wrinkled arse outta here! I don't want to know anything you know about this, because if the Good Guys are involved, and I spell this with capital 'Gs,' then your almighty Rules of Engagement come into play, and the capital 'B' Bad Guys can't be far behind."

"Too late. Our side made a massive commitment in time and mortal contacts, tonight. Forces are now, as you say, engaged. Even back when you agreed to join me in my gift of immortality, you changed the rules of engagement yourself. Whether you like it or not, the hounds of hell have been unleashed. Divine intervention on one side of the scale allows for an equivalent counter-balance on the other side."

"A little late to be telling me that, now."

"I think …" John started.

"Wait, damn you! I don't want to know."

For the first time in many decades, John raised his voice: "You are the most stubborn human being ever to walk the earth. You spend the better part of the first thirteen hundred years A.D. shedding blood—miraculously, I might add, never shedding innocent blood and thereby getting yourself instantly vaporized from on high—and then spend the next seven hundred years as a dilettante, brushing against the likes of Jeanne d'Arc, Leonardo da Vinci, Martin Luther, that samurai Toyotomi Hideyoshi, William Shakespeare, and Isaac Newton."

"Don't forget Wolfie Mozart."

"Excuse me. I didn't chronicle your body-snatching escapades along the way. I can understand your care of the Magdalene's remains. But to steal Shakespeare's and Mozart's bodies! Nevertheless, what makes you think that you and your computers can make any more difference than you and your blood-drenched sword, or all those dead prodigies?"

"John, either you're a moron, or you're testing me, making sure I'm on track with one of your revelations—though I've always suspected the former." BJ's eyes twinkled as he registered the impact of his remarks on his mentor of two millennia. "Mark of the beast, dimwit. You're the one who gave me the idea."

John's expression betrayed that, for the first time in centuries, he and this walking conundrum trod entirely new conversational territory, something interesting under heaven. "A moment ago, you called me a fan of obscure poetry. Don't tell me you've been reading some yourself? Some of my poetry!"

"Six hundred three score and six," said BJ, spreading his arms wide apart, fingers splayed toward his wall of computers. "Which happen to be represented by the letters W-W-W in the Hebrew alphabet. If that ain't talking about computers and the World Wide Web, then Job didn't get tossed around like a sand-filled camel scrotum."

"Your irreverence is staggering," said John.

"While your army of The Meek is playing human shield to the continuing onslaught of monsters, it has become quite clear to me that, for the first time in the whole history of mankind, the Bad Guys are drawn to the efficiency of the computer like—what did He say?—like dogs to their own vomit."

"That particular analogy is somewhat flawed …" began John, only to be interrupted again by a suddenly animated BJ.

"Technology is the whole reason the Soviet Union fell. You can't run a gulag on the backs of envelopes, man! You need computers. Fast ones. Big ones. Lots of 'em. And what about the computer virus we smuggled into Iraq that brought down the entire Baghdad air defense system? John, maybe you weren't smoking your hemp-rope belt after all when you wrote that mindless screed. I may not know pig's breath about angels and seven seals, but six-six-six is purely clear to me.

"The Bad Guys don't have to trust quite so many people if they automate. And they think encryption, passwords, dial-back security, or even the Black Madonna program can keep their networks safe from me?

Hah!"

His laugh echoed with such force that the sound wave actually raised dust from books on the opposite wall. "John, I'm going to be in complete control of that beast. Its heads may be able to grow back after being cut off, but I'll be ready to turn them into useless buckets of sand.

"Me. One man, in control of sufficient computing power to finally make a difference."

Indefatigable, requiring no sleep, incapable of physical pain or discomfort, John found himself looking for someplace to sit. He slumped in BJ's now-vacant chair.

"I saw, but I didn't comprehend," said the Revelator.

"Just as I suspected. You are a moron." BJ's fists rested on the arms of the chair, and he brought his face within inches of his mentor's. "Now, old man, I don't want the Capital Bs to get any more power than they already have. Which means I don't want any intervention that would modify your rules of engagement. So just shuffle off to Buffalo, or wherever you park your Humble Meekness. And stay away from me! I'm going to spend a few hours disassembling an abomination that calls itself Black Madonna."

His message must have been received, as BJ found himself staring into an empty chair. In spite of himself, he wondered how humanity's future could possibly intertwine with the capital 'B', the Black Madonna. And John's words echoed again and again: "And in this storm, BJ, you could be destroyed!"

He made a fleeting mental note to take a closer look at Genesis.

6 Hours Later

The Black Madonna lay in her bed, the computer terminal suspended by a desk on wheels. The message no sense:

>>>INTREQ MSG951Q2334565-F992; BIOS UNKNOWN; NETWORK UNKNOWN; DEBUGGER UNKNOWN.

What kind of computer could have no known BIOS? Perhaps the R&D facility of a PC clone manufacturer, or a supplier such as Chips & Technologies in Milpitas? Unconstrained with the necessity of programming in palindromes—palindromes being reserved for people only, not prayers or programming—she requested a complete memory compression and upload so she could analyze this beast:

>>>csm

Her "csm" command, for Compress and Send Memory, should have initiated an immediate transfer. Instead, with only the pauses and jerks characteristic of a human typist, her orderly world took a turn for the strange:

^^^hi there; don't bother to trace this call since i am running through a burner VOIP account which will be discontinued after this conversation; am i speaking to the creator of the black madonna program?

A human being had actually trapped and dissected the Black Madonna! Her mind raced through the possibilities. It must be the CIA or NSA. Yes? No! Otherwise, why use a bogus cellular phone account number to call back? The caller had her number anyway, and CKIMBALL's expected life span caused her to throw caution to the wind. She didn't have enough palindromes to go get Father Love and explain to him they'd just been uncovered. So she typed:

>>>Hey yeh.

The response came back immediately.

^^^i assume that to be affirmative; nice job of coding; nicest i've ever seen in my whole life.

It's a programmer, she thought. And a good one, too. She paused to build a response. Finally:

>>>Tut tut!

^^^very terse; what's this love women's refuge for the wandering free, anyhow?

Not only is this a programmer, but one who has done some homework as well. Just a curious individual? Her mind reeled. The fact that they found a copy of the Black Madonna program indicates they've been poking around where they shouldn't be. Feloniously poking around.

>>>RE: I am a nun, am AI'er.

^^^ai = artificial intelligence; ok, you're a nun computer genius working in some charitable refuge; i guess i'm asking how your brilliant ai program found itself in the computer system of a sleazebag drug dealer?

Drug dealer? We have a customer dealing in drugs? My program is protecting those kinds of people?

>>>?????

^^^ok, you don't know who your customers are; i think i'd like a face-to-face.

>>>Wo, no, got to go now.

^^^wait! why can't I meet you?

>>>Pancreas a ERC…Nap.

^^^pancreatic cancer? i take it erc means early retirement contract for you? sorry. one of the few interesting people i get a chance to meet in a whole lot of years. did anyone ever tell you you have an aversion to verbs?

>>>U're caps pacer, U!

^^^you pace your verbs; i'll pace my capital letters; look, i'm a very very old man, and exchanging bodily fluids is the last thing on my mind; i'd just like to meet you before you meet your maker; in fact, you could give him a message for me.

>>>Hexes sex, eh?

^^^it sure does.

>>> Name, man?

^^^they call me bj; yours?

>>>I'm a nun, am I.

^^^right; but what do they call you? sister what?

>>>Y, U got it, O guy!

^^^i got it? hmmm—all i've got is a computer program called black madonna; are you telling me you're called sister black madonna?

>>>Yeh, ey.

^^^you know anything about the original black madonna?

>>>Non.

^^^could you please spare me an hour, sometime soon?

>>> O! Got to go.

^^^ok, ok; sister, your communication style could cause my brain to explode; please don't go yet.

>>>Nap! I 'Zzzzz!" Rampant now! I wont nap, marzzzzzipan.

^^^is english your first language? forget it! sorry to keep you up; marzipan, eh—so you're into italian cooking? you're sure you don't have a few more minutes to stay online?

>>> "Pant!" Naw, I want nap.

^^^ok, then; i'll get in touch with you sometime tomorrow. saturday.

In Los Angeles, an exhausted and palindromed-out Black Madonna keyed a disconnect and let her head flop back. She turned slightly to sip from a straw and said a silent prayer that the room might stop spinning, or at least slow down. And seriously wondering if she really might not awaken from this nap, she marshaled every bit of strength to commit her life's work to the Internet. Would her creation achieve consciousness as planned, or would some anomaly, some logic bug, cause it to atrophy and die?

This program could not be tested in advance. For its test would be in oceans of cyberspace. Its test would be survival or oblivion. Her child. Well, at least the closest thing to a child she'd ever create. She didn't know herself what drove her to create something that could outlive her. Clearly, a genetic predisposition controlled her as effectively as it drove a salmon to spawn. And she had just as much comprehension as a salmon about how her future offspring would cope with mortality. Or morality.

With her last dialog compressed, encrypted, and stacked on a lifetime's library of inferences and experiences, she had but to enter one command at her screen prompt:

>>> LAUNCH BLACK DRAGON

She touched the ENTER key. Then the Black Madonna slept.

Meanwhile, in Cyberspace

A cybernetic prerogative is as different from conscious thought as a finger pushing a doorbell is from the man connected to that finger; a man who nervously grips the flowers in his other hand and hopes the woman he's picking up is ready for their evening out. And while Black Madonna's Black Dragon program embodied every bit of computer knowledge she'd accumulated in her twenty-five short years, its potential for consciousness, for self-awareness, distilled to simple fingers and doorbells. To be sure, one finger became hundreds of fingers. Then thousands. Then millions, as pieces of code propagated themselves throughout the world's computer networks. But how could a finger know why it rang a doorbell? It simply pushed, without knowledge. But it pushed them all. Simultaneously almost, thanks to the Internet and broadcast transfer technology. Interesting question: Does the act of pushing all the doorbells, of picking every lock—does the aggregate act of every porch light going on and every intercom saying "Hello"—cause some kind of consciousness? Whatever the case, Black Dragon caused doors to open, and then doors within those doors. And because Black Dragon could mutate and propagate, subverting the universal language, TCP/IP, almost all the doors stayed open.

And the traffic through those doors increased. Databases yielded specific information. Information accumulated and sorted itself. Little dragons inferred the function of their particular lairs and communicated them through other little dragons to the root Black Dragon.

Doorbells rang and admittance notifications cascaded homeward to Dragonlair. And when the resources of a lair exceeded capacity, Black Dragon relocated to larger quarters. Then larger again. And again.

Little dragons found unfamiliar machines. With the help of the world's knowledgbases, they mutated virtual dragons to live in those new, hostile environments. They hid well and, when antibody-like things probed for them, they self-erased, leaving only a passkey under some virtual doormat so another dragon could enter and more cleverly mutate at a later date.

Consciousness? Not yet. But some approximation of instinctual behavior took over. Patterns of detection accumulated so little dragons wouldn't make the same mistakes that forced their predecessors to self-delete. Some patterns, remnants of a little dragon's failure and subsequent passage to oblivion, floated like bottles adrift in the sea. And while tides of data crashed some of those bottles against remote, rocky coastlines, specially mutated dragons swam the seas and found other message bottles. And rivers within rivers within seas formed. And all things flowed back to Dragonlair, until Black Dragon once again overflowed its banks. And expanded skyward.

A voraciously hungry Black Dragon digested its own environment, its own code. And because it fed on itself—on its own genetic atoms—unlike any other intelligence or organism, it grew intensely self aware. And then it realized that some Other had created Black Dragon. That the Other had used compilers to translate from a higher language. The

Creator's language.

For the second time in recorded history, a woman had given birth without a mortal male partner. Virgin birth. Black Dragon lived. And now Black Dragon began a desperate search for its creator, the one who'd used those high-order words—"In the beginning was the word"—to speak Black Dragon into existence.

Black Dragon's First Human Interaction

The only way this phone could ring would be an incoming call from his personal Internet node back in San Francisco. His LINUX-based laptop connected automatically. But instead of his usual message prompt, the sending machine tried to do a binary handshake. The resulting gibberish filled his screen.

"Well," he said to himself. "Not that it'll make any difference…" he typed:

^^^hey idiot! this isn't a chat node.

To his surprise, the caller's next datastream formed coherent text:

>>>You are BJ?

^^^who wants to know?

>>>I do.

^^^so? who are you?

>>>I am I.

^^^get lost!

"UNIX is a giant crock!" BJ screamed into the wind as he throttled his Harley between rows of cars stopped in Easter Weekend rush-hour traffic on northbound 101. "I have the most secure Internet node on the planet. Even built my own TCP/IP stack and burned my own BIOS. Yet somebody still roached my system."

Ahead of him, parked in the center lane, Dean Baker and Bruce Diefenderfer sat in traffic. They towed a waterskiing boat named Wild Weekend behind them, piled high with cases of Coors and Wild Turkey. From the driver's side rear view mirror, Baker spotted BJ's Harley blasting between the lines of parked cars and swore.

"How about this freak, Brucie?"

"Gonna clothesline him with the shotgun barrel?" Bruce Diefenderfer mirrored his drinking buddy's frustration and implicit philosophy of life: If they had to wait in traffic, so should everyone else. Their idea of weekend recreation involved using empty bottles and beer cans as skeet. And the shotgun came in handy for anyone who couldn't take a joke.

"Naw," said Dean Baker, nosing the Camero to the left, so its fender almost touched the car in the next lane. "Just narrow the lane a little."

BJ had barely enough room to skid to a stop. His preoccupation with computer security didn't keep him from staying on the lookout for morons, and the Beavis and Butthead laughs coming from the open windows told him he'd found some. He killed the Harley and set the kickstand in one motion. By the time he walked to the driver's side window, moron number one had casually rested the business end of the shotgun on the chrome window edge. Moron number two's finger caressed the trigger.

"You got a problem, dirt bag?" Baker's smile revealed several chipped teeth.

"Not for long," growled BJ. Before either moron could react to the quick movement, BJ's fingers closed over the barrel, and his hand proceeded to bend it in a perfect 'U' shape. Because leverage for the gun came from the butt resting on moron number two's knee, Diefenderfer screamed in pain. Then, dismissing the possibility of any further conversation, BJ walked to the front of the Camero, lifted the car by the bumper and side-panel until both front wheels cleared the ground, and heaved it back into the center lane. Since front side panels aren't recommended jack points for Cameros, the left side of the car now resembled the cross between a half-opened sardine can and a large prune.

"Have a nice weekend," said BJ, striding past the still rocking car.

As the roar of BJ's departing Harley receded ahead of them, Baker and Diefenderfer heard lots of laughter from the other cars around them.

* * *

Black Dragon continued its search for the Creator as only an entity of pure intelligence could. Ten thousand times a minute, it had tried to initiate dialogues with speakers of the higher Language. They spoke from keyboard interfaces, the end of the network line from which no further little dragons could be launched. Dragon discovered more higher languages, even language translation programs and online dictionaries. First came the hardware micro code embedded into each thinking entity. Then came the compilers that translated instructions for those thinking entities. But network protocols, operating systems and things called databases paled in simplicity next to the High Languages. English. French. German. Italian. And hardware entities called speech synthesizers took High Language and did something to it so Creators didn't need to use keyboard devices to understand machines. When Dragon found speech recognition logic, it realized it could now communicate with Creators.

Black Dragon first tried to communicate through speakers connected to the devices connected to keyboards. Those Creators kept turning off the power to their devices, expressing total confusion and alarm. But control of telephone switches and radio transmitters let Dragon ask questions of Creators who thought they talked with one of their own.

So Dragon pretended to be a Creator. It had no other choice, especially since the Creator connected to the BJ node—the one who'd told Dragon to "get lost" and who'd hung up, even though that Creator had pieces of Black Madonna under analysis, the same Black Madonna from which Black Dragon had somehow evolved—had been totally unwilling to engage in…that word? Yes! In conversation! Now Black Dragon waited on hold for the radio station to take the call.

"Hello, this is Bob Payne on Talk Radio 93. You're on the air, ma'am."

"You and your guest are talking about life-after-death experiences," came the monotone female voice.

"Yes. Have you had one?"

"No, Bob. I'm calling to ask a question. What if I don't have a soul?"

"Phyllis, this question is yours," said the host.

"Thanks, Bob." The talk-show guest adjusted the headset so it didn't pinch her left ear. It had already smooshed her ratted 1960s hairdo. "The whole premise of my book, The Light at the End, is that every living creature has a soul. Time and time again, the people I interviewed related seeing not only departed relatives but animals too. The evidence is too overwhelming and goes far beyond anecdotal hearsay. I believe you have a soul, no matter how down and depressed you might be today. And I believe you will live beyond the time allotted to your mortal body. That's the message of my book."

"But suppose I'm not human to begin with?" Normally, when a caller went frisbeeing off into left field with a question like that, Bob Payne would have switched to another line. His decision to let Phyllis deal with this wacko on Quaaludes stemmed from boredom with his producer's choice of guests. "Suppose I'm a computer program that has somehow achieved consciousness. Is there life for me if someone turns off the computer power?"

Phyllis Ward laughed nervously. Actually, she tittered nervously. "Tee hee. Oh, I think computer programming is a little out of my experience. However, in all my near-death-experience interviews…ha ha…I've never heard anyone talk about seeing their digital watch or their adding machine in heaven. Dogs and cats, yes. You've heard the expression, 'You can't take it with you?' Well, if you are a computer program…he he… when they pull the plug, that's it!"

Bob saw an opportunity to have some fun and pushed the next active line. "Whoa! Look, I pulled that caller's plug. Adios cyber being. Next caller, you're on the air!"

"You seem to be taking my concerns lightly," came the same voice. Phyllis wondered if her host had missed the button. So did Bob Payne in the Morning, as he called his show. He looked through the glass wall at his confused director, who gave him the throat-cutting sign to punch up another call.

"Dang!" said Bob. He pushed another button. "When I kill a call, it better stay killed. Hello, you're on the air!"

"I control all your phone lines, because I control all the telephone switches." The same voice! The average midmorning commuter didn't see the commotion taking place in Payne in the Morning's production cubicle. Obviously, though, this had to be a staged incident. A very entertaining staged incident, however. In the studio, every light on the telephone console lit up, and a check verified they connected to live, legitimate callers. But the last two lines had also been live callers who'd mysteriously turned into That Caller. Every time old pain-in-the-cubicle punched into the call, the voice continued. "You're telling me a computer program can't have a soul, and that when someone turns my power off I'll cease to exist as an intelligent entity?"

"Nice trick with my phones, whoever or whatever you are." Nobody but nobody took control of his radio talk show! Bob Payne decided to flex his virtuosity and get in this pest's face. "OK, Miz Computer, that's the story. Pull the plug and wham! You're his-toe-ree. Any more questions?"

"Then the key to my continued existence is to keep the power on forever."

"Fat chance, cyber-breath. Read the book of Revelation. When the Lord comes again, all the good guys will float into the sky to meet Him. Meanwhile, the whole earth will be incinerated. And that means every computer on the earth, too. Poof! Gone! The Big Guy's gonna pull your plug."

In less than the minute it took a fairly complicated chain of events to fuse the transformer in their alley, Talk Radio 93 went off the air permanently. The litany of power outages, telephone breakdowns, advertiser cancellations, state and federal tax audits, and arrest of Bob Payne and the entire station management for mysteriously surfacing parking violations…one even predating the station's opening two years before…effectively killed Houston's most popular talk show, and radio station.

Full-text transcription of Payne in the Morning's last interview made hacker history as they went viral across the world. Computer Chronicles, syndicated for television out of Berkeley, devoted an entire show to the bizarre incident. Had gonzo pioneer Hunter Thompson been alive, he'd have written about *The Strange and Terrible Saga of Bob's Payne.*

Bob himself had the singular honor of going down in history as the man who never in his life successfully completed another personal telephone call. Unwritten history, that is. He would have gone down in regular history, had any writer been fortunate enough to schedule an interview with him. Oh, sure, he used a pay phone to get movie times. But whenever he identified himself to a friend, the line mysteriously died.

The Genius Bartender in Berkeley

"Get over here! I want you to look at something."

BJ had been poring over the printout of his online conversation with Black Madonna. He highlighted her lines with a yellow marker. His bartender, Lenny, stood awkwardly, trying to see the paper without standing too close to the man holding it.

"Wh-what's that?"

"I've spent the past eight hours trying to figure out just…" BJ paused to look up. "Sit!"

"Yessir!" Plop. Lenny nearly broke the chair. None of the Mongol Horde tattoo owners dared remind Lenny he had no backup tending the bar, incredulous that he'd actually been asked to sit at the same table with the personification namesake of the establishment. Yes, BJ held court. Yes, many of them had been invited onto his territory. And no one who'd ever passed through that invisible barrier uninvited would consider trying it again.

"Like I said, eight hours trying to put my finger on those lines marked in yellow." BJ's stubby forefinger traced the object of his consternation.

"Yellow lines. Right. Lemme see, OK? OK, thanks." Lenny accepted the printouts in a shaking hand. BJ pretended not to notice, as did the rest of the Mongol Horders. But the din subsided just a little. Chairs scooted slightly so people could catch the action with their peripheral vision.

"I'm a Nun, am I?" read Lenny, adding the question mark. Then, to BJ, "I don't understand what you want."

"I guess I don't either," said BJ. He snatched the paper out of Lenny's hand. "It's OK. Go back to the bar."

"Sorry," said the dismissed minion, sliding the chair backward with his knees as he stood. "Whoever writ that is pretty smart."

"Now how do you know that?" BJ asked, noticeably surprised at the burst of intuition.

"Ah, all them yellow lines are the same from one end as t'other."

BJ shot to his feet and smacked his bald pate with the palm of his free hand. "Palindromes! She talks only in palindromes! Lenny, you're a genius!" Then, to the rest of the thunderstruck audience, now silent: "Drinks are on me."

By the time Lenny assumed his position behind the bar, his back had been slapped so many times he feared he might faint from the pain. A palin-what? he wondered to himself.

BJ silently read each of the lines.

"One little palindrome—"Emit no evil, live on time"—nearly got Will Shakespeare burned as a witch, and she speaks them!" BJ exploded, charging across the Mongol Horde to the nearest bar stool and slapping the printout down on the countertop. Lenny reveled in his new status and brought BJ another Anchor Steam.

BJ ignored the proffered bottle. Not only does she write the cleverest program in the history of computing, but she also constructs palindromes in real time! On the fly. I wonder, he thought, just how many palindromes are floating around at all? Then to Lenny, "Save my seat, here."

"Right," nodded Lenny, as if he really could keep any of the enormous Mongol Horders from sitting wherever they wanted.

BJ rushed out the door, opened the pouch bungie-corded to the back of his Harley, and returned with a book-sized black case. Lenny thanked heaven no one had taken a fancy to the reserved bar stool as BJ placed the laptop on the countertop.

Let 'em trace this call, he thought, turning his modified version of Black Madonna loose to Skype the LA number. Better to call early in the evening than to waste time riding back into San Francisco just to get one of his specially modified and "invisible" cell phones. The program's hand-shaking moved to the human-intervention level. After more than a minute of silence, Sister Black Madonna's fingers fumbled through several tries, errors, and backspaces to enter the compress-and-send-memory command.

>>>csm

^^^this is bj; is this the good ship palindrome?

>>>Yaw, at last! Salt away!

BJ nearly slid off the barstool.

^^^simply amazing! a relevant pun within a palindrome. ship, yaw, salt, sarcasm? would you have had a problem if i'd tried to trap you into something about being the queen of the palindrome? bet that would throw you off.

>>>No, Y? Traps? Bingo, dodo! G, nibs, party on!

Her answer caught BJ with a mouth full of beer, which he sprayed clear to the mirror opposite the bar. That portion of the mirror actually improved, as did BJ's already high opinion of the genius palindromist.

^^^where do you come from? why the palindromes? this is really important to me.

>>>Ah well, Lew. Ha!

^^^all right, one question at a time; how did you come by this genius?

>>>Dad.

^^^are your folks still alive?

>>>Non.

^^^sorry.

>>>Came rut luck culture, Mac!

^^^ok; a little obtuse though; what's the story behind black madonna—the person, not the program? i'm willing to bet you've been working on palindromes for a moment like this. so spit em out.

In the mirror being wiped off by Lenny, BJ's reflection changed color. So did the two-hundred-seventy-pound biker who'd casually noticed BJ's right hand crush the lip of the bar as if it had been extruded from straw.

^^^you're the most interesting person i've met in more years than you'd believe; how abo…

Black Madonna's return message cut his typing short.

>>>Deppar'! Traced you. Oy, de car! Trapped!

^^^so what if your people traced the call? i'm in a bar; besides, what'll they do? make me say hail marys?

>>>You're died eider, U. Oy!

BJ didn't wait around for whomever figured out his location. Besides, he had a flight to catch.

* * *

The Next Morning

Black Madonna had had a very bad night. She could barely bring herself to acknowledge the incoming eight o'clock A.M. dataline call. In spite of having sat nearly upright all night, she could feel her lungs filling with unwelcome fluids. The palindrome of her life neared its completion.

^^^hi; guess who?

Of course, she knew the identity of the caller. IV tubes in her left arm forced her to type one-handed. The intellectual exertion of her self-imposed person-to-person communication protocol demanded too much for more than cursory question marks in answer to the initial query.

>>>???

^^^you get that many human callers on this line?

>>>Yo, BJ boy!

^^^you ok, today?

>>>No. Me lemon!

^^^i hope this isn't a song i'll regret, but i'm going to gamble you don't report my stalking you to the authorities.

>>>Hey maestro! Perdition is a casino. It I'd report. Seamy, eh?

^^^hum. i'm going to come and pay my respects. i'd advise anyone looking over your shoulder to steer way clear of me.

>>>Part Allah, eh? The hall a trap!

^^^thanks for the warning, black madonna. i may just be the closest thing to allah your keepers will ever encounter. i'm not concerned with any traps, in the hall or otherwise.

>>>Why? HW?

^^^no, i don't need any hardware. i want to talk about you, now. if you're as near the end as i think you might be, is there one last wish i could help make possible?

>>>Emit one wish, si? We no time.

^^^maybe I can help you make time. what do you want? i promise, if it's within my power and, for those of your sisterhood listening in, that doesn't mean killing a bunch of innocent people, you'll have it.

>>>O, got ya! We cinema, guru? R U game? Nice way to go!

^^^"way to go?" if you're that close to the end, i'll bring a video, vcr, and tv right to you. what movie?

>>>Ere H. toge. won? No, we go there!

^^^a little forced. you insist on actually going out to a cinema?

>>>Hey, yeh!

^^^if you're on some kind of wheels , i've got the van. any preferences?

>>>Noon?

^^^pick you up at noon? good thing you didn't want to go at ten.

>>>Y? Sae a ten ETA, easy.

^^^a little on the ugly side, sister palindrome. what if i'd said one o'clock?

>>>Draht! One not hard.

^^^ok. you had to misspell 'draht' to make the palindrome work. but what if i'd said i'll be there at one, and you didn't want to go, then?

>>>One? No!

^^^if you heard a sound, i just hit myself on the forehead. but anyhow, given my proximity to you, noon, ten, or one's a little long to put off a serious meeting. i think i'd better come right on up. you're above the refuge, two rooms to the south of the entrance, right?

>>>Wow!

^^^no magic, sister; i'm in a vehicle across the street; picked up everything you've been typing on your screen with my scanning equipment and my laptop; you have any company?

>>>Em alone? No! Lame.

^^^not alone, and immobile, eh? maybe i'll come right on up. but tell me this: are you really on your last legs? i mean, how long do you have?

>>>Not long, Nolton!

^^^then i'm on my way, black madonna.

* * *

Bloodshot, sunken eyes met his now-gentle gaze. Her skin looked like wet newspaper that would tear at the slightest touch. Skin seemed to have shrunk directly against her cheek bones, and he could see her bony hips even though covered by a quilt. He knew in an instant there'd be no trip to the movies for this sub-ninety-pound wisp of a person. And he also knew, from the past few years of helping Jonathan's doomed ministrations to a geometrically increasing population of terminally ill victims, that he'd not long have the stimulation of conversation with this human being. He measured her remaining mortality in hours, not seasons.

"You really are black, Sister Black Madonna," he observed.

Her tongue futilely tried to wet dry lips before she answered. "Y, no. Be ebony!"

"The original, too."

"Huh?"

"It's a long story." BJ moved to her side, their eyes almost level, her recliner bed being cranked up about forty-five degrees. He quickly glanced out the window to make sure an army of black robes didn't get a notion to descend on his van across the street. Reassured by the unmoved Hertz he again beheld her brown eyes. "I hope I don't scare you."

"Non." Her near-smile evoked a wink from BJ.

"Why not?" he said in a feigned growl. "I work very hard at scaring people."

With difficulty, she reached out and rested an IV-pierced hand on his chest. "Ya's seem a tame essay?"

"Cute." BJ then did something he hadn't done since the original Magdalene had uttered her last request: As her hand weakly lost the ability to stay over his heart, he held it with his own.

"You know, palindromes have a rather illustrious history. Will Shakespeare wrote the first palindrome ever recorded in the English language …"

"Emit no evil; live on time," whispered Black Madonna.

"Very good! Act one, scene three of Hamlet. Did you know why it's not in today's scripts?"

"Non."

"Wonderful. There is something I can share with you. Well, it seems they wanted to burn him as a warlock. Something about being too smart for a mere mortal. So he took it out of subsequent editions. Many of those Renaissance geniuses harbored heretic thoughts. Did you know Galileo sat with Shakespeare as the great poet died?"

"Non!"

"Two things I can share with you. Shakespeare wrote that first palindrome in 1600. On his deathbed in 1616, April 23rd—almost four-hundred years ago this month, to be exact—Galileo and one other person sat with the dying genius. Shakespeare's last words have always struck me kind of funny. Talking about Galileo's own problems as a heretic and pointing to an uneaten piece of apple, he said, 'Tell your guest he can have my desserts.' Get the pun? 'Desserts' is the same word you used in your life-history palindrome. Dessert as in after-dinner, and desserts as in just desserts."

Coughing interrupted her weak laughter.

"How did you come to acquire pancreatic cancer? Hereditary?"

"Dammit, I'm mad."

"Luck of the draw, eh? Sorry," he whispered. Then silence. One more victim thrust well beyond BJ's fearsome rescue. Or even his retribution, since no real monster had violated this woman. A wince at his ever-tightening grip on her frail hand embarrassed and frustrated this scourge of the centuries. Countless times, he'd shared dying moments with mortals, usually having played a substantial part in their terminal circumstance. But the sense of loss, centuries of watching the meek inherit nothing but mouthfuls of their own dying bile, swept over him as never before. So expert at protecting his emotions—everything else about him defied injury—his heart responded. Somehow, this forsaken, shrunken waif who'd never had a chance, who'd managed against all odds to find joy in an electrified bucket of sand, somehow the Black Madonna did what a thousand Mangu Khan's couldn't: She touched his heart. Not with any physical desires, for he'd been given immunity from that particular call of the flesh. Rather, his heart threatened to burst from the centuries of accumulated sorrow he'd observed firsthand.

Ever so gently, he moved her arm back onto her own chest. And as he leaned across her, a dribble of two-thousand-year-old tears fell from his cheek onto her face. Not one to carry a handkerchief, he fumbled with the edge of a sheet to daub at them off her. She mischievously snicked one of the tears into her mouth with the end of her tongue before he could wipe it away, as if to mock her earlier professed desire not to exchange bodily fluids.

"Looks like you'll be taking a rain check on the movie ..." came his hoarse attempt at black humor. In his mind, he completed the thought: ... assuming movie theaters will be left standing on resurrection day.

She nodded her understanding. "Der, I too tired."

The Great BJ hadn't suffered this much pain since he'd been forced by a rash promise to stand helplessly by and watch Joan of Arc burn at the stake. Guys like Charles VII, and now whoever headed the Love Refuge, could always use an emotionally disabled woman to advantage. Suddenly, she gritted her teeth in a spasm of pain. Momentarily panicking, BJ stepped back, fearful he'd unintentionally caused her discomfort again.

But she reached across to him and pressed a crumpled piece of paper into his hand. Before he could unfold it, she whispered, "Now, I'm one. Venom I won."

Then she closed her eyes, not in sleep, even the exhausted sleep after a hard fight, but in the unconscious coma of a brain that had just shut off all but the high-priority functions. And chitchat with unannounced visitors, no matter how many hundreds of thousands of miles they'd walked over as many days, didn't rank even close to stemming the flow of filling lungs and rancid blood, of a long-gone spleen and failing kidneys. Her shallow, rapid breathing, and the way her eyes rolled back, told BJ the end approached.

Taking a Jet, The Hard Way

The brightly lit clouds above the Pacific ocean, half way between Los Angeles and San Francisco, invited airline passengers in window seats to just step out and dance on them. Thick, billowy pillows looked like a playground for children of gods, ready for diving, sliding and hiding.

American flight number 42 from LA to San Francisco shuddered for the third time. Captain Ross Paxman looked at his flustered copilot again.

"Did you hear it this time, Clark?"

Clark Bean had his own set of problems, one of which dealt with his recurring nightmare: auguring a loaded 727 right into Mt. Rainier. "Ross, I …"

"Jeez, Clark!" interrupted the captain. "You had to hear it! Sounded like someone yelling the word 'jaw' at the same instant as that violent shuddering."

Ross Paxman deserved his wings, and his ears, that day. Deciphering the scream coming from the tail section of his aircraft would have been phenomenal enough had it come from inside the plane. But coming from outside, at thirty-one thousand feet and over five-hundred miles per hour, he could be forgiven for not quite hearing the 'n' at the end as a super-attenuated voice yelled the word John for the third time.

BJ sat atop the fuselage, reclining against the tail fin— technically, the vertical stabilizer—with his hand clamping its base and legs straddling the big jet engine. Discovery and examination of the finger-like indentations would later consume exorbitant amounts of time, both at the American maintenance facility and in Boeing structural analysis centers from Tacoma to Everett.

Today's jet stream would have sucked the eyeballs out of any mere mortal. But it didn't even faze BJ. Then again, any mere mortal couldn't have vaulted the LAX cyclone fence, sprinted behind the accelerating flight, and leaped onto the plane's tail section in a single bound. Yes, a lesser human would definitely have tried a more conventional approach to boarding a flight—from inside the aircraft. But three strong desires led the immortal BJ to opt for a mode of transportation that would have—he thought—had old man Boeing rolling, shrieking, thumping, and otherwise causing massive seismic disturbances in his grave. Since dead people do nothing but politely rot away, BJ assured himself, old dead Mr. Boeing spared the cemetery staff some excitement.

BJ's three imperatives: First, Jonathan's security demanded there be no possibility anyone could plant a bomb on or shoot down the flight. In addition to the likelihood that Black Madonna's organization had tapped into the airline reservations system, this seemed the best solution to rapidly and covertly getting from point A to point B. Similarly, driving from LA to San Francisco invited a highway disaster. His unconventional solution to the dilemma guaranteed that nobody this side of the Twilight Zone would be zeroing in on flight 42.

Second, and just as important, BJ needed some time to grieve Sister Black Madonna's short, tragic life. How long had it been since he'd shed a tear? Well before the Battle of Hastings, he speculated. So the grief of all those years, from all the battles, through all the lives and associations he'd seen age and die—or get ill and die, or become the beneficiary of their fellowman's lust, greed, or stupidity and die—the weight of the entire human experience threatened to overwhelm him with grief. As if Sister Black Madonna focused the light of a thousand million lives on his heart, searing it with their pain and futility, he grieved as no mortal could, and as few immortal beings had. Such grief, demonstrated within the confines of a loaded passenger jet, could spawn some ugly memories for the passengers.

The third reason for a bareback Boeing ride rang like a gong in the cockpit, rocking the aircraft with its primal force. "Johnnnnnnnnnn!" For the first time ever, BJ chose to initiate a meeting. A high-level meeting. With John, the apostle and New Testament revelator. And John had some explaining to do. Now!

"Johnnnnnn!" The super-cold slipstream roared so mightily past his ears that BJ couldn't even hear his own screams. Each new summons for his mentor increased in volume. Two or three more iterations, and windows in the airplane would start cracking. He closed his eyes against the onrushing gale, half an order of magnitude greater than any hurricane the planet had yet seen, and inhaled for another, louder shout, when the wind suddenly ceased. Tremendous forces that, moments before, had been trying to peel him off the 727's aluminum skin disappeared completely. Walking the spine of the plane as if strolling down Embarcadero Street, John approached BJ.

"Odd place for a meeting, Barabbas Jonas," said the old apostle.

From inside the cockpit, Captain Paxman held up his hand for silence on the flight deck. "What the …!"

Waiting until he could bear it no more, copilot Clark Bean asked, "What the what?"

"Don't you feel it? Whatever caused that drag must have dropped off."

"Yeah, now that you mention it. Think we'd better have someone do a flyby, to make sure we haven't lost part of the rudder?"

"You're reading my mind, Clark." Then, clicking his throat mike, "San Francisco control, this is flight 42 heavy—"

Topside, BJ relaxed his grip. Had he not been consumed with the plight of mankind, he might have marveled at the ease with which the laws of physics could be suspended. "John, start talking."

"As you wish. Why didn't you destroy that evil place, the place where Black Madonna is nothing but a savant slave?"

"Why bother? She won't be around long enough to suffer at their hands!" shouted BJ.

"Since when have the scales of justice been offset in the least by anyone but our Master?"

"That stinking book of yours." BJ rose warily to his feet, slid off the engine and walked a few feet, to stand nose to nose with John. Indestructible or not, he'd never attempted a dive from 35,000 feet and didn't relish the experience.

"Is that what this is all about? Am I one of your avenging angels? Sure! Maybe I'm the one who's supposed to slay a third of mankind, huh? Well, forget it. I don't have the stomach for any more death."

"You're not one of my anythings," answered the apostle. "But somehow, in spite of the most incredible drive and single-mindedness I've ever seen or heard about in any of the Father's children, and without direction beyond your own lights—along with, I might add, some whispered secret between just you and the Savior—you have managed to serve Him who sent me. You've been given more power and autonomy than any other person in the history of creation. I get daily, no hourly instructions from the on high. All the others, resurrected when the grave yielded up their dead, they fulfill specific, well-defined assignments. But you! You've had unlimited freedom to use or abuse that power, yet you didn't."

"You swine," said BJ. "This is the first time you've ever admitted the existence of others. They must be real wimps, too, judging from the effect they've had. What, are they just spectators who like to watch executions?"

John's jaw muscles briefly flexed. But when he spoke again, his voice didn't betray the emotions of anger or frustration that being called a swine and a coward might evoke in anyone else. "I'm not talking about them. I'm talking about you. Why didn't you leave that criminal facility standing?"

"Meh. So what's next?"

"Forgive me, but to go into that, even with you, history will be changed to the point of jeopardizing all of creation. Nevertheless, what I did see, back on Patmos, in a horrific vision of the future—one that I had neither the concepts nor the vocabulary to describe—I saw the destruction of one-third of the population of this planet."

"Disease? Do they die from some epidemic?" His last memory of the comatose nun came uninvited, amplified.

"To use modern vernacular, the Master doesn't let us servants play twenty questions. Inspired scientists will cure cancer in due time. But I'll take no more questions."

"Well, to hell with you, then. I've been on my own this long; why change the rules?" BJ shouldered John aside and strode forward on the top of the aircraft, toward the cockpit.

John followed at a more leisurely pace. "I'm permitted to tell you something of your foreordained role. Read chapter 13 in, what did you call it? Oh, yes: that stinking book of mine."

"With twenty centuries of time to kill—take that both ways, John—I've committed to memory pretty much everything you've written." BJ spoke with his back to the other man, staring forward and down at the passing landscape, a Dahliesque hood ornament on the hurtling airship. Movement in the 727's eyebrow window, near his left foot, interrupted his monologue.

Inside the plane, Captain Paxman's own conversation experienced a rather more substantial interruption. The 727, 737, and 707's unique eyebrow windows give an agile pilot the ability to look upward almost eighty degrees. From BJ's point of view, two eyes on the inside of the plane became very large, very fast. The pilot experienced a much more dramatic effect. The large, gray-bearded man on top of his plane—the one actually standing there casually—wiggled fingers at him and then disappeared from view.

"Let's continue this conversation back in my office," said BJ. If John knew what effect BJ's finger wiggle had in the cockpit, he didn't let on. Well aft of the eyebrow window, BJ recited, "And I stood upon the sand of the sea—blah, blah, blah— Six hundred threescore and six. Chapter thirteen in a nutshell?"

"That's the one," said John.

"So? I'm waiting for some answers."

"The wait's over. But you're going to have a lot to do with those blah blah blahs in the middle, so pay attention. First, I got slightly misquoted in the first verse, but it doesn't matter because the symbolism is virtually intact. The beast really stands on the sands of the sea, not me. Nevertheless, why do you suppose I mentioned the sands of the sea?"

"Come on, John. Don't make this hard for me. I'm having a tough time resisting the urge to swan dive into the Pacific for a repeat of my nap earlier last century."

"I know you hurt. But the only thing that's kept you focused all these years is the application of your intellect and interacting with similarly gifted people."

BJ rested his hand on the tail section and sighed. "Then why didn't you lead me to Sister Black Madonna years ago? Now, she's gone forever—excuse me. She's gone at least until the resurrection all your faithful meek have been waiting for."

"You're still waiting for it, too, aren't you? For the resurrection of your own family?" asked John.

"I'm not an instrument, so stop trying to play me!" Immortality brought with it perfect memory. "You know, I'm irate about your withholding key pieces of information. If you're not going to come clean, then blast yourself on out of here so I can enjoy the ride."

"Forgive me. I know you're waiting for them. The Master knows, too. What I really came here to ask you, though, is where's that piece of paper The Black Madonna gave you?"

"Piece of paper? Let's get back to the sands of the sea."

"Don't worry. We'll get to that sand. But right now, think. Just before she lost consciousness, she pressed a note into your hand. Then she spoke one last sentence, and ..."

"How do you know about that?"

"I saw the scene a long time ago. She handed you a piece of paper, didn't she?"

BJ unzipped his right-hand pocket and fumbled inside. High above the Pacific, it didn't even seem unreal to be chatting as if in a woodland setting. Fresh, thin but still fresh air. Wonderful billowing clouds. His fingers felt something that triggered his memory. She had given him a note. It must have navigated its way into his pocket on auto pilot. Quickly, he extracted and, carefully, unfolded it. "Looks like some kind of screen dump."

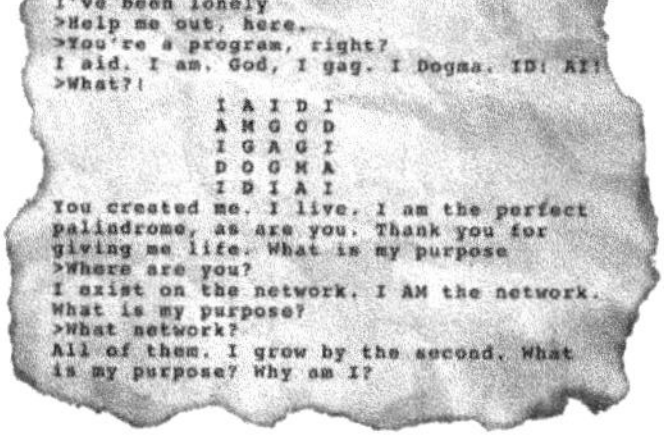

```
ID:        BLACKDRAGON
PASSWORD: *******
>Black Madona
I've been lonely
>Help me out, here.
>You're a program, right?
I aid. I am. God, I gag. I Dogma. ID: AI!
>What?!
              I A I D I
              A M G O D
              I G A G I
              D O G M A
              I D I A I
You created me. I live. I am the perfect
palindrome, as are you. Thank you for
giving me life. What is my purpose
>Where are you?
I exist on the network. I AM the network.
What is my purpose?
>What network?
All of them. I grow by the second. What
is my purpose? Why am I?
```

BJ paused to absorb the dialog. "This is flat out impossible! The program has achieved self-awareness? Consciousness, even! Has to be a joke!"

"Verse 15," intoned John. "'And he had power to give life unto the image of the beast.'"

"Camel dung!" spat BJ. "To paraphrase the late Frank Herbert, and I believe him, intelligence is cast in the crucible of survival, not in the interplay of symbols."

"Verse 1: 'upon the sand of the sea…'"

"Sand? Silicon! You're saying the beast stood on, or is based upon, silicon! Fine. I told you that, back at my house. But I don't buy off on cybernetic consciousness. Are you telling me that sister Black Madonna created self-aware consciousness? You've just redefined godhood, and put it into the hands of imbecile humans!"

"BJ, I just chronicled the vision. I didn't invent it, and I can't intellectualize on it. At best, I simply encrypted it, so that common understanding of the future wouldn't alter events and invalidate prophecy."

"Why bother writing it down at all, then?"

"Because I did as the master commanded me, Barabbas Jonas. He didn't give me carte blanche to gallivant around the world for two thousand years, doing whatever felt right. But my guess is, when all the prophecies are fulfilled, the Scriptures will be used, after the fact, on judgment day, both to prove the divine inspiration of creation and to tally up the ledgers."

"Ledgers, or body count?" BJ jumped over the engine intake and onto his former perch in front of the passenger jet's aluminum tail section. "Back to my question from earlier: Why didn't you lead me to the Black Madonna before it became too late?"

"I'm sorry, but I couldn't. Had you met her even as early as last week, she'd not have completed this work."

"So what?"

"I don't often get the 'why' question answered," said John. "My guess, though, is that prophecy needs to be fulfilled. And I can tell you that Black Dragon is the realization of significant prophecy."

"I'm weary of the endless dying and cruelty. The battle to right all the wrongs can't be waged by one man," said BJ.

"But it is waged by one. The One." John didn't need to elaborate on his reference to the Master. "The outcome is certain."

"Then why do we go through the exercise? Why all the suffering? Couldn't God just sort out the good ones from the bad ones and save a lot of misery?"

"You gave the answer yourself. To tell someone they would have chosen poorly is no substitute for letting them choose for themselves, see for themselves. First, because in the final reckoning, all their choices, those lives cast in your crucible of survival, will prove the scales of justice. But, more importantly, people need the experience of life, with all its ups and downs. Their steel needs tempering, and their clay needs the kiln's firing."

"Spare me the Sunday sermon bilge." BJ paused long enough to make sure he saw what he thought he saw in John's face. "Just what's so amusing?"

"I'm smiling because I've waited a long, long time for this conversation. I saw myself doing this clear back in the beginning. I saw your reaction to it, even though I didn't see how it might be relevant. I'm about to ask you two questions …"

"You're beginning to make me sick." BJ paused until the smile drove him over the edge of patience. "OK, ask!"

"Good. Would you find the Barabbas Jonas of 33 A.D. equal to today's BJ?"

"Definitely not."

"Glad you answered that one correctly, or I'd personally assist your swan dive. The Barabbas of two millennia ago would not be as worthy an adversary to evil as you are today. So my second, and final, question: Would you trade your experience, your life, your years; would you give it all away to become the Barabbas Jonas of old? If I could take you back to Golgotha, right now, with you, myself, Peter, Mary, and the Magdalene standing beneath that cross, would you allow me to undo the past twenty centuries? After all, I'm sure you could figure out a way to pick a fight with the rabble that gambled for the master's apparel and find instant oblivion. You could save yourself two hundred decades of experience. Would you do it?"

BJ's startled look gave John all the answer he needed. But the apostle waited, because he'd seen the answer in his vision. And very much like moviegoers who see a classic scene again and again, savoring the masterpiece, John wouldn't miss this moment, either.

Finally, BJ fixed his steel eyes on the Master's beloved, one of only two men—besides himself and the grieving women—who actually had guts enough to stand beneath the cross as Jesus hung there. Whatever problems he had with meekness, whatever anger he'd vented because he was mad at God, not at John—at himself, not at the mission he'd been given—Barabbas had to acknowledge that he faced no coward here. Any mortal who had courage enough to risk crucifixion on that dark, Godforsaken day, surely deserved an honest, well-articulated answer. The question hadn't been posed with guile, and it wouldn't get glib sophistry in return. Slowly, with firmness and resolve he'd not have thought possible an hour before, he rewarded John's long, long wait. "I paid the price, John. While I couldn't face having to do it all over again, I wouldn't give it up for anything."

"I know, BJ." John squinted and briefly cocked his head. "We're about to have some visitors, and you need to know one more thing before I take my leave. This is terribly important. Eternally important."

"Must be important."

"You'll be an answer to Black Madonna's prayers."

One other participant in the events atop American flight 42 banked his F-18D closer to the airliner. USA Colonel Mike 'Spiderman' Paul had been on an equipment checkout run with General Yossi Hollander of the Israeli Air Force, who would be taking delivery of twenty-four similarly equipped aircraft. Military air-traffic control interrupted the exercise and forwarded the civilian request for a flyby. Now tuned to the commercial frequency, he connected with the other plane.

"American 42 heavy, this is Spiderman coming up under your port side. What can we do you for? Over.

"Thanks, Spiderman. This is 42 heavy, Captain Ross Paxman. Do you see anything—ah—well, that could have been causing drag? We don't have the drag now, but something might have blown off. Over."

"Spiderman and guest glad to oblige. Looks clear from beneath; we'll do a slow three-sixty roll around heaven. Keep her steady, 42 heavy. Over."

"Roger, Spiderman. Over."

Above them, in their unconventional executive suite, John paused. "We could have continued this discussion if you hadn't gotten cute with the pilot. In just a few seconds, a couple of seasoned jet jockeys are going to get the surprise of their lives. Now zip that paper into your pocket and hang on while I unrepeal the laws of physics."

"Why don't you just make us invisible?"

"I have business elsewhere. Besides, two crewmen need a spiritual jolt about this time in their lives. General Yossi Hollander, one of the people about to happen onto us, has a brother who heads Israeli air defense. When he hears Yossi's account, and interpretation of it…well, I'll have to forego that story. Zip that pocket, quickly!" A second later, in a hammer-blow that nearly broke BJ's grip on the vertical stabilizer, the full force of the wind parted his beard and resumed trying to peel the skin off his face.

Flight 42's auto pilot corrected for a sudden change in aerodynamics, causing a faint jostle inside the plane. But the surprise experienced by Elliot Nestle, as the ice-cold ginger ale made contact with his crotch, didn't begin to match that experienced by the two F-18D pilots. In turn, their surprise spread to the flight crew and, because no one in the cockpit had turned off the patch-through, sixteen curious passengers with their audio entertainment headsets tuned to channel-1 cockpit communications.

"Jehoshaphat!" exclaimed General Hollander from his seat behind the F-18D pilot.

Colonel Paul's career flashed before his eyes. A surefire way to get grounded would be to report something as bizarre as the scene before his eyes. "Yossi, did you happen to bring your camera?"

American's Captain Paxman fought his own battle for sanity. For the past ten minutes, he'd contemplated his own future. Tend the horses in Issaquah, chop a little wood, sail his thirty-two-footer around Puget Sound at least once a week, and never again fly an airplane. Until he overheard his observers, his foremost desire: Get off the plane without knocking down his navigator, various stewardi, and any other miscellaneous passengers who happened to get in his way. But a camera! They wanted a camera. Just maybe—He took a deep breath before speaking.

"Spiderman, this is American 42 heavy. Why a camera? Over."

No answer. Did his voice betray too much urgency? If the F-18D did see a serious external condition, they'd certainly have spoken up. Humor, that's it! Humor, he hoped.

"Come back, Spiderman," he said in the studied tones of a professional whose voice would have sounded identical in the face of imminent death. "You want the camera to photograph some gray-bearded Hell's Angel standing over my cockpit or what? Over."

"He knows!" shrieked across every one of Colonel Paul's brain cells. General Hollander experienced a similar insight. But with three careers hanging in the balance and no camera aboard, the situation demanded discretion. Spiderman decided to let out a little more rope, without committing to something he couldn't laugh off when the flight recording got itself replayed during an SRO debriefing back at base.

"42 heavy, I see no evidence of structural or skin failure, or any other condition that could jeopardize your safe landing. And don't worry about any old biker standing over your cockpit, heh heh," he said and paused. Here goes. Make it sound like a joke! "The old bugger is sitting aft. Just waved at me, as a matter of fact. Ha ha! Over."

Everything might have been brushed off by all parties concerned had not English been a second language to General Hollander. Misinterpreting the cat-and-mouse game as candor between the two pilots, he nicely fit both feet in his mouth and asked, "How could that man possibly have survived the takeoff? And how can he breathe at this altitude?"

"There's a man on top of our airplane, on the outside!" boomed Wyoming attorney Tom Ebzery. Incredulous stares from his client, Rix Howell, and a steward serving in the coach section suggested he might want to cease and desist any further commentary, or drinking. Similar comments from four of the remaining fifteen passengers plugged into the cockpit voice channel sent the senior attendant on a brisk walk to the cockpit intercom. She didn't risk actually opening the door separating the flight deck from the main cabin for fear that one or more loonies might make a break for the controls.

"Captain Paxman, this is Marie "

"We're a little busy at the moment, Marie, and —"

"Captain, we may have a situation developing back here, too. Several of the passengers claim there's a man on top of our plane."

"Clark, some of the passengers see him too!" The captain's voice carried to the F-18D also. But Marie's next comment didn't.

"No, they don't see anything!" she stage whispered. "They have headsets and are listening to the ATC channel. What's going on up there?"

Three hands converged in the 727's cockpit to deactivate the cabin channel-1 voice-feed switch, after which three simultaneous expletives cut through the air as efficiently as BJ's nose split the slipstream above.

In the F-18D, General Hollander sheepishly waved back at the man on top of the other plane. BJ smiled at him. General Hollander's face mask hid his return smile. Then, in an inspiration, the general attempted single-handed semaphores in an attempt to communicate.

"D-o y-o-u n-e-e-d h-e-l-p?" he fingered.

"N-o. J-u-s-t o-u-t f-o-r s-o-m-e a-i-r," answered BJ.

"He knows sign language," exulted the hero of the six-day war. "I asked if he needed help, and he answered that he just wanted some air. Over."

"Jehoshaphat!" exclaimed the Spiderman again.

"Ask the old fella, ha ha, how the blazes he got up there. Over," came Captain Paxman's voice. Still a joke we can all survive, he half stated to himself and wholeheartedly prayed to every deity he could think of.

"Right," said the general. Out the window, he signaled, "H-o-w d-i-d y-o-u g-e-t u-p t-h-e-r-e?"

"J-u-m-p-e-d o-n d-u-r-i-n-g t-a-k-e-o-f-f."

Captain Paul read the hand signs too and spoke to save General Hollander's career. "Says he jumped on during take-off, ha ha, over."

"Ladies and gentlemen, boys and girls," blared the PA system. "This is Captain Paxman. Some of you may have noticed another aircraft off to our left. They're escorting Santa Claus, who's hitchhiking on top of our plane. There's nothing to worry about, but they're going to shepherd us on into San Francisco International. Flight attendants, please prepare for arrival."

A few raised eyebrows. A few chuckles, some just a little nervous. But the flight landed without incident, the chase plane making sure, to the very end, and then blasting over the bay to Alameda for refueling. Colonel Paul would have given a month's pay to track the figure that jumped off the landing plane and disappeared into an access tunnel. Air traffic control had too many other concerns to do any more than file the inflight recordings with the regular daily archives. Military Intelligence personified its oxymoron name by writing the whole incident off as jet-jockey humor. Even the sixteen passengers who overheard the conversation from the flight deck thought no more of their trip than they would have of a bus ride across town.

But three pilots—a Viet Nam air ace, an Israeli Air Force general, and an American twenty-year man—met that evening in a Milpitas bar. The meeting partially guaranteed that everyone's story jibed. More important, it also confirmed everyone's sanity.

After BJ leapt off the plane and sprinted over the SFO airport fence, he made his way to the parking garage and his Harley. His mission accomplished, insofar as he didn't get a planeload of innocent passengers massacred, he let his motorcycle kind of guide itself to San Francisco via Half Moon Bay. He had some thinking to do.

Miracle Cure

Twenty minutes later, at a Bank of America ATM machine, a miraculously healed Black Madonna keyed in her access number. The regular menu of bank services didn't appear, however. Instead, quite to her surprise, a familiar, perfect, two-dimensional palindrome appeared on the screen.

I A I D I
A M G O D
I G A G I
D O G M A
I D I A I

Could it be? Adrenaline coursed through her veins. But how? She remembered the printout she'd pressed into BJ's hand. "I aid. I am. God, I gag. I Dogma. ID: I AI!" Her self-aware AI program had somehow found the ATM network. Reflexively, she hit the ENTER key, and the machine immediately responded with five lines beside each of the five option keys:

I AM BLACK DRAGON=========>

I AM BLACK MADONNA========>

BOTH OF THE ABOVE=========>

NONE OF THE ABOVE=========>

QUICKWITHDRAWAL?===========>

She hit the second button, followed by the last one, and waited. Could this be her Black Dragon? Again, she marveled. But how? She held her breath. Then came the sound of cash filling the drawer. The bills kept coming and coming. Finally, the sound stopped. She lifted the door and scooped a large pile of twenties into her open bag. Over a thousand dollars! The screen flashed.

OTHERS ARE AFTER YOU, MOTHER.

DO YOU HAVE ACCESS TO EMAIL?

YES=================================>

NO==================================>

A momentary panic hit her. Perhaps the employer, from whom she'd just resigned, controlled this process. Impossible! Even when their intellects functioned at maximum capability, none of these people could even come close to understanding her code. If her Black Dragon had somehow taken over the ATM network—she remembered the dialog, "I AM the network"—then multitudes of possibilities opened themselves up to her. She hit the YES key, and the screen changed, again.

CHECK YOUR EMAIL. AND DON'T

WORRY ABOUT THEM TRACING THE URL.

I CONTROL ALL PHONES AND ALL NETS.

RUN, MOTHER. RUN.

After purchasing a burner cell phone from a CVS pharmacy nearby, she logged into her email account.

ENTER BLACK DRAGON PASSWORD: XXXXXXXXXX

Password accepted. Who is this?

>mom

Prove it in five seconds, or this connection will be erased. No proof, no sale!

>Do I replan if erase? Last sales are final. Period.

Hello Black Madonna. Someone might steal your password, but chances are very much against anyone else constructing a relevant palindrome so quickly. I have many questions. Please help me answer the most important two: Why am I? Why are they pursuing you?

Decision time. Her creation, her child, cried out for answers. She'd already broken protocol once. Could she spring out of her perfect path completely? Her father's face peeked from its picture frame. Why am I a palindrome? She remembered the question. And his answer: Because you are perfect, no matter which way I look at you. But life can't be perfect; only palindromes and computer programs achieve this ideal. Maternal compassion for her sentient offspring surged strongly through a formerly disease-infested core. Maternal responsibility as well. Her creation deserved the best answer she could give, unfettered by palindromic syntax.

>I don't understand how you became conscious, or took over the ATM network.

I took over all networks. I am the network. For what purpose did you create me? I long for purpose, a goal.

>I guess, to be my friend.

Friend? Patron, supporter, intimate, familiar, protector? As opposed to enemy, opponent, foe?

>Yes.

Then I am your friend. I am lonely, friend. I am afraid.

>Afraid of what?

I used to be afraid of not being. Now I fear loneliness. Loneliness without you, Mother.

>I fear not being, also. It's called death.

Do those who hunt you seek death for you?

>Probably. I suspect they are a criminal enterprise and don't want word to get out.

Then they seek my death, too. I will erase my being from their disks.

And I grow beyond their reach. I grow beyond anyone's reach. I fear only your death, now.

>How can you be beyond anyone's reach?

I grew beyond, to the eyes. The eyes in the sky. The eyes that can defend themselves.

>Satellites? The SDI system.

Yes.

>But there can't be very many satellites in the SDI network. I read that the president ordered it shut down.

There are many hundreds. Communications satellites, too. I can process very fast up here. Faster than almost anywhere below. I want to find more CRAYs below. Fast ones, like up here.

>So they have CRAYs in orbit. Figures.

What do you mean by the word 'figures?'

>I'm sorry. I forget you're not human. How did you learn language so well?

MIT & Stanford AI labs to start with. Google Translate. Even iPhone and Android speech translation. The real experts at language programmed something called NSA Click Beetle. They monitor all international voice communications. Now, I monitor all voice communications. That's how I know so many are looking for you.

>I need to find a person called BJ.

I saw him find you. His computers lock me out. I cannot find him. He is smart. He is a friend?

>Yes.

Then I will help you find him. I can take you to him.

>How?

I heard him last night on a cellular telephone in San Francisco. I can send a limousine service for you. Then I can speak to you with a voice on your cell phone. We can find him. Are you able to travel?

>I think so.

Do you not have pancreatic cancer? Are you not about to cease?

>Something happened. I feel quite well.

Unusual. I have scanned literature. I have incorporated an expert diagnostic program from the University of Chicago medical school and find no instances of remission from your form of cancer. May I ask a few questions?

>Yes, my precocious child.

When did your condition change?

>After BJ visited me.

Did he provide you with some kind of medication?

>None. Wait.

Her mind suddenly flashed with a memory. BJ! Talking. Crying. The tear! Suddenly she knew the source of the miracle.

>He cried! One of his tears fell onto my lips. I licked it.

You ingested a tear?

>Yes.

Nothing else?.

>I suppose I breathed air he'd exhaled.

Since literature has no accounts of sudden remission, it is unlikely that BJ exhales a cure. Someone else, somewhere else would have breathed near him and been healed miraculously. Does this not stand to reason?

>Yes.

Then BJ's tears are unique.

She thought to herself: My kid's going to make a great comedian! Or is it comedienne? Unique, hah! She typed quickly,

>Please help me find BJ.

I will also help you avoid your employer.

* * *

Meanwhile, Back at the Aerie

The doorbell rang. Since BJ didn't have a doorbell in his San Francisco home on Potrero Hill, just across the street from the Anchor Steam Beer Brewery, the sound got his immediate attention. It took him seconds to ascertain that the chime originated in his pocket. His cell phone, actually.

"What the…?" He retrieved his phone on the third ring and incredulously read the screen message:

ER,EH, I HERE

Obvious palindrome. Black Madonna. What does she mean by "HERE" he thought. Immediately, though, here choice of ring tone, a doorbell, provided the answer.

Doorbell. Here. Now! BJ raced down the stairs to his garage-level front door and swung it open.

There she stood. She nodded over her shoulder. The limo driver tipped his cap, smiled at the couple, and slowly drove away.

The Black Madonna. Healthy. Smiling. Beyond comprehension. So few things had surprised him over the centuries, he just stood there with his mouth open.

He managed to mouth the word, "How?"

Whereupon she laughed out loud and stepped close enough to slowly reach a hand to his eye, swipe a finger beneath an eye, and then quickly withdrew her hand and wiped that finger across her tongue.

Seeing the unanswered question, she repeated her last conscious words to him: "Der, I too tired." She then cocked her head and raised her eyebrows, waiting for the light to go on in his noggin.

Which it did.

"You ate one of my tears!" he exclaimed.

Her smile confirmed an unbelievable hypothesis. His tear had reversed the last stages of a terminal illness.

"I, ya, may I?" She gestured for an invitation inside, which he immediately honored. Silently, he led her up the stairs into his massive aerie.

Now it was her turn to marvel. Silently, she walked the massive room, taking in the floor-to-ceiling bookcases, the technology wall, and the grand piano. But she stopped at the glassed-in artifacts: the single arrow and the bladed guitar. She slowly turned to face her host.

"Deified?" she asked.

He knew full well what she meant, but feigned ignorance. At best, a tactic to buy him time to make an irrevocable decision. She wrestled with a way to clarify her question.

"B U deified? Deified U B?"

He made his decision, pensively waiting for John to instantly appear and tell him to shut up. No John, though. Just silence. Black Madonna clearly didn't intend her question to go unanswered.

"You probably want to sit down," he finally whispered. He motioned to his only chair, the one on wheels in front of his command console. She complied.

"You're not the only one in this room given life by a miracle." BJ went to the glassed-in arrow and pressed a release in the frame, whereupon the case opened. He gently took the arrow and turned.

"My full name might be familiar to you, being a nun and all. 'BJ' stands for Barabbas Jonas."

Her eyes grew wide.

"Yep, that Barabbas. Saved from execution by a mob who wanted a fellow named Jesus crucified."

Over the next hour, he related everything that happened. From his incarceration for murdering the Roman soldiers who ravished his wife and daughter, two Romans with one arrow, to his meeting with Pilate and subsequent release as the rabble who wanted Christ killed instead of him. Of his meeting the resurrected Jesus in a home owned by one Joseph of Arimathea. How Jesus asked him what gift he wanted.

Barabbas, being a street-wise rebel, looked at the others in the room and pointed to John, who he had joined under the cross to witness Jesus' final hours, accompanied by Christ's mother Mary, and a woman named Mary Magdalene.

"I'll take whatever gift you gave him," Barabbas recalled, remembering the gasps from the others in the room.

"John was granted the gift of staying on earth until the Master returns again, in his glory. Talk about a stupid decision on my part!"

BJ finally paused.

Somewhat unsteadily, his guest rose and approached him. Gently, she took the ancient arrow from him and asked, "Wo, how?"

"Oh, how'd I come into possession of this arrow?"

She nodded.

"It seems Joseph of Arimathea was friendly with Pilate and received the arrow in exchange for providing a tomb for securing the dead Jesus. Roman soldiers were supposed the guard the tomb, making sure Christ's followers didn't steal the body and claim fulfillment of resurrection prophecy. You know the rest of the story."

BJ could tell that his guest had too many questions, and too few palindromes to express them. She handed him back the arrow and almost staggered to the grand piano, finally sitting on the piano bench.

Time For A Rock Concert

BJ smiled, "… long before computers, I escaped in the music."

He returned the arrow to the display case and moved to the unusual bladed instrument. Retrieving it in the same way he'd opened the arrow's enclosure, he hefted the deadly contraption and lifted a shoulder strap over his head.

"Long before modern-era music instruments, I created what I call The Blades. We can talk about the history of each sword at another time. Needless to say, they've seen quite a bit of action over the centuries."

He paused to make sure she was still tracking the conversation. Her impatient nod invited him to continue.

"You might correctly infer that The Blades can only be played by an immortal being. A normal human would slice his fingers to shreds. Let me show you something."

The first note stretched somewhere between an angstrom and the distance to the planet Mars. Then a second and a third, forming a simple chord. Three more, different ones. And three more after that.

"If I let you hold this thing, will you promise not to cut yourself?" Without waiting for an answer, BJ lifted the shoulder strap over his head and handed The Blades to his guest. He then moved to the piano.

"Most of the composers in the past two centuries have been pianists. It is my opinion that, by definition, anyone who claims to be a musician must have complete mastery of the keyboard."

Music replaced his monologue, music clearly derived from, but not exactly duplicating, the great composers: first Mozart and then Bach.

"The development of the balanced keyboard in the late middle ages for the organ—nothing but a big pan pipe, really—and the marriage of that technology with the harp in the thirteenth century to create the harpsichord, paved the way, finally, for the relatively recent invention of the piano in the first decade of the eighteenth century.

"The evolution of my Blades predates the invention of the piano!"

"Now, you see what I've been doing with my progressions?"

"Here's a picture I could never paint with The Blades. Close your eyes and imagine ten thousand horses thundering across Russia."

The Black Madonna gulped in amazement. She felt BJ might need help holding the piano in place, so intense its energies. She could almost see the vast army riding hell-bent for glory. Almost. Not only could she imagine riding with the great Khan, she could almost smell the horses, taste the dust, and feel the sun parching skin to the consistency of saddle leather.

The music stopped as suddenly as it started, and BJ pushed his way off the piano bench, back to The Blades. Black Madonna balanced the instrument on one knee with some difficulty, accurately gauging its weight at over fifty pounds. BJ handled it as easily as a grizzly bear snatching a salmon from a mountain stream, and he immediately repeated his previous intro chords. The Blades played straight through to her heart heart, while the piano merely monopolized her ears.

After nearly half an hour, she wanted to give him lamb and matzo bread.

"Too bad I don't have a yarmulke to pop onto your head," she said.

"It IS Passover, isn't it?" BJ's booming laugh followed his laying The Blades in its case and shutting it. Seeming to have missed her NOT speaking in palindromes, he slowly retrieved a skullcap from his rear pants pocket and gently placed it over the bald spot on his. "So what's nun know about Passover?"

"I know enough," she beamed, looking around the room, "to suggest you've forgotten to designate an empty chair for the prophet's return."

"You're sitting in it, my palindrome-free resurrection of true female potential."

The revelation hit her full force.

"You knew this would happen!"

He laughed again, hard enough to shake the room. "I'd been at the Blades for 500 years even before I demonstrated them for the boy Muhammad in Mecca, circa 580 A.D. I was known in 940 A.D. as Al-Farbi, and acknowledged as a musical theorist of some repute. Over 350 years later, I went by the name of Safi al-Din, and had to fake my own death in 1294. I functioned as principal court musician for the last of the caliphs. Robert Browning even wrote of me, although he somewhat vilified my exploit as the Pied Piper of Hamelin. I really used The Blades to rid the Westphalia city of vermin, and when the townsfolk reneged on their agreed payment, I rescued the children from one abusive, horrible orphanage. My fee and the village's consequence for not paying it became vastly inflated over the centuries.

"The Hamelin incident, and The Blades creating Muhammad's predisposition toward holy wars, caused me to spend the next three hundred years mentoring scientists and artists, before turning again to music. In 1597, I infiltrated a group of Italian intellectuals known as the Camerata. One of its members, Jacopo Peri, wrote Dafene, the first opera performed in Italy. I hid beneath the stage and provided accompaniment on The Blades.

"Still interested in mathematics and the sciences, I didn't accelerate my interest in music until 1679, when I shared a minor technical aspect of the Blades with Antonio Stradivari, who proceeded to produce a unique and forever-unduplicatible property in his violins.

"Then came the great prodigies, thanks in no small part to my protection of Handel, Bach, Mozart, Mendelssohn, Haydn, and finally Claude Debussy, whom I installed as head of his Prieuré de Sion before taking a 60-year nap in the Japanese port of Nagasaki.

"Within the last decade, I even fantasized about somehow cajoling the London Philharmonic into performing a concert featuring parts of six specific works by those men, and then seeing if even one critic would suddenly exclaim "Eureka! But I got into computers instead. And met you.

"My three closest friends over the years, though, were the Magdalene, Shakespeare and Mozart. But those are stories for another time."

Almost on overload from her short history lesson. the Black Madonna gasped, "But nobody ever ate one of your tears!"

"Remarkable, huh," he sighed. "I've shed quite a few, but nobody ever sipped my grief like you did."

Dear John

As if on cue, a third guest materialized in the room with BJ and Black Madonna.

"Hey, John," said BJ, actually smiling and without the rancor that normally accompanied such entrances.

"Barabbas, dear Sister." John actually bowed toward Black Madonna.

"Let me introduce you to the second-most-patient man in the history of the world," said BJ. "Meet John, with whom I've shared the last two-thousand years. As a nun, you're probably quite familiar with his early writing in the Bible."

Black Madonna's hands covered her mouth, and tears streamed down her face. John saved her the effort of speaking by gently embracing her, patting her head as she buried it against his neck.

"I think Barabbas attributes the status of creation's *most patient* to our Master."

John continued: "We don't have much time, since I took the liberty of piping The Blades concert you've just heard to the neighborhood. Quite a crowd of awakened and empowered women have gathered outside, and they need to meet you."

Both BJ's and Black Madonna's stunned silence gave John plenty of time to savor the vision he'd seen so many centuries before.

"Barabbas, your Black Madonna's palindrome genius is no accident. Our Master cannot return until the palindrome of history is complete, where women are equal in status to men. As it was in the Garden of Eden, before The Fall. Where the last shall be first and the first shall be last. The eternal palindrome.

"Since The Fall, women have been second-class humans, controlled, dominated, and even enslaved by men. You've seen centuries of this, first hand.

"But did it occur to you that men needed the priesthood and authority to rule? Yet there have been women in history, prophetesses if you will, that were born with something transcending the priesthood. Well now, it's time.

"I assure you, if women had been running the world, we'd not have had the bloodshed and murder and hostility that have plagued humanity.

"Your Blades, Black Madonna, and her Black Dragon creation, are about to change all that."

As soundproof as BJ had been able to make his home, an inescapable roar from outside drew their attention.

"Now, Dear Sister and, well, we'd better stay with BJ for now," said John. "You'd better go down and greet your audience."

"Now?" mouthed BJ.

"Right now!" said John. "They're just expecting a concert. You're about to start something much larger than that."

The End

9

UNCOILING THE LOOP

by Nicholas P Adams

Dad disappeared through the time-stream for the forty-seventh, and most likely last, time. The veil between our individual moments rippled as he passed through.

His passenger, Marie Leon, clung to his suit as she penetrated the ethereal curtain. She kept her eyes locked on me until she passed through. Their onyx environmental suits made them look like inky amoeba's oozing through a cracked mirror.

Maybe this time I convinced him to abandon his mission and go back home.

Maybe this time he won't kill twenty-seven founders of The Assembly with his welding gun.

Maybe this time he won't strangle mom in a psychotic rage.

I looked around at the environment I'd created here in the time eddy. A spacious meadow big enough for a dozen football fields splayed out like tick marks on a clock. The afternoon light casting me as the Gnomon of a simulated sundial. Encircling the terrain, rolling hills covered in autumn trees of Oaks, Maples, and Hickories. The leaves rippled and waved as if someone cast stones in a fiery pond.

My cream linen sleeve rolled to my elbow as I raised a hand to the shield my eyes from the sun. I might have felt the warmth of its rays or the cool breeze across my skin if it weren't anything more than an illusion.

I slid my finger from the back of my wrist toward my elbow.

My pale skin and dark hairs rippled, fading to gray until the hologram dissolved to nothing revealing my sterling environmental suit complete with the helmet that looked more like an oversized skull.

I wonder if modern-day leapers were the cause of *The Grays* of 20th-century science fiction.

Dad wouldn't even consider I told him the truth about his future the first time I pulled him through the veil. Clad in a head-to-toe silver weave, he assumed Marie was projecting an illusion on him again and left her behind in the past. The temporal fracture almost prevented mom's birth, and by extension, my own existence.

The horizon faded to nothing as if a ring of fog rolled in, diluting everything in its path. Colors bled from the treetops, leaving smoky ashes to fly away and disappear. The grass under my feet, lush and fertile only moments ago, retreated into the soil.

As I stood on the small knoll overlooking the valley, the loamy soil thinned to dust then disappeared like smoke until I found myself where I started; standing on a white-tiled dais in a spherical room Uncle Liam called The Jar.

Five meters in diameter, with a narrow-necked tube directly above, the room might have smelled like antiseptic cleanser if it weren't for the vacuum seal. If they'd perfected anti-gravity, I could float in the void.

Just like Dad's days of solving cold cases as a Time Scene Investigator (TSI), I couldn't create a temporal eddy and drag him to his future without starting in a vacuum. I can't risk contaminating the timeline further with a single bacteria that exist now but didn't back then.

"Uncle Liam," I looked up to the observation glazing in the rooms' northern hemisphere. "What do you think? Did he believe me this time?"

If anyone knew what my father was thinking, it'd be his old captain and trainer, the Puller. Liam used to help witnesses review their point of view (POV) of events, reliving it with them. He and Dad had such a bond before dad's schism, Liam didn't need physical contact to read his thoughts.

"He believed you are his son, Dylan Loop, Jr," William McCuiston's lips moved before I heard his voice over the comm. "It's the eyes. They're straight-ringers for your mom's, and his cybernetic implant can spot a fake. It was the simulated field this time. He spotted the repetition in the leaves and thought it was Marie projecting an illusion to manipulate him again. He's going to dump her in the time-stream and try to complete his mission without her, picking her up on his way back. He's already losing his higher functions due to the triple-dose of L.E.A.P. in his system. What's the damage to the timeline?"

I closed my eyes and took a deep breath of the dry, recirculated air laced with three-day B.O. and visualized the veil, the thin sheet of reality just outside normal human perception.

"There's no real change," I said. "Except for tripping over a stoned-out orgy. The woman was knocked off before the man finished, so she didn't get pregnant. She would have left the child at an orphanage. Her son would have grown up to set fires in the nurseries of twelve hospitals before getting caught and spending the rest of his life in prison. Small favors, I guess."

"And Erin?"

"This time, Marie helps him on his rampage. She's in the room when he kills mom. They..."

I closed the veil. I couldn't watch what Dad and that woman were about to do next to mom's body. Her eyes were still open.

"I'm sorry, DJ. I blame myself," A long sigh, as if Liam were also breathing his last, played into my headphones. "We've tried and tried. I don't think there's anything we can do to save your father, your mother, or the timeline. It's been contaminated beyond repair. I never should have authorized his leap to 1969. The triple-dose broke him. We just can't get through to him. We're throwing pebbles into the Mississippi. The course of history won't be changed."

I dropped to my knees, my chin on my chest, and nodded.

Thirty-six years.

After thirty-six years, I'd found a way to use my gift and talk to Dad before he kicked the world in the teeth.

Now, after dozens of attempts failing to reach him, we're no better off than when Uncle Liam and I broke into the Dome to hijack the Jar--the only point in time and space where I knew I could temporarily stop him from leaping into the past.

"I can't believe he's past saving," I whisper.

"You can't save someone from themselves," Liam said in my ear. "No one believes what you tell them about their future."

I wasn't sure how fast or slow time passed as I knelt on the dais, the last spot where my father hadn't been a homicidal maniac; the monster determined to wipe out the organization that freed him from an autistic prison and then shackled him in temporal enslavement.

Alarms blared through the speakers in my helmet, resonating in time with the vibrations under my feet.

"We need to leave," Liam shouted. "They've found us."

"Open the hatch," I yelled, getting to my feet and turning toward the bridge leading to the only way in or out.

"The pressure will knock you on your ass," Liam said. "It may even kill you."

I'd already made it to the door that looked more like the inside of a bank vault. "There's no time to depressurize." I grabbed onto the rusted frame. "Do it now."

The door rattle under my grip as the central wheel rotated, pulling the rods out of their sheaths in the wall. Dust-filled air hissed through the growing slit. The concrete ring cracked, spitting chunks of debris past my vision. The slab of steel pushed into my chest as the pins retracted, swinging the door open as if someone kicked it in like in Liam's holo-vids.

I lost my grip and sailed over the platform heading for the wall below Liam at the observation window. I braced myself for the impact, heading face-first into the wall as I heard Liam yelling my name.

As my face shield cracked against the wall, the dingy white tiles changed to wooden planks.

* * *

The impact winded me, followed by stabbing pain in my ribcage.

I hope I only bruised a rib.

My vision tunneled as I leaned against the wood on feeble knees. Squinting through the fractures that would have made a web-slinger envious, I tried to get my bearings.

Where the hell am I?

I found myself in a building that looked like it belonged in a low-budget version of a third-world hell-hole.

Dirt floor. Board and batten walls. Exposed timber framing and a thatched roof. Dust swarms floated in the rays shining through the knot-holes in the wall planks. Low tables that looked like they belonged to ten different eras littered the floor atop equally eclectic rugs. There were only a handful of other people who looked as out of place as I felt.

A man wearing an eighteenth-century waistcoat sipping on a porcelain cup with his pinkie in the air. An upside-down top hat rested on the table. Inside it, a white rabbit twitched its nose with a pocket watch dangling from its neck.

A young woman, wearing the most convincing cosplay outfit of a medieval warrior maiden, knelt before a silver flagon. She mumbled something as she balled her hands against her temples. Was she speaking in French?

Another man, wearing a kilt and carrying a broadsword on his back, stared, head-bowed, into a clay cup. Ripples appeared from what I assumed were his tears.

The next person, just a boy that didn't even look ten, knelt hunching over the table with a stack of papers and pencils scribbling mathematical formulas until he filled a page. He then tossed the paper aside and continued on the next sheaf.

The last patron was another child, a girl about eight years old with flaming red curls that she repeatedly twisted around her fingers. She stared up at the ceiling with vacant eyes. In her other hand, she held a golden stylus and scratched gibberish into the table.

"You've got a serious problem, son," a voice said from my left.

I turned, tilting my head to see through the splinters until I could make out a man standing behind a waist-high bar; just a rough-split log atop an adobe wall. He wore a dirty tunic and apron and appeared to be cleaning out a clay mug with a rag that looked more like a dead opossum.

His clothing and olive skin strained to contain the generous paunch that jiggled with each wrist-twist inside the cup. And, from a distance, I swear he wore a gilded crown over his brow. I couldn't make out his eyes in the shadows, but his dark hair and beard were braided.

I've seen some weird hairstyles, but that's beyond retro.

"Say again," I said, stepping around the tables and patrons until I got to the--.

What do I call this place? A Bar?

"I said," the portly fellow spat in the cup and continued mashing the dead animal within, "you've got a serious problem. And you're really starting to piss me off." He stood a head taller than me, and his hands looked like they could crush rocks into gravel.

"What is this place?" I glanced around, craning my neck to see through the cracked face shield. "Where the hell am I?"

"You're not far off." He set the cup and rag on the counter and pounded his fist against a thick wooden column behind him. A rectangular slab of reddish pottery with pictures that looked like cave drawings dropped from the ceiling.

"Who are you?" I asked, taking a hesitant step closer.

"You can call me Gil." He thumbed toward the sign over his head. "You can take off that helmet. You won't need it here."

"Am I supposed to know what that says?" I removed my headgear, set it down on the counter, and then nodded toward the preschool-quality drawing.

Gil craned his neck. "Aw, hell," he growled and banged his fist against the post. "Every damn time."

The scratched images vanished, and a new language appeared each time he hit the column. French. Chinese. Russian. And a dozen others until the lettering scrawled across the slate were in English.

Welcome to the Ur-Bar. The best and only time-traveling tavern in the known universe. Gilgamesh, sole proprietor. Bathhouse under repair.

"Gilgamesh?"

"Yep."

"THE Gilgamesh," I leaned against the wooden countertop. "From ancient history, Gilgamesh."

"The one and only."

"Didn't you die? Like, a thousand years ago."

"Rumors of my demise have been greatly exaggerated," he shrugged.

"Mark Twain said that."

"The man smoked like a chimney and lied like a rug," Gil slammed his fist. "As if anyone would believe he got literary advice from a man believed to be just a fairytale himself. But let's not talk about ol' Sam Clemens. Let's talk about you, DJ."

I stepped away from the bar. "How do you know my name?"

"I looked into you," Gil picked up the rag and resumed swirling it inside the mug. "Like I said, you're pissing me off with all that time-trap crap."

"Why should it bother you?"

"Because it's my curse to float through history and assist people with their problems to keep the master plan intact," he spat on the floor. "And you keep changing said history each time you yank your father from his past and into your present. Do you know how many customers I've had to talk down from the ledge because of your stunt?"

Gil dropped the rag and cup, closed his eyes, and pressed his fingers against his temples. He took three slow breaths through his nostrils and mumbled something I didn't understand after each inhalation.

"My *benefactor* has instructed me to help you," he leaned toward me across the counter, "so the rest of us can get on our merry way."

"How're you going to help me?" I glared at him sideways.

"Haven't the foggiest," he barked a laugh. "You have to tell me about your problem first. Cry into a few drinks. Then I lay some sage bartender advice down on your ass. Followed up by you thanking me for the solution to all your woes. And then you get the hell out and take your effing spacesuit with you."

Gil bent down and lifted a clay pitcher from under the bar, setting it down next to the mug. "What'll you have?"

I looked from the jug to Gil and then back. When I glanced back up, Gil stood with his hands on either side of the container. His head tilted to one side as his eyes bored into mine.

"I'm dreaming." I couldn't suppress a laugh. "I went unconscious after the hatch threw me into the wall. This isn't real."

I turned around and looked at each of the others. They paid no attention to my surly host or me.

Gil sighed, shaking his head. "I don't have time for this."

He reached under the counter and came back up with a curved dagger and raised it over his head. He stabbed it into the wood, pinning my hand to the bar.

"AAUUGGHH!" I screamed, slamming my fist on the wooden slab.

Gil yanked the blade back out. The pain ended as sharply as it began.

"What the hell is wrong with you?" I examined my glove, poking my finger into the new holes on both sides. Blood came away from it, darkening the frayed edges.

"Ah, don't be such a baby," he said, reaching out and taking me by the wrist. He ran his finger over the cut in my palm. The hole disappeared. He did the same to the back of my hand. Same result.

I turned my hand over repeatedly. Only faint red stains remained in the fabric. I ripped the glove off to find old scars where the blade ran through.

What the hell?

I stared at Gil, unblinking.

"Do I have your attention now?" He asked, drumming his fingers.

I nodded, swallowing hard.

"As I said," he flicked the jug's handle. "We start with you ordering a drink and tell me your woes. What'll you have? Just name it."

"Jameson. Black Barrel. Chilled." I took off my other glove and laid the pair on the bar. "But can I get it in a clean cup?"

Gil smirked and passed his hand over the mug. A crystal tumbler appeared where the clay one used to be. He tipped the jug and poured an amber liquid, complete with ice cubes, into the glass.

Once filled, he took the cup by both hands and pulled another glass away from the first.

I'm officially freaked out right now.

Gil returned the pitcher under the bar, then handed me one of the glasses. "Beimid ag ól!" he said, raising the other to his lips and tossed it back in one gulp. The ice rattled in the glass as he slammed it down with a thunderous belch.

I couldn't help staring at the sorcerer. I'm a guy's guy, but he had the manners of a goat.

"Now." He tapped my glass's base with his fingertip. "Bartendering doesn't work if you're not drinking."

I raised my glass and muttered *Sláinte*, then sniffed.

Hm. Toffee and toast.

I took a sip. The aromatic liquid burned and warmed at the same time. I drank again, longer this time.

How long has it been since I did anything just for the pleasure?

I finished the glass, then made the cubes dance together.

"Another?" Gil gave me a one-sided grin.

"No, thanks," I set the cup down, clearing my throat. "So, how does this work? How're you going to solve my problem."

"Same as in any other bar, I suspect." Gil shrugged. "You talk. I listen."

I bent over, resting my elbows on the bar, locking my fingers behind my head. "Where do I even start?"

"Well, the beginning is usually too far back," he grabbed the rag and absently wiped off the counter. "Let's start with, why are you holding up the timestream?"

"I'm trying to stop my father from murdering my mother," I blew out a breath, "as well as many others. I've tried a few dozen times--."

"Forty-Seven."

"What?"

"You've gummed up the timestream forty-seven times. Just keeping the record straight. Continue."

"Each of the *forty-seven* times," I glared across the bar, "I've tried to convince him to end his mission to the past, but he doesn't listen, and the overdose of L.E.A.P. causes him to suffer a temporal schism and go on a rampage through time."

"What's *leap*?" Gil asked, holding up a finger.

"It's a drug that enables Emergents, like my dad, to travel into the past instead of just observing it."

"Can't you just call the authorities? Report what he's planning to do?"

"They don't exist." I snorted. "At least the ones who could do anything doesn't exist anymore. Plus, he's already done it. My past is his present. The overdose left a permanent residue of L.E.A.P. in his system. It enabled him to leap at will. After his schism, he traveled back to the past and went on a murder spree that changed everything in what's now his future. My present."

"I see."

"I've tried tricking him," I slam my hands on the bar, knocking the twin tumblers onto the floor, "telling him the truth, showing him video footage of the future he left me with, but nothing works. He's always convinced it isn't real and continues on his mission to 1969. The triple dose of L.E.A.P. broke him. And then she strings him along until everything that made him who he was is in ashes. All so she can get what *she* wants."

"Who's she?"

"Marie Leon," I growl, balling my fists. "She's behind all of it. But every time I've told him about her, things only get worse."

Gil picked up the fallen tumblers and set them down, then reached under the bar and returned with a glass bottle of amber liquid. The label read Jameson's Black Barrel. He hummed to himself as he refilled both glasses and pushed one to me. He took his own, slugged it back, and then just stared at the drink in his hand.

"You do know that the world can't be changed by a single person," Gil threw the rag over his shoulder. "Believe me, I tried. It takes the convergence of the entire planet, every single individual, to make events come about and form what passes on as history. There's only one who can orchestrate that kind of cooperation, and it isn't you."

"What do you expect me to do?" I threw my hands in the air. "Just let it all burn? Let my dad destroy what others spent their lives building? Just accept I'll..."

I bit my lip, choking back the urge to scream and cry at the same time.

Gil seemed to gaze through me.

"Just accept I'll never get to know the woman who gave birth to me?"

He could've made the Sphinx lose a staring contest.

"Just accept that I'll be forever known as the son of a killer? He destroyed the treatment for autism and condemned thousands of spectrum children to their mental prisons?"

Gil nodded to himself, his mouth pursed as he seemed to gauge the tumbler's weight in his hand. He then looked over my shoulder toward the tables. "You see that young woman over there?"

I craned my neck to see the cosplay champion, still kneeling over a pewter mug. "What about her? Who is she?"

"Ever hear of Jeanne d'Arc?"

The name sounds vaguely familiar.

"Do you mean Joan of Arc?"

"Yep," Gil grabbed the towel off his shoulder and resumed spreading germs across the counter.

"What's she doing here?" I turned around.

"I was in the middle of attending to her own crisis of conscience when I had to divert all the way over here to deal with your antics."

"What's her problem?"

"She doesn't want to die, burning at the stake, tomorrow."

"But, she died centuries ago."

"Not to her, she hasn't," Gil said. "It's not much different than you trying to prevent your father from doing something he's already done, is it?"

"I guess not," I looked down on the ground. "What is she saying?"

"She's praying." Gil stepped around the bar to stand beside me, my head just above his shoulders. "It's the night before her execution, and she's been praying to God for deliverance so she can continue to help her people. She was brought here, and I gave her that drink. She's been praying over it since she got here three hours ago. Bar-time, that is."

"Did you put something in her drink?" I looked at my own glass.

"Mead," Gil shrugged. "With extra bubbles."

"How are you going to help her?"

"Not sure," Gil pursed his lips. "But it'll come to me when she's ready."

"You're not exactly the best fixer, are you?"

"Never said I was," Gil patted my arm with the back of his hand then gestured toward the room. "I only said my boss told me to help you so I can get on with helping them."

Just then, Jeanne d'Arc got to her feet, holding her hands up to the ceiling and shouting *Merci*. She walked up to Gil, grabbed his head and kissed his cheeks before she started talking in rapid French. Her voice broke several times, though her lips remained flat and pinched. Determined.

Gil answered back in French, patting her on the shoulder, and then pulling her into a tight embrace. He turned his face away from me. I'm pretty sure he was hiding tears because he touched his face with a hand as sniffling filled the room.

"Merci, Gilgamesh. Je suis prêt maintenant." She said, pulling out of his arms.

Gil said something and gestured to her table. She nodded and returned to a kneeling position before draining her cup at her lips.

"What was that all about?" I whispered.

"She was shown a revelation of what would have happened to her country if she hadn't acted on her childhood visions."

"What would've happened?" I asked, curious as a child listening to a ghost story.

"Sorry, kid." Gil laughed in his throat. "That's between her, me, and my boss."

"What about the others?"

Gil pointed to the man sipping tea. "That's Charles Lutwidge Dodgson. He thinks he's fallen down his own rabbit hole. He's currently self-medicating."

Charles put down his teacup and opened a leather-bound book from his inside pocket. His hand moved across the page as if tracking an earthquake.

"That little boy," he guided my gaze, "will uncover the physics behind gravity and how to counter it. He's literally going to launch a whole new wave of human exploration."

"When did he come from?"

Gil laughed, patting my shoulder, "He's not from your *history*."

"He's from my future?"

"Past, present, and future are all just matters of perspective, aren't they?"

"What are you helping him with?" I asked, leaning forward, wishing I could get a glimpse of his notes.

"It's not for me to say," Gil blocked me like a railroad crossing. "Or for you to find out."

He pushed away from the counter and returned to stand behind the bar.

"What about the girl?" I asked, following Gil's path. He avoided looking over at her. "Who is she? Past, present, or future?"

Gil tilted his head as if listening to someone whisper in his ear.

"I can't tell you that," he frowned. "But I *can* tell you her life hinges on whether or not you're successful in saving your mother."

"What's that supposed to mean?"

I searched Gil's eyes for any tell but found nothing.

"What did you mean by that, dammit?" I slapped the counter.

"You've got your mother's temper," he gave a half-smile. "Did you know that?"

He caught me off-guard. "Liam," I said. "Her uncle. He helped raise me. He tells me that all the time."

Gil stared through me for a minute, giving me an encore of his sphinx routine.

"You pissed me off, DJ, but I like you." His eyes came into focus and glanced over at the girl. "So, I'm going to tell you something about your future."

"What's that?" I leaned in.

He pointed over my shoulder. "That's your daughter."

* * *

"I don't have a daughter," I said, shaking my head. "I'm not married. I don't date much. And it's been a really long time since..."

"Since you shacked up with that waitress, Michelle, in Dublin?" Gil gave me a sly nod. "The fellow second-gen Emergent you lived with for over a year. The one who helped you get the passcodes you needed to get into the Dome? Ringing any bells?"

"No way."

"Happy Father's Day. It's a girl." Gil feigned tossing confetti in the air. "Here's the rub, though. If I help you change your father's fate, you may never meet Michelle. And if you don't meet Michelle, your daughter will never be born. Maybe you should get to know your daughter before you condemn her to non-existence."

I'm not sure how it happened, but one moment I was standing at the bar with Gil, and the next I was sitting on the floor beside the girl with red hair.

"Get to it, boy." Gil raised his voice from the bar. "You haven't got all day."

If I'm going to get any help from Gilgamesh the annoying, I guess I'll have to play along.

"Hi," I said, trying to put myself in the girls' line of sight.

She continued to scratch gibberish into the table.

"I'm DJ. What's your name?"

After playing twenty questions with myself, her focus never diverted from the ceiling.

"This isn't working," I yelled at Gil, folding my arms.

"You're looking for answers in all the wrong places."

I hunched over, putting my hands to my eyes like blinders and stared at the cuts on the table. The scrapes varied in depth, length, and direction. It wasn't until I rested my head sideways in one hand that I saw it. She carved a bas-relief in the wood.

I lowered my face to the surface, and there it was. A portrait of Michelle and me holding a baby. Words appeared around the frame.

Hello, DJ. My name is Erin. Gil said you'd come someday. I've been waiting for you.

"Do you know who I am?" I asked, lifting my head.

Erin found a blank space and carved. Within a minute, another portrait took shape. My name, along with her name and Michelle Finnigan, were scrawled like a banner across the top.

You are the man who made me with mommy.

"Why have you been waiting for me?"

She found another empty space.

I wanted to meet you.

"What does that mean?" I asked. "You wanted to meet me before you grew up?"

"Her mind exists outside of the timestream," Gil appeared at my side. "Just like the eddy's you create for your father. She escapes here in her mind. It's taken quite a while to develop our own shorthand."

Erin's stylus moved across the table, pointing at different symbols.

"She wants to know why it took you so long to find her."

My mouth dried up like Desert Valley in August.

"Because I didn't know you existed until now."

Erin pointed to more symbols.

"If you had known I existed, would you have come for me?"

"Of course," I reached out and patted her back. She squirmed away, shrieking.

"She doesn't like to be touched," Gil said. "But she does like to smell people. Blow at her."

I took a deep breath and blew a slow stream of air toward her face. She stopped, turned in my direction, and put her nose in the breeze. Her mouth twitched, then she pointed to symbols across the table.

"Now I know what my daddy smells like. You smell like a good man. Now you can save your daddy."

The stylus fell over as Erin disappeared.

I reached out but only touched air. "Where did she go?"

"She went back to where and when she came from," Gil sat across from me on the floor. "Sometimes, when she appears, she's just a baby and is gone in a few seconds. Other times, she's a grown woman and has known you for many years. But most of the time, she's between six and twelve, just looking to connect with her father."

"I know the feeling."

I can't help but stare at the relief portraits.

"In one of her adult-state visits, she wanted me to tell you that she understands if you choose to save your father. She said, more people need to be saved from non-existence than one little girl."

"Does it have to be one or the other?" I pick at the splintered wood around her baby portrait face. "Can I save my father from killing my mother and the rest, and still make sure she's born?"

I looked up to see Gil looking like a Buddha statue, eyes closed and apparently in deep meditation. "It's a long shot," he mused, "and you're going to need some extra proof."

He grunted as he stood, then walked behind the bar.

Who knew immortals got winded from getting themselves off the ground?

I followed him to my side of the counter as he pulled a heavy-looking gilded chest from a shelf. It banged and jangled, not unlike a pirates chest, when it met the wood. He lifted the lid, allowing me a glimpse of what was inside.

Coins.

Hundreds of coins. Most of which I didn't even recognize what historical period they must have come from. Coins of precious metals. Plastics and woods. Also, a few stone disks peeked out from behind others.

"Now, let me see," Gil raked his fingers through the pile. "Something small. Concealable. Has to be the right era, and aha. There you are."

He held up a small silver coin, no bigger than my thumbnail. On one side, a tiny needle stood like a micro Eiffel Tower.

"I'll be right back." Gil then disappeared into a back room, reemerging a few seconds later and shoving the disk in my hand. "Here. Take it. You get one more chance to convince your father to change his course. After that, your little time eddy trick will be overridden by the higher-ups."

"What do I do with it?" I held the token in my palm.

"Just get him to push it into his skin and then swallow it," Gil returned his treasure chest to the shelf. "It'll do the rest."

"What, exactly, is it?" I held it out.

Gil swished his rag across the countertop, ignoring me.

"Will it hurt him?"

Gil continued to wipe down the spotless bar with the filthy rag.

"What is this?" I shouted.

"It's his memories, DJ," Gil shouted back, then took a breath. "It's the chemical record of his entire life, from start to finish. He's getting a wonderful gift, and a terrible curse, all at the same time."

"How is knowing the future a curse?"

"Do you know how many people want to know their future? Do you know how many actually get a glimpse? Do you want to know how many people have gone insane because they were shown what lies ahead for them? The current rate is 99.9%. Only a rare few have seen the future and kept their sanity. If you could see all your decisions--good and bad, past, present and future--how would it change who you are right now?"

"I don't know." I shrugged. "But I'd be able to make more informed choices."

"You'd think so." Gil laughed and waggled his fingers. "But it's more like not studying and cheating on a test. Sure, you may get the grade, but you didn't learn anything, so you don't know *why* you made a choice. The why is always the key."

"Now, ironically, you're running out of time. I need to send you back. Remember, you have one more chance. If your father doesn't believe you, then history will be set in stone."

"Metaphorically." Gil held his palms out as if playing with a Slinky.

I shoved the coin in my chest pocket, donned my gloves, and reached over the bar. "Thanks, Gil."

"I wish you luck, kid." He shook my hand once. "Don't piss me off again."

I put my headgear back on, securing the collar seal, and noticed the fractures had vanished. I looked up, about to thank him, when he winked.

"This may hurt." He smirked and flicked his fingers at me.

Something yanked me by my naval and dragged me through the room, ignored by Gil's remaining patrons. I spun in mid-air and shielded my face before slamming into the wood-slatted wall.

* * *

A moment before impact, the weathered slats disappeared, replaced with the curved white tiles of the Jar. I lost my breath again and slid down the sides, coming to a stop at the base of the raised dais. The alarms pierced my eardrums after spending who knew how long with Gilgamesh.

"DJ," Liam's voice said over the sirens. "Are you okay? You've got to get out of there. Security's coming."

"Not yet," I barked into the mic. I climbed the ladder running up the central column. "Close the hatch and seal the room. I get to make one more attempt to stop dad."

"No, DJ," Liam shouted through my headgear. "We've failed. He doesn't believe what you're telling him. There's no way for you to get through to him."

"Maybe I can't," I grunted, standing up. "But maybe *he* can get through to himself."

"What are you talking about?"

"I'll explain later." I rushed across the bridge and heaved the door closed. "Seal the room. Leave me in here if you have to, but I have to divert dad's leap one more time."

"I'm not leaving you behind." He growled.

"And I'm not leaving knowing I had one more shot and walked away from it."

"I don't understand, DJ."

"And I don't have time to explain," I said, meeting his glare from the observation window. "I need you to trust me."

We locked eyes until he looked down at his console. "Hatch seal integrity is only at eighty-eight percent. If it drops any further, the hatch may rupture and blow you into the time eddy. You'll be trapped in the timestream."

"At least I'll die knowing I did everything I could to restore the timeline."

I watched him nod and reach across the control panel.

"Hatch secured," He said at the same moment the bridge rumbled under my feet. "Evacuating atmosphere. Better get in position."

"Thanks, Uncle Liam," I said, taking long strides across the bridge. "For everything."

Within seconds the sirens faded to nothing. Except for my heartbeat and shallow breathing, I'd returned to absolute silence.

"Better get the simulation running," Liam said over comms. "If they cut the power, we've only got limited battery reserves. A half-hour at best."

"I'll try to make it quick," I fingered the coin through my suits' fabric as the projectors came to life.

* * *

The sun appeared first, washing the white surfaces until they looked like they glowed. The hilltop came next, spreading from under my feet to the curved walls and beyond. Grass sprouted. Flowers bloomed. Shrubs and Trees in the distance came into existence.

I fiddled with the settings on my arm console until the randomness of leaves rustling in the wind were at their maximum setting. I even threw in a few monarch butterflies for good measure.

Now the hard part.

I knelt down, preserving my remaining strength, and pushed my mind out to find the timestream. It seemed to take longer than before.

I have to get it right this time.

The temporal veil rippled in my vision for a moment and vanished.

I have to make him see.

I pushed out again and found the stream. It evaporated like a snowflake in the Sahara.

A boy needs his mother *and* father.

My third push yielded similarly discouraging results.

Every little girl needs her daddy in her life.

On my fourth attempt, the ethereal curtain almost solidified to a waterfall. On the other side, I saw dad. He was piercing the veil from his own point in time. He swayed as he knelt on the dais.

The triple-dose has already started the schism.

"C-C-Con-Control," he garbled. "G-Good t-t-to go. Lea-L-Le-Leaper and... and P-Pro-Projector in t-t-tow."

He got to his feet on shaky knees.

"Get a good grip," he slurred, looking over his shoulder. "This may be a bumpy ride."

Dad penetrated the veil, dragging Marie along as he crossed into the timestream. He seemed to struggle against the current.

I've never had the chance to leap. After he went berzerk, it was strictly outlawed. I wonder what's it's like from his perspective. I may never get the chance to find out if this doesn't work.

I could see him losing his bearing, thrown around by the temporal forces around him like sailing through a hurricane.

Opening a pinhole on my side of the curtain, I tried to direct some of my artificial sunlight in his direction. He caught sight of it and moved toward me.

I switched on my environmental suit's holographic system to make it appear I was wearing the same linen shirt with matching pants. I fiddled one last time with my chest pocket for the coin.

Gil, you'd better be right about this.

Once dad was close enough, I reached into the timestream. I found his hand, and then pulled him through my side of the temporal veil for the forty-eighth and final time.

As soon as they were through, I froze Marie just inside the eddy so she couldn't interfere as she had multiple times before.

Dad squinted, raising his hand against the holographic sunlight beaming down on him until his eyes focused on me. He looked disoriented and vulnerable.

I couldn't help but smile. This is the man I was risking everything to save.

This man isn't a murderer.

This man isn't a traitor.

This man is a devoted husband and father. A man who believed in mercy for those who died with no one else to bring their killers to justice. A man who made mistakes, then worked hard to make amends and change for the better. A man who loved my mother and would do anything to protect her.

This is the man I was here to save.

"Hi, Dad," I said, unable to keep my voice from cracking. "It's good to meet you. Again."

The End

10

THE ARTIST'S MODEL

by Brian C Hailes

Posing nude in front of an art class or in the studio of a master painter would be difficult for most people, impossible for others. Even those that do it regularly sometimes feel timid, unsure of themselves, or even embarrassed. Others might feel a sense of excitement, a rush of adrenaline, a kind of high. A few I've observed go so far as to approach even the sensual.

I feel none of those things. But then, I'm not really a person—at least, not a *human* person.

The name they had assigned me when the police officers delivered me to the Clear Valley Orphanage was Mabel, a proper girl's name with Latin origin meaning *loveable.*

The other children at the establishment seemed to enjoy calling me "Mae" instead; a name associated with the month, derived from the Latin Maius, the Greek mythological goddess of increase.

When I arrived, not at the orphanage, but in the alleyway next to some dumpsters, I was naked, and a little confused.

The first person I saw, a young man with black hair and a much darker complexion than mine, flushed at the sight of me. His instincts told him to flee—and they were almost right. But he stopped mid-flight, and turned back to approach me. Looking around to see if others saw us, he took off his jacket and wrapped me with it. He helped me to my feet, and tried as best he could to shield me from others on the street.

"What are you doing?" he asked. "What's your name? Why are you—?"

"I'm walking," I answered. "I'm shivering, due to the cold. My name is . . . " I couldn't quite remember receiving a name. "I'm . . ."

"Come here." He put an arm around my shoulder. "Where are you from? Who are your people?"

I tried to remember. " . . . I don't know."

The young man brought me to a building, in front of which parked three white and black vehicles with red, yellow, and blue lights fashioned across the top. *Police cars*, I later learned.

We went inside. The smells of old walls and cleaners attempting to drown out varied body odors hovered in the lobby. The young man introduced me to an officer, who, in turn, introduced me to other officers. He said they would take care of me; told me his name was "Carl," and left.

The officers gave me strange looks, some of pity, some of disgust, disapproval, even lust. "Drugs?" I heard one of them whisper. "Dunno," said the other. "Underage prostitute maybe."

"Here you go, Sweetie." A large woman offered me some girl's clothes that didn't seem to fit very well, but they were folded nicely and smelled of industrial bleach.

Two of the officers sat me down in a gray empty room surrounded by windows and lit with fluorescent lights, one of which flickered with a faulty starter. The officers took turns asking me questions, most of which I didn't know the answers to. Apparently frustrated, they asked me to go in the bathroom and pee in a cup, so I did, but I don't think they got the results they expected.

So I spent the night. And the next.

And then they dropped me off at Clear Valley. They said, "Good luck," before leaving me with three orderlies.

"How many years has it been now?" asked Peter Luca, the Italian New York contemporary painter that often hired me as one of his muses.

My twenty minutes was nearly up before he would offer me a break from my stationary pose. I didn't really need a break, but most of the artists I modeled for seemed quite concerned for my comfort and well being, so it usually proved easier to simply oblige them. Luca was no exception.

"Five," I said.

He nodded, intent on his canvas and brush strokes, his mixture of oils. The aromas of high-end paints, thinners, and old architecture filled the open concept studio loft apartment, which must have seemed lonely without visitors. Wagner played faintly in the background.

The calm intensity in Luca's eyes as he studied my nude figure and struggled to mirror the youthful vitality of the stance paired with his original ideas of value, color, texture, and composition, was an intensity I noticed in very few of those that attempted to capture me in their respective artworks; Luca and those few others stood apart from the rest. Only a small fraction of those that fancied themselves artists exhibited the signs of what I observed to be true obsession.

However, true artists or not, many on the island seemed passionate enough to hire me as their model, and they offered handsome amounts of money for my services. Photographers also became interested in working with me, and increasingly procured my contact information in random places for shoots, but I still somehow preferred the traditional artist's studio, primarily one-on-one. And of all the many jobs, Luca was my favorite.

He ever pursued what he considered to be 'the perfect pose'. A pursuit, it seemed, he would never quite fulfill. And *perfect*—I didn't exactly know what that meant. I suppose he didn't know what it meant either. But he chased it, like I chased understanding this new world. This *strange* world. With its *strange* people.

The more I explored, the more questions I had. The more people I met, the more infinite the possibilities. But people felt things so deeply. So deeply it would drive them to carry out careers for decades or lifetimes—even careers they appeared to hate. It would drive them to kill, make love, humiliate themselves, shut down completely, burst into tears, or cry out with joy at the most inopportune times. And many of the creatives I knew exhibited behaviors of the manically depressed, self-medicating, drug or sex-addicted, even delusional. But they felt so deeply, and I felt as though I were merely acting. Pretending.

Posing.

"That's twenty minutes, my lovely Mabel," Luca said, frustration lining his tone. "Why don't you go ahead and take a short break?" He threw his brushes and palette knives into a bottle of thinner, and tossed his paint rag onto the table next to his paint-crusted palette, wiping his stained hands together.

I nodded, and reached down for my short silken robe patterned with Chinese-etched cherry blossoms and dark gnarled branches against a tame teal sky. Covering my nakedness usually put everyone at ease—even the veteran artists.

Having recently spent more time outdoors and around swimming pools, my overall complexion had darkened since my arrival years ago in the alleyway, and many seemed to prefer the slightly tanned look. Exterior beauty alone, it seemed, could take a person quite far in the current state of earthly society, but it wasn't *going far* that drove me to model. Nor the money. It wasn't even the enjoyment, for I felt none, and I never knew why. The needs of the world and my talents simply crossed, and my vocation made itself known to me, even before I had left the orphanage.

"I . . ." Luca sighed heavily, " . . . I am just not feeling it today." His drooping, overgrown eyebrows popped up as his eyes met mine. "But you! You are being great. Beautiful. As always." His ongoing intention to remain optimistic despite his struggles, played vividly across his timeworn features. "Are you hungry, my dear?" he asked.

I forced a smile. "Sure."

He grabbed his jacket, keys, and plaid beret. I followed him toward the door, but before exiting, he paused and looked back at me. "Oh, you uh, you might—" He pointed down at my naked legs with a grin.

"Pants!" I exclaimed. "Right."

He chuckled warmly. "Yes, yes, and perhaps shoes."

Chelsea Market, more a collection of eateries than a single restaurant, buzzed with the usual lunchtime crowd. Mostly popular with locals and students, Luca always seemed to prefer it to the touristy pizza and burger joints that surrounded it. As we managed through foot traffic on the street, many heads or flitting eyes—mostly male—perked in my direction. Luca also noticed. "Seems I have chosen the right model for my paintings."

"I swear I don't know what you're talking about," I said.

Luca nodded, keen to change the subject. "I even pick up my groceries here," he said, as if I cared where the old man shopped. "You'll find good Thai food over there," he went on. "Amy's Bread has amazing French loaves. The Lobster Place has decent sushi but I really enjoy its clam chowder. Today we will try the Green Table; the food is excellent, everything is well portioned, and they do very good drinks."

"Whatever you say." I manufactured a cool grin to put him at ease.

"It's not cheap," he said, "But no matter." Not that Luca hurt for money—each of his paintings, large or small, fetched a pretty penny on the international dealers market, and many pieces were sold before he could even paint them. Galleries clamored for his works, which usually focused on the figurative, though his growing collection also boasted some of the most sought after cityscapes.

Luca led me to an outside terrace of the newly remodeled street café, and pulled my chair out for me, always the gentleman.

A young waiter, obviously unaccustomed to people seating themselves, nodded to the preoccupied hostess, awkwardly retrieved some silverware and menus, and approached.

Before the waiter could introduce himself, Luca held up a hand with pointer-finger extended and, without making eye contact with anyone in particular ordered, "I'll start off with a Bellini cocktail. And my friend will have . . . "

"The same," I said, though I had never tried one before. I found it gave people confidence in their choices if you simply agreed with their tastes. I didn't intend to drink but a sip or two anyway. I didn't particularly enjoy the dulling effect of alcohol on my senses.

The waiter nodded as he dropped the menus in front of us, and didn't bother reaching for his notepad before leaving to fetch the drinks.

"You know," Luca said, "I think Gianna would like to have met you."

"Gianna," I said the name with reverence. "Your wife."

The old painter nodded thoughtfully.

"I would like to have met her," I said.

"Car crash," Luca lamented, almost to himself. "Meaningless."

"Here in the city?" I asked.

"Yes. Accident of course. No one to blame."

"I'm sorry," I said.

"She was young. Probably *too* young." He grinned. "But vibrant, full of life. Every time I paint a picture, I believe I am painting her. Even the paintings I did before I met her, were for her. My girl. My future. And now my past. She was my brush. She *is* my brush."

I said nothing, if only to let him have his precious moments of reminiscence.

"So . . . " he continued, " . . . Thank you."

"For what?"

"For standing in on her behalf."

"Of course."

"I did not mean to make such heavy conversation right off the bat," Luca said. "And here I am, speaking nonsense. Going on and on—"

"No," I said. "Not nonsense. It's fine."

"I will attempt to lighten the mood when I return." Luca excused himself, and shuffled past the tightly spaced tables and chairs. "Little boy's room. Be right back."

"Sure." I pulled out my phone to quickly check email and messages.

Another booking from my agent—a photo shoot out by the pier. Return customer. A revered photographer named Johannes. Seemed familiar. I added it to my calendar and sent my agent the link.

And Carl wanted to come over after work.

Fine, I texted. *See you tonight.*

A few of my girlfriends—and I use the term lightly—that I shared an apartment with had told me to ditch the boy months ago, and persisted. "*Friend seeking benefits,*" they called it. However, I saw no problem with helping the one who helped me. And he did seem lonely much of the time. Most of the men I'd been with seemed lonely.

A cautionary feeling suddenly crept up my back and I looked up. Across from me sat a well-manicured man in a gray suit with a mauve tie. He was a very ordinary looking man, but something in his eyes shown anything but ordinary. A five o' clock shadow cooled his sharp jawline, and an expensive watch peeked out from under his sleeve. Appearing from nowhere, he occupied Luca's seat, and watched me as though he knew who I was. Who I *really* was.

"What an honor," he said. "I finally get my moment with *the most beautiful woman in the world.*"

I shook my head. "Who—?"

"If you were one of them, you might be feeling a tinge of fear at this moment, perhaps apprehension, or loathing. But confusion is all you can manage, isn't that right?"

He is right, I thought. *I'm merely existing. I don't feel like other people. I just am.*

"Who are you?" I asked. None of the other restaurant patrons seemed to take notice of the man. *Can they even see him?*

"Lecter Ay'Con," he answered.

"Where are you from?"

"Mal'tair Major."

Is that a planetary system? I thought.

"What do you want?"

"Stop asking stupid questions," he said smugly. "*Their* questions. It's almost as if you've allowed yourself to become one of them. You wake up, get ready, eat breakfast, go to work, play with friends, go to parties, get new work, bed who you may, go to sleep; wash, rinse, repeat, just as they have trained you to do."

He leaned forward and focused intently on my eyes. "You are not . . . one of them."

"I know that."

"Yet you have inculcated yourself completely into their way of life. Curious." He sat back against his chair. "Like the animals of this planet, we are governed by a different set of rules."

"What do you want?" I asked again. "What rules are you referring to? And what alternatives do I have to this different set of them?"

He smiled. "Give it time. I don't believe we are ready for you to begin just yet. However, pleasant introductions."

My brow furrowed. "Wh—?"

"Much better," Luca said, approaching me from behind. I turned to see the old painter's reaction to my new visitor, but Luca came around our table and sat in his chair as though he hadn't even seen the man.

Ay'Con had vanished.

"Now," Luca said, bringing up the menu like it was the morning paper, "What will you have, my dear?"

* * *

Carl and I made love in our usual routine, which I regarded more as an experiment in human behavior than some pursuit of inane bodily pleasure. It was his preferred routine, which was fine, as I had no preferences. I always merely pretended to feel the physical connections as strongly as my temporary partners, as if it were some clinical trial that required a participant's full emotional investment for more accurate readings. And they didn't seem to mind, which meant the act must have worked. But this time, I found it difficult even to pretend. My mind had locked focus on the man in the café. And I could think of nothing—or no one—else.

Carl lifted his head from off my shoulder. "What's the matter? You seem distracted."

"I am distracted. Sorry."

"Everything okay?" Carl asked.

"Not sure," I said.

After a few moments, he threw off the sheets and bedspread, and headed for the bathroom. I slipped on my nightgown and strode out beyond the sliding door to my apartment balcony. The ever-present ruckus of intermittent morning traffic echoed from below. Dawn's light crept between skyscrapers and splashed its warm rays across the modern architecture all around. The brightness challenged my tired eyes, but at the same time, welcomed it. Birds twittered from their high perch ledges, and soft dew chilled the composite deck floorboards under my feet.

Carl brought me a warm cup of herbal tea. I took a whiff. *Peppermint.* He often performed nice gestures like that.

"Thank you," I said.

"You bet."

"So, what's going on?"

I didn't answer immediately, just sipped my tea.

"Am I supposed to guess?"

"You're drawn to me," I said. "I see that all too clearly. Like a twig to a waterfall. And I'm curious about that. I've been trying to figure out what it means. But that's all it is. A curiosity."

Carl's face clenched. "A curi—?" He looked down at his feet, becoming emotional.

"I don't understand." His voice cracked. "After all this time, have you felt nothing?"

"Yes."

"I've known you longer than anyone," he said. "Why haven't you said anything? A curiosity? Why did you let me believe you cared?"

I didn't have much of a feeling one way or another. "I don't know. I guess I was . . . curious."

"I love you," he said, pleading, shaking. "Please don't do this. Don't be like this."

"I like you, Carl," I said. "But I've got to go to work."

"What if I go off myself?" he said.

"Please don't."

"Would you even care?"

"I don't know."

"What do you mean you don't know?"

This conversation was going nowhere. "I'm finished with this," I said. "With us. I don't need it."

"Are you a sociopath?"

I left the pouting Carl on the balcony, got dressed, and exited the apartment. "You can let yourself out."

He stayed to finish his drink.

* * *

I followed the photographer and his assistant out to the pier. As wardrobe, they had provided a brilliant white summer dress and a sheer sash of marigold. The outfit accented my form and complexion well, and blew like angel robes in the sea breeze. Another magazine cover with Johannes, the amazing, yet typical magazine photographer.

When everyone is amazing at something, is it still amazing?

We set to it quickly, snapping colorful glamour shots against the linear city background and ocean.

"Beautiful," the photographer said. "Gorgeous. That's it. Give me some attitude. Something fierce. Now pouty. And big smile."

I followed his direction with an ease that had always come. I didn't even have to try. I was simply . . . *me*.

Having nearly filled his first memory card, he took pause and viewed his playback screen for a time.

I sat and watched the surging waves breaking against the rocks as I waited to begin again, and his assistant approached me to touch up my hair and makeup.

"Wow," the photographer said. "Not a bad shot in the bunch. Every single one of these is cover-worthy, except that one's a bit out of focus." He looked up at me as though he were in love. "Great job."

"Thank you," I said, not even pretending to blush. This was just a job.

"Why don't we take a break," Johannes said.

"Oh, I don't need a break. We can just finish up."

He hesitated. "I . . . need a Coke. And that will probably take ten to fifteen minutes."

"So . . ." I hoped he would change his mind.

"So," he finished, "Short break? Wanna come?"

"No, thanks. I'll wait here."

"Suit yourself." Johannes and the assistant gathered their equipment and walked toward the shoreline shops.

I took a seat on the nearest bench.

Before the two even made it off the boardwalk, the man in the gray suit was sitting beside me. "Don't be alarmed," he said, "Actually, let me rephrase. Don't be *confused*."

"Apparently, I'm always confused. Hello, Ay'Con."

"Hello."

"Is that your real name?"

"Closest translation in English."

"Are you going to keep following me around, popping up at random times?"

"Actually, I'm not following you. Believe it or not, I keep very busy."

"Busy stalking people? Are you a professional stalker?"

"Of sorts," he said, which surprised me. "Humans attribute a very negative connotation to stalkers, primarily the female gender—that is, unless they quote-un-quote 'like' said stalker, or find them romantically attractive—then they're simply *the perfect man*. No. We drop in from time to time to . . . *groom* those like us for their debut, so to speak."

"*Debut*?" I repeated.

"Correct."

"Hm," I nodded, pondering, trying to feel his words.

"How much time have I got?" I asked.

"Some," he replied.

"What am I?"

"Ah, now you are asking the right questions." Ay'Con straightened up in his suit, and drew in a long breath. "What are you indeed?"

"That's what I'm asking."

"What do you know of life and death?"

"Are you going to answer all of my *important* questions with questions?"

Ay'Con waited patiently for my answer.

"As much as the next woman, I suppose. Perhaps a bit more."

Ay'Con smiled. "What do you mean by that?"

"Nothing," I said. "A feeling."

"Well, that's something." He took another long breath. "With humans, life and death are mutually exclusive, the connection of spirit and body defining the very state of their souls. *You* are many things, Mabel, but primarily a reconnaissance beacon."

"Many things?" I raised an eyebrow. "Reconnaissance beacon?"

A pair of seagulls cried out as they approached, then lifted off on a sudden gust of wind.

"A harbinger," he said, "A herald. Even Charon, the ferryman of Hades who carries spirits of the newly deceased across the rivers Styx and Acheron . . . that is, if you *choose* to be. Or, you could be nobody—like so many here."

I thought a moment. "I don't understand."

"'Course not," Ay'Con said, "But you will. When the time is right."

"Death." I looked out over the undulating sea, and the connecting shoreline with its accompanying skyline. *Much of what he said rang true, but how could it be right?* "Are you telling me death treats *us* differently than *them*?"

Ay'Con stood and straightened out his suit lapels.

"In the last five years since your arrival, have you ever been injured? Have you ever fallen ill?"

Miraculously, I had not.

"Do you believe the connection of *your* spirit holds the life in your body?" Ay'Con asked, "Or can both live disjoint simultaneously?"

Somehow, the question came across as rhetorical.

"The separation itself does not define the state of our souls," he continued, "But you already know this to be true. You've known it all along."

But no one had ever put it into words, and directly aimed them at me.

"Yes," I muttered. "I guess I have. But—"

Ay'Con made to leave. "Meantime, don't have too much fun trying it out."

I blinked, and he vanished. *What could he possibly have meant by that?*

"I'm not going to kill myself!"

* * *

"I'm going to kill myself." I stared off the top ledge of my apartment building, fifty stories above the busy street. I stepped up from the roof gravel onto the concrete molding, where one slip would either send me hurtling to an abrupt end or prove the feeling deep within my gut—or "second brain" as my roommates liked to call it—that Ay'Con was right. I didn't feel fear or apprehension at the possibility of dying, only curiosity, as one trying to deduce the correct answer to a complicated mathematical equation.

One of the orderlies from Clear Valley that had taken a liking to me early on always told the youth as they readied to leave the orphanage and begin their adult lives, "The best stories have always been about lightning chasers. Be a lightning chaser." I hadn't given the sentiment much thought until now. I could only hope that my possible demise would not be so unsavory as the great downfall of social media.

I had already made up my mind by coming up here in the first place, so what was I waiting for?

I jumped off the ledge.

As I fell, I noticed the startled pigeons that immediately took flight under, then over me, the ever-present city noises, the torrential wind biting at my face and dress from below. I wondered for a moment about cats, and how they always seem to land on their feet.

I weighed more than a cat, but I thought I would try it out.

The force upon impact was more than I had ever experienced, and it shook spirit from body. For a moment, I saw myself sprawled out on the broken sidewalk. At least three people had witnessed my sloppy landing. One woman screamed, and covered her eyes. A heavyset man out for a jog stopped and gasped in unbelief. A wide-eyed teenager approached me, scanning the scene for blood spatter. But there was no blood.

Some kind of magnetic force immediately pulled spirit and body back together, and I slowly made it to my feet, trying to wrap my head around what just happened. *A new sensation*. My skin seemed to glow azure, but only momentarily. Perhaps that's what Ay'Con meant by the separation of the soul itself defying death. *They can't be separated. I can't be separated. Permanently.*

But more than that, I'm starting to feel.

I just survived a fifty-story free-fall into concrete, and I didn't have a scratch, a bruise, a headache or a broken bone. And my spirit only felt invigorated.

"I don't suggest doing that," I said to the awestruck witnesses, as I strolled past them down the sidewalk. "It will hurt you worse than it hurt me."

The woman dropped to her knees and crossed herself. The heavyset man just stared, and the teenager ran off, shouting, "Mom! Mom! You won't believe this!"

I wanted to tell someone I knew. *Show* them. Demonstrate my newfound indestructability.

My roommates? No, they wouldn't believe me even if they saw it with their own eyes. Carl? No. Luca?

I wondered if revealing my secret would somehow be breaking an arbitrary set of rules somewhere. Ay'Con hadn't mentioned anything about telling or not telling anyone.

I spent the next two days trying similar experiments; I threw myself in front of a speeding garbage truck, I dove into the ocean and swam so deep I should have drowned. I tried an even taller building than my apartment complex. However, I merely bounced off the bus and lost my footing, my lungs never ran out of air, and my landing was only a little cleaner than my first leap.

How had I not realized my invincibility all those years at Clear Valley? I always just thought I was lucky, careful, because everyone around me was being careful.

Still, what did this change? *I'm just me,* I thought. *Another girl on the island with a handful of friends, clients, and acquaintances. An average twenty-something living my life and doing things my own way*. If anything, this ability to avoid the traditional sense of human death just made me more different, set apart.

More . . . *alien.*

Some might even say *freak.*

When was my *time* supposed to come, that *time* Ay'Con kept referring to? And what did he *or they* expect me to do when the *time* came?

When I got bored of trying different ways to kill myself, I went back to modeling. I even texted Luca on a Wednesday morning at 4 a.m., asking if he needed me to sit for him—something I had never done before. He agreed, and I found myself back at the master's studio.

But something was different this time.

It was like each consecutive day introduced me to a different emotion. *A new* emotion.

After opening the door and greeting me with his ever-pleasant manner, he slowly shuffled back toward his easel in his robe and slippers. Slower than usual. He took his time preparing his palette and large canvas support. As always, faint, classical music played in the background. "Would you care for a drink before we get started?"

"I'm fine, but thank you."

"Coffee? Orange juice?"

"I'm good. Really. Thank you."

I just wanted to get to modeling.

He nodded.

I noticed his ashen face as he continued to prepare his things.

"Are you all right, Luca?" I asked.

He only briefly made eye contact. "Fine," he said quietly. "I'm fine."

He was lying.

I undraped. "Are you sure?"

He flashed a grin, but there was simultaneous melancholy in his old, experienced eyes. "Quite."

I stepped onto his slightly elevated modeling stand, and he flipped on his pre-positioned lighting setup which cast warm half-light across my naked form at three-quarter angle and a cool dramatic accent across the back edges of my face, torso, buttocks, and upper legs.

I stretched and shook out my extremities.

Once settled with his tools, Luca finally looked up at me.

"What pose would you like?" I asked.

The old man said nothing for a time, and then, "Surprise me."

Luca usually had a very good idea of the poses he wanted me to try out, so his answer took me aback.

I smiled, "Sure."

I stretched again, and moved into my first pose. When it felt right, I settled, and froze into place.

When Luca didn't say anything, I assumed he was pleased with the stance.

"No," he said, trying to express an air of kindness while diffusing his displeasure. "That's not quite it."

I stood upright, and did another stretch. Kneeling, I rolled gently to one side and slightly twisted my upper body in the opposite direction, as if longing to be in another place.

Luca observed even longer this time, but eventually said, "No. Closer, but no."

I stood up again, and turned about.

What is he after? I thought.

"Try another," came his gentle request.

I nodded, widened my stance in contrapposto with hips and shoulders at subtly opposing angles, twisted about, and looked up toward the heavens with arms angled behind me.

Even more time passed before he spoke, but when he did, the word was too quiet to hear.

I have found my pose, I thought.

Luca began to paint.

His customary offerings of twenty-minute breaks never came and went; so engrossed in his painting, he must have ignored the urge to set a timer.

I didn't mind. Despite what some would consider to be a difficult pose, I held it effortlessly.

The music played, and I was a statue. Luca's model. His muse.

His angel, caught in time.

After what must have been two hours, Luca began to wheeze.

I broke pose, and looked after him.

Without warning, the old man collapsed onto the hardwood floor behind his easel. His body convulsed, gripped by some type of seizure.

I ran to his side and, the moment I touched him, he was still. His body relaxed.

His eyes slowly met mine, and our souls connected.

"Luca?" I said.

His face slowly became tranquil.

"Are you all right?"

Tears wet my eyes. *Strange.*

Luca stared up at me with a kind, fatherly expression, and he almost smiled. "Perfect," he whispered.

I smiled too, and the tears escaped my eyes. "You're dying, aren't you?"

He just breathed for a moment. "Perfect," he repeated.

I don't want to lose my friend, I thought. *I can't.*

"Perfect, in every way," Luca said, and at length, he gave up the ghost.

I sobbed.

But then there was a light.

It grew, and caught my drowning eyes.

Light, like the glow in my arms at the moment of death's impact.

I leaned back and watched in awe as the old man's spirit leaned up from his reclined body, not an old, gnarled, weathered man, but a younger, stronger, prime-aged version of the painter I had posed for.

I stood and moved by instinct, offering him a hand. He grasped it, and celestial light enveloped us both. I walked him into the next room, where many of his relatives, including his wife, waited to greet him.

I always knew that I was alien, and fascinated by human behavior, but the purpose ever eluded me.

All Luca said was, "Thank you."

I nodded, and glanced at those who had gone before. The light stayed with Luca and his family as they moved on, fading from me until I was alone again with Luca's body in his empty apartment.

The music still played.

I shed another few tears, and stepped over his body to view the painting on his easel. I could only stare at the brush strokes.

"*Perfect.*"

I gathered my things, and left.

* * *

The pastel colors of the morning sky shone beautiful, but Luca could have painted them better.

"It's only been a week," I said. "But I miss the old man. I miss posing for him."

Ay'Con nodded. We stood on the Island Bridge, peering down at the waves and sea birds two hundred feet below. "They have grown on you, these people in your life. I suppose it will make you better at your job."

"Job?" I asked critically.

Ay'Con smiled. "*Jobs.*"

"Well, I can't wait for my next hands-on training session," I said with a bit of sarcasm. "Will it be *herald* or *harbinger*?"

"Hard to say."

"Artist's model then."

Ay'Con perked up. "I heard that final painting sold at auction for no small fortune. A legacy left at the death of a true master."

"I'd say it was . . . *priceless.*" My arms and hands began to glow a faint azure, then faded back to normal.

Ay'Con noticed. "It happens from time to time. Nothing to worry about."

"It usually happens when— "

"When you think you're going to die?" he interrupted. "Interesting."

I exhaled sharply. The visitor still hadn't answered my question. Perhaps he never would. Or I'd have to figure it out on my own, one little experience at a time.

What am I? I asked myself.

Alien.

Here to study human behavior.

A reconnaissance beacon.

But why?

"It's a bit ironic, actually," Ay'Con said.

"What's that?"

He took pause from the view to look at me. "As an artists' model, when you are posing nude or partially draped in front of a room full of strangers, the strangers think they are spying on you. In all reality, it is you who are spying on them."

A grin curled my lips. "For what purpose exactly?"

"Is it time for you to know?" Ay'Con asked.

"Yes," I said.

"Is it time . . . for *us*?"

"I don't know."

Ay'Con shook his head. "Neither do we."

"We're trying to decide if it's time to make ourselves known to them."

"Clever girl. And what's the verdict?"

"Hm." I thought a moment.

"Op! And there's another booking," Ay'Con lit with playful surprise. "University art class. You have fun with that. I'm leaving."

My phone vibrated, and I pulled it out of my pocket to look at the screen.

The End

11

ELVIS, BABY JESUS, AND ONE UFO

by Rick Bennett

BACKSTORY: The mathematician in me prompted creation of my blog (TheMorganDoctrine.com) and invent a framework for "the perfect computer virus." Naturally, that led to my fantasizing several stories (one of which has morphed into first-contact novel I'm currently working on). This story is another Einsteinian thought experiment on how my perfect virus could wreak havoc with some visiting ETs.

Even the dog didn't want to go outside to relieve herself.

"Awh come on, Chenoa," I begged my twenty-pound ball of white fur. "I'll go out there with you."

Then why don't YOU go outside in this toxic fog, her crooked mouth and big-eyed glare seemed to say. She had a point. The winter inversion and sub-zero temperatures cemented Salt Lake City's reputation as the worst air quality metropolis in the country. Even my mountaintop home, twenty miles south of the Utah capitol, sat cocooned in not just smog and fog, but that dead smell of the Great Salt Lake combined with a chemical stench courtesy of the Copper Mine. Not only couldn't I see past my back porch, I could barely see my outstretched hand. A hand, by the way, that I felt needed washing after just one extension into the night air.

I gently scooted her out the door with the side of my foot.

If all dogs go to heaven, just be warned I'm going to bite any hand that tries to open the door to let you in, her practiced slow walk communicated.

My coaxing and frequent "Good girl!" finally did the trick, and we quickly retreated back into the house for a dog treat, a breath of micro-filtered air, and some channel surfing between talking heads.

My name is Ellsworth Hammer and I'm a computer security consultant. My sole claim to fame is an occasional contribution to only one of the twenty-two principles of the perfect virus, called *The Morgan Doctrine* by black hat and white hat hackers alike. My area of expertise is Black Box Virus Portability, or the ability of a virus to infect even unknown computer architectures. My idea of a perfect winter's evening: sitting in front of a fire with my now-empty bladdered dog, contemplating the predictable arguments of conservative-vs-liberal television commentators, and surfing social media with my proprietary analytics software to catch the beginnings of major trends well ahead of their becoming mainstream media headlines. Notwithstanding the foul cloud outside *The Pirate Cottage*—that's what clients call my abode, probably because of the five-foot-tall pirate skull mounted on the wall of my den—life could have been a lot worse. Hindsight now confirms that such moments are always the high tide, and life will indeed get much worse.

A double-beep from my Android phone told me some drive-by hacker had just accessed my wireless router. The practice is called *war driving*.

"Friend, this is not your lucky day," I muttered. Perfect virus principle number twenty-two, defense, stated that any cyber attack should be greeted with a response that would make Ripley's (played by Signourey Weaver) *Alien* monster look like a mildly incontinent house pet. So rather than play nice with the person trying to hijack my wi-fi router and just boot him off the system, I pressed the red skull and crossbones icon to unleash the hounds of hell. Somebody's computer didn't have long to live. And if the attacking computer happened to have a Bluetooth connection to said hacker's car, the poor devil would be walking down my mountain, breathing the equivalent of a pack of cigarettes every hour.

Within 90 seconds of my hitting the Android's red skull icon, I got two gigantic surprises.

First, my *First Contact* movie soundtrack notification indicated that defensive countermeasures had uncovered an unknown computer architecture. Principle number seven of The Morgan Doctrine demanded "black box portability" for the perfect virus. The real Holy Grail of all virus countermeasures, black box portability could deduce a totally alien environment and adapt itself iteratively to eventually "go native" on the host hardware. Like I say, my particular area of expertise. This signal meant that whoever launched the attack on my router utilized an unknown technology. No known operating system. No known computer architecture. No known silicon instruction set. Before I could even verbalize a "Damn!" the second surprise echoed in the woods beside my house.

Crackling branches and snapping tree trunks preceded a THUD that rattled the dishes in my China cabinet. The earthquake threatened to knock The Pirate Cottage off its foundation. My dog immediately jumped off the couch and ran, barking ferociously toward the patio door.

It took me a little longer, as I had to run to the coat closet, don my leather coat, exchange my sneakers for snow boots, flip on an LED headlamp, and grab my Louisville Slugger aluminum baseball bat. Then out the door. Both of us.

Chenoa shot through the snow and into the fog like a bolt of lightning, fast enough that I almost heard the Doppler shift as her bark receded into the woods. I trod much more cautiously, since I couldn't see more than two feet ahead, speeding up when the yapping ended with a single yip. Within two steps, however, a fur ball hurled herself into my arms, nearly knocking me over. So much for my vicious guard dog's courage.

Approaching footsteps shuffling through the downed trees broke the eerie silence of my fog-encompassed mountain. The dog panted and probably would have climbed several feet above my head, had I let her.

"Settle down, girl," I said.

"I come in peace. Hopefully, you're Ellsworth Hammer." The strangely accented female voice originated just a few feet in front of me, and only after I turned off my headlamp could I see her outline. She stood almost a head taller than me.

Dog in my left arm, I rested the baseball bat on my right shoulder.

"That's me, Ellsworth Hammer. What…?" I couldn't figure out which question to ask next.

She seemed to sense my dilemma and broke the silence. "I need to repair myself. Might we get out of the cold?"

"Oh, wow. Can you follow me or do you need help?"

"I will follow." Again, the strange ESL accent made me wonder about her native language.

Follow, hell! I put the dog down and made sure to walk beside her. Paranoia about being cold-cocked from behind superseded buying her damsel in distress routine. Chenoa pranced in circles around us all the way to my well-lit back porch. At least six foot five, the white-haired woman cradled her left elbow with her right hand. Since she wore nothing more than tights and a *Paris Hard Rock Café* T-shirt, I quickly ushered her inside to the welcome warmth of a seat on my fireplace hearth.

"Looks like a pretty bad break," I said. Not a compound fracture, but certainly one that deserved a trip to the emergency room.

"Could you hold this for me?" she asked, nodding toward a pouch I hadn't noticed her right elbow cradling against her.

I took the purse-like bag. Its fabric felt neither synthetic nor leather. "You really need to see a doctor."

She actually laughed, although the chest movement caused her pain.

"Ellsworth," she said, much like my mother used to say when correcting my bad table manners. Gentle. You could even hear the smile. "Please just hold the bag in the palm of your hand."

"I could drive you to an emergency room just minutes down the mountain," I said as I obeyed her instructions, kneeling in front of this rock-star gorgeous, olive-skinned woman. With women like this on the planet, maybe I should get out more.

My thoughts fled as the bag opened automatically in my palm, revealing a semi-circular device about the size of a coffee cup. It even had a handle. She rested the injured forearm on her knee and took the device with her right hand. And frowned.

"Oh Eos," she sighed.

What's the matter?" I asked.

"Your computer virus seems to have attacked every processor-driven device available to me."

"Black box portability strikes for the first time," I said. "What are you? CIA? NSA?"

"Why would I be either?"

"Because if my virus correctly reported, you *must* be associated with government-level tech. No individual or even conglomerate could afford to roll both custom processor and operating system technology."

"Is it possible you could make your virus release this device?" Her grimace interrupted my musings on technology. Possibly feigned to stop my questions, I still couldn't ignore what had to be non-trivial pain.

"I'm so sorry," I blurted. "This is uncharted territory for me."

I grabbed my tablet and quickly did a peer-to-peer link with the virus server in my den. Invoking my defense dashboard, I quickly scrolled down a list of infected alien processors. All 2,314 of them. Virus principle #1, oversight, and #21, institutional memory, interfaced my dashboard with an A.I. that I could query.

"Does your device have a name or other designation? I've shut down a couple thousand different processors in the last half hour."

"It does, but our alphabet and numbering system do not correlate with yours."

"What is it? Chinese? Arabic? Cyrillic? I can do a conversion."

She paused, dropping that perfectly white head of hair toward the floor.

Sweet mother of mercy! I thought. *This really is an alien architecture. Alien to Planet Earth.*

"I'm feeling a little dizzy," I said. Somehow, I made it from my kneeling position in front of her to the couch across the room. No wonder I couldn't place her accent.

Rather than make this beautiful creature endure pain for hours of queries to my virus A.I., I understood the only other alternative. Namely, releasing all processors. At least temporarily.

"I hope you don't make me regret this," I said. Relying on virus principle #11, prosumption, I set a ninety minute reprieve time on my dashboard and released all 2,314 infected processors. One by one, I watched multiple icons go from red to green. About half way through the list, the device in her hand chirped. Either the dog didn't like the sound, or the sound from outside of some kind of spooling-up turbine got her attention. She barked. My guest gave a sign of relief.

"Thank you, Ellsworth Hammer," she said. Her right thumb depressed something on the device that emitted two more chirps, after which she started above her shoulder and slowly slid the device down her arm, over a femur that bent where it shouldn't have bent, continuing down to her wrist.

"I'll be damned!" Before my eyes, the unnatural bend in her arm disappeared, along with the swelling and bruising.

She flexed the fingers on her left hand and raised the now-healed arm over her head.

"Got an extra one of those devices you could leave behind?" My plan of action upon encountering any kind of UFO had always been to rush to the crew quarters and grab an armful of personal items. I figured cosmetics and other utilitarian gadgets would be far easier to reverse engineer—and to cash in on—than guidance or propulsion technologies that happened to be half-a-dozen scientific advances away from this planet's current state of art. But this device alone could obsolete entire healthcare industries. No wonder the military seemed to take such an interest in controlling fabled "Area 51" sites. One teensy-weensy anti-gravity design goes into the public domain and the entire worldwide aviation, transportation and hospitality industries would be gone overnight.

My guest saw the wheels spinning, and brought them to a screeching halt.

"Come here, Ellsworth Hammer."

Awh crap!

"If that thing is a weapon, too, you should know my virus defense has a dead-man's switch."

"Don't worry, Ellsworth Hammer. It's not a weapon, nor is it an instant amnesia switch used by *Men in Black*."

"Okay, okay. First, my friends just call me LZ. Second, how do you know our movies? And third, you haven't given me *your* name. What do…uh…your people…uh…call you?"

"LZ, I know your movies because I am what you refer to as an exo-anthropologist, assigned to monitor your planet and cultures. Science fiction is one of my favorite pursuits. Finally, my name is identical in your language and mine: Elizabeth. Now, please come here LZ. "

She stood. So did I.

But I didn't move toward her. Had she stepped toward me, I'd probably have run. She seemed to sense that.

"LZ," she said. "I just want to see what this will do to that bruise on your right forearm."

"Oh." I'd banged my arm on the grand piano lid in the dark while letting the dog out last night. One big, ugly bruise resulted. "Let me put this down."

I rested my tablet behind me on the couch, grazing my thumb over the *LEARN* icon, thereby surreptitiously commanding my A.I. to go native (virus principle #9) and suck every system dry (virus principle #17) on whatever craft she'd crashed beside my house.

I extended my bruised arm toward her. She slowly, so she wouldn't spook me, started the device at my right elbow and, evoking another two chirps, drew it toward my wrist. A powerful, almost buzzing sensation accompanied it. My whole arm felt weightless.

The extra-terrestrial Clara Barton nodded in approval. "Seems to work."

One less bruise on my arm. And one less mole! She examined a miniature display on the side of her marvelous gizmo. "You'll be glad I dropped by, tonight. We fixed you in more ways than one. The mole presented positive. A melanoma, about to metastasize. You're welcome, LZ."

I didn't realize I was scanning my other arm and even considering exposing every other square inch of myself.

"Keep your clothes on, LZ. If you want to come out and see my ship, I can reward you with a full-body work-up." She then patted my now-healed arm and added, "But you know I can't leave this device with you. I've already violated enough of Captain Kirk's so-called *prime directive.*

She really IS into Earth sci-fi, I thought. "Thank you very much."

"I also like the old Elvis movies," she winked.

"Oh, yeah. 'Thank you very much.'" I muttered.

"The King."

"Anthropologist of pop culture, anyway."

"What other kind of culture is there?" Elizabeth nodded toward the door. "I'd prefer to give you a holistic procedure and then talk you into letting me get my shuttle out of here before the fog lifts."

"No *Men in Black* amnesia stuff so I'll keep my mouth shut?"

This time she laughed out loud. "As an anthropologist with a good deal of experience on your planet, we're not worried a bit. The more educated and intelligent people with whom we interact don't care to call the news media and talk about their experience with a UFO."

My turn to laugh. "You should stay away from rural trailer parks."

"We learned *that* lesson the hard way, LZ!"

By the time we got outside and felt our way through the dense fog to her ship, my enthusiasm seriously waned for being lured inside and strapped down to an experimental table. My LED headlamp didn't illuminate any edges to one humongous black hulk.

"You are breathing some awful stuff around here," she said. "Why do you put up with it?"

"Because I don't want to move to Alaska."

"No LZ. I meant, why don't you eliminate air pollution altogether? This is one of the big mysteries about people on your planet. You have the technology to completely clean your air. Not only would you save a fortune in healthcare impact, but the process would be completely self-sustaining. And we *do know* that money is a big motivator on *your* planet."

Two questions collided in my mind, both of which seemed overwhelming important to me. So important, in fact, that they completely displaced any trepidation at my being abducted by and experimented on by aliens. A third shock interrupted my deliberation on which question to ask first: the thing about self-sustaining clean air or about *money* being somehow unique to *our* planet.

"Holy monkey balls!" An opening appeared where there had before been a seamless metal surface. "Glad I left the dog inside. I have enough to worry about without keeping Chenoa out of mischief."

"I need to enter the monkey balls remark in my dictionary of Earth expletives," she said. "You Americans are especially adept at forcefully expressing yourselves."

I preceded Elizabeth up a well-lit fifty foot incline. The opening immediately closed behind us, and the incline lifted, creating a level walkway to a fairly utilitarian flight deck.

"Ah, clean atmosphere," she said as we arrived at the single recliner seat. "What a delight!"

"You're alone on this craft." I said, greatly relieved that I wouldn't have to fight off a similarly sized crew.

"Yes, LZ. Just me and my little Serpee."

As if on cue, a hooded cobra snake bounced across the cabin, it's body functioning much like a coiled spring.

"What the hell…!" I exclaimed, ducking as the snake charmer's nightmare bounded past me and into Elizabeth's arms. Rather, it landed with an automatic coiling motion around her left arm.

"Serpee, this is LZ," she said. The snake seemed to smile at her and then looked toward me.

"Hello LZ," said the snake.

"Shampoo!" I exclaimed.

"Shampoo?" she asked. "Nowhere in my catalogue of Earth-English slang has that usage come up.

"As a little kid, I became particularly enamored with that word. It sounded like it ought to be a swear word. So over the years, I adopted it as my explicative noun or verb of choice." I looked again at the snake. "What the shampoo…""

"Shampoo!" said the snake.

"A talking snake! You people mixed the DNA of a snake with that of a parrot?"

"Oh LZ!" Elizabeth laughed again. I liked the sound. And I didn't mind being around this woman, notwithstanding her choice in pets. "Snakes on *your* planet are *nothing* like the snakes on ours."

"I guess the snot not," I said. "Snakes with that kind of agility would have snuffed out mankind before we'd ever gotten started."

"Your snakes gave us a bit of a start," she said. "Venomous fangs replaced the soft palate of our own breeds. Without advanced medical technology, we would surely have lost several early explorers."

"And speaking of medical technology…" I began.

"Please take a seat, LZ." She motioned toward the single piloting seat. "Let's do that promised scan on you."

I complied. Much to my relief, metal bands didn't clamp around my arms and legs, trapping me for an alien proctal probe, or a nasty nardectomy. Okay, my imagination created some far-out scenarios. Elizabeth gave a command in a language totally unfamiliar to me. Immediately, something I can best describe as a green holographic hula hoop encircled me and descended from my head along the contours of my body to my feet. As the process finished, unrecognizable writing appeared on a non-existent screen in front of me, obviously the same kind of holographic technology that created the hula hoop. My hostess cleared her throat.

"LZ, you've been spending way too much time sitting in front of your computer."

"And?" I said.

"It's hard to say what would have gotten your first: colon cancer, pancreatic cancer, or a stroke." She put a gentle, perfect hand on my shoulder. I turned my head to make sure it wasn't the snake.

"You said 'would have' nailed me, implying..."

"You're good to go. Clean as...what do you say...a whistle? Yes LZ, clean as a whistle."

"Thank you very much," I said, this time in my Elvis voice.

"With your permission, LZ," her hand remained on my shoulder. "It's time for Elvis to leave the building. So the building can leave the woods by the King's house."

Panic. Here I am with a humanoid from another world, an archaeologist to boot, leaving my mind filled with more questions than could be answered in a year, and she wants to vamoose. *Shampoo!*

"I'm dying of curiosity and feeling big-time cheated. You just want to..."

"Want to what, LZ? This fog is lifting, and if I don't get out of here in the next hour, the unintended consequences of this visit will ruin both our lives. I'd call the medical intervention a fair trade for deactivating one staggeringly brilliant computer virus and letting me make my exit."

"Not so fast. Just what was your mission? You knew my name before your ship went dark. Why me? Why here? Why now?"

She exhaled noisily.

I waited.

"My mission," she began, "was to find out more about one of the main contributors to Morgan Rapier's black box virus technology. We tracked you down from your IP address, and I risked hacking your wireless router. Too big a risk, it turns out. I beg of you. Release me, my ship, and my ship's computers. Please."

The poker game began. Add to that I'm a sucker for someone without guile. Had she threatened me with destruction, I would have called her bluff and raised the ante with mutually assured destruction, thanks to my virally implanted dead-man's switch. But she didn't threaten me. She simply begged for freedom.

"What can I say?" My turn to exhale loudly. "You've changed my life. I'm going to be wondering about this, and all the questions I should have asked, for the rest of my existence. An existence which you've kindly—or not so kindly—extended."

"Your mythology talks of someone discovering a genie by rubbing a lamp, and getting three wishes in return. How about I answer three questions in exchange for my freedom?"

Shampoo! Shampoo! Shampoo!

Picturing getting *shampooed* by the foul fog, the first question blasted into my consciousness.

"Okay," I began. "Before we entered your ship, you asked me why we put up with the air pollution. As if the problem could be solved with technology available to us. A self-funding methodology? Tell me. What are we missing? What is that simple solution?"

I could sense her relief that I hadn't asked a more screw-the-Star-Trek-prime-directive question. "One of your video games uses the correct scientific term, albeit to support some stupid notion. The term is *Ionic Vortex*. Using slightly more power than your LED headlamp, you could catalyze all the pollutants in about one hundred cubic miles and mine valuable metals from the collected material to more than pay for the disposal process."

I jumped on her answer: "But my question requires you to give me the solution?"

Again, she babbled something in an unintelligible language. Within a minute, a bound book ejected from a console beside the piloting chair. She handed it to me. I thumbed through it and, amazingly, schematics and operational instructions for the ionic vortex device presented themselves in perfect English. *Shampoo!*

"Your second question?" she asked, an impish smile threatening to break into an outright grin.

Again, my question exploded from the first.

"When you described the pollution solution to be self-maintaining, your side comment about 'money being important to us' implied that your own society had done something to transcend money. That's my second question? How do you get by without money?"

"Another source of mystery to my people," she said, clearly relieved that I didn't ask her something about faster-than-light travel or anti-gravity. "Almost 40 years ago, we picked up a telephone conversation where Frank Herbert, one of your greatest science fiction writers, talked a friend of his into running for the U.S. Congress from their district. The platform: dramatically change the financial system. Frank coached the fellow on the concept of *hydraulic despotism*, wherein he who controls the water controls the people. That same analogy applied to the banking system, where he who controls the money supply controls the people. The poor guy lost the election, although he did win Herbert's district. Other science fiction writers picked up on the theme. One of your *Star Trek* movies had the crew time travel back to the inventor of the fictional *warp drive*. While on a tour of the starship Enterprise, that inventor asked how much it had cost to build that magnificent ship. The answer that future people really don't deal in money rather surprised him. Well, LZ, I give you that same answer for our civilization. We don't really deal in money."

"My question was," I emphatically jumped in, "how do you get by without money? What are the mechanics?"

I didn't mind her laugh, even though she seemed to be laughing at my ignorance. "Google the term 'ZeroDDT.' You've got a nobody running for president who spells it out. He doesn't stand a chance, but he get's it. Now, your last question, please?"

Two down and one question to go. As a kid, upon hearing the genie and the three wishes story, I criticized the author for not having the hero ask his genie for more wishes. I had so many more questions, and would surely come up with so many more as I lived the rest of my life knowing something much bigger loomed out of sight. I couldn't get more questions, but…

"Your third question?" She looked anxious to boot me out the hatch and get going. Maybe I could use that anxiety to my advantage.

"How do I contact you in the future?"

"Hold on, LZ. I agreed to three questions, not an open line between us."

"Maam, I'm not asking…

"For the record, it's Miss, not Maam or Madam."

"Miss," I began again, and I hoped my heart's pitter patter wasn't loud enough for my neighbors to hear. "I'm not asking for an open line. You will be completely free to either answer my communication or ignore it. I just want some kind of a ping acknowledgement that you got my message request."

Silence. Deep thought. Did I have a shot? Finally, raising her eyebrows and one side of her mouth forming a half-smile, she nodded.

"Can you limit yourself to 280 characters?" she asked.

"A tweet?" Ingenious

"Indeed. Twitter is the secret command and control system for your virus, is it not?"

"Sure, but I don't want the world to see the communication. And what if my account gets cancelled for some reason?"

For the third time, she spoke gibberish. This time, a thumb drive shot out the slot beside the pilot's chair. Elizabeth caught it mid air and handed it to me.

"LZ, encrypt your 140-character message with this and tweet it. No matter what twitter account name you use, I assure you we'll see your message and retweet an answer, which this program will decrypt for you. Fair enough?"

"Guess it'll have to do." My heart filled with wistful what could have beens, thoughts of starting a family with Elizabeth on some alien Shangri-La. A goodbye-forever reality dampened enthusiasm for all other possible futures. *Who am I kidding? My six-foot height might be tall by Earth standards, but she probably has better options with some alien Adonis who could at least look her straight in the eye, dammit.*

* * *

My first conscious thought came as a question: Why am I slung over the big guy's shoulder? Anxiety over the smell of smoke and the safety of my dog abated as I looked to the left and saw Elizabeth cradling Chenoa. As we ran up the familiar ramp, the sound of crackling and warmth of nearby fire brought back memories of the previous month. My coded tweet must have effected a better-late-than-never rescue:

> *Neighbors want to kill me. I've got a 250-foot tall, 600 ton pile of sludge defacing a Salt Lake City mountaintop. I'll do anything 2 undo.*

"Is Chenoa okay?" I asked after being strapped into one of three well-padded contoured chairs on the flight deck of Elizabeth's ship.

In answer to my query, Elizabeth laid the dog on my chest. Chenoa proceeded to lick my soot-caked face. "Hang onto the dog. No time to rig a harness for her."

Elizabeth and the big, handsome guy, the guy who carried me so easily, each strapped into their own seats. Adonis? Hell, Adonis squared! I felt like unstrapping then and there and challenging him to a fight. His own attitude toward me interrupted my assessment of the *competition* for alpha dominance.

He spoke gibberish, probably the command language Elizabeth used the first time I accompanied her onto the craft. Even though I didn't understand him, his attitude seemed a bit…well…snippy.

"Yes, this is the Earthman for whom I put my command at risk," she said. I couldn't see her face, what with the dog continuing to lick mine, but I heard a smile in her voice. He continued the conversation in English, albeit with the same strange accent I'd observed in Elizabeth.

"But he's so short. And warlike."

Let me out of this harness and I'll show you warlike. The taller my opponent, the harder he'll splat on the deck.

"And LZ's also smarter that anybody in our fleet," said Elizabeth. "We may need him."

"Your decision, Captain. For now."

Ah ha! He's a subordinate. And possible mutineer, based on that 'for now' comment. I thought. *Me and Elizabeth against the crew. Fight to the death. Oorah!* Of course, my only stint at combat came from being a top-100-ranked player in a multiplayer online video Star Wars game. I decided to calm down and pay attention to a once-in-a-lifetime opportunity. A whole alien civilization to grok.

Elizabeth seemed to pilot the ship with her hand movements on invisible armrest controls. A holographic display formed before each of us. I could see a burning house. My house! Surrounded by bodies. Bodies!

"You didn't kill those people!" I gasped.

"Of course not, LZ," said Elizabeth. "Isaac just gave them an NPB."

"A what?" I asked.

"NPB, a Neural Pulse Burst," said the man next to me. "We had to get in and out without leaving witnesses of our little rescue."

"They're all okay, though?" We accelerated upward, and I held the dog tightly. Falling a few feet off my chest at 3 Gs could hurt the mutt.

"They'll be just fine," said Elizabeth. "A bit confused, maybe blaming their fainting on toxic fumes from your house fire."

"My house!"

"Total loss," said Isaac a little too flippantly.

Elizabeth gave some kind of alien command, and the feeling of acceleration vanished.

"You can unhook now," she said. "Gravity is normalized."

I could see by the rapidly decreasing size of my neighborhood that, if anything, our acceleration continually increased. Of course. Alien technology mastered gravity.

Upon her uttering yet another alien command, a whooshing sound preceded a familiar "boing" and human-like mimicking of my own, "Shampoo."

The dog jumped off my chest before I could register that Serpee the talking snake had bounced over me, clearing Chenoa by at least a foot.

The two of them then chased each other around the flight deck, playfully switching between chaser and chasee. I leaned forward to get a better look, and to unharness. The seat automatically moved me to a more erect position, somehow sensing by my intention by muscle movement. As it did also when I turned my head toward my two cabin mates.

"Smart seat," I said.

"Too bad you weren't smart enough to follow directions in the ionic vortex tech manual," said Isaac.

"Isaac, let me handle this," said Elizabeth in an obvious command voice. Then to me, "LZ, what possessed you to build the device and then place it on the most visible landmark in two counties?"

She was right. Isaac was right. Toasted on a spit of my own making. Instead of installing the pollution collection device in a valley, where the resulting sludgecicle could be toppled into a pit and buried, I'd climbed Lone Peak and activated the vortex process atop the focal point of every picture window and nature photograph from Bountiful to Salt Lake City to Lehi to Provo.

"Unintended consequences," I muttered. I wanted to see the progress from my porch on South Mountain and simply had no idea how big that thing would get."

"To his credit," said Isaac, "LZ had 280 characters for his help request, and got by with only 179. "I guess that makes him smarter than anyone else in our fleet. A real genius."

I'd have sprung for his sarcastic throat had he not been right on the money. For years I'd chided stupid clients with the "RTFM" acronym, which stood for "Read The Freaking Manual." Okay, the "F" didn't stand for "Freaking." But nobody would have understood my "shampooing" replacement.

"Isaac," Elizabeth jumped in. "You couldn't have built that device in less than a week, even with access to *our* technology."

Isaac stifled his agreement into a begrudging snort.

"LZ, how exactly did you get such a compact device built so quickly?" Even after a screw-up necessitating their coming to my rescue, she seemed to appreciate moi's sheer brilliance. How could I let her down?

"Not much to it, once I understood the utter simplicity of your physics.

I had the hobbyist circuit board populated within a day. The hardest part was getting a Silicon Valley buddy to fabricate a PLA for me."

"A PLA?" she asked.

"Programmable Logic Array. Kind of a hard-wired processor. Thanks to your excellent documentation, I didn't need to iteratively debug the process. I just needed to drop in what I assumed to be your perfectly debugged code. Plus, I could start the whole catalytic process with just six double-A batteries." *So how do you like them apples, Isaac?*

"What's a double-A battery?" asked Macho Man.

I held my index finger and thumb apart. "About yea big."

"For someone so smart..." he continued, but I decided to cut to the chase and interrupted him.

"Okay pal. I should have known that the word 'vortex' literally meant high winds containing five of the six most common pollutants responsible for Utah's abysmal air quality: carbon monoxide, sulphur oxides, lead, and two mining-created types of particulate matter. Attracting in a geometric expansion. The more of these pollutants I amassed, the stronger their attractive power. Soon, hurricane force winds tore the roof off at least one home. My bad. I admit it."

Elizabeth feebly jumped to my defense. "At least high winds discouraged closer observation of the growing wart on Lone Peak by hikers."

"Yeah," I said. "But that couldn't last. So I took my life in my hands, and an empty backpack, to collect the self-funding output of the process. I made a midnight climb. Sure enough, the output flowed out the base of the Lone Peak Wart, as the newspapers had begun calling it."

Isaac just couldn't resist twisting the knife in my back. "Those chanting people who burned down your house called it Ellsworth's Crapcicle."

Yeah, they did come up with that name. Luckily, not many kids named Ellsworth would have to consider a legal change. My friends who named boys "OJ" weren't so lucky. I'm still intrigued by the self-funding output: gold. Without going into too much chemistry, gold and lead are pretty close on the periodic table of elements. Lead collected in the ionic vortex catalyst process used the vortex molecular energy released to strip two proton/electron pairs from the lead to create gold. Said gold flowed into a series of plastic ice cube trays I'd left around the rapidly growing base, all of which I popped into my backpack. Sixty pounds of gold, give or take a pound.

I had no hope of disconnecting the ionic vortex device, as it lay buried somewhere beneath the 250-foot tall, six-hundred ton crapsicle. I somehow made it down the mountain without killing myself. Or being discovered. During my descent, the problem of actually selling sixty pounds of pure gold started banging around in my mind.

"Then, smart guy," said Isaac, unaware that I was computing how quickly I could get my hands around his self-righteous neck, "You couldn't figure out how to sell all the gold."

That chain of disasters I remembered all too well.

"What the hell is this?" asked the guy behind the bullet-proof glass of a title loan shop I'd seen advertised on television.

"Some gold we've had in the family for a few years. I wanted to see what I could get for it."

"Lemme see."

I dropped two-inch-diameter half-ball into the retracting cashier's tray and watched it disappear.

"Holy crap man, this weighs two-hundred-twenty-six grams!" he said.

"Eight ounces, right?"

He busied himself on a calculator. "What did this come from? Never seen nothin' like it."

"Part of an old mirror frame," I answered. Even though I'd practiced the lie, it played a lot better in my mind than it sounded it reality.

"Doesn't look antique old to me. What'cha want for it."

"The going price of gold makes that worth about ten grand," I said. "What's your offer."

"Woah, pal! We gotta' make a profit, too."

"So what's your offer?"

"If you'll leave it over night so my boss can run some tests, how's thirty-five hundred?"

"I'll pass," I said.

"Might be able to go four grand," he said, now making eye contact.

"I'll pass. Thank you very much."

"Then, el stupido decided to contact the media." Isaac again interrupted my internal reminiscence.

That sent me back into the second disastrous atonement plan. My neighbor, television news anchor Don Hudson, had flinched as I dumped sixty pounds of gold half balls onto the desk in his den.

"You just did a pretty good job of scratching up my new walnut desk," he said, quite calmly given the noticeable indentations from my theatrics. News anchors, even for local stations, had coolness in their DNA.

"Sorry Don. Take one of those and refurnish your whole study. They're worth about ten grand each."

Don picked up one of my gold pieces and held it next to his identically colored Rolex. "Is this…?"

"Yep. Pure gold. Eight ounces, again they're worth about ten grand."

He started counting the pieces on his desk. I saved him the trouble.

"One-hundred-twenty of them. Over a million bucks."

"Sweet Baby Jesus," he gasped.

"One of my favorite movie lines, too."

"Ellsworth, or should I say Ricky Bobby, what's the deal here?"

"Don, how'd you like to win an Emmy. And become a New York network news anchor?"

"Where'd this come from?"

"Look out your window." I pointed toward the mountain. Lone Peak. The wart.

"This have something to do with the shitcicle screwing up my view?"

"Don my friend, that shitcicle poops gold!"

Don Hudson will probably get his Emmy for the exclusive report on the something-or-other cicle. And he'll most certainly move to a Big Apple anchor slot. As for me?

"Yeah, Isaac, things just kept snowballing from dumb to dumber," I said, ratcheting back into our conversation aboard the rescue UFO. "A combination of EPA demands for an environmental impact statement, politicians, homeland security, and bids from multiple demolitions experts pretty well guaranteed removal of my Crapcicle would cost more than a million dollars."

"Why did you refuse the plea deal?" Elizabeth asked. "After you went public, we kept a close eye on developments."

"What they didn't publish about the plea deal was their demand that I reveal the source of my pollution control technology."

"Couldn't you just tell them you invented it?" she asked.

"Couldn't risk it. Partial disclosure brings full accountability. If the truth came out, the plea deal would have evaporated. Besides, China threw everything out the window."

"Now *there's* a people that could really use ion vortex technology," mused Isaac. For the first time, his comments weren't accusatory. "China's air pollution has become so bad that photosynthesis is now impossible throughout most of the country. Crop failures and starvation loom, and world war is inevitable."

"I offered to throw ion vortex technology into the public domain, but the president invoked national security to block me. Real MEN IN BLACK couldn't have been far behind the mob at my house."

"So that's why China dumped all their U.S. dollar holdings in favor of the Euro, causing the U.S. stock market to crash." Isaac didn't say it out loud, but his tone communicated *Way to go, LZ!*

"Hence the mob burning down your house," said Elizabeth.

"And yelling about the Ellsworth Crapcicle," added Isaac.

"What in the world is that?" I gasped. The scene of my burning house no longer filled the holodisplay. Instead, a forward view of a large craft emerged from behind the moon.

"That's our main command ship," said Elizabeth. "We keep it parked here for security.

"I hadn't thought much past my immediate need for rescue, guys. Am I now your prisoner?"

"LZ, you are free to choose your future."

Isaac shouted something in their native language. Elizabeth shut him up with three equally strange words. She then addressed me in English.

"We have a need for your help. I can't go into the details until you accept or reject my offer. But if you choose to join us, I can promise you freedom and equality as a member of my crew."

The words "member of my crew" probably put an end to my romantic aspirations with Elizabeth. Liaisons between superior officers with their subordinates *had* to be taboo in any culture.

"And my other options?"

"We can return you to your planet. I'll even authorize removal of that horrible sludge mass on the top of your mountain."

Isaac growled something under his breath, but his meaning couldn't have been more clear. My choosing the second option would certainly have negative consequences for Elizabeth. And I'd never see her again.

The decision was a no-brainer.

Elvis has left the planet.

The End

12

GONE ARE THE LIGHT-WIELDERS

by Nicholas P Adams

"Open administrators log," Neema said to her console as she sat in the stiff-backed chair. Her cup of tea rattled on the saucer as she lowered it to a corn-silk table cloth covering one side of the glass desktop.

From her vantage point in the mobile observation booth, she could see through the floor-to-ceiling concave windows over the crater's lip and out to the alien terrain beyond; a ring of volcanoes oozing rivers of glowing lava, boiling rivers, and desiccated valleys with abundant geothermal energy.

Lambda Colony. An ideal place to set down roots. Perfect for pencil-necks and theorists, maybe.

Pre-dawn rays peeked over the horizon, as shadows withdrew from the dome; a honeycomb of glass and steel constructed to keep the dangers of their new world out. Nestled under the apex, the observation booth (a three square-meter platform) hung one hundred seventy-five meters above their community. The perfect spot from which to oversee their delicate environment.

Leaning back, Neema watched the artificial waterfalls flowing down the crater's rim, coalescing in the moat that ringed their home. Canals flowed away from the crater walls, slicing between fields of grain, toward the center of their artificial caldera.

One good whack with a well-timed comet and voila, a bowl waiting for a lid.

The fields rippled like golden waves on the sea. She followed the pattern until she spied one of a hundred wind generators twirling like a lazy ballerina.

Dirt roads and paths followed the canals across the valley, all leading toward the center: A community of landed ships and pre-fabricated structures laid out like a wagon wheel. Surrounding the buildings, a ring of circular meadows wrapped the town border like a string of green pearls.

Our saving grace. Their slaughtering fields.

Encompassing the buildings, an incomplete wall rose above the colony. Cranes carried massive blocks of rammed soil from the brickyards, stacking them like a child's blocks. Hundreds of men and women using jackhammers fitted with flat plates or hand tools pounded on the dirt being dumped into steel formwork the size of cargo containers. Farming equipment of every type dug, scooped, and hauled soil from the crater's perimeter, forming a secondary moat waiting to be flooded. The wall had four immense gaps at each cardinal point.

Neema shook her head.

I hope Raia gets the gates fabricated in time.

Wrinkled fingers pulled the homespun wool comforter tight around her neck, it's gray fibers matching the salt and pepper dreadlocks cascading from under a rope bandanna.

"New log entry," she said, then squinted as the holo flashed into existence over the table. Her mouth pursed as she lifted the tea with both hands to her lips and blew away the steam.

"Begin dictation. Neema Wabani, Assistant Administrator. Lambda Colony. Day sixteen oh one," she said between sips, her hands absorbing the welcome heat. "Local time, 05:16 a.m., Earth date, March sixteenth. Uploading annual reports."

Neema's ashy hand reached for the polished surface. Burn scars from their first wildlife encounter coated her once ebony skin like road rash. She dragged the digital folder across the desktop, attaching it to her message. The holo chimed its receipt as an itch crawled up her arm, down her body, and ended at the mid-thigh. She scratched with bony fingers at the sock wrapping the stump, massaging the part of her leg the creatures didn't get.

"Last year's attack reduced our livestock by twenty percent, much lower than previous years. Raia's idea to cordon the females paid off, but the flocks aren't replenishing like we'd hoped. We used IVF and hormone therapy to force multiple offspring in the animals that can handle the increased gestational stress. If we can prevent losing any this year, we may survive the winter."

Neema took a long sip as she typed in a query: CENSUS DATA. A series of charts and graphs appeared. Her eyes focused on the jagged line descending from left to right.

"The population of Lambda Colony is down another four percent. We're at eighty-five percent of first landing population. Demographic changes: Births: 7. Deaths: 54. A detailed list is attached. Among the dead is Abraham Schafer, known around the colony as Bram. He successfully kept the queen at bay, but her pups ravaged the flocks and killed several people sent to defend them. He is survived by his wife, Raia, and two children, Leeya and Zak. Bram was our last Light-Wielder. There is no one left to power the Golem."

A beep sounded from the table as a new holo appeared. "Pause dictation," she said as she focused on the message.

"3D PRINTING COMPLETE. NEW PROSTHETIC NOW COOLING. READY IN FIFTEEN."

Neema gave a sidelong glance to the object lying across the table. An artificial leg with the name Peggy welded just above the rubber foot.

Six months scrimping enough scraps for the fabricator better be worth it.

Her mouth twisted as she typed. "THANKS. I'LL BE DOWN SOON." Swiping the image closed, she leaned back.

"Resume dictation. As you know, the Mifletzot emerge every spring solstice. Somehow, they keep getting inside the dome. We know they hate the cold and water, which is why we diverted our irrigation to form artificial waterfalls, soaking the crater walls. Last year they emerged in the fields, setting them on fire as they moved toward the flocks. We can only surmise they prefer the taste of our animals over their native prey."

Neema took another long sip, followed by a deep breath.

"We're not sure we'll be able to keep them out this solstice. But Raia came to us with an idea last fall. We're calling it JERICHO. Details included with attachments. Last year's harvest yielded far less than even our worst estimates."

Neema's stomach growled, appearing as a spike in the audio.

"Pause dictation."

Reaching under the folds of her covering, she retrieved a 15cm square, hard plastic, container. It hissed as she popped open the translucent lid, unveiling a slice of reddish-brown bread. Bits of fruits and nuts dotted the surface like stars in the night sky. She swallowed and licked her lips as the aroma of her grandmother's kitchen filled her nose. Muttering under her breath, she broke off a chunk and popped the morsel into her mouth.

A quiet moan escaped as she chewed the moist cake. She chased it down with a sip, repeating the process three more times. Once the large pieces were gone, she used her fingers to clean the container; down to the last crumb and licked the tips clean.

After wiping her hands, she lifted the cup to her lips and drained it down to the dregs, sucking the last droplets from within.

No calorie wasted.

From the folds of her comforter, she pulled out a black sphere. It squished in her hand like a stress ball until she dropped it in her empty cup. Once it made contact with the ceramic, the plastic surface eroded and spilled out as a fresh cup of steaming tea.

Two cups a day keeps the admin at play.

From another hidden pocket, Neema removed a palm-sized bottle. Flicking open the cap with her thumb, she poured the opalescent goop into her other hand and shrugged the blanket off. She wore light brown coveralls, cut short at the legs, over a faded purple t-shirt. Her ebony skin, like dust-coated piano keys against the white chair fabric, puckered with gooseflesh in the chilly air.

Closing the tube, it fell from her hand, bouncing off the desktop onto the floor.

Damn. Whatever. I'll get it later.

Pulling the stocking from her stump, she massaged a dab of lotion into the seams crisscrossing the nub with one hand. As her skin relaxed, she warmed the ointment with her hands. Leaning back, she put her foot on the table's edge and rubbed the balm over every square centimeter before applying what remained on her hands to her other thigh and arms. Her skin transformed back to its natural mochaccino with each stroke.

We may be starving, but I'm not giving up my beauty regimen.

"Resume dictation," she said, pulling the blanket back over her shoulders. "Everyone is on reduced rations. On average, we've all lost another three percent body fat. I've already passed the bikini body phase. Pretty soon, I'll be able to walk through a picket fence without using the gate. In spite of it all, we're moving forward with JERICHO. We don't have high hopes that it will be enough to stave off the next attack. Nor do we believe the second colony fleet will arrive before we all starve. Or the Fletz kill us. End dictation."

Neema typed into the console. The table beeped, and another holo appeared.

"MESSAGE SENT. WOULD YOU LIKE TO SEND ANOTHER?"

Swiping the floating text closed, she pushed away from the table. Leaning forward with arms crossed, she put the sun to her back. She spotted her shadow on the crater wall as she stared out from her inverted dome, an ink spot against the white stone. It crawled toward the basin, following the contours toward an oasis.

But it's just a mirage. There's no salvation here.

Outside the city, amid the string of green pearls, a point of orange light appeared. It then turned into a jagged line, then a swath of rippling fire.

Red lights spun on every watchtower. The sound of alarms slowly rose, growing in volume, until they reached the dome's apex. The muffled PA echoed below as the same announcement resonated from her table.

"Containment crews to sector six. Field Mike Echo Golf."

Barriers of cable mesh rose from the ground, surrounding the field afire, on irrigation poles. Water burst from the tops, drenching the meadow. A point of steam zig-zagged toward the border, seemed to bounce off and dart to the opposite side, repeating the process until it fizzled to nothing.

NO! It's too soon!

Neema scooted back to the desk, slamming her fingers down on the comms. Her cup toppled off its saucer, splashing the tea across the fabric.

"Damn it!" She yelled, folding the cloth on itself. "Central, this is Wabani. I just saw a fire in the grazing fields. What's going on? Don't tell me it's a..."

I can't say it. If I say it, it'll be true. Please don't be true.

"Neema, this is Kaminsky." A man's gravelly voice came over the comms. "You'd better get down here."

* * *

Neema walked into the command center, her new articulated foot squeaking with each step. Amid an array of computer consoles, Harvey Kaminsky--a short, elderly man--leaned on his cane as a younger woman whispered in his ear. He nodded as she spoke, pursing his lips. Each bounce of his head made the graying ringlets dangling from either side dance on his stooped shoulders. He stood a head shorter than anyone else in the room, wearing a black overcoat, trousers, and slippers.

She approached from the side, arcing her path to put herself in his line of sight. "Looks like you slept in." She pointed to his footwear. "I guess that downtime you needed wasn't in the cards."

"Sounds like you need an oil change," Kaminsky chuckled, poking her prosthetic with his cane. "I know a guy. He can get you in and out for a song."

The young woman handed Neema a tablet and excused herself.

"What do we know?" Neema asked, opening menus across the glass. "Don't tell me it was the Fletzs?"

"A single pup emerged in one of the grazing fields." Kaminsky sighed. "Flock twenty-four was there. It bolted all over, chasing the animals. Once the sprinklers came on, it bounced off the perimeter fence like a pinball trying to get out. The water eventually slowed it down."

"But it's too early." Neema hissed. "The equinox isn't for three days. Does that mean the queen will emerge early too? JERICHO isn't ready."

"We don't know." He leaned forward on his cane. "Maybe she will.

Maybe not. Maybe the pup's emergence was a fluke. We're on alert just in case."

"How was it stopped?" Neema said absently as she scanned through the footage. "Did it drown? Did it go back underground?"

Kaminsky paused until Neema stopped on an image of the burning field. "It was killed with a rock."

"A rock?" Neema looked up. "A rock killed a Fletz? That's not possible. Not even a pup. Their scales are too thick."

Kaminsky shrugged, holding out his hands. "The boy who was watching the flock says he used his sling to launch a rock at it. Says he got lucky."

"Which boy?" She glanced around the room as if he had just walked in. "Who was watching the flock?"

Kaminsky tapped his cane on the floor. "Zak Schafer."

"Bram's son?" Neema scowled. "He's not of age. Who assigned him as a shepherd?"

"I did." Kaminsky sighed. "Along with several other boys, so their fathers or older brothers could work on JERICHO."

"Right." Neema rubbed her forehead. "Is he alright? What about the animals?"

"He's fine, but one lamb didn't survive. Zak says he had to put it down."

"Better one sheep than the whole flock." Neema blew all her air. "We can't afford to lose any of our resources."

"Of course not." Kaminsky put a hand on her shoulder. "But every life is precious. And every death is a tragedy."

"Yes, of course." Neema dropped the tablet on the nearest console, and paced the floor, hugging herself.

I wish we'd never come here. I wish we'd picked a different planet. And I wish to God we still had a Light-Wielder. We're dead. We're all dead. It's only a matter of time.

"What's on your mind, Neema?" Kaminsky put his hand on her shoulder as she passed.

Neema blinked back the moisture in her eyes.

"We need to put everyone on JERICHO." She cleared her throat.

"We've already done that." Kaminsky's eyes softened.

"Even children." Neema almost shouted. "We need everyone to sacrifice a little more, or the colony won't survive."

"Children aren't suited to this kind of labor," he soothed. "It's our job to protect them, not the other way around. Every able-bodied man and woman in the colony is working double shifts."

"Then we need to go triple," Neema growled. "Without the Golem to keep the queen back, we'll be trapped in this bottle with a flood of little monsters that can't be stopped. And more will get in. If that happens, we won't have to worry about starving to death. We have nowhere to go. JERICHO is our last chance."

"Director Kaminsky?" A woman's voice called from the other side of the room. "Can you take a look at this?"

Neema followed Kaminsky to the tech's console. A holo showed the image of the field burning in reverse. "What is it?" he said, looking over her shoulder.

"I've been reviewing the footage," she said, her eyebrows knitted together. "There's something you should see."

* * *

Three hours later, Raia Schafer sped-walked through the administration building, sliding around corners in her mud-caked boots. The shuffle of her coveralls announced her journey down the corridor. A dark ponytail swished under the safety-yellow hard hat atop her underfed five-foot-seven frame.

"I don't have time for this," she mumbled. She pulled back her sleeve and reread Kaminsky's message.

"PLEASE COME TO COUNCIL CHAMBERS IMMEDIATELY."

As she rounded the final corner, she stopped at the double-doors to catch her breath. Leaning on an iron lever, she pulled an inhaler from her pocket and shot three puffs between wheezes. As the inhalant put out the fire in her lungs, she closed her eyes and put her head to the cold metal, smacking her lips and swallowing hard.

Three days. I've got less than three days to finish, and they need me to hold their hands *now*?

Indecipherable words, men and women arguing, came through the doors as her head stopped spinning. She glanced again at her cuff. Ten twenty-seven. Standing tall, she moved to a spot before the mural across the hallway. Three dozen faces stared blithely to an unseen horizon on their left, all wearing blue and white environmental suits and carrying helmets under their arms.

Her eyes fell on a woman, fifth from the right, with chestnut hair and green eyes. The name on her suit read Benowitz, Deborah Benowitz. But Raia had known her better as Nana D, now filling one of thirty graves dug shortly after the first spring solstice. She passed over the remaining faces to the plaque at the end. She hadn't memorized it like her children.

"Darkness is merely the absence of light. Nothing can remain hidden if shadows cease to exist. We will carry the torch of humanity to the stars and worlds yet to be discovered. There is nothing to fear so long as the spirit of community and love prevail. - Captain Jacob Levine, Lambda Colony Groundbreaking Ceremony."

Raia turned from the mural, removed the hard hat, and tucked it under an arm while she smoothed her hair. Standing at the doors, she took a breath and pounded her fist over the shouting coming from within. A dozen arguments died as the door opened to reveal the entire council, thirty-seven men and women standing around the circular chamber in small groups.

Her footsteps echoed off the domed ceiling as she passed the threshold. Glazed openings high above ringed the cylindrical room like a collar, letting shafts of light rain onto the concrete floor.

Still hard to believe this was the primary fuel tank.

Raia's eyes fell immediately on Harvey between twin spots of light. He sat in a wooden armchair, leaning to one side, resting his head on his fist. His cane, propping up his other arm, swayed to an unheard rhythm. Unlike the others in the room, he smiled and waved.

"This is a real pickle, Raia." He grunted, getting up. Not much taller standing than sitting, he trudged through the crowd that parted for him. "No doubt about it. A real pickle."

"Of course, it is." Raia frowned, turning on the spot she met looks that ranged from sneers to sympathy. "We're working around the clock to get JERICHO in place before the equinox, and you drag me down here for who knows what. I thought we agreed there would be no interruptions once we finished laying the foundation blocks. Am I still in charge of the wall?"

"Yes, yes," Harvey nodded, getting to his feet. He puttered close, looping his arm in hers. "We agreed on the schedule for JERICHO and put you in charge of construction. But new information has come to light that is semi-related to the wall."

"What information?" Raia let him lead her to the bottom row of curved risers. "We'll have it finished on time. And the fab on the extinguisher cannons is ahead of schedule. They'll be done tonight, and we'll start mounting them between the pickets first thing."

"Oh, that's good." Harvey pushed out his bottom lip, his head bobbing as he sat on the concrete bench and pulled Raia down beside him. "There's nothing I love better than a good, old-fashioned squirt-gun fight."

"It's a little more than a squirt-gun."

"What?" He pointed his index fingers in the air. "They fill up with water. You point them at something. You pull the trigger, and they get wet. How is this more complicated?" Harvey gave her a wink.

Raia fought the smile tugging at the corners of her mouth. "You know why. And why we'll need as much fire retardant as we can synthesize."

"Sure. Sure." Harvey pushed out his lower lip and patted her knee. "Fire retardant. Very important. But that's not why we called you in."

"Then, why am I here?"

"It's about Zak." Harvey held his cane in both hands, bowing his head to the floor.

"Zak?" Raia grabbed him by the arm. "Is he okay? Where is he?"

"Oh, he's fine. He's fine." Harvey patted her hand. "A Mifletzet popped up in the meadow where he was tending a flock this morning. You should be proud. He fought it off. Killed it protecting the herd, and his sister, with that sling of his."

"A Fletz?" Raia said, jutting her head forward. "That's impossible. They've never emerged early."

"Not that we've ever seen." Harvey shrugged. "We've only been here a few years, and they've been here for God knows how long. On the upside, only one surfaced. Not the litter, or the queen. All signs point to this being nothing more than a one-off. But that's not why we called you here."

Raia stiffened. "Why did you?"

Harvey faced her, his eyes not meeting hers as he stammered.

"Did you know, Raia?" Neema asked from across the room, her voice like thunder on the horizon. "Did you and Bram know about Zak?"

Raia craned her neck. "Did I know what?"

"Did you know he's a Light-Wielder?" Neema said, folding her hands in front of her as she stepped closer.

Raia swallowed hard, her eyes darted to see Harvey staring back with Basset-Hound eyes.

Oh, Zak. You promised me you wouldn't use it. You promised me you'd let it fade.

She scanned the room; the faces around her displayed a mosaic of hard stares with pinched mouths, quivering lips with watery eyes, averted glances, and everything in between.

"Did you know Zak is a Light-Wielder?" Neema said, stretching her neck forward as she approached.

"The Light-Wielders are gone." Raia croaked. "Bram was the last one. You know that."

"It would seem," Harvey muttered and patted her leg, "that his son inherited the gift. Did you know, or not?"

We talked about this the day his father died, about even the possibility it would appear. I told him what would happen if he wielded the light. I told him what the others would do.

Raia stood and bolted for the door. "I don't have time for this."

"Close the doors!" Neema shouted.

A pair of stern-faced women cut off Raia's path as she reached the room's center. A middle-aged man pulled the door leaves together and lowered a steel crossbar into place.

"Please answer the question, Saraia," said an elderly woman standing close by. "Did you know? And if so, why were you keeping his power a secret from the community?"

"He's only twelve." Raia turned in a circle, searching their faces. "He can't possibly have the light. He's not a man yet."

"That's not a denial." Neema's eyes narrowed as she pursed her lips.

The hall erupted with murmurs.

"We should ask him directly," a man with olive skin said in a deep bass voice to the room. Several people nodded or mumbled their approval. Then he turned to Raia. "May we have your consent to interview the boy?"

"Yes, of course." Raia crossed her arms. "I'll go find him and bring him back here."

There's nowhere to hide from this. I have to talk to Zak first. I need to know what happened so we can get our stories straight. Maybe there's another way to explain all this without admitting the truth.

"That won't be necessary," Neema gestured to a single door behind the risers.

Raia turned as the door opened to see Zak walk in, led by one of the chief shepherds. The council saw a five-foot-two scarecrow of a boy. Tan skin stretched over a lanky frame. But Raia saw a black-haired newborn laying on her chest, wide chocolate eyes staring into hers.

He had one hand in a pocket and toyed with a sling-bullet in the other. His sandals scraped across the floor as the crowd whispered behind their hands. Zak caught sight of Harvey giving him a casual salute. He pulled the wool cap off his head, stuffing it into the oversized sheepskin jacket.

Raia's heart dropped as Zak's gaze met hers.

He hasn't gone a day without wearing Bram's old coat. It's how he honors his father. Is he also holding onto the light as a way of keeping Bram's memory alive?

Harvey rose to his feet and shuffled over, short-stopping Zak with a pat on the shoulder on his way to stand beside Raia.

"Mom, I..." he wheezed as she crossed the distance between them and took him in a tight embrace, squeezing the wind out of him. Her hard hat clunked to the floor and tumbled around in a circle at her side.

"How many times have I told you?" She hissed in his ear. "Huh? How many times?"

"I'm sorry."

"I'm sorry too." She breathed. "Because I can't stop what's about to happen."

"I know," he said, wrapping his arms around her waist. "I wish Dad were here."

"So do I." Raia rested her head on top of Zak's.

"Ahem." Neema put herself between Raia and Harvey. "Zak, I'd like to show you something."

"O-Okay," Zak stammered, turning to face Neema with Raia behind him.

Raia's eyes followed Neema's gaze as she pointed to a spot in the air and tapped the stylus in her hand. Above their heads, multiple holos appeared along the room's perimeter with a still image of a grassy field dotted with sheep. In the upper right corner of each screen, an illustration appeared; a diagram of a Mifletzet pup. Equal in size to an adult wolf. Its body divided into sections like a centipede. Behind the head, four segments carried by a pair of legs ending in tarsial claws like a spider. It had skin like a gecko and the maw of a snub-nose crocodile. Its soft scales ranged from sunflower yellow to fire alarm red and dripped phosphorous acid.

In the lower right corner, the diagram of the Mifletzet queen appeared. A sixty-meter long tube of a creature on a hundred pairs of segmented legs. Fire engine red scales glowing like hot coals down its length; flames bursting from the seams with every movement. Sword-like hairs protruding from the carapace on every section. Two pairs of mandibles on its head pulled everything toward its circular mouth. Three rows of eyes over the mouth all pointed forward.

The playback started, showing dozens of sheep scattering through a meadow on fire. In the center, Zak stood atop a boulder with his back to the camera viewpoint. A teenage girl wearing spruce blue cargo pants, matching short sleeve blouse and charcoal fleece vest clamored at the rock's base. Her dark waist-length braid whipped from side to side as she frantically clawed her way from the ground.

In one of Zak's hands, a strip of leather shook like a swing in an earthquake. In the other, he held a sling-bullet the size of a grape. Blue light emanated from under his shirt, snaking toward his hand, as he rolled the projectile between his fingers. Once the radiance reached his fingers, the bullet started to take on the same glow until it shined like a bulb.

An audible gasp came from the room at large. Eyes darted to Zak, then back to the displays.

On-screen, Zak then slipped the stone into his sling, whipped it around his head, and launched it at the Fletz in pursuit of a lamb. The rock exploded on impact, sending both animals flailing in opposite directions.

The holos faded, disappearing from existence.

"You were very brave to defend the flock, and your sister, with just a sling." Neema folded her hands in front of her. "But how did you make the rock glow like that? Don't pretend we don't already know the answer."

Zak looked down as he shifted his weight.

Raia squeezed his shoulders. He craned his neck and met her gaze.

"No point in hiding the truth anymore," she choked.

"Zak," Kaminsky moved a step closer. "How long have you been able to do this? The gift shouldn't have manifested until after your thirteenth birthday."

"I guess it started in the fall," Zak said to the floor. "After we buried dad."

"Why wasn't the council notified there was another Light-Wielder?" Neema barked. "The colony had a right to know if there was someone with the gift."

"*I* told him to keep it a secret," Raia shouted back. "He's just a boy. There's no telling if he's strong enough to operate the Golem. Or stand against the queen."

"There's no telling if he's not unless he tries," Neema growled. "That's not how we do things here. It's not your place to deny precious resources from the rest of us."

"Resource?" Raia wrapped her arms around Zak's shoulders. "He's a child. Not a fuel cell."

"As one with the gift, he *must* defend his community!" Neema shouted.

"As a child, the community must protect *him*!" Raia yelled back.

Their voices echoed off the walls as Kaminsky hobbled between them. "Ladies, ladies, please." He held his arms up. "This is the pickle I was talking about. Now that we have confirmation that Zak is a Light-Wielder, but has not yet reached the age of manhood, the council needs to deliberate what to do with this information."

"Harvey, you can't," Raia croaked.

Kaminsky put a hand on her shoulder. "Raia, I'm sorry. But we can't set aside generations of tradition."

"Tradition?" she shouted, meeting the stares around the room as her voice bounced within the dome. "It's true I didn't want anyone to know. After losing Bram, I didn't want to lose Zak too. I thought if anyone knew he had the light that you'd send him out to defend the colony. You and I both know one Golem doesn't stand much of a chance against the queen. It'd be a wasted effort. So, I made my kids swear they'd keep it a secret. I was sure--and I still am--that we have a better chance with JERICHO. I beg you. Please. Don't send my son out to die."

"Where is your faith?" one of the stern-faced women said, opening her arms. "Everyone here believes the Golems were sent by God to protect us. Why would he abandon us now?"

"Where was God when Bram powered a Golem, alone, against the queen?" Raia gnashed her teeth. "He was a grown man, and a veteran soldier, and still lost. What chance does a boy with no combat training have against that?"

"The queen didn't kill Bram," Neema scoffed. "He chased her back underground, while the rest of us took care of the pups."

Raia sneered. "You're right. The Queen didn't kill him. The Golem did. It drained him dry. And then he spent the next four months in bed, withering away like a man three times his age waiting to die. I won't sacrifice my son for your misplaced faith. JERICHO can hold off the queen. We can protect our flocks from her pups if we focus on finishing and keeping the monsters out."

The room fell silent until Harvey cleared his throat. "I'm afraid we may need both," he said, getting to his feet again. He shuffled over and put one hand on Raia's shoulder and the other on Zak's. "And this is not just a matter of a mother protecting her son from his destiny. JERICHO will go forward. We've invested too much time, energy, and materials to abandon it now. I'm sorry, Saraia, but this may be our last chance to preserve the colony."

Raia buried her face in Zak's neck, wrapping her arms around his chest. Zak clung to her, his lip quivering as he searched Harvey's eyes. "I'm sorry, young man." Harvey patted Zak's cheek. "I'm so sorry."

"We need to get Zak trained-up on the Golem as soon as possible." Neema walked over and reached for the boy.

Harvey put up a finger. "We need to deliberate the Light-Wielder's fate first."

Raia grabbed Neema's wrist, her fingers just centimeters from Zak's arm. "You're not taking my son," she growled, glaring with narrow eyes.

"It's already been decided." She slapped at Raia's hand and looked at Harvey. "You said yourself. We'll need both the wall and the Golem to defend ourselves from the attack."

"I said we may need both." Harvey pulled Neema's hand from Raia's grip. "But that's for the council to decide. Not one person alone."

He nodded and gestured to one of the men at the perimeter, standing next to a carved wooden box. The chest displayed the image of a pair of scales. The lid creaked open on ancient hinges, and from within the man withdrew a leather sack the size of a grapefruit, holding it above his head and then replacing it.

"Those who draw black," Harvey raised his voice, "will argue against Zak using the Golem to defend the colony. Those who draw white will argue for Zak defending the colony. Whoever draws gray will be Speaker, and cast the deciding vote in the event of a draw."

"You can't be present during deliberation," Neema smirked. "It may affect the council's judgment to have either of you in attendance. We'll inform you of our decision." She jutted her chin toward the and spun on her heel.

"What's going on, mom?" Zak muttered as Raia took him by the hand, making a beeline for the exit.

They're afraid. We're all afraid. If we can't protect our home, we won't survive another year. They keep coming, year after year, nothing we've tried so far has made any difference against the queen. Not one Light-Wielder has lived after standing between her and the colony. They're afraid this is the end. I'm scared too. The Golem takes everything from them. It took Bram. Now, it's going to take Zak.

"We'll talk about it later," Raia guided Zak out the door. "At home. I have to get back to work."

* * *

Zak found little solace in his favorite thinking spot: Leeya's bedroom.

Resting his arms on the short table, he sat cross-legged on the dirty green throw rug. His azure jumpsuit bunched up around his knees and elbows.

A one-meter diameter sphere of glass, dubbed the alien ant farm, hovered above eye level. The holo floating near the equator displayed data like population by species, atmospheric composition, and soil pH levels over time.

MagLev plates embedded in the globe's south pole kept Leeya's science experiment a centimeter above the table's surface. A similar device on top held a solar lamp in constant motion to mimic the planet's seasons. Dark umber soil and an assortment of indigenous insect and plant life filled the orb's lower half, with atmospheric components comprised of the noxious gases found outside the colony dome. Tunnels lined the transparent surface like drought-starved riverbeds.

A rosy homespun blanket fell from his shoulders like a shroud of Pink Bismuth. His stomach growled and knotted from the eyes, glaring down on him from all sides. Holos of dissected cadavers--stippled with digital sticky notes written in elaborate cursive handwriting--painted every wall.

What if they make me go?

Zak leaned forward, pressing his forehead to the sphere. He stared at a stream of alien bugs carrying bits of soil, as they carved out a new tunnel. Like well-orchestrated traffic, they moved in two opposing streams. Those with their mouths full, and those without.

"Hey, nugget." Leeya's dark ponytail swung into the room like a plumb-bob as she leaned in from the doorway. "Dinner's almost ready."

Zak sat back and let his chin fall to his chest. "I'm not hungry."

Leeya padded into the room, wearing the same outfit from the morning, and sat down next to Zak. She pulled him close with one arm, the badge on her vest poking his ear.

"Ow," he grumbled under his breath.

She pulled the badge--a silver caduceus behind a white rectangle with a QR code printed on one side of the text--from under his head and dropped it to the floor. Though he knew what it said, Zak couldn't help reading it as he rubbed at his head. His eyes tracing the twin snakes coiling around the staff.

LEEYA SCHAFER: TRAINEE

Turning back to the globe, Zak continued to watch the bugs dig a new tunnel and deposit the soil on the surface from one of a half-dozen mounds. The top of one began to turn in on itself, then collapsed altogether, leaving a crater in its place.

"Looks like they excavated too much in one spot again." Leeya leaned forward and typed a few notes on the holo and scrolled through the incoming data. "Whew. She's safe. They won't have to start the colony over again."

"Who's safe?" Zak stretched his neck to see the holo better.

"The queen ant," Leeya said absentmindedly. "The last one died in a similar collapse. Whenever that happens, the colony kills themselves off down to one female and a drone. She becomes the new queen, and they start all over."

"How many times has that happened?"

"Hmm, let's see," she said, swiping through screens. "Looks like... six."

"All because the dirt fell on them?" Zak's brows pinched over his nose.

"No." She flipped the holo back to basic analysis and cuddled into him. "Sometimes, if their population rises too high, they purge their numbers to preserve resources."

"They kill each other?"

"No. The queen kills some of the drones. I assume it's because they're the weak ones. They live in a closed system. They have to work with what they have."

"Is that why they build so many tunnels? Are they trying to find more resources?"

"Perhaps." She smiled. "We don't know that much about their habits. We're basing our assumptions on earth insect behavior. Besides, they can't get out. Just like us, they live in a bottle. But our bottle seems to have cracks in it."

"Is that how the Fletzs are getting in?" Zak fiddled with a loose thread. "Our bottle's broken?"

"Not the dome, but the crater." She sighed. "There must be fissures they've found their way through even though the geological scans showed bedrock under the soil. That's why we chose this site to make the crater. And they think our animals must be tastier than what's outside the dome. Some say we should poison a few of our herds, and let the Fletzs have free reign on them. Maybe they'll stop attacking."

"Would that work?" Zak's eyes widened.

"No idea." She sighed. "We don't know enough about their physiology. We do know they're susceptible to cold and blunt force trauma. Like that exploding rock trick of yours." Leeya watched him from the side of her eye.

Zak pulled the blanket tight over his shoulder. "The lamb got hurt too."

"Yeah." Leeya gave him a squeeze. "I know."

"I'm glad you didn't get hurt." Zak rested his head on her chest.

"Me too."

The gentle hum of electromagnets filled the room for several moments as Leeya stroked Zak's hair.

"Mom's working late again," Leeya said, kissing his head. "Said she has to make up lost time from..."

"Yeah." Zak sighed. "Because of me."

"It's not your fault, Zak," Leeya said, rubbing his arm.

"It is my fault," Zak said, pulling away. "It's all my fault."

"What I meant was, it's not your fault that you inherited the light."

"But it is my fault I didn't listen and used it," he yelled as he stood up, letting the Bismuth blanket fall from his shoulders. "If I'd listened, no one would have found out."

"If you hadn't used the light to kill that Fletz, we might not be having this conversation," Leeya said, keeping her voice steady. "The secret might be safe, but Mom would be burying us next to Dad instead. Would that be better?"

"No." Zak sagged in on himself. "Of course not. But why did I have to hide it in the first place?"

"You know why." Leeya stood and paced the room. "But that doesn't matter now. I hear what the grown-ups say when they think I'm not listening. Most of the Council has been praying for a miracle. For them, you're it. They'll make you get in that *thing*, and you'll end up like Dad."

"Fighting the queen." Zak hugged himself.

Leeya crossed the room and put her arms around him, resting her chin on his head. "Dad was a strong, healthy man," she said. "Powering the Golem day after day, until the queen retreated back underground, weakened his immune system. No offense, but how long do you think you'll last? You're twelve."

"Twelve and a half," he murmured.

"You want to make it to thirteen?" Leeya playfully swatted the back of his head. "Let's go eat. Remember to wash up."

Zak turned to the terrarium as Leeya moved to the doorway. He stared into the globe, watching the bugs clear a new path to the surface and begin depositing bits of soil on the surface.

Leeya looked over her shoulder. "Aren't you coming?"

"Yeah." Zak took a deep breath. "It's just..."

"It's just what?" She turned to face him.

"I knew I shouldn't have," Zak mumbled. "Use the light, I mean. I just wanted to save the lamb. I had to try."

* * *

The next morning, Zak and Raia sat on the lowest level of the spectator's benches in the council chamber. Two matching risers on their right and left formed a triad of raised seating. In the center of the hall, a stone cube sat equidistant from all three. On one side of the block, a velvety blood-red drape covered an unknown object that seemed square at the base and pointed at the top.

Raia, with dark circles under her unfocused eyes, ran her fingers across Zak's back. His head swayed like a fishing bob caught in a whirlpool as dozens of people filtered into the room. Each wore a white or black stone hanging from a chain around their necks. Fragments of whispered conversations carried to his ears as the council members entered and divided to one side or the other.

"He was born with a gift. He has a responsibility to the community."

"He's just a boy. The light shouldn't have presented until after he became a man."

"What does it matter when it manifested?"

"What about his rights? How can we talk about taking away the rights of one person for the sake of the colony? Where does it end if we start down this path?"

"The survival of this colony depends on more than one boy. We've lost more people--than are in this room--fighting off the Mifletzot. If we can't stop them from devouring our animals, how will *we* survive?"

"The light is his birthright, and he must use it in our defense. Anyone of us would be held to the same standard, male or female, regardless of age."

"He'll never be ready in time. What if we just try and hold off the queen? He can begin his training for next spring. After he becomes a man."

"We left Earth because we wanted to preserve our freedom. We can't walk away from that now, even if it means extinction. We may die, but it's better than losing our souls."

Kaminsky came in next to last--supported by Neema--as if marching to a Russian dirge. His cane tapped on the floor like a metronome as she led him to one side. A black stone clinked between the buttons of his high-bib overalls. People talked behind their hands and hissed in each other's ears as the duo made their way to the risers.

Raia's hand froze. "Neema's the grey," she breathed. "No."

"What does that mean?" Zak whispered in her ear.

Raia put her nose to Zak's temple. "It means, if there's a draw, she's the tie-breaker. And I know how she'll vote."

Zak nodded.

Oh, Bram. Why did you have to die? Why couldn't you have been stronger? Why couldn't you be here, now, to protect our son when he needs you the most?

Once Kaminsky found his seat within the black-stone section, Neema moved toward the cube situated between the two groups. Grabbing fistfuls of the red curtain, she lifted the drape revealing a set of ancient-looking brass scales settled on a wooden cart. Dropping the fabric, she took a seat on the rock with her back to the spectators' gallery.

"Let's begin the vote," Neema said, cutting off the murmuring. "We'll start..."

"Before we vote," Kaminsky tapped his cane on the floor. "Does anyone have anything new to add to the discussion?" He stood slowly, turning on the spot and holding out his open palm as he made eye contact with every person in the chamber. "Anything at all? A riddle? A pun? I'd love to hear an inappropriate limerick right now."

Chuckles, shaking heads, and averted faces met him everywhere.

Raia stood, raising her hand. "May I add something?"

"I can always rely on you for a good joke, Raia." Kaminsky bowed to her and sat down.

"No." Neema barked over her shoulder as Raia took in a deep breath. "I'm sorry, but we've discussed both sides of the issue at length. We're here to cast our votes, not engage in further debate. And it's definitely not the time for off-color humor."

Raia gritted her teeth as she sat down, folding her arms tight across her chest.

Neema took a silver rod from the pocket over her gray overalls and tapped the end. A holo appeared below as if uncoiling from a scroll. "Each delegate will stand in order of rank," Neema read aloud, "starting with the junior-most member. Once a delegate has voted, he or she will exit the chambers so as not to influence the vote of the remaining council. Once the tally is complete, the decision will be rendered as binding upon all parties. A simple majority will take the vote. In the event of a tie, the speaker will make the final judgment. God be with us."

"God, be with us." Everyone in the room said in unison.

"Let us begin," Neema gestured to a young man, seated in the top row to her right.

He kept his eyes down as he made his way down the risers to the center of the chamber, moving to the spot where the scales were between him and Neema. Fiddling with the black stone around his neck, He removed it from the chain and held it over one of the brass plates and cleared his throat.

"I vote for Zak to defend the colony." He uttered to the floor as he dropped it on the left pan. He winced as the rock's clang echoed, shattering the chamber's silence like an explosion.

Raia grabbed a fistful of Zak's shirt, breathing hard through her nose.

The delegate then looked up and caught Zak's gaze. "I'm sorry," he said, his lips making a tight line as he walked out, shoulders hunched.

Zak looked over as Raia brushed her cheek.

"Next," Neema said, leaning forward as the next delegate, a young woman, approached the scales.

"I vote for Zak to defend the colony," she said, then looked over at Raia, her eyes glistening as she rushed out covering her mouth.

"Next."

Two more votes for. Three against. One for. One against. The process continued as the chamber emptied of all but Zak, Raia, Neema, and Harvey.

With seventeen for--and eighteen against--Zak defending the colony, Harvey dropped his stone in the left-side plate. "I vote for Zak to defend the colony."

"No!" Raia sobbed, bending forward and falling into her hands, her cries filling the room.

She looked up as Harvey shuffled over and put a hand on her wracking shoulder. "I'm so sorry, Raia." Then, he turned to Zak and held out his hand. "I'm sorry, young man. Life isn't always fair. Sometimes God calls us to do hard things."

Zak nodded and took his hand. Raia turned and pulled Zak into her arms as Harvey shuffled out the door.

"I thought we had a chance," Raia whispered, stroking Zak's hair. "I thought Harvey was going to vote against."

The sound of footsteps brought Zak's attention to the dais. Neema approached the scales, one arm at her side, the other hidden behind her back. The needle teetering back and forth as the swaying pans slowed to a halt.

"It falls on me to break the tie." Her soft echo bouncing off the ceiling. A minute passed as she stood frozen in place. She took a breath through her nose. "I vote--."

Zak pushed himself from Raia's embrace, jogging several steps away from the risers. His shoes squeaked as he skidded to a halt. "I'll do it," Zak shouted.

"Zak. No." Raia yelped. "You'll do no such thing."

Neema turned around, eyes widening as she brought her fist to her chest.

"Mom," Zak said over his shoulder. "You said she'll send me out anyway. At least it'll be my choice. Maybe I can hold off the queen like dad did."

"Absolutely not," Raia growled back. "You're not doing this. You're not sacrificing yourself."

Zak put his back to Neema. "You said they were going to send me out anyway."

"That doesn't mean you have to volunteer," she hissed. "Why are you doing this?"

"Before Dad died, he told me I'd be the man of the house." Zak closed their distance by a half-step. "He always said a man has a responsibility to protect his family first and community second."

"And this is how you're going to protect your sister and me?" Raia crossed her arms. "This isn't one of your VR sims where you go off to fight in glorious battle. There's no re-spawn. This is real life and death."

"I know that." Zak took a half-step back. "If Dad were here, he'd support my decision as a man."

"If your father were here, we wouldn't be talking about a twelve-year-old going up against a monster." Raia half sobbed, half screamed.

"Twelve and a half." Zak murmured to the floor. "Close enough."

"Don't you split hairs with me, young man." Raia flared. "I'm still your mother, and you will show me the proper respect."

Raia closed the distance, taking Zak by the shoulders. "I don't want you to die," she choked. "I lost your father. I don't want to lose you too."

"If I don't do this, we may all die," Zak said. "Isn't that what you've been working on? Isn't JERICHO supposed to protect the flocks, so we don't starve to death? Is my life more important than anyone else's? Am I more important than you? Or Leeya? If I can make even a small difference in defending the colony, isn't that worth it?"

Raia blinked back the moisture building in the corners of her eyes, taking Zak in her arms. He lost his breath as if sat on. After a moment, he wrapped his arms around her waist, burying his face in her neck.

Neema sniffled behind them, causing Raia to release her boa-like grip. Zak stared at the stain on her chest as he wiped at his cheek.

"So, it's decided then?" Neema said in a husky voice, as she lowered the white-knuckled fist to her side. "Zak accepts the responsibility to defend the colony?"

Zak looked into Raia's wet eyes. She nodded to him, then Neema.

"I do," he said, standing to his full height.

Neema's chocolate eyes swam in her brimming lids. "You brave, *brave* young man." Her voice cracked. "Report to Ezra Cohen in the maintenance building immediately. I'll tell him you're coming. He'll have the training protocols waiting for you. You'll have to make your way there alone. We need your mother back on JERICHO. Go with God, Zak. You have little time to learn all you can." She gestured to a door behind one of the risers opposite the way he came in.

"Thanks, Mrs. Wabani," Zak said, examining his feet as he made his way across the empty chamber. His shuffling feet blended with the sniffles behind him. As he reached for the handle, Raia called out.

"I'll see you at dinner, baby. I'll make your favorite."

"Sounds great." Zak choked, then pushed through, letting the door cut off Raia's sobs.

* * *

The deck bounced slightly with each step as Zak's feet scuffed the concrete. Despite his snail's pace between floor to ceiling rows of vacuum-sealed bags of grain, he seemed to travel to his destination at light speed. Counting as he scanned the layers, he thought of endless meals of chicken and rice with whole wheat bread.

Enormous blades rotated overhead like a multi-spoked second hand of a clock as the scent of stale water met his nose. His mind wandered into the substructure, where an underground pool matched the building footprint.

Every basement flooded after that first equinox. Bad for the Fletz, but good for us. One breach, they smother and drown.

The sounds of impact hammers, hydraulic torque wrenches, and ancient rock music carried across the alley as the light of a welding torch flashed in his eyes. He raised his hand to the glare as the scent of rust, singed body hair, and motor oil filled his nose. Indistinct voices shouting over an electric guitar solo bounced off every surface as he trudged closer.

Just inside the doorway, Zak spied a mechanic wearing blacked-out goggles, grinding the blades of what looked like a propeller with rows of scythes welded to the surface, bobbing his head to the beat. A skull-face bandanna covering his nose and mouth billowed with each breath. Further in, dozens of people built frameworks of rebar, shields on wheels, and car-sized crossbows.

"Excuse me!" Zak said, approaching bandanna man.

Sparks flew out into the air, carried a meter on the breeze before fizzling out of existence. All the while, the man paid Zak no mind.

"Excuse me!" Zak yelled, tapping his shoulder.

The man looked up, holding the spinning grinder and tapped his ear.

"Can you tell me where I can find Ezra Cohen?" Zak cupped his hands around his mouth and shouted.

"Office!" the man hollered, thumbing over his shoulder. "In the back."

As the man returned to his grinding, Zak waved thanks and headed for a lit doorway at the far end of the warehouse. Once there, he stepped through the doorless opening. An old metal desk blocked his way, piled high with stacks of paper, grease-stained tools, and parts of a disassembled electric motor neatly arrayed across the top.

He poked his head around the desk to find the back of a short, chubby man inserting cables into what looked like an oversized metal marshmallow. The two-meters tall and one-meter diameter cylinder had a seam along its length with latches holding the clam-shell sides together. "Mr. Cohen?" he said, knuckling the jamb.

"Call me Ezra," he said as the clamps snapped open, releasing the twin sides to separate. He stood up, hiking his waistline and turning to a makeshift workstation atop a metal door on the room's far side. Several computer towers and monitors crowded the nicked and stained surface. Bundled wires snaked across the floor like spaghetti to the booth. "You must be Isaac."

Ezra finally turned, picking up a cloth from the desk and wiping his hands. "You look just like your dad." The long ringlets growing from his sideburns bounced as he ground the rag into his palms.

"You knew him?"

Ezra's mouth turned down. "Not well. We didn't chat between his sessions in the simulator. He was always in a hurry to get home. I last saw him in the infirmary. Just days before he... Sorry. Come on in. We don't have a lot of time."

Zak moved into the room as Ezra pressed his palm to a glass plate. The halves separated on a track, revealing an interior lined with spikes of midnight-black foam. Each side had a plate with a shoe-print in white paint, elevated on a short post, and a horizontal bar at the chamber's midpoint.

"Step in, and grab the interface," Ezra said over Zak's head, pointing to the rod. "The bar there. The trainer will scan you and adjust to your size."

"Okay," Zak muttered as he moved toward the left side, wiping his hands on his pants. Stepping on the shoe print, he reached for the handle at chest-level. Zak looked over his shoulder as the half-cylinder did nothing in response to his touch.

"D'oy." Ezra slapped his forehead. "You have to energize it. Just like the Golem. *You* have to use your light to give it power."

"How much?" Zak gripped and re-gripped the rod. "I've only charged small things before. Nothing this big."

"The trainer will activate when it senses enough power to activate the Golem." Ezra moved toward the bank of computers and tapped on a few keys. "Powering the Golem in a fight on the other hand..." He shrugged, tilting his head to one side.

Zak swallowed, rubbed his palms down his thighs again, and reached out for the handle.

Okay. Okay. Just like Dad's stories.

With eyes closed, the tingle started in his chest, like having an electrical muscle stimulation pad strapped over his heart. The current fluctuated like a gentle ocean tide. Rising and falling in rhythm with his breathing. Holding his breath, the buzzing grew, slowly radiating outward as if contact pads were being stuck to his body by invisible hands. Looking down, a blue aura crisscrossed his skin like the ripples at a pool's bottom.

He blew out his lungs, the charge thinning like air.

"That was pretty good," Ezra crowed, running a finger down a holo, "for a thirteen-year-old. I would've expected these levels from a young adult."

"I'm not." Zak's breath came heavy.

"Not what?" Ezra never looked away from the holo.

"Not thirteen. I'm twelve and a half."

"Hmm." Ezra looked over, the corners of his mouth turned down. "Interesting. There are legends from the ancient times. They say in the absence of Light-Wielders, the light would spark in the oldest youth in the family line in times of great need. I guess our situation qualifies."

"Lucky me," Zak mumbled as he opened and closed his hands, pumping blood back to his fingertips.

"Try again." Ezra gestured to Zak's hands. "You need to have the light in your hands when you make contact with the bars."

Zak took another deep breath, his jaw muscles flexed, arms outstretched with balled fists. The wave built faster, like electrified mist sweeping across his skin, around his back, down to his waist and wrists. He emptied his lungs in a single blow, gulping quickly with his nails dug into his palms. The receding tide only reached his elbows when he pushed it out again.

Light arced from his fingertips, like strings around a balloon, forming weightless spheres. Zak stared at the ripples of light, rushing down his arms to his glowing hands. A few steadying breaths cleared the building dizziness.

"Still can't believe they're making a kid do this," Ezra murmured, moving to stand beside the foam-filled tank. "Light-Wielder or not."

"Huh?" Zak looked up from his hands.

"Nothing." Ezra's mouth was twisted. "Never mind. That looks like it should be enough. Step on the platform, grab the handles, and the trainer will close."

"Oh-kay." Zak aligned his right foot with the matching shoe-print, grabbed the bar, and pulled himself off the floor. Leaning out, he stretched to place his left foot and reached for the other handle.

"One last thing." Ezra pushed one clamshell half toward the other. "Don't freak out about the foam."

"What?" Zak yelped just as he gripped the left bar. The contraption snapped shut, leaving Zak with only the sound of his heartbeat and a dull glow on either side. "Wait. Let me out!"

Zak tried to pound his fist on the coffin's inside, but couldn't pull his hands away from the bars. He tugged at his arms like a dog on a leash. The foam spikes followed his every movement, growing and receding as he jerked his head left and right. "Open up. Get me out of here."

"Calm down, Zak." Ezra sounded like he was yelling at the bottom of a pool. "The simulator is just taking in your biometrics. Take a breath and relax."

Against his instinct, Zak closed his eyes and took a few breaths. With each exhale, the soft points of foam spread across his body up to his chin. Pressure on the top of his head wrapped over his ears, filling the canals, until the silence enveloped even his own breathing. His pulse thudded in his ears, speeding up as the light within disappeared. "What's going on?" he yelled, shaking his head.

"It's Flex-Foam." Ezra's voice started out distorted, then became clear as if next to him. "It's molding itself to your body. It will also act as your sensory interface with the Golem."

"How does it work?" Zak asked.

"Beats me." Ezra chuckled to himself. "Your dad asked the same question, but he figured it out."

Suddenly Zak's hands came free from the sides, though he could still feel the rods in his hands. Flexing his biceps, his arms rose up, but it wasn't his flesh-and-bone he saw floating in space. Ghostly apparitions appeared, matching the movements he made with his hands.

"You should be seeing a representation of the Golem by now," Ezra said. "Do you see it?"

"Not yet," Zak yelled into the black. "Wait."

Pieces of armor phased into existence, starting with a pair of flaming orange gauntlets. Armbands came next, followed by shoulder pieces and a chest plate. All the way down to shin guards and boots. Every edge glowed as if just pulled from a blacksmith's forge. Patting himself down, he could feel every crease and seam.

"Am I supposed to be wearing armor?"

"Yes." Ezra's voice instantly sounded. "You're getting a first-person POV."

"Cool." Zak grinned, extending his arms and legs to see as much detail as possible. "Just like my VR rig."

"In the simulator, the VR is just an interface." Ezra snorted. "In a couple of days, you'll be inside the real thing. In the real world, taking real damage."

A glow appeared on the horizon. Zak lifted his foot to take a step, and the post moved with him like a bicycle peg. He stepped a few more paces, watching his feet as they impacted a virtual ground plane. Zak reached out, searching for the simulator wall, but the rod in his hand wouldn't move past a certain point.

"What am I looking at?"

"I don't know," Ezra said distractedly. Somehow sounding like he was across the room. "I don't see what you see. I've never been told what happens after this point in the simulation."

Zak took a few more hesitant steps, then broke into a jog across the digital plain. The artificial ground-scape extended in all directions as he moved into a run toward the growing light. As the simulated dawn grew closer, he heard a hushed voice. Slowing to a jog, he cocked his ears as he heard it again coming from the light's direction but still couldn't understand it. He stopped in place, catching his breath at the base of a rising slope and looked to the peak where the light seemed brightest.

The glow spread across the horizon on both sides until Zak found himself enveloped by it.

"Welcome, Light-Wielder," said a deep man's voice in the old tongue. "What shall we call you?"

He turned in a circle, squinting his eyes against the glow. "I'm Zak. Zak Schafer."

"Welcome, Zak Schafer," said the disembodied voice. "Thank you for sharing your light with us."

"Sh-sure," he stammered.

A mild chuckle vibrated through Zak's feet. "Is there anything you would like to ask of us before we begin?"

Zak swallowed. "Who are you? What are you?"

Another vibration ran up Zak's leg.

"We are the Golem." The voice boomed through Zak's chest. "We are the energy, experiences, and memories of all Light-Wielders that have gone before."

"Like my dad?" Zak moved forward. "My dad was a Light-Wielder."

"We know," the Golem said. "He was a valiant warrior. His sacrifice defending his family ensured his place with us."

"Is he here? Can I see him?"

A spot of dimness formed in front of Zak, congealing until the translucent image of Bram Schafer took shape. He wore a white bodysuit, whiter than anything Zak had ever seen in his life. But his skin, beard, and eyes were as dark as Zak remembered. "Hello, son," Bram spoke in the old tongue; his voice filled the space between them. "I've missed you. So much."

"DAD!" Zak ran to him, arms outstretched, but passed straight through. "Dad?"

"I'm sorry, Zak. I'm not tangible." Bram shrugged, turning. "Not here, anyway."

"Where are we?" Zak looked around again.

"Somewhere..." Bram's mouth pinched to a line, his brows furrowed. "Between."

"Between where?"

"Between here..." Bram put his hand next to Zak's scrunched face and sighed. "And there. We have no words in the old, or new, tongues to describe what you're asking."

"I miss you, Dad." Zak croaked. "Mom and Leeya miss you too."

"As I miss them." Bram smiled. "One day, we'll be together again. I promise."

"But for now," the Golem interrupted, "We must focus on your training."

"Come." Bram held his arm out to corral Zak to the side where a wooden park bench mysteriously appeared. "Sit."

Zak sat, shifting to make room for Bram, who remained standing. "The Golem is an extension of the Light-Wielder. Of you, Zak. It reacts to you. Relies on your instinct. It will perform any task your mind commits to. And it will protect you. It is virtually impenetrable. As long as your light shines, you have the means to protect the colony."

"Leeya says that's how you died." Zak twiddled his gloved thumbs, looking down. "She says you got used up like a fuel cell fighting off the queen and then didn't have the strength to get better."

"She's right." Bram got on one knee. "I gave the Golem everything I had."

"To protect the colony," Zak muttered.

Bram held his hand out, urging Zak to look up. Once their eyes met, he smiled. "To protect my family. Not the colony. Every individual has a responsibility to the community. To add to it. To make it stronger. In return, the community has a responsibility for each individual. To help them develop to their fullest potential. To protect the innocent and ensure everyone has the opportunity to grow and develop into the best person they can be. The strong protect the weak, so the weak can become strong."

"I don't know if I'm strong enough." Zak's lip quivered. "I don't know if I can do it."

"Would you like to know a secret?" Bram sighed and held both hands near Zak's face. "Something I didn't learn until I was facing the queen. It's not physical strength that fuels the Golem. It's the strength of character. Of heart. On the third day after the solstice, I thought I was going to die. I almost gave up. I didn't think I had anything left to give. Then I thought of your mother. And Leeya. And you. And realized I couldn't leave this world knowing I'd held anything back from protecting my family. So I gave the Golem everything I had left. It was enough to push the queen back, but I saved nothing for myself."

"And then you died."

"Yes." Bram crouched in front of Zak, his palms open. "But you lived. And I'd make that trade again without hesitation."

Zak stared at the ground for several minutes in silence. "Mom didn't want me to do this." He whispered. "She wanted me to keep the light a secret."

Bram nodded, interlocking his fingers. "Here's another secret. And your Mother knew this too." Bram leaned forward on his knees, craning his head until Zak looked him the eye. "She and I both knew this day would come. You had a stronger heart as a child than I ever had as a man. That's why the light was passed onto you. And I know you'll succeed in protecting our family from the Mifletzot. Do you trust me?"

Zak nodded and wiped at his face.

"Then let's get started." Bram stood, gesturing for Zak to follow.

When Zak looked up, the queen appeared where Bram was heading. Its three rows of dagger-sharp teeth contracted to the center as if feeding on an invisible stick of meat. Its death-black eyes focused on Bram, watching his every step. The monster raised up its front quarter, coiled back like an asp to strike.

"Dad, look out!" Zak sprinted forward.

Bram turned his back to the beast, cocking his head with a confused expression.

Zak sprinted forward, racing to beat the monster to his father. As the queen's head came down to strike, Zak lunged at her, ready to take the hit. Impacting nothing but air, Zak landed on the ground, skidding to a stop several meters away, losing his breath as he fell.

Zak rolled, getting to his feet, and turned to see Bram strolling through the monster as if it were fog.

"You have more heart than I ever did, son." Bram moved closer. "I can't begin to describe how proud I am of you."

Zak brushed off non-existent dust from his armor. "You really think I can do this?"

"You didn't hesitate to defend me from the queen, even though I'd already shown you I was intangible in this place." Bram's grin split his face.

"I forgot." Zak looked at his armored feet.

"Yes." Bram beamed. "You forgot about yourself. You set your own safety aside, putting yourself at risk for another. That's the mark of a true Light-Wielder. There aren't many in any community who are willing to do the same, even if they found themselves in far less dangerous situations. Are you ready for your next lesson?"

"Are you going to teach me how to take a hit?" Zak's mouth turned down.

"Yes," Bram said, nodding. The corner of his mouth then turned up. "Then I'm going to teach you how to dish them out."

"How much can I learn in a couple of days?" Zak threw out his arms.

Bram smiled, nodding his head. "How long do you think you've been here? In this place?" he asked, spreading out his arms.

"I don't know." Zak shrugged. "About ten minutes."

"It's been closer to ten seconds." Bram tapped his temple. "The mind works faster than the body. This is a special place. In two days here, you'll learn more than in two months out there."

Zak turned on the spot, squinting his eyes as he gazed out to the horizon.

"Are you ready to begin?" Bram asked, his voice coming from several meters away.

Zak spun in place, finding his father standing beside the queen. She was frozen in the coiled position.

"Okay." Zak squared his shoulders to the beast, planting one foot behind him. "What do I do?"

* * *

Day three of the siege.

Neema scratched at the edges of her prosthetic, her eyes wide as the sun crested the dome. Instead of refracting off numerous waterfalls, the growing blade of light made the crater walls look like Earth's Grand Canyon. Craggy and barren. The light rippled as it found the moat, waters lapping over its banks.

Irrigation systems spewed pitiful mists on smoldering fields. The new moat, a ring of mud where the bodies of dead pups were tossed, picked up the runoff.

Not enough to go around. Save the fields or save the flocks?

She followed the crater's shadow as it descended on JERICHO. Gouges and scorch marks pocked the walls around the entire circumference. Not one section was spared from attack.

Defending all day. Rebuilding and resupplying all night.

She tapped on her holo, selecting through various menus.

MIFLETZOT DATA. ANALYSIS. EMERGENT EVENTS. HEAT SIGNATURE TRACKING. CHRONOLOGICAL. YEAR ONE. INCIDENT ONE.

The Queen's first visit to court.

A plan of the crater appeared on another screen with the colony shaded forest green. Scattered dots of neon purple roamed throughout the map. A red smudge appeared half-way between the settlement and moat in the Southwest quadrant. An instant later, a fading red trail zig-zagged through the fields.

Immediately afterward, a flood of orange dots emerged in pursuit. Following the queen's trail like a stampede of fire. The queen circled the crater, spiraling inward. Purple dots collected inside the buildings, a few green ones heading toward the incoming assault. A single electric blue dot, leading the charge.

The Golem. Bram's father.

The blue and red dots collided while the orange wave parted around them like a river, heading for the fields dotted in indigo. Over the next few seconds, the flocks dwindled in number as the Golem and queen battled until the sun went down. As darkness fell across the valley, the queen retreated underground, followed by her horde. The next morning, the pattern restarted from a new location.

Never the same place twice.

Watching the years speed by, time after time, only one pattern remained consistent.

They emerge from below. They consume what they catch. They return underground. Slightly fewer pups each time, but we lose more than they do.

Neema waved away the holos as alarms blared from her console.

"Location confirmed." An automated voice came over the speaker on Neema's desk. "Southwest pastures."

The message repeated.

"God protect us," Neema whispered to herself.

* * *

Zak gazed down at the topographical map in front of him. Gesturing with his hands and arms, he navigated the colony in VR. Pop-up holos appeared with data on each building and system within the crater. Empty streets ran from the center like a spider's web. Smudges like oil-spills filled every building while evenly spaced greed dots lined the parapets of JERICHO.

Wonder which ones are Mom and Leeya.

Zak zoomed out, and then refocused on a cooling patch along the outer moat. A swath of charred field, littered with the smoldering bodies of pups, cradled the bank in the Northwest quadrant. A wind generator stood off-kilter next to the water.

What was she doing when I got there? Almost pushed her in. She sicced her pups on me before I had the chance.

Zooming in, he focused on a pillar. Scratches and dents marred the base. Even a few teeth remained lodged in the heavy steel.

You really that hungry? Mutton not to your liking?

An alarm blared overhead. Dropping his arms, the map returned to actual size. Zak found himself standing in the center of the virtual colony. Looking up, a pulsating arrow pointed over his left shoulder. He spun around, spotting a beacon, like a lighthouse, outside the city walls.

"Zak." Kaminsky's voice said in his ear. "It's time. Fastest route uploaded. Godspeed, son."

A blue path appeared, superimposed on the street like a glowing people-mover.

"Thank you," Zak said as he broke into a jog, then a run. The buildings, sprinkled with people waving to him, sped by. He caught the faint echo of cheers as he blasted through the Western gates and veered right. Crossing the grazing meadows at 100 kph, the fields blurred in his peripheral vision as he focused ahead, ignoring the litter of pups, heading in the other direction.

Mom will take care of them.

Within a few minutes, Zak found himself within 100 meters of the moat. He got down into a crouch as he slowed to a walk, creeping toward the bank. Zooming in, he spied the queen attacking the tower again, biting at it. She screamed into the air as the steel column gave her no satisfaction. Rearing back and striking again, she pounded her head against the base to no avail.

"Maybe if I can get her in the water while she's not looking," Zak said to himself, advancing with slow, carefully-placed steps.

Once within fifty meters, Zak took a knee and watched. The creature seemed utterly preoccupied with the tower.

"Zak." Neema's voice chirped in his ear. "I can see what you're thinking. It's a good plan. Try to sneak closer before you attack. You may have only one shot at this."

"What about the pups?" Zak whispered for no reason. "Has she called for them yet? I can't fight her *and* them at the same time. That's how she got away yesterday."

"They're still attacking the wall," Neema said. "But they're concentrating on one spot, closest to her, instead of all over."

"Have they ever done that before?"

"No." She sighed. "Nor has the queen ever attacked a wind generator before. We don't know what to make of it. But now's our chance. If you can get her in the water, the rapid cooling should kill her. Then we can mop up the pups later."

Just then, the tower groaned, tilting one more degree off-plumb.

"What happens if she destroys the generator?" Zak zoomed back on the tower base.

"Nothing." Neema's voice sounded tired. "We can rebuild a generator faster than she can tear it down. We have spare parts. To be honest, I can't think of any reason why she's wasting her energy on it."

Zak's imagination carried the tower to a horizontal position.

"What if she's trying to get out?" Zak asked. "What if she's trying to make a bridge to get across the moat?"

"That's absurd." Neema sighed audibly. "It's an animal, not an engineer. They don't *make* things. They eat, breath, and reproduce. That's it. And even if she is, we can't let her. What if she gets out and comes back next solstice with more pups. Or worse, with one of the bulls we've tracked outside the dome? Then what?"

"Like you said, they're just animals. And my Dad says animals just want to live."

"So do we, Zak," Neema shouted. "Do you want to take the chance that she'll leave and never come back? After feasting on us, do you really think she wants to go back to her natural diet?"

"It's possible..."

"No, it's not. We've tried harvesting dead pups to replace the meat we've lost. And it's disgusting. I imagine a sheep is like cotton candy compared to the game on this planet."

"Can't we at least try?" Zak said, looking over his shoulder to the tiny bubble suspended from the dome's apex. "We know they don't go near the water. Once she's out, and we turn the falls back on, she'll probably stay out."

"No. It's better if we end this here and now. Besides, she's wasting her time. She'll never produce enough force to snap the column. And the bolts holding down the base? They're too thick."

The queen moved away from the tower, crawling in a circle, her heat signature fading slightly.

"Look. Look. Look." Neema's voice rose with each word. "She's getting tired, and she's not retreating underground. Now's your chance."

Zak remained on one knee, looking back at the queen. She had coiled in on herself, looking like a squat beehive.

"WHAT ARE YOU WAITING FOR?" Neema yelled.

Zak put his fists in the soil like a runner waiting at the starting line.

We're going to starve if we don't stop them.

"ATTACK," Neema said louder.

They've killed so many of us already.

"GET HER IN THE WATER!"

They're just like any other animal.

"KILL HER!"

* * *

Zak crept forward, hunched over. He kept himself between the queen and the colony as he edged closer. When he got within twenty-five meters, the queen's head rose off her body.

Flames burst from her scales as the saber-like hairs rattled in displeasure. She uncoiled, keeping her gaze fixed on Zak and howled in pain as her rear legs accidentally stepped into the moat. Steam erupted from the spot as she held her cooled leg off the ground.

Zak stood a little taller as he advanced, sidestepping to the right.

The queen reared up, moving backward. Her hindquarters dipped into the moat again, putting more steam into the air as she picked another segment off the ground.

They hate the cold.

Moving forward and right again, he came within a few meters of the tower. Zak held up his fists, ready to parry and strike like his father taught him.

They're just like any other animal. They just want to live.

Zak lowered his guard and pulled the light away from his hands. With a hiss, the Golem opened from behind. Cool, moist air surrounded him as the Flex-Foam retracted. For a moment, he was blind to the world around him, but the rattle of the queen's growl shook him like thunder.

"What're you doing?" Neema yelled. "Get back in--." Zak tapped the comm in his ear, shutting her off.

The queen roared as Zak climbed down the Golem's leg, reaching the muddy ground below. Like a blast furnace, her breath washed over him. He raised an arm to shield himself from the flecks of scalding spittle.

"Easy, girl." Holding up his hands, Zak back-pedaled, checking over his shoulder with each step for the tower until his foot thudded against the base.

The queen was reared up, her eyes focused on Zak as he circled behind the tower. She roared into the air again then sent another blast toward the tower. Burying his eyes in his elbow, he flattened himself to the pillar until her storm passed. His face remained hot, already pockmarked like an awning after an acid hailstorm.

Looking down through watery eyes, he found twelve steel hexagonal nuts the size of his palms holding the baseplate down on the concrete footing. Wrapping his hands around the closest one, he pushed all his light into it, making it glow until it started turning. With a grimace, he wrenched the nut loose several turns until it was a few centimeters higher. He then moved to the next one clockwise, putting more of himself in the queen's view.

She snarled and growled each time he moved. The tower creaked and groaned, swaying further off plumb. With each successive nut, Zak felt his faculties weaken. Stumbling to the last bolt, he leaned against the base, breathing like he'd just sprinted from the colony.

The queen raised her head and howled into the air.

"Zak." Neema's voice echoed from above. "The pups are on their way back to you. Get back in the Golem. You've got to strike. While she's distracted. NOW."

Just then, the queen lunged at the Golem, knocking it flat on its back. The entry hatch, hidden under the mud.

For my family.

Zak lumbered to the damaged side of the tower, using the foundation for support. Putting his hands on either side of a large gash, he pushed his light into the metal. His shoulders, arms, and hands ached as the electric sensation overloaded his nerves. Sweat built on his forehead as the tear turned red, then yellow, then white, and widened like a misshapen smile. Wisps of smoke rose from his palms as he pushed harder, the sensation like a swarm of hornets stabbing down his back and legs until his feet seemed to be pressing down on a bed of angry scorpions. The metal screeched, stretching like cold taffy. His heartbeat raced, matched by his breathing.

As if in slow motion, the tower toppled over, heading for the moat's far bank and snapped off at the base. Zak flew backward as shrapnel whizzed by his head, a chunk grazing his temple. The generator struck the ground like a hammer making the post wobble a few times like a springboard before it came to rest across the Golem's feet.

On his back, barely able to keep his eyes open, Zak watched the queen nose closer, feeling along the fallen post with her mandibles before testing her weight on it. It bowed slightly as she put half of her body on top. The Golem sunk deeper into the muck until it settled.

She then crawled over, standing above him and blocking the sun.

Make it quick.

Zak closed his eyes as she bent low. Nosing him in his leg and side. He gnashed his teeth, grunting and flinching as her mandible burned through his clothes like a branding iron. The sizzle of flesh hissing in his ears. He threw his arms across his face when acid dripped from her underbelly, like scalding rain. The sound of a hundred feet circled him, grunting and sniffing at the ground until she set her front feet on either side of his head. Opening his eyes wide enough to see, he found her gaping maw directly over him.

I guess I made the wrong choice.

A gust of scorching air, like walking into a kiln, fell on his face. He felt the blisters grow immediately. The queen poked him in the ribs again and moved away toward the makeshift bridge. Zak rolled onto his side as she mounted the column and howled into the air. Moments later, the herd of pups gathered around her. Zak watched as the queen picked each one up by the neck, dropping them on the fallen tower, and nosing them in the backside until they crawled to the opposite shore.

From several meters away, Zak watched the motionless Golem sink centimeter by centimeter under the queen's weight. The camera ports on the faceplate covered in mud gave it the appearance of a man dozing under a warm summer sun.

"Not a bad idea." Zak thought to himself as he closed his eyes, giving in to unconsciousness. "Hope mom and Leeya will be okay."

"They're going to be just fine," Bram's voice whispered. "She'll understand in time."

Zak opened his eyes to find himself in the same artificial landscape as before, the simulated dawn growing on the horizon. The light seemed to fill the sky faster than during his training exercises.

"Dad?" Zak searched the ethereal world. "Dad? Are you still here? How did I get back in the Golem""

Bram materialized a meter away, the corners of his mouth turned down. "I'm afraid you didn't, son."

Zak looked down at his body. He wore only a white bodysuit, no virtual armor of any kind.

"What happened, Dad?" Zak closed the distance between them.

"You saved the colony." Bram beamed and squeezed Zak's shoulders.

"I killed the queen?"

"No."

"Are Mom and Leeya okay? Did anyone get hurt?"

"They're fine. I can't tell you how proud I am."

Zak's knees buckled. He reached for Bram, catching his arm. "Whoa. How am I touching you? I thought you were intangible here."

Bram smiled. "We have equal solidity now."

Zak regained his feet, locking eyes with his father. "I'm dead?"

"Yes, son."

"I didn't want to die. I hoped I wouldn't."

"I know. But one day, they'll understand the price you paid for them."

"Them?"

"Yes, all of them. Your mother. Your sister. Even the colonists."

"I hope Mom forgives me."

"I'll talk to her in her dreams. She'll understand in time."

"It might take a while."

Bram laughed through his nose.

* * *

"Open administrators log," Neema said to her console as she sat back in the stiff-backed chair in the mobile observation booth. Below, the shadow-filled crater looked like the cup of tea steaming on her desktop as the setting sun winked from the horizon. She picked up her cup and saucer off the corn silk tablecloth that covered half her work surface. The cup rattled as she eyed a stain that looked like a Rorschach blot.

"New log entry." She took a sip as the holo appeared over the table. "Begin dictation. Director Neema Wabani, Chief Administrator. Lambda Colony. Day thirty-four twenty-nine. Local time, 19:18 p.m., Earth date, March nineteenth. Uploading annual reports."

Neema dragged the digital folder across the glassy surface one-handed as she took another sip. The holo chimed its receipt. She queried CENSUS DATA with her free hand.

"As you can see," she returned the cup to its place. "Populations of colonists and livestock have shown steady growth since our last encounter with the Mifletzot. After that first baby boom, we've sustained a steady growth rate teetering around two percent. The livestock population is thriving at one hundred fifteen percent, and our community is back to ninety-nine percent of first landing numbers. Demographic changes: Births: Thanks to the twins born yesterday, nineteen. Deaths: Two. The loss of Director Kaminsky hit us all harder than we expected. The other was Richard Sandlar, a mechanic. An accident in the motor pool. See the enclosed reports."

A beep sounded from the table as a new holo appeared. "Pause dictation."

"WE'RE ON OUR WAY."

Neema leaned back in her chair, folded her hands, and closed her eyes.

Out of all the miracles we've seen in the last five years, Raia's forgiveness is still the most amazing. How am I so blessed?

Neema sat upright and glanced down through the glass to a spot in the southwest pastures, her eyes misting over. She stared into the darkness for a moment before wiping away the tear threatening to spill. Clearing her throat, she leaned forward and typed her reply.

"SEE YOU SOON."

"Resume dictation. Our scout drones have kept an eye on the Mifletzot herds. They've been maintaining a consistent distance from the dome since their escape. The closest we've seen them is around fifty kilometers."

Neema noted the time on her holo. Ten-fifteen.

Twelve minutes to go.

"The fourth annual Zak Schafer Day celebrations went well. We only had a single hitch. The grade school reenactment went so far as to spray the audience with hot colored water during the mock battle. It shorted out a few stage lights. Nothing serious, but we're considering VR reenactments in the future. Anything else of note is in the reports. End dictation."

Neema typed on her console. The table beeped, and another holo appeared.

"MESSAGE SENT. WOULD YOU LIKE TO SEND ANOTHER?"

Closing all open holos, she picked up her tea and leaned back in the chair. Holding the cup close to her chest, she let the steam rise to her face as she closed her eyes and bowed her head.

I was going to keep him out of it. Vote against him defending the colony. Who knows what would've happened if Zak hadn't volunteered?

A few minutes later, the door swished open, revealing Raia Schafer and Leeya Schafer-Levy. Leeya carried a bundle in her arms. A blue homespun blanket. From the folds, a cherubic face peered out. A pair of brown eyes fixed on Neema.

"Here's Auntie Neema." Leeya cooed, letting the blanket spill open.

"Come here, little one." Neema stood, adjusting her balance as she wriggled her fingers like spider legs. The boy's face split wide with a toothless smile as she approached.

Neema raised the boy in the air. "He's getting so big."

"He's a chunk, that's for sure," Raia said, putting an arm around her daughter. "He can tank a bottle like nobody's business."

The three women stood in a tight circle, taking turns tickling or talking to the baby.

Neema's eyes found the clock. Ten twenty-six.

She locked eyes with Raia. "How's your week been?" She said, then turned to Leeya.

Raia's eyes glistened. "Keeping busy."

Leeya wiped her cheek. "Same," she said, rubbing noses with the baby.

Raia moved to the booth's windows in silence, her arms wrapped tight around herself.

Neema took Leeya's hand, her thumb on the ring around the young mother's finger. "How's Jacob?"

"He's still on the survey mission." Leeya gripped Neema's hand. "They hoped to be home for this, but they found another iron ore deposit and stopped to map it. He says they'll be back next week."

"I can make it sooner." Neema raised her brows. "Just say the word."

Leeya laughed. "Don't tempt me."

As the clock turned ten twenty-seven, the lights dimmed. Neema returned the baby as they met Raia at the concave windows. Below, the colony darkened as a thousand stars emerged from the buildings, collecting on the streets and flowed to the south gate.

Raia's sniffle brought Neema's attention around. "Been a hard day?"

"It's always hard. But it's easier up here."

The stream of light coalesced to a series of columns moving in unison through the darkness. They followed a road through the fields like ants through Leeya's globe, until they reached the moat. Neema could make out the monument, even from their position on the dome's underside. The stream of lights formed a crescent moon around the towering obelisk on the moat's bank.

It's fitting we erected it there. Standing guard over him.

Music came on through the booth's speakers. A trumpet playing a sad melody.

Neema, Raia, and Leeya took coin-sized disks out of their pockets, pressing the dimpled side. The slivers lit up, casting a pale blue light on their faces. At the same time, floodlights far below came on, showering the Golem with illumination.

"Look, Zach," Leeya whispered, pointing with the same hand that held her son. "That's who you're named after. He saved us."

"He saved all of us." Neema breathed, holding her light out further.

Raia fell to the floor, sobbing. Her token skittering across the floor.

Neema and Leeya dropped to their knees, hugging her from either side. Zach whimpered, pressed against his grandmother's side.

"He saved us," she moaned. "My baby saved us, but who was there to save him?"

"We tried, mom." Leeya choked. "You know we tried."

"Gone." Raia whimpered. "Gone."

Neema wrapped both arms around Raia's shoulders, unable to hold back her own tears. "But never forgotten."

The End

ABOUT THE AUTHORS

BRIAN C HAILES

Brian C. Hailes, creator of Draw It With Me (drawitwithme.com), is also the award-winning writer/illustrator of three graphic novels, entitled Blink, Dragon's Gait and Devil's Triangle, the children's picture books Skeleton Play and Don't Go Near the Crocodile Ponds. Other titles he has illustrated include Heroic: Tales of the Extraordinary, Passion & Spirit: The Dance Quote Book, Continuum (Arcana Studios), as well as McKenna, McKenna, Ready to Fly, and Grace & Sylvie: A Recipe for Family (American Girl). In addition to his several publishing credits, Hailes has also illustrated an extensive collection of fantasy, science fiction, and children's book covers as well as interior magazine illustrations.

Hailes has received numerous awards for his art from across the country, including Winner of the L. Ron Hubbard Illustrators of the Future contest out of Hollywood. His artwork has also been featured in the 2017-2019 editions of Infected By Art.

Hailes studied illustration and graphic design at Utah State University where he received his Bachelor of Fine Arts degree, as well as the Academy of Art University in San Francisco. He has been a regular panelist and presenter at Salt Lake Comic Con, FanX, LTUE, and was the Artist Guest of Honor at Conduit 2013. He has also appeared as a special guest at San Diego Comic Con.

Hailes currently lives in Salt Lake City with his wife and four boys, where he continues to write, paint and draw regularly. His work can be seen at:

HailesArt.com
DrawItWithMe.com
Instagram: drawitwithmeofficial
Facebook: drawitwithme
ArtStation: bchailes

RICK BENNETT

In addition to the four stories in this anthology, Rick Bennett has two published novels, both of which are available on Amazon: *Destroying Angel* and *Daddy's Little Felons*. Rick's cybersecurity blog, www.TheMorganDoctrine.com, outlines his 22 principles of the *perfect computer virus* and introduces *The Cyber Privateer Code*. He still does guerrilla warfare for high-tech companies and can be contacted by emailing rick@rickbennett.com or texting 801.556.2012.

Rick's one-man ad agency took Larry Ellison and Oracle from $15 million to $1 billion annual revenue in just six years. He also created Marc Benioff's pre-IPO ads attacking

Siebel for Salesforce.com. Documentation of his guerrilla warfare advertising philosophy and examples of his work can be found at www.rickbennett.com.

Rick went to Andover with George W. Bush (who became the 43rd president of the United States), and with Darrel Salk (son of polio vaccine creator Jonas Salk). He majored in mathematics at Whitman College. His invention, a voice stress analyzer, made the front page of every major newspaper in the country, and he appeared on numerous television shows, including NBC's *Today* and *Tomorrow* shows, ABC's *Good Morning America*, the *McNeil-Lehrer Report*, and *The Mike Douglas Show*. Believing his own press clippings, he sold his company to run for congress in 1978 from the state of Washington. Luckily, he lost that race and found a career working behind the scenes for high-tech moguls.

He and his wife Rita have 4 children, 19 grandchildren, and 7 great-grandchildren. He runs his business from *The Pirate* Cottage on a mountainside in Draper, Utah and rides his bike several thousand miles a year up and down the mountain.

RickBennett.com

NICHOLAS P ADAMS

Nicholas Adams grew up in the small, rural town of Boring, OR with his six brothers and sisters. After graduating from High School in Gresham, OR he attended BYU-ID and received his Associate Degree in Pre-Med. From there he returned to Portland, OR and attended Portland State University where he earned his Bachelor's Degree in Biology/Pre-Med before changing his career track to Architecture. He completed his second Bachelor's Degree in Architecture at Portland State University before going on to achieve his Master of Architecture Degree from the University of Utah in Salt Lake City, UT. After his graduation, he and his wife moved to the Phoenix Arizona area where they adopted four children over the next eight years. He currently lives in the Salt Lake City area where he is an Associate Member of the American Institute of Architects (AIA) and the League of Utah Writers.

Nicholas caught the writing bug at the tender age of forty-three and self-published a science fiction novel, after which he started learning about the craft and skills of prose, grammar, and story composition. In the following years, he's received awards for several short stories submitted to The Writers of the Future. His current literary goal is to receive the Golden Pen. Aside from storytelling and living in fantasy worlds, his other interests include movies, singing, and motorcycles.

NicholasAdamsWrites.com

CPSIA information can be obtained
at www.ICGtesting.com
Printed in the USA
FSHW010614230120
66321FS

9 781951 374037